Q
4047
·I77
A6
1973

A Vittorini Omnibus

By Elio Vittorini

A VITTORINI OMNIBUS
WOMEN OF MESSINA

A Vittorini Omnibus

IN SICILY

THE TWILIGHT OF THE ELEPHANT

LA GARIBALDINA

by Elio Vittorini

A NEW DIRECTIONS BOOK

Manufactured in the United States of America
First published clothbound (ISBN: 0–8112–0498–7) and as New Directions
Paperbook 366 (ISBN: 0–8112–0499–5) in 1973
Published simultaneously in Canada by McClelland & Stewart, Ltd.

New Directions Books are published for James Laughlin
by New Directions Publishing Corporation,
333 Sixth Avenue, New York 10014

Contents

Publisher's Note

In Sicily, the first of Vittorini's novels to be translated into English, was written in 1937 and published in the author's native Italy. Italy, in 1937, was a Fascist country, and Vittorini was not in sympathy with the government. On the contrary, he was writing an anti-Fascist book. This explains why, in his novel, he resorts to an occasional ambiguity; it was necessary, if his book was to get past the Fascist censorship. Being a genuine poet, Vittorini never uses ambiguity to pervert the truth, but only to shield it, and that is why, once the reader understands the circumstances under which *In Sicily* was written and published, the obscurities vanish and the truth stands revealed.

JAMES LAUGHLIN

Introduction

Elio Vittorini is one of the very best of the new Italian writers.
He was born July 23, 1908, in Syracuse in Sicily and spent
his boyhood in various parts of Sicily where his father was
a station master on the railways of that island. He is not a
regional writer, for Italy is certainly not a region, and Vittorini
from the time he was old enough to leave home without permission at seventeen learned his Italy in the same way American boys who ran away from home learned their own country.

The Italy that he learned and the America that the American boys learned has little to do with the Academic Italy or
America that periodically attacks all writing like a dust storm
and is always, until everything shall be completely dry, dis-
persed by rain.

Rain to an academician is probably, after the first fall
has cleared the air, H_2O with, of course, traces of other things.
To a good writer, needing something to bring the dry country
alive so that it will not be a desert where only such cactus
as New York literary reviews grow dry and sad, inexistent
without the watering of their benefactors, feeding on the dried
manure of schism and the dusty taste of disputed dialectics,
their only flowering a desiccated criticism as alive as stuffed
birds, and their steady mulch the dehydrated cuds of fellow
critics; such a writer finds rain to be made of knowledge,
experience, wine, bread, oil, salt, vinegar, bed, early mornings,
nights, days, the sea, men, women, dogs, beloved motor cars,
bicycles, hills and valleys, the appearance and disappearance
of trains on straight and curved tracks, love, honor and dis-
obey, music, chamber music and chamber pots, negative and
positive Wassermanns, the arrival and non-arrival of expected
munitions and/or reinforcements, replacements or your
brother. All these are a part of rain to a good writer along
with your hated or beloved mother, may she rest in peace

or in pieces, porcupine quills, cock grouse drumming on a basswood log, the smell of sweetgrass and fresh smoked leather and Sicily.

In this book the rain you get is Sicily. I care nothing about the political aspects of the book (they were many at the time) nor about Vittorini's politics (I have examined them carefully and to me they are honorable). But I care very much about his ability to bring rain with him when he comes if the earth is dry and that is what you need.

He has more books about the north of Italy that he knows and loves and about other parts of Italy. This is a good one to start with.

If there is any rhetoric or fancy writing that puts you off at the beginning or the end, just ram through it. Remember he wrote the book in 1937 under Fascism and he had to wrap it in a fancy package. It is necessarily wrapped in cellophane to pass the censor. But there is excellent food once you unwrap it.

ERNEST HEMINGWAY

Cortina D'Ampezzo, 1949

Author's Note

In order to avoid misapprehensions I would like to point out that the protagonist of this story is not the Author, just as the country which provides the protagonist with a background and bears him company is called Sicily merely by accident; merely because the word Sicily sounds, to me, more harmonious than Persia or Venezuela. Moreover, I expect that all manuscripts come out of a single bottle.

IN SICILY

(Conversazione in Sicilia   1937)

PART ONE

1

That winter I was haunted by abstract furies. I won't try and describe them, because they're not what I intend to write about. But I must mention that they were abstract furies—not heroic or even live; some sort of furies concerning the doomed human race. They had obsessed me for a long time, and I was despondent. I saw the screaming newspaper placards, and I hung my head. I would see my friends, pass an hour or two with them in silence and dejection. My wife or my girl would be expecting me, but, downcast, I would meet them without exchanging a word. Meanwhile it rained and rained as the days and months went by. My shoes were tattered and soggy with rain. There was nothing but the rain, the slaughters on the newspaper placards, water in my dilapidated shoes and my taciturn friends. My life was like a blank dream, a quiet hopelessness.

That was the terrible part: the quietude of my hopelessness; to believe mankind to be doomed, and yet to feel no fever to save it, but instead to nourish a desire to succumb with it.

I was shaken by abstract furies, but not in my blood; I was calm, unmoved by desires. I did not care whether my girl was expecting me, whether or not I met her, glanced over the leaves of a dictionary, went out and saw my friends, or stayed at home. I was calm, as if I had not lived a day, nor known what it meant to be happy; as if I had nothing to say, to affirm or deny, nothing to hazard, nothing to listen to, devoid of all urge; and as if in all the years of my life I had never eaten bread, drunk wine or coffee, never been to bed with a woman, never had children, never come to blows with anyone; as if I had not thought all such things possible; as if I had never been a man, never alive, never

3

a baby spending my infancy in Sicily, among the prickly pears, the sulfur mines and the mountains.

But the abstract furies stirred violently within me, and I bowed my head, pondering mankind's doom; and all the while it rained and I did not exchange a word with my friends, and the rain seeped through my shoes.

2

Then came my father's letter.

I recognized the handwriting on the envelope, and did not open it at once. Recognition made me hesitate, and I realized that I had once been a child, and had enjoyed a childhood of sorts. I opened the letter, and it said:

"My dear boy,

You and your brothers know that I have always been a good father to you as well as a good husband to your Mama, but now something has happened to me, and I have gone away. But you must not think ill of me. I have remained the same good man that I was, the same good father to you, a good friend to your Mama and, what's more, I will be a good husband to this—let us say—new wife with whom I departed. My sons, I speak to you with no sense of shame, as a man to men, and I do not ask your forgiveness. I know I am doing harm to no one; not to you all who were the first to leave me, and not to your Mama whom, after all, I deprive solely of the bother of my company. With me, or without me, she will still continue to whistle and sing in her home. And so I set forth on my new path without regret. Don't worry about money and so on. Your mother will want for nothing; every month she will receive the full amount of my pension as an ex-railwayman. I shall live by giving private lessons, thus fulfilling an old dream whose realization your mother always thwarted. But now that your mother is alone,

4

I beg of you to go and visit her sometimes. You, Silvestro, were fifteen when you left us, and ever since then you've never been to see us. Well, for the eighth of December, instead of sending the customary greeting card on her birthday, why don't you take the train and go down and see her? I kiss you, your dear wife, and the children.

Your affectionate father,
Constantino."

The letter, I saw, came from Venice. I realized that he had written identical words to each of us five sons of his scattered through the world—a circular. It was extraordinary. Rereading the letter I recognized my father, his face, his voice, his blue eyes, his gestures, and I visualized myself as a boy applauding him while he recited *Macbeth* for railwaymen, in a waiting room at a little station on the line from San Cataldo to Racalmuto.

I recognized him and realized that I had once been a boy, and remembered Sicily and her mountains. But this was all my memory revealed. I recognized him and saw myself as a boy applauding him, while he was reciting *Macbeth* in his red suit; and those eyes of his, those blue eyes shone, as if he were now once more acting on a stage called Venice and I was once more about to clap. No sooner did my memory disclose this than all was dark again. I was overcome by my quiet hopelessness, as if I had never had those fifteen years of childhood, of Sicily, of prickly pears, sulfur, *Macbeth*, and mountains. Yet another fifteen years had passed, a thousand kilometers away from Sicily and from my childhood, and I was almost thirty now; and I felt as if I had experienced nothing, neither the first fifteen years, nor the second, as if I had never eaten bread, never enjoyed possessions, tastes and sensations in all those years, as if I had never been alive and was an emptiness—yes, that's it—an emptiness. I was ruminating upon the doomed human race, and quiet in my hopelessness.

I had no desire to see my girl's face again, but was glancing over the pages of a dictionary which was the one book that I was now capable of reading, when I began to hear within me a lament like a pipe's mournful note. I went to work every day as a linotype operator, did seven hours of linotyping every day, under an eyeshade, in the sweltering heat of the lead machines; all the while within me sounded the pipe and stirred the countless mice, which could not be precisely described as memories.

There was nothing but mice, dark and shapeless, three hundred and sixty-five of them, and then another three hundred and sixty-five, the dark mice of my years, yet only my years in Sicily and the mountains. And I felt them stir within me, hordes of mice numbering fifteen times three hundred and sixty-five, and I felt a vague nostalgia come upon me to relive once more my childhood. I took up again my father's letter, reread it, and looked at the calendar. It was the sixth of December. For the eighth, I would have to send the usual birthday card to my mother. It would have been unspeakable to forget now that my mother was at home alone.

I wrote the card, put it in my pocket, and, it being Saturday and the end of a fortnight, I drew my salary. I went to the station to post the card and passed by its brightly lit hall. Outside it was raining, and the water was getting into my shoes.

My way home lay either through the rain or by way of the steps. So I climbed the steps, which lead to the illuminated hall, and there I saw two placards: one was a newspaper's, screaming of new slaughters; the other, that of the Italian Tourist Agency. "Visit Sicily," it said. "Fifty per cent reduction from December to June; Third Class Return Fare to Syracuse—250 Lire."

I found myself for the moment at the parting of the ways: one led back home again, to those obsessions about slaughtered multitudes, to the still hopelessness; the other to Sicily, the mountains, the pipe's lament within me, perhaps to a stillness less black and a hopelessness less stark. The human race was doomed whichever path I took, and I knew a train was leaving for the south at seven o'clock, in ten minutes' time.

The pipe sounded shrill within me, and I did not care whether I left or not. I asked for a ticket which cost 250 lire, leaving in my pocket a hundred lire of the fortnight's salary just drawn. I went on into the station, amid the lights, the high engines and the yelling porters.

Thus began a long journey by night, but it would have made no difference were I to have stayed at home, skipping through my dictionary or sleeping with my wife.

3

Toward midnight I changed trains at Florence, then again about six in the morning at the Termini Station in Rome, and about midday I reached Naples. There it was not raining, and I sent off a telegraphic money order of fifty lire to my wife. I wired to her: "Returning Thursday."

Then I took the train for Calabria. It began raining again, and night came on. It all came back to me, the journey, and I as a child on my ten flights from home and Sicily, traveling back and forth through a countryside of smoke and tunnels, the rending whistles, of the train halted by night in the jaws of a mountain or by the sea, and the names—Amantea, Maratea, Gioia Tauro—evoking dreams of ancient times. And so, suddenly, the mouse within me was no longer a mouse, but scent, savor and the heavens, and the pipe no longer played mournfully, but merrily. I fell asleep, awoke, fell asleep again and awoke once more, until at last I found myself on board the ferryboat for Sicily.

The sea was black and wintry. Standing on that high plateau of the top deck, I saw myself once again as a boy breathing the air, gazing hungrily at the sea, facing toward the one coast or the other and gazing hungrily at the sea, with all that garbage of coastal town and village heaped at my feet in the rain-swept morning. It was cold, and I remembered myself as a boy feeling cold yet remaining obstinately on that elevated windy platform, with the sea speeding swiftly by below.

We were a tight fit. The boat was full of little Sicilians

traveling third-class, hungry, frozen, without overcoats, yet mild-looking, jacket lapels turned up and hands dug into trouser pockets. I had bought some food at Villa San Giovanni, some bread and cheese, and I was munching away on deck at the bread, raw air, and cheese, with zest and appetite, because I recognized the old tang of my mountains, and even their odors—herds of goats and wormwood—in that cheese. The little Sicilians, bowed with backs to the wind and hands in pockets, watched me eat. They had dark, but mild faces, with beards four days old. They were workers, laborers from the orange groves, and railwaymen wearing gray caps with the thin red piping of labor gangs. Munching, I smiled at them, and they looked back at me unsmiling.

"There's no cheese like our own," I said.

No one replied. They all stared at me, the women in their voluminous femininity seated on their great bags of belongings, the men standing, small and as if scalded by the wind, hands in pockets.

Again I said: "There's no cheese like our own."

Because I felt suddenly enthusiastic about something—that cheese, its savor in my mouth, with the bread and the sharp air, its flavor clear but acrid, and ancient, its grains of pepper like sudden embers on the tongue:

"There's no cheese like our own," I said for the third time.

Then one of the Sicilians, the smallest and gentlest and darkest of the lot, and the most scalded by the wind, asked me:

"But are you a Sicilian?"

"Why not?" I replied.

The man shrugged his shoulders and said no more. He had what looked like a little girl with him, sitting on a bag at his feet. He bent over her, and taking a great red hand out of his pocket, he seemed to touch her caressingly while he adjusted her shawl to keep her warm.

Somehow this gesture made it clear that she was not his daughter, but his wife. Meanwhile Messina drew near, and it was not a heap of garbage on the sea's edge, but houses and moles, white tramcars and rows of dark-hued wagons

8

in the railway sidings. The morning seemed wet, though it was not raining. Everything on the top deck was moist, the wind blew moist, the sirens from the ships sounded moist, and the railway engines ashore whistled with a moist note; but it was not raining. And suddenly we saw the lighthouse tower sailing by in the wintry sea, very high, heading for Villa San Giovanni.

"There's no cheese like our own," I said.

All the men, who were standing, pressed toward the deck rail to gaze at the city, and the women too, seated on their bags, turned their heads. But no one made a move toward the lower deck to be ready to disembark. There was still time. From the lighthouse to the jetty, I remembered, took fifteen minutes or more.

"There's no cheese like our own," I said.

Meanwhile, I finished eating. The man with the wife who looked like a child bent down once again; in fact, he knelt; he had a basket at his feet, and watched by her, he began to busy himself with it. It was covered by a piece of wax cloth sewn with string at the edges. Very slowly he undid a bit of the string, dug his hand under the wax cloth, and produced an orange.

It wasn't big or very luscious or highly tinted, but it was an orange, and without a word, without rising from his knees, he offered it to his baby wife. The baby looked at me; I could discern her eyes inside the hood of the shawl; and then I saw her shake her head.

The little Sicilian seemed desperate, and remained on his knees, one hand in his pocket, the other holding the orange. Then he rose again to his feet and stood with the wind flapping the soft peak of his cap against his nose, the orange in his hand, his coatless diminutive body scalded by the cold, and frantic, while immediately below us the sea and the city floated by in the wet morning.

"Messina," said a woman mournfully. It was a word uttered without reason, merely as a kind of complaint. I observed the little Sicilian with the baby wife desperately peel his orange, and desperately eat it, with rage and frenzy, without the least desire; then without chewing he gulped it down and seemed to curse, his fingers dripping with the orange juice in the cold, a little bowed in the wind, the peak of his cap flapping against his nose.

"A Sicilian never eats in the morning," he said suddenly. "Are you American?" he added.

He spoke with desperation, yet gently, just as he had always been gentle while desperately peeling the orange and desperately eating it. He spoke the last three words excitedly, in a strident tense voice, as if it were somehow essential to the peace of his soul to know if I were American.

I observed this, and said: "Yes, I am American. For the last fifteen years."

4

It was raining on the mole of the Pier Station, where my little train was waiting. Of the crowd of Sicilians from the ferryboat, a number, with jacket lapels turned up and hands in their pockets, with their women and bags and baskets, stood immobile, as earlier on board, under the portico.

The train waited while the carriages which had crossed over on the ferryboat were hitched on. And this was a long process. I again found myself near the little Sicilian with the baby wife, who once more sat on her bag at his feet.

Sometimes when he looked at me he smiled; he was desperate, with his hands in his pocket, in the wind and cold, yet his lips shaped themselves into a smile, under the peak of the cloth cap that covered half his face.

"I have some cousins in America," he said. "An uncle and some cousins...."

"Oh, have you?" I said. "Whereabouts? In New York or the Argentine?"

"I don't know," he replied. "Perhaps in New York. Perhaps in the Argentine. In America."

"Where are you from?" he added.

"I?" said I. "I was born in Syracuse...."

He said: "No. From what part of America?"

"From...from New York," I said.

We were silent an instant after this lie, I watching him, and he watching me with his eyes hidden under the peak of his cap.

Then almost tenderly, he asked: "How are things in New York? All right?"

"There's no money to be made," I replied.

"What does that matter?" he said. "You can be all right without making money. It's better, in fact...."

"Who knows!" I said. "There's also unemployment there."

"What does unemployment matter?" he said. "It's not always unemployment that does the harm. It's not that. I'm not unemployed."

He pointed to the other little Sicilians around them. "None of us is. We work. In the groves we work."

He stopped, and, changing his tone, he added: "Have you come back because of unemployment?"

"No," I said, "I've come back for a few days."

"Ah, yes," he said. "And you eat in the morning? A Sicilian never eats in the morning."

And he asked: "Does everyone eat in the morning in America?"

I could have said no, and that I, too, as a rule, did not eat in the morning, and that I knew so many people who perhaps did not eat more than once a day, and that it was the same throughout the world and so on. But to him I could not speak ill of an America where I had not been, an America which was not even America, nothing real and concrete, but just his idea of the kingdom of heaven on earth. I could not say no; it would not have been right.

"I think so," I replied. "In one way or another."

"And the afternoon?" he asked next. "Do they all eat in the afternoon, in America?"

"I think so," I said. "In one way or another...."

"And in the evening?" he questioned. "Does everyone eat in the evening in America?"

"I think so," I said. "More or less...."

11

"Bread?" he said. "Bread and cheese? Bread and vegetables? Bread and meat?"

He spoke with hope, and I was unable to say no.

"Yes," I said. "Bread and other things...."

The little Sicilian stood mute with hope for an instant. then he looked down at his childlike wife at his feet, the impassive, dark, fully enveloped shape seated on the bag, and he became desperate. Desperately, as earlier on board, he bent down and undid a bit of the string from the basket, drew out an orange, and still stooping with his legs bent, he proffered it to his wife. After a wordless refusal on her part, he was in a frenzy of humiliation with the orange left in his hand. He began to peel it for himself, and ate it swallowing as if he were swallowing curses.

"They're eaten in salad," I said, "among us here."

"In America?" asked the Sicilian.

"No," I said, "among us here."

"Among us here?" asked the Sicilian. "In salad with oil?"

"Yes, with oil," I said. "And a clove of garlic and salt...."

"And with bread?" said the Sicilian.

"Certainly," I replied. "I always used to eat them... fifteen years ago... as a boy...."

"Oh, you used to eat them?" said the Silician. "Were you doing well then, too?"

"So so," I replied.

And I added: "Never eaten oranges in salad?"

"Yes, sometimes," said the Sicilian. "But there's not always oil."

"Exactly," I said. "There's not always a good harvest.... Oil can be dear."

"And there's not always bread," said the Sicilian. "If you don't sell the oranges, there's no bread. And you've got to eat the oranges... That's it, see?"

And he desperately ate his orange, his icy fingers dripping with its juice, looking at his childlike wife at his feet, who did not want oranges.

"But they're very nourishing," I said. "Can you sell me some?"

The little Sicilian finished gulping and wiped his fingers on his jacket.

"Really?" he exclaimed. His hand dived into his basket, groped about inside under the wax cloth, and produced four, five, six oranges.

"But why?" I asked. "Is it so difficult to sell oranges?"

"They don't sell," he said. "No one wants them."

Meanwhile the train, lengthened by the carriages that had been brought over, was ready to leave.

"They don't want them abroad," continued the little Sicilian. "As if they're poisoned. Our oranges. And our employer pays us like this. He gives us the orange.... And we don't know what to do with them. No one wants them. We've come on foot to Messina—and no one wants them here. We went to Reggio and Villa San Giovanni to see if they want them there, but they don't want them....No one wants them."

The guard blew his little trumpet, and the engine whistled.

"No one wants them....We go backward and forward, we pay our own fares as well as the freight for them, we go without bread, but no one wants them....No one wants them."

The train started, and I leapt at a carriage window.

"Goodbye, goodbye."

"No one wants them. No one wants them. As if they were poisoned! Cursed oranges!"

5

I had scarcely sunk down on a wooden seat in the moving train when I heard two voices in the corridor discussing what had happened.

Nothing had happened that could be called a real incident, a fact, or even a gesture. A man, that little Sicilian, had shouted at me those last words of his, the end of his tale, when it was too late and the train had already started.

A question of words, that was all. And here were the two voices discussing the matter.

"But what did that fellow want?"

"He seemed to be protesting...."

"He had a grudge against someone."

"I'd say he had a grudge against everybody."

"That struck me, too. He was starving."

"If I had been down on the platform I would have arrested him."

They were two cigar-smoking, vigorous, drawling voices, sounding pleasant in dialect. They were talking Sicilian.

I poked my head into the corridor and saw them standing by a window, two massive, square-built men in hats and over-coats, one with a mustache, the other without, two Sicilians of the drayman variety, but well-dressed, prosperous-looking, unbending about the neck and back, yet rather affected and boorish perhaps from timidity.

"Two baritones," I told myself. And, in fact, the one without a mustache had a somewhat melodious, sinuous voice like a baritone's.

"You would only have been doing your duty," he said.

The other, under his mustache, had a raucous cigar smoker's voice, yet pleasant when speaking dialect.

"Of course," he said. "I would only have been doing my duty."

I withdrew my head into the compartment, but continued to listen, picturing to myself as the baritone and raucous voice alternated, their two faces, the one shorn and the other with a mustache.

"Such fellows must always be arrested," said No Mustache.

"Yes, they must," said Mustache. "You never know...."

"Every starving man is dangerous," said No Mustache.

"Of course. Capable of anything," said Mustache.

"Of stealing," said No Mustache.

"Goes without saying," said Mustache.

"Of murder," said No Mustache.

"Undoubtedly," said Mustache.

"And of perpetrating political crime," said No Mustache.

They looked at each other in the eye and smiled—I could

14

see that from the one's face and the other's back; and so they continued to talk, Mustache to No Mustache, of what they meant by political crime. A lack of regard and consideration is what they meant, it seemed; they said so and accused all mankind; mankind was born to commit crime, they said.

"No matter what class.... No matter what creed," said Mustache.

And No Mustache: "Whether they are ignorant. Or whether they are educated."

Mustache: "Whether they are rich. Or whether they are poor."

No Mustache: "They're all alike."

Mustache: "Shopkeepers."

No Mustache: "Lawyers."

Mustache: "My delicatessen man at Lodi...."

No Mustache: "At Bologna a lawyer...."

Again they looked at each other in the eye and again they smiled; I perceived this again from the one's face and the other's back, and through the din of the train rumbling along between the sea and the orange trees I heard them recounting to each other about the Lodi delicatessen man and the Bologna lawyer.

"You see," said Mustache, "they have no respect."

"They have no consideration," said No Mustache.

Mustache: "My barber at Lodi...."

No Mustache: "My landlord at Bologna...."

They told each other about that barber at Lodi and that landlord at Bologna. Mustache said he had once arrested that barber of his and locked him up for three days; and No Mustache said he had done the same thing to a butcher of his at Bologna, and I could tell from their voices that they were satisfied, overcome with satisfaction and almost on the point of falling into each other's arms from the conjoint delight of knowing how to arrest people and keep them locked up.

And they exchanged other trivial bits of information, always without resentment, always with mournful deprecation, but in the end with satisfaction. Then they became perplexed and asked themselves why, after all, did people view them with disapproval.

"Well, it's because we're Sicilians," said Mustache.

"That's it, because we're Sicilians," said No Mustache.

They discussed what it was like to be a Sicilian at Lodi and at Bologna, and suddenly No Mustache let out a sort of grief-stricken cry, and said that at home in Sicily, it was even worse.

"At Sciacca I...." said No Mustache.

"At Mussumeli I...." said Mustache.

They elaborated how it was worse at Sciacca and Mussumeli, and No Mustache said that his mother did not say what his calling was; she was ashamed of saying it and said that he was employed at the Land Registry.

"Employed at the Land Registry!" repeated No Mustache.

"It's a question of preconceived notions," said Mustache.

"I know. Old prejudices," said No Mustache.

And they declared how impossible it was to live in their native places.

As the train sped clatteringly between the orange trees and the sea, No Mustache said: "What orange trees!" and Mustache said: "What a sea!" and both of them said how lovely it was at home, at Sciacca and Mussumeli; but again they affirmed that they could not live there.

"I don't know why I'm going back there," said Mustache.

"As if I do!" said No Mustache. "My wife's from Bologna, my sons are from Bologna...yet—"

Mustache: "Without fail every year as soon as I start my leave...."

No Mustache: "Without fail...especially about Christmas time."

Mustache: "Especially during this month. And what do we get out of it?"

No Mustache: "Rotted bowels...."

Mustache: "Poisoned blood."

Here the door of the compartment was shut with vigor—I would say, banged—by the man sitting opposite me. Suddenly shut off, the voices were soon drowned by the noise of the train. And the train flew through the orange groves between the mountains and the sea.

High snow appeared in the distance and vanished. The wind had blown the sky clear, though the sun had not yet emerged. The journey became familiar to me and I observed that we had reached halfway between Messina and Catania. I no longer heard the two voices outside. I looked about me, concerning myself with other Sicilians.

6

"Don't you notice the stink?" said the man opposite.

He was a large Sicilian, perhaps of Lombard or Norman stock from Nicosia, a drayman type like the owners of the voices in the corridor, but sincere and forthright, and tall, with blue eyes. He was not a young man; his age was about fifty. And I thought that he possibly resembled my father as he now would have been, although I could remember my father only as a young man, slim and lithe, reciting *Macbeth,* garbed in scarlet and black. The man must have hailed from Nicosia or Aidone; he still spoke the almost Lombard dialect with the Lombard "u" of those Lombard districts in the Val Demone.

"Don't you notice the stink?" he said.

He was a man with a little pepper-and-salt beard, blue eyes, and an Olympian brow. He sat without his jacket in the cold third-class compartment—the drayman perhaps only in this and nothing else. He rumpled his nose above his sparse mustache and beard. Yet he was hairy to a degree, a fact revealed by the rolled-up sleeves of his shirt which was designed with little dark squares and on which he wore an enormous waistcoat with six little pockets.

"Stink? What stink?" I asked.

"What! Didn't you notice it?" he said.

"I don't know," I answered. "I don't understand what stink you're talking about."

"Oh," he said. "He does not understand what stink I'm talking about." And he turned to the others in the compartment.

They were three.

One was a young man in a soft cap, wrapped in a shawl, minute, emaciated, and yellow in the face. He was sitting diagonally opposite me, by the window.

The second was also young, but ruddy, powerful, with curly black hair, his neck black, a plebeian, certainly a Catanian. He sat at the other end of my seat, facing the sick man.

The third was a tiny old man without a single hair on his face, dark, his skin hidelike with cube-shaped scales like a tortoise's, incredibly tiny and dried up; a dry leaf of a man. He had got on at Roccalumera and was sitting—if one can call it sitting—on the edge of the bench, between the Great Lombard and the sick man, with his back against the wooden elbow rest, which he could have folded up out of the way, but had omitted to do so.

The Great Lombard, turning to his companions in general, addressed him in particular.

"He doesn't understand what stink I'm talking about," he said.

There came a sound like a puff of wind, an incipient whistle, a lifeless, disembodied voice: "Eeh." The tiny old man was laughing. But this was not the first time he had laughed. He had been laughing from the first moment he had got on, with his eyes, with his acute, lively eyes, laughing fixedly, gazing before him, at me, at the seat, at the young Catanian, and laughing—joyously.

"Incredible! He doesn't understand what stink I'm talking about," said the Great Lombard.

They all looked at me and became hilarious, the sick man with the silent, dim hilarity of illness.

"Ah!" said I, likewise hilarious. "I really don't understand...I don't notice any stink...."

Then the young Catanian intervened.

He leaned forward, ruddy, with his great curly head, his massive arms and thighs, his enormous shoes, and said:

"The gentleman refers to the stink that was emitted from the corridor."

"From the corridor?" said I.

"But, really! It's incredible," shouted the Great Lombard. "He didn't notice it."

"The gentleman refers to the stink of those two...." said the Catanian.

"Those two?" I said. "Those two at the window? Were they making a stink? What stink?"

Again I heard the lifeless sound, the disembodied whistle from the tiny old man, and I saw that his mouth was like the slit in a money box. I also saw the sick man, motionless and silently hilarious in his shawl. The Great Lombard was almost raging, but with gaiety in his eyes that looked like the blue eyes of my father.

Then I understood what the stink was, and laughed.

"Ah, the stink!" I cried. "The stink!"

Everyone became merry and contented, regaining his composure; meanwhile those two in the corridor were paying a visit to their home villages, where they had spent their childhood.

"It's strange," said I. "There's no place in the world where they are more frowned upon than in Sicily.... Yet they are almost all Sicilians who practice this profession in Italy."

"All Sicilians?" cried the Great Lombard.

"It's true," I said. "I've been traveling around Italy for the last fifteen years...I've lived in Florence, I've lived in Bologna, and Turin; and now I live in Milan, and everywhere I've found a Sicilian practicing this profession."

"Exactly. That's what my cousin who travels also says," observed the Catanian.

"Well, it's understandable anyhow," said the Great Lombard. "We are a sad people, we Sicilians."

"Sad?" said I, looking at the little old man with the tiny hilarious face, with the tiny eyes brimming with hilarity.

"Very sad," said the Great Lombard. "Even mournful...Everyone always eager to look on the dark side of things."

I kept looking at the tiny face of the old man, and said nothing.

The Great Lombard continued: "Always hoping for something else, for something better, and always despairing of being able to attain it....And always tempted within ourselves to commit suicide."

"Yes, that's true," said the Catanian earnestly.

And he began to scrutinize the toes of his enormous shoes. Without turning away from the old man's tiny face, I said: "Perhaps it's true....But what's that got to do with practicing that profession?"

"I think it's got something or other to do with it," said the Great Lombard. "I think it's got something to do with it. I can't explain how, but I think it's got something to do with it. What does a man do who's abandoned? When he's lost and cast off? He does what he most hates doing....That's the reason, I think. I think it's understandable if they're almost all Sicilians."

7

Then the Great Lombard began to talk about himself. He had taken the train at Messina, where he had been to see a specialist on account of a peculiar kidney disease of his, and was returning home to Leonforte. He came from Leonforte, up in the Val Demone between Enna and Nicosia. He was a landowner with three beautiful female children—that's how he expressed it: three beautiful female children. He had a horse, on which he rode about his estate, thinking himself a king the while, so tall and proud was his horse. But he did not think it enough to think oneself a king when astride a horse, he would have liked to acquire—as he said—other perceptions in order to feel that he was changed, with something new in his soul; he would have given all he possessed, even his horse, and his land, just to feel himself at peace with men, like one—so he said—like one who had nothing to reproach himself.

"Not that I have anything particular to reproach myself," he said. "Nothing at all. Nor do I speak in the sense of the confessional....But I don't feel at peace with men."

He would have liked to have a fresh conscience—as he said, fresh—one which would have required him to perform other duties, not the customary ones but others: new and higher duties toward men, because there was no satisfaction in the fulfillment of the customary duties; one felt as if one had accomplished nothing: one was discontented and disappointed with oneself.

"I believe that man is ripe for something else," he said. "Not only for not stealing, not killing, and so on, and for being a good citizen.... I believe that he's ripe for something else, for new and different duties. It is this that we feel, I believe, the want of other duties, other things to accomplish. Things to accomplish for the sake of our conscience in a new sense."

He stopped talking, and the Catanian spoke:

"Yes," he said.

And he stared at his enormous toes.

"Yes," he said, "I think you're right."

He kept looking at his shoes. Ruddy and bursting with health though he was, he had the sadness of a powerful but unsated animal, of a horse or an ox. "Yes," he said again, with a persuaded, convinced air, as if a name had been found for a malady of his. Yet he spoke not a word about himself, but merely asked:

"Are you a professor?"

"I a professor?" exclaimed the Great Lombard.

And the little old man beside him made himself audible with his "Eeh," like a dried leaf, a disembodied voice. He was like a dried straw that uttered words.

"Eeh," he said twice. "Eeh."

Filled with laughter, his eyes shone brightly in his dark, leathery face like a tortoise's carapace.

"Eeh," he said, with his mouth like a slit in a money box.

"Nothing to laugh at, little Grandpa, nothing to laugh at," said the Great Lombard turning to him.

Again he talked about himself, from the beginning: his trip to Messina, his properties above Leonforte, his three female children, the one—as he said—more beautiful than the other, his tall and proud horse, and himself, who did not feel at peace with men and thought that a new conscience

21

was needed, and new duties to accomplish, in order to feel more at peace with men; all of which was from time to time addressed exclusively to the tiny old man who looked at him and laughed and uttered his "Eeh," like the sound of an incipient whistle, a disembodied voice.

"But why?" said the Great Lombard suddenly to the old man. "Why are you sitting in that uncomfortable way? This can be lifted."

And he raised the wooden armrest which supported the little old man as he perched precariously on his seat. "This can be lifted," said the Great Lombard.

The old man turned round and looked at the lifted armrest, said "Eeh" again a couple of times, and continued to maintain his uncomfortable posture, balanced insecurely, his tiny leathery hand gripping a knotted wooden stick as high as himself with a serpent-headed knob.

It was while the old man was turning round to look at the armrest that I saw the serpent's head, and then I saw something green in its mouth, three little leaves on the twig of an orange tree. The little old man saw me, and again said "Eeh." He took the little twig from the serpent's mouth and put it into his own, that was like a slit in a head that was no less like a serpent's.

"Ah, I think it is precisely this," said the Great Lombard, addressing himself to the company at large. "We feel no satisfaction any longer in performing our duty, our duties. ...Performing them is a matter of indifference, and we feel no better for having performed them. And the reason is this: those duties are too old, too old and they have become too easy. They don't count any longer for the conscience...."

"But aren't you really a professor?" asked the Catanian.

He was ruddy, bull-like, and with a bull's sad air, he kept staring at his shoes.

"I a professor?" said the Great Lombard. "Do I look like a professor? I'm not ignorant, I can read a book if I like, but I'm not a professor. As a boy I was with the Salesians, but I'm not a professor...."

So we reached the last station before Catania, and were already in the suburbs of that city of black stone, when the little old man who said "Eeh" like a dry straw, got out. And when we arrived at Catania, there was sun in the streets that passed before our gaze, streets and houses of black stone directly below the train. Then we reached Catania Station, and the Catanian got down as well as the Great Lombard, and, looking out of the window, I saw that Mustache and No Mustache had also got down.

In fact, everyone left the train, and the journey was resumed with deserted carriages in the sunshine, and I wondered why I, too, had not got down.

In any case my ticket was for Syracuse, and I continued the journey in the empty carriage, in the sunshine, across an empty plateau. Returning from the corridor to my compartment, I was surprised to find the sick young man with the yellow face still settled in his seat, enveloped in his shawl, with his soft cap on his head. Exchanging a silent stare with him—yet I was happy in his company—I journeyed on and on through the sunlit empty plain which was engulfed at last in green, malarial swamps. We had reached Lentini. It stood at the foot of long green slopes covered with orange groves and marshes. The young man, enveloped in his shawl, alighted and shivered in the sunshine as he stood on the deserted, malaria-ridden platform.

Now I was alone, and the train ran through a rocky landscape along the sea, toward Syracuse. I lifted my eyes and there was No Mustache motionless in the corridor.

He was looking at me.

8

He smiled.

He was standing in the corridor with the sun on his back, turned away from the rocky landscape and the sea. We were just two, he and I, in the whole carriage, perhaps in the whole train, speeding through the empty countryside.

23

His shorn, cigar smoker's face smiled at me, as he stood, portly, in his aubergine-colored overcoat and hat. He entered the compartment and proceeded to sit down.

"Will you allow me?" he said, when he was seated.

"Good heavens!" I replied. "But, of course!"

And he was happy to be able to remain seated with my leave, happy not just to sit—he had an entire carriage from which to pick a seat—but to sit there, where I was, where someone else was, a man.

"I thought I saw you get down at Catania," I observed.

"Ah, you saw me?" he said, happy. "I saw a friend of mine off on the train to Caltanissetta...I jumped on again at the last moment."

"Oh, yes," I said.

"I jumped on the last carriage."

"Oh, yes," I said.

"I was just in time."

"Oh, yes," I said.

"There was a first- and second-class carriage in the middle," he said. "I had to stay down there parted from my luggage."

"Oh, yes," I said.

"But I got down at Lentini and came along here," he said.

Again I said: "Oh, yes."

He stopped talking, sitting silent for an instant, happy, and satisfied to have explained everything; then he signed, smiled and said:

"I was worried about the luggage."

"Quite," I said. "One never knows...."

"That's true, isn't it?" he said. "One never knows....With these dreadful fellows wandering about."

"Quite," I said. "With these dreadful fellows...."

"Like the fellow who got off at Lentini."

"Who?" said I. "That muffled-up one?"

"Yes," said he. "That muffled-up one....Didn't he look like a criminal?"

I did not reply, and he sighed, glanced about him, read all the little enamel-plated notices in the compartment, gazed

24

at the countryside, empty, uniform with its bald rock, curving swiftly along the sea, and said at length:

"I'm employed at the Land Registry."

"Oh!" said I. "Really? And.... What are you doing? Are you going home on holiday?"

"Yes," he replied. "I'm going home on leave.... I'm going to Sciacca, to my native place."

"To Sciacca," I said. "And do you come from far?"

"From Bologna," he replied. "I work there. And my wife's from Bologna. My sons, too."

He sounded happy.

"And you are on your way to Sciacca from here?" said I.

"Yes, from here," he said. "Syracuse, Spaccaforno, Modica, Genisi, Donnafugata...."

"Vittoria, Falconara," I said. "Licata."

"Aaaah!" he said. "Girgenti."

"Agrigento, please," I said. "But wouldn't it have suited you better to go on via Caltanissetta?"

"It suited me well enough," he said. "And I would have saved eight lire. But it's along the sea, throughout, this way."

"Do you like the sea?" I asked him.

"I don't know," he replied. "I think I like it. In any case I like this line...."

And he sighed and smiled. Then he rose, saying:

"Will you excuse me?"

He went to the next compartment and returned with a boy's lunch basket. It was small and made of fiber, and he set it out on his knees and squat legs, opened it, took out some bread.

"Bread," he said smiling, and giving a little, contented grunt.

Then he took out a long omelet and again smiled.

"Omelet!" he said.

I smiled in response. With a penknife he cut the omelet in two and offered me a half.

"No, thank you," I said, warding off his hand that was thrusting omelet at me.

His face darkened.

25

"What?" he said. "Won't you have some?"

"I'm not hungry!" I said.

He: "Not hungry? One's always hungry on a journey."

I: "But it's not even one yet. I'll eat at Syracuse."

He: "All right. Begin now. And you can carry on at Syracuse."

I: "But that's impossible. I would spoil my appetite."

His face grew still darker. He kept on insisting. "Oh! I'm employed at the Land Registry!" he said again. "Don't be so unkind! Just for the sake of accepting...."

So I accepted and ate the omelet with him. He was glad, and so was I in a way; happy in a way to make him happy, chewing omelet and soiling my hands with omelet as he was. Meanwhile Augusta had gone by, with its mountain of moribund houses rising from the sea, with its ships and seaplanes and salt mines lying in the sunshine. Syracuse was approaching. Through the empty country the train ran along its bay.

"You'll have more of an appetite at Syracuse," he said. And he added: "Are you stopping there?"

"I'm stopping there," I replied.

"Do you live there?" he said.

"No," I replied. "I don't live there."

"But don't you know anybody at Syracuse?" he said.

"No," I replied.

"You're going there on business, then?" he said.

"No," I replied. "No."

He was put out as he looked at me, eating his half of the omelet and watching me eat mine.

I said: "You have a fine baritone voice."

He blushed instantly.

"Oh!" he said.

"Eh? Didn't you know it?" said I.

"As to knowing it, I do," he said, blushing and happy.

And I said: "Naturally. You couldn't have lived until now without knowing it. It's a pity you work at the Land Registry instead of singing...."

"I agree," he said. "I would have liked to sing!—*Falstaff, Rigoletto!*—On every stage in Europe."

"Or even on the streets, what does it matter? Anything's better than being an employee."

"Oh, yes, perhaps...." he said.

He stopped talking, rather disconcerted, and remained silent, chewing. Beyond the curve of the rocky landscape rose the rock of Syracuse Cathedral, against the sea.

"Here we are at Syracuse," I said.

He looked at me and smiled.

"So you've arrived," he observed.

We said good day as the train entered the station.

"I think I'll get my connection at once," he said.

I alighted at Syracuse, the place where I was born and whence I had set out fifteen years before, a station in the journey of my life. Once again as he took down his luggage, the so-called Land Registry employee, No Mustache, in fact, nodded to me.

"So long," he said. "But what will you do at Syracuse?"

I had got far enough away not to reply, so I walked off toward the exit, and never saw him again.

So I was at Syracuse.

But what could I do at Syracuse? Why did I come there? Why did I buy a ticket just to Syracuse and not to any other place? Choice of destination had certainly been a matter of indifference. And certainly being at Syracuse or elsewhere was a matter of indifference. It was all the same to me. I was in Sicily. I was visiting Sicily. And I could just as well get on the train again and return home.

But I had met the orange man, Mustache and No Mustache, the Great Lombard, the Catanian, the tiny old man with a voice like a dry straw's, and the malarial young man enveloped in his shawl, and it seemed no longer a matter of indifference being at Syracuse or elsewhere.

"What an ass!" I told myself. "Why didn't I go to see my mother instead? For the same money I'd have been in the mountains by now...."

And in my hand I found the unposted birthday card for my mother, and I remembered it was the eighth of December. "Damn!" I thought. "Poor old woman! Now unless I take it to her myself, it won't reach her today." And I went to the branch line railway station to find out whether I had enough money on me to continue the journey to my mother's in the mountains.

PART TWO

9

It was three o'clock on that sunny December afternoon. Accompanied by the rumble of the hidden sea, the little train with its diminutive green carriages entered a rocky gorge and then a wood of prickly pear trees. It was the Sicilian branch line railway that ran from Syracuse, through the mountains, to Sortino, Palazzolo, Monte Lauro, Vizzini, Grammichele.

We passed the stations, the wooden shacks with the stationmasters' scarlet caps that caught the sun, and the prickly pear trees. A light gleamed. A gray donkey waded through They seemed to be carved out of blue stone, all those prickly pear trees spreading around us endlessly. The only living creature we happened upon was a boy, wending his way along the railway line and picking the coral-colored fruit with their crowns of thorn that grew upon the stony trees. He gave a shout at the passing train.

The wind was blowing inside the caverns of the forest; when the train stopped, one heard a rumbling like that of the sea earlier, a crackle of minute explosions. A little red flag would flutter, the train would stop, then move off again. Dwellings peeped through the dense wood of prickly pear trees; the train halted on the arch of a bridge amid a cluster of roofs; it passed through a tunnel and was lost again in the trees and the boulders of rock, with no living soul but a boy in sight.

He yelled at the scurrying train, and the sun blazed down on his cries, the red flags, and the stationmasters' red caps.

Then suddenly a red cap, a red flag and a boy's cry were robbed of the sun, and it was dark under the prickly pear trees. A light gleamed. A gray donkey waded through a watery path. The train mounted and crept through tunnels.

Long mountain ridges came into view and, when the train stopped, below in the valley lights shimmered in little clusters of four or five, that were villages.

A torrent roared and a voice cried: "We are at Vizzini." Now the torrent was roaring at the foot of the train; we had stopped. We stepped down by the stream into the black night, with a mountain on one side and the sky on the other.

This was Vizzini, and there I passed the night in a carob-scented room. There was no mail going my way, and I could do with a couple of nights' sleep, and was frozen besides. I didn't mind finding no coach available; all I wanted was sleep, and instantly I dropped off into the most profound slumber with that scent of carob around me. In the carob-flavored morning, drenched as I now was in the flower's perfume, I awoke by the light that stole through a shutterless window. As if I were still asleep, I set out in the mail from Vizzini, perched high above its three valleys, and followed the course of the torrent, climbing for three nights, higher and higher into the mountains, until someone cried, "Snow!"

10

"Just imagine, I'm at my mother's!" I said to myself, as I alighted from the mail at the foot of the long stairway mounting to the more elevated parts of my mother's village.

The name of the village inscribed on a wall, was written just as I wrote it on the card I sent each year to my mother; and the rest—the stairway rising between the aged dwellings, the mountains, and the snow-daubed roofs seemed to me as they had been, I suddenly remembered, once or twice in my childhood. I felt that being there was not a matter of indifference, and I was glad to have come, and not to have stayed in Syracuse, not to have taken the train back to North Italy, not to be yet at the end of my journey. Most important of all was not to be at the end—perhaps to be at the very beginning instead! That is what I felt, at least, gazing up at the long stairway, at the houses and cupolas above, the rocky slopes studded with houses, the roofs in the valley below, the smoke from some gable-end, the patches of snow, the straw, the little group of children around the cast iron fountain in the sunshine, barefooted on the ice-crusted earth.

"Just imagine, I'm at my mother's," I thought to myself again. I found my presence there unexpected, just as one encounters oneself unexpectedly at a certain point in one's memory—and even unreal. I felt that I had begun a journey in the fourth dimension. Nothing had happened it seemed, or nothing more than a dream, a spiritual interlude, between my being at Syracuse and my being here. Moreover, my being here appeared to be the product of a mere decision on my part, of a movement of my memory, not of my person; and so, too, were the morning, the cold mountain air, my pleasure at being here. Nor did I feel any regret at not having got here the previous evening, in time for my mother's birthday, as if this daylight were still of the eighth of December, and not of the ninth, or of a day in the fourth dimension.

I knew that my mother lived higher up, because I remembered mounting the stairway during a visit to my grandparents. So I began to climb. On the steps, as I mounted, were great bundles of fuel wood piled before some houses, and every few yards a patch of snow. In the chilly sunshine—it was almost midday—I finally reached the top of the stairway overlooking the vast landscape of mountains and valleys streaked with snow. Not a soul was about except children with bare feet ulcered with chilblains. I walked here and there among the cottages, and around the cupola of the large mother church that I also recognized as something remote in my memory.

I wandered about with the birthday card in my hand. It bore the name of the street and the number of the house where my mother lived, and I was able very easily to find my way guided, like a postman, by the card and, to a slight extent, by my memory. I also insisted on inquiring at a shop where sacks and barrels were on sale. And thus it was that I called at the house of Signora Concezione Ferrauto, my

30

mother, searching for her like a postman, with the birthday card in his hand, and her name, Concezione Ferrauto, on his lips.

Astride a tiny garden, the cottage, with a short flight of steps in front, was the last in the street. I climbed the steps bathed in sunshine and looked again at the address on the card. I had arrived at my mother's. I recognized the threshold, and I did not feel indifferent at being there; it was the climax of my journey in the fourth dimension.

I gave the door a shove and entered, and a voice from another room called: "Who's there?" I recognized that voice, forgotten for the last fifteen years. That voice of fifteen years ago I now remembered. It was high-pitched and clear. I recalled my mother when she would talk from another room in the days of my childhood.

"Signora Concezione," I said.

11

The lady appeared, tall and fair-haired, and I fully recognized my mother, a tall woman with chestnut, almost golden hair, a hard chin and nose, and black eyes. She wore a red blanket round her shoulders to keep her warm.

I laughed. "Well, happy returns," I said.

"Oh, it's Silvestro," said my mother, and came to me.

I gave her a filial kiss on the cheek. She kissed me on mine and said: "But what on earth brings you to these parts?"

"How ever did you recognize me?" I said.

My mother laughed. "That's what I'm asking myself, too," she said. We got the smell of roasting herrings, and my mother added: "Let's go into the kitchen...I have a herring on the fire!"

We went into the next room, where the sun shone on the dark iron rail of the bed, and then into the little kitchen, where the sun shone on everything. On the floor, within a

31

wooden fender, a copper brazier was burning. On it lay the herring roasting, smoking. My mother bent to turn it. "It tastes good, you'll see," she said.

"Yes," I said, as I inhaled its odor. I did not feel indifferent, I liked it, and I recognized what my meals used to taste like in my childhood.

"I'm sure there's nothing better," I said. And I asked: "Didn't we eat them when I was a boy?"

"Of course, we did," said my mother. "Herrings in winter and capsicums in summer. That's what we ate, always. Don't you remember?"

"And broad beans with cardoons," I said remembering.

"Yes," said my mother, "broad beans with cardoons. You were mad about broad beans with cardoons."

"Ah!" I said. "Was I mad about them?"

And my mother said: "Yes, you always wanted a second helping.... And also of the lentils cooked with onions, dried tomatoes, and bacon...."

"And a sprig of rosemary there was, too?"

"Yes.... And a sprig of rosemary," said my mother.

"And I also wanted a second helping of that, didn't I?" I asked.

"You certainly did! You were like Esau.... You would have given away your birthright for a second helping of lentils.... I can see you when you got back from school, at three or four in the afternoon, by train...."

"That's it," I said, "on the goods train, in the luggage van.... First I alone, then I and Felice, then I, Felice and Liborio...."

"Cheeky sparrows you were!" said my mother. "Your fine heads of hair, your black faces, and your hands always black. ...And you wouldn't lose a moment before you'd ask: 'Is it lentils today, Mama?'"

"You mean, in those line-keepers' houses along the line where we lived," said I. "We'd get off at the station, at San Cataldo, at Serradifalco, and Acquaviva, all those places where we lived, and we'd have to do a kilometer or two on foot to the house...."

"As much as three kilometers sometimes," said my mother. "The train would go by and I'd know you were on

32

the way home, and I'd begin to heat up the lentils and cook the herrings. Then I'd hear you shout: 'Land, land.' "

" 'Land'? Why 'land'?" I asked.

"Yes, of course, 'land'! Some game of yours," said my mother. "And then once, at Racalmuto, the line-keeper's hut stood on an ascent, and the train had to slow down. And you boys had learned to jump off the moving train, and you'd get down in front of the house. I was terrified you'd be run over, and I waited for you outside with a stick."

"And did you beat us?" I said.

And my mother said: "I certainly did! Don't you remember? I'd give you a sound hiding with that stick. And sometimes I'd leave you without any food."

She stood up again with the herring in her hand, held it by the tail, and scrutinized it, first one side and then the other. And in the herring's odor I recalled her face, just as it was when she was young, just as I now remembered it to have been, together with the face that had been shaped anew by the years. My mother, then, was this: the memory of her fifteen or twenty years ago, young and awe-inspiring, with a cane in her hand, waiting for us as we leap from the goods train; there was this remembered vision and, in addition, there was her present self created during the years of our separation; thus she was endowed with a two-fold reality.

She kept examining the herring, first the one side, then the other, fully cooked yet none of it burnt. Of the herring, too, my mind perceived its image in the past and its present shape. Thus everything possessed a two-fold reality: the memory and the present actuality. The sun, the cold, the copper brazier in the middle of the kitchen, and my awareness of this corner of the earth where I was, everything possessed this two-fold reality. That was why perhaps my presence here was not a matter of indifference to me, because it was a journey to something that had a two-fold reality; everything, the journey all the way from Messina, the oranges on the ferryboat, the Great Lombard on the train, Mustache and No Mustache, the green malarial swamps, Syracuse, and, finally, Sicily itself —everything had a two-fold reality, and a fourth dimension acquired during the journey.

12

The herring was tidied up, put on a plate, sprinkled with oil, and I and my mother sat at table—in the kitchen, I mean. My mother sat with her glistening chestnut hair and the red blanket about her shoulders, turned away from the sun that was streaming through the window. The table stood against the wall, and I and my mother sat facing each other; on the floor was the brazier and on top of it the plate of herring almost overflowing with oil. My mother flung me a napkin, handed me a little plate and fork, and drew a half-eaten loaf out of a drawer.

"You don't mind my not laying a tablecloth?" she asked.

"Oh, no," said I.

And she said: "I can't every day...I'm old now."

But Sundays and feast days apart, I remembered, we had always eaten without a tablecloth in my childhood, and my mother always said she couldn't wash every day. I began to eat the herring and bread, and asked: "Why is there no soup?"

My mother looked at me and said: "How was I to know you were going to turn up?"

I looked at her and said: "But I'm thinking of you. Don't you make soup for yourself?"

"Thinking of me?" said my mother. "I've hardly ever eaten soup in my life...I used to make soup for you boys and your father, but as for me, this is what I used to eat: herrings in winter, roast capsicums in summer, lots of oil and lots of bread...."

"Always that?" I asked.

"Always. Why not?" said my mother. "Of course with olives, too, and sometimes pork sausages, when we had pork...."

"Did we keep a pig?" I asked.

"Yes, don't you remember?" said my mother. "We used to keep a pig some years, in those line-keepers' huts. We'd feed it on prickly pears, and then we'd kill it...."

I recalled what the countryside was like around a line-keeper's hut along the railway track, with the prickly pear trees and the shrieks of the pig. We were happy then, I thought to myself, in those line-keepers' huts. All the countryside to roam about in, without having to cultivate it, no peasants, only an occasional sheep, and the men from the sulfur mines returning from work at night, when we were already in bed. We were happy then, I thought to myself....

"Didn't we keep chickens, too?" I asked.

"Yes, we kept a few, of course," said my mother.

"We used to make mustard," said I.

"We used to make all sorts of things..." said my mother. "Tomatoes dried in the sun.... Prickly pear cakes."

"We were happy," I said, and thought it too, recalling the tomatoes drying in the sun during the summer afternoons, without a living soul about throughout the vast countryside. It was dry, sulfur-colored country, and I remembered the great humming in the summertime and the engulfing silences, and once more I thought how happy we were. "We were happy," I said. "We used to have wire netting."

"Those places," said my mother, "were infested with malaria."

"The terrible malaria," said I.

"Terrible, certainly!"

"And the crickets..." said I. Beyond the wire netting that covered the windows and the veranda, I remembered, was a wood teeming with crickets in the sunlit solitude. "I thought it was the crickets, the malaria!" I added.

My mother laughed. "Perhaps that's why you caught so many?"

"Did I catch them?" I said. "But it's their chirping I thought was called 'malaria,' not they. Did I catch them?"

"You certainly did!" said my mother. "Twenty or thirty at a time!"

I said: "I think I caught them because I thought they were grasshoppers. What did I do with them?"

My mother laughed again. "I have an idea you ate them."

"Ate them?" I exclaimed.

"Yes," said my mother. "You and your brothers."

She laughed. I was put out. "Could it be possible?" I asked.

"Perhaps you were hungry," said my mother.

"We were hungry?"

"Perhaps."

"But we were so contented at home," I protested.

My mother looked at me. "Yes," she said. "Your father got his money at the end of every month, and then for ten days we were all right, we were the envy of every peasant and sulfur miner.... But after those ten days we were like them. They'd be eating snails."

"Snails?" said I.

"Yes, and wild endives," said my mother.

"Did they only have snails to eat?" I asked.

"Yes, as a rule, the poor people only had snails to eat," said my mother. "And we were poor the last twenty days of the month."

"Would we be eating snails for twenty days?"

"Snails...and wild endives," said my mother.

I pondered over it, smiled, and then said: "Anyhow, I expect they were pretty good."

"Excellent.... You could cook them in so many ways," said my mother.

"How, in so many ways?"

"Just boiled, for instance. Or with garlic and tomatoes. Or dipped in flour and fried."

"What an idea!" I said. "Shell and all?"

"Of course!" said my mother. "We ate them by sucking them out of their shells. Don't you remember?"

"I remember, I remember..." I said. "You got the flavor in sucking the shells."

"We used to spend hours sucking..." said my mother.

13

We were silent for a minute or two eating the herring. Then my mother began to speak again describing various ways of cooking snails, in order—as she informed me—that I should teach my wife. But I told her that my wife didn't cook snails. And my mother wanted to know how my wife cooked things generally, and I said that she boiled them generally.

"Boiled? Boiled what?" exclaimed my mother.

"Boiled meat," said I.

"Meat? What meat?" exclaimed my mother.

"Beef," said I.

My mother looked at me with disgust. She asked me what it tasted like. I told her that it didn't have any special flavor, and that the soup would contain macaroni or something of the sort.

"And the meat?" asked my mother.

I told her that usually, in fact, there was no meat left once the soup was eaten. I dilated on the matter, describing how the soup consisted of carrots, celery and a piece of so-called meat, which was bone. I explained it carefully so that she should realize that we were better off in North Italy, at least nowadays, at least in the cities, than in Sicily, and one ate fairly well on the whole.

But my mother maintained her look of disgust. "Oh!" she exclaimed. "You mean every day?"

"Of course!" said I. "Of course, not just on Sundays. So long as you work and earn money, at least!"

My mother was disconcerted. "Every day! Don't you get sick of it?" she said.

"What about you? Don't you get sick of your herring?"

"But herrings are tasty," said she, and began to tell me about all the herrings she thought she had eaten in her life. She said that in this—her capacity to consume numberless herrings—she was like her father, that is to say, my grandfather.

"There's something in herring that's good for the brain," she said. "They also give you a good complexion." She enumerated the human functions and other things for which she thought herrings were good, and she announced, moreover, that my grandfather owed his greatness entirely to herrings.

"Was he a great man—my grandfather?" I asked. I vaguely remembered growing up, in my most distant childhood, under a hovering shadow. That must have been the shadow of my grandfather's greatness. I asked: "Was he a great man, my grandfather?"

"He certainly was! Didn't you know that?" asked my mother.

I said yes, I knew it, but I asked my mother what he had done that was great. My mother shouted that he had been great in every respect. He had brought into the world large and beautiful children; all girls, she cried; and he had built this house where she was now living, with his very own hands, though he was not a mason.... "He was a great man," she said. "He could work eighteen hours a day, he was a great Socialist, a great hunter, and great when he rode his horse in the procession on St. Joseph's Day...."

"Did he ride in the procession on St. Joseph's Day?" I said.

"He certainly did! He was a great horseman, the best in the village, and also in Piazza Armerina," said my mother. "D'you imagine they'd hold the procession without him?"

"But he was a Socialist..." said I.

"He was a Socialist..." said my mother. "He could neither read nor write, but he understood politics and he was a Socialist...."

"How could he ride in St. Joseph's procession if he was a Socialist?" said I. "The Socialists don't believe in St. Joseph."

"How stupid you are!" said my mother. "Your grandfather wasn't a Socialist like other Socialists. He was a great man. He could believe in St. Joseph and yet be a Socialist. He had brains enough to do a thousand things at once. And he was a Socialist because he understood politics....Yet he could believe in St. Joseph. He said nothing against St. Joseph."

"But surely the priests looked upon him as an opponent?" said I.

"D'you think he cared about the priests?" said my mother.

"But the procession was a matter for the priests," said I.

"You are an ignoramus!" exclaimed my mother. "The procession was of horses and men on horseback. It was a mounted cavalcade."

She rose and went to the window, and I realized that it was up to me to follow her. "See," she said. The window looked on a slope of roofs, and beyond were the valleys, the torrent and the woods in the wintry sunshine, and still further away the mountain with its crags streaked with snow. "See," said my mother. And I saw with greater intensity the smokeless rooftops, the torrent, the groves of carob trees, the patches of snow. I saw these with greater intensity, or rather, grasped their two-fold reality.

My mother continued: "The cavalcade set out from there, opposite us in the direction of that telegraph pole.... There's a little church there on that mountain, though it can't be seen. They used to illuminate it inside and outside so that it shone like a star. Well, the cavalcade started from the church, with lanterns and bells, and came down the mountainside. Of course, it was always at night. One could see the lanterns, and I knew it was my father at the head, a great big horseman. And everyone would be waiting in the square down below or on the bridge. Then the cavalcade entered the groves, and the lanterns were no longer visible and you heard only the bells. A fairly long interval passed, and next the cavalcade turned up on the bridge with all the bells ringing and the lanterns—and there was my father at the head looking as if he thought himself a king...."

"I seem to remember," said I, and indeed I seemed at least to have dreamed of something like that, of clattering hooves and a great star adorning the mountain in the depths of the night.

But my mother said: "Nonsense! You were hardly three, the only time you saw the procession."

I gazed again at the Sicily that was outside, then at my mother's figure all draped in her red blanket, from her golden head to her feet; and I saw that she had a man's shoes on her feet, my father's old shoes when he was a line-keeper, cut high and possibly with nails on the soles—the sort, I remembered, she always used to wear at home for added comfort, or in order somehow or other to feel grafted on the man, and herself to feel a bit of a man, a rib of a man.

14

We returned to the table, and observing me look at her in silence, my mother said:

"What are you looking at me for?"

"Can't I look at you?" I said.

"Well," said my mother, "if you want to look at me, look at me, but finish eating first."

I cut another slice of bread which was hard and white-crusted, as if it had been badly baked, and said: "What came over Father—going off with another woman in his old age?"

My mother seemed surprised, even offended, and looked as though she was bound to object to everything I said. "What d'you know about it?" she cried.

"That's what he wrote to me," I said.

"Oh, the coward!" cried my mother. "Did he write to you that he met another woman and left me to go off with her?"

I said yes, that that is what I had understood, and she cried: "What a coward!"

"Why?" said I. "Isn't it true?"

"How can it be true?" said my mother. "Don't you remember what a coward he was?"

"Coward?" said I.

"Of course," cried my mother. "When he used to beat me and then start crying and beg my pardon."

An exclamation escaped me. "Oh!" said I. "It's clear he didn't like to."

"Didn't like to!" cried my mother. "As if I couldn't defend myself! And didn't I give him what for! Perhaps that's what he didn't like."

"Ha ha!" I laughed heartily, as I thought of my father, nimble as a boy, with his blue eyes, and my mother, heavy and powerful with her great shoes on her feet, savagely at grips, lamming out at one another and at everything around them, kicking the chairs, smashing the window panes, caning the tables, while we boys would be laughing and cheering. I laughed, and my mother said:

"You see what a coward he was? And when I was in labor he cried too. I had the pains, but I didn't cry; he did. Now if my father had been there!"

"I expect he didn't like to see you suffer," said I.

"Didn't like it!" cried my mother. "Why shouldn't he like it? I wasn't going to die. If he'd only lent me a hand instead of crying...."

"How could he help?" I asked.

"How could he help?" said my mother. "Would you do nothing if your wife were in labor?"

"Well, I'd hold her..." said I.

"You see?" said my mother. "But he didn't even hold me....We were alone in those lonely places, and there was so much to do, prepare the hot water and so on, but all he could do was cry....Or he'd run to the neighboring line-keeper's hut to fetch the women from there....He'd love that, having other women about the house. But they'd never come at once, and I'd be needing help, I'd call to him to help me, to hold me, to help me walk, and he'd be weeping. He didn't want to look...."

"Ah!" I exclaimed. "He didn't want to look?"

My mother looked at me with a sort of squint. "No, he didn't want to look," she said, adding: "I think you boys would see more than he would. You used to come out of your room...."

I interrupted her: "We'd see more than him?"

"Yes, you boys would want to see....You'd come out on the landing from your room and stand near him. But he wouldn't lift his eyes, while you would have yours wide open. You'd see him weeping and me trying to walk by holding on to the chairs and tables. Then I'd shout to him to send you away, but he couldn't even do that....Now if only my father had been there!"

"Your father?" said I.

"Certainly!" cried my mother. "He was a great man, a great horseman, and a peasant who could hoe the soil eighteen hours a day, and he was courageous, and did everything when mother was in labor....I'd like to have seen him in your father's place! I'd be telling him to send you all away, but he'd do

41

nothing. He didn't understand, he didn't raise his eyes, he was afraid of looking. And I'd be calling him coward, telling him to help me, telling him to hold me because of the pains, and he—you know what he'd tell me? He'd tell me: 'Do wait till they arrive.' "

"Who was supposed to arrive?" said I.

"He meant the women he'd been to fetch..." said my mother. "But the women didn't always arrive in time. Once I felt the baby's head popping out—it was the third one of you—and I flung myself on the bed and told him: 'Run, it's come!' "

"And were we watching?" said I.

"Of course," said my mother. "He hadn't sent you away. But you were very small, you and Felice. You were two-and-a-half, and Felice just over a year. And the baby was the third one of you...I saw his head out...."

"And we were watching?" said I.

"Yes, of course!" said my mother. "And the baby was too, with his whole head out and his eyes open. He was a beautiful baby. And I yelled at your father to hurry and pull him out. D'you know what he did? He raised his arms to the heavens and began to invoke God just as he did when he declaimed his tragedies...."

"Oh!" said I.

"Yes, that's what he did," said my mother. "The baby looked at me and his face became violet. He was a beautiful baby, and I didn't want him to be strangled...."

"I expect someone arrived then," I said.

"What a hope!" said my mother. "It was two in the morning and no one arrived....But I seized the flask of water on top of the cabinet, and I was in such a great rage, I flung it at your father's head...."

"Did you hit him?" said I.

"My God, I have a good eye!" said my mother. "I hit him and so he brought himself to help me. And he did help me. He pulled out that baby safe and sound as if he were some other man and not himself. But of course, I had to push harder than he pulled. His face was all blood and sweat...."

42

"You see he wasn't a coward?" said I. "He didn't want for courage. I should say he had something more, which left him when he began to bleed."

"Something more?" my mother exclaimed, looking at her empty plate. "What more d'you want him to have? He wasn't a man like my father!"

She rose from the table and vanished into a dark room beyond the kitchen, into the attic perhaps. It was strange how lightly she walked in her clumsy shoes.

15

"Where are you off to?" I called after her.

She replied in a voice sounding suffocated, as if coming from under a pall of dust: "I'm getting a melon!" And I felt sure that she was in some unused room with a low roof—the attic.

I waited. There was no longer any herring on our plates, nor the smell of herring in the kitchen. My mother returned with a long melon in her hand. "A fine one, isn't it?" she said. "A winter melon!"

She smiled, and she seemed a ghost, herself and the memory of her, twice real with the melon in her hand, as in the line-keepers' cottages in my childhood.

"We used to have melons in winter, too," said I.

"Yes," said my mother. "I used to bury them under the straw in the hen coop. Now I keep them here in the attic. I've got about ten of them."

"In the hen coop?" I said. "It was always a mystery where you kept them! We could never find out. You seemed to be storing them inside yourself. And every so often, like on a Sunday, you'd produce one. You'd vanish like you did now, and return with a melon. . . . It was a mystery. . . ."

"I expect you all used to search for them everywhere," said my mother.

"Of course," said I. "If they'd been in the hen coop, we'd have found them."

"They were there all the same," said my mother. "But in a hole dug in the ground with the straw on top."

"Ah, that's where they were!" said I. "And we used to think you stored them somehow inside yourself. . . ."

My mother smiled. "Is that why you used to call me Melon Mummy?" she asked.

"Did we call you Melon Mummy?" said I.

"Or Mummy of the Melons perhaps. . . . Don't you remember?"

"Mummy of the Melons!" I exclaimed.

The melon, laid on the table, revolved gently toward me, once, twice. The green of its hard rind had delicate veins of gold, I bent down and sniffed.

"Ah, that's it!" I said. "That's it all right."

Not only did I get the penetrating smell of the melon; but the old smell like that of wine in the wintry solitude of mountains, along the deserted railway line, and like that of the tiny dining room, with its low roof, in the line-keepers' cottages.

I looked about me.

"Isn't there any piece of our furniture here?" I asked.

"Not one," said my mother. "Some of the crockery and the kitchen things are ours. . . . The blankets, and the linen. We sold up the furniture when we came here. . . ."

"But what made you decide to come here?" I asked.

"I made the decision. This is my father's house and there's no rent to pay. He built it bit by bit, on Sundays. . . . Where did you expect us to go?"

"I don't know . . ." said I. "But it's certainly very far from the railway! How can you live without even seeing the line?"

"What d'you want to see the line for?" said my mother.

"I'd have thought. . . . Without ever hearing a train go by!"

"What d'you want to hear a train for?" said my mother.

"I'd have thought it mattered to you. . . . You used to go out and stand at the barrier with a flag when it passed."

"Yes, if I didn't send one of you," said my mother.

"Ah, you sent one of us sometimes?" I exclaimed.

Her reply did not matter. I could remember that I was on special terms with the train, as if we had engaged in a dialogue together; for a moment I found myself trying to recall the things it had told me, as if I looked upon the world in the light of what I had learned from it during our conversations.

I said: "There was a certain place where we lived right near the station. Serradifalco, I think. We couldn't see the station, but we could hear the goods trucks banging against one another during the shuntings. . . ."

I remembered the winter, the vast emptiness of the undulating landscape, not a tree to be seen, not a leaf, and the earth smelling wintry, like a melon; and that noise.

"I'd like to hear that noise!" I said.

"Cut the melon," cried my mother.

I pressed on the hard skin, and the knife instantly sank in. Meanwhile my mother had brought wine and glasses. The wine was poor stuff, but the melon lay halved before us and we inhaled the perfume of wintry melon.

16

"And then?" I said.

"Then?" asked my mother.

"Yes, then," said I. "What happened about Father then?"

My mother seemed again put out.

"Why talk about that?" she mumbled. "It's the same to me, with him or without him. . . . And if it's the same to him, being without me, well, I don't care."

"Then it's true he's gone off with another woman?" said I.

"Gone off?" said my mother. "Gone off, nonsense. I sent him away. This was my house, here."

"My, my!" said I. "So you got sick of him and sent him packing?"

"Well," she said. "I stood him for several years. But it became too much. I couldn't bear to see him fall in love at his age. . . ."

"How on earth did he fall in love?" said I.

"But he's always been like that with women," said my mother. "He always wanted other women about the house, to play the cock of the walk with them around him. You know he wrote poetry. He wrote verses to them."

"There's no harm in that," said I.

"No harm? Turning up their noses at me to hear themselves called queens in his verses—no harm?"

"Did he call them queens?" said I.

"Yes, indeed. And queen bees! Grubby railwaymen's wives, school mistresses, and stationmasters' wives—queen bees, indeed!"

"But how could they know he meant them?" said I.

"Well, when a woman saw him being nice to her, looking at her at feasts, while toasting the most beautiful woman, and then declaiming those verses with his arms flung out toward her—what more did she need to know?"

I laughed. "Ah, those feasts! Those gatherings!"

"He was a madcap," said my mother. "He couldn't live without a din. . . . Every six or seven days he was bound to get up something or other. He'd ask over the railwaymen all along the line, with their wives and daughters, and he'd play the cock of the walk! Sometimes there were parties every evening, either at our place or at someone else's. Dancing, card games, or recitation. And he'd be in the center of the show, with his shining eyes. . . ."

I could remember my father with his glinting blue eyes, holding the middle of the stage during my childhood amid the solitude of the Sicilian mountains; and I also remembered my mother, not really unhappy, when she officiated as hostess at home, handing the wine round, radiant, smiling, and by no means unhappy with such a cock for husband.

"There he showed his greatness," continued my mother. "He never tired of dancing, and he wouldn't miss a turn.

When the record was finished, he'd run and change it. Then he'd seize a woman and dance off with her. He could lead a quadrille with some clever step at every phrase of the music. And he could also play the accordion and the pipe. He was the best piper in the mountains and his great voice could fill a valley. Ah, he was a great man! Like an ancient warrior. . . . And you saw that he felt he was a king on his horse. And when the cavalcade appeared on the bridge, with lanterns and bells, with him like a king leading it, we'd all cheer. . . . Long live Papa, we'd shout."

"Who are you talking about?" I asked.

"I'm talking about Papa, your grandfather," said my mother. "Who did you think I was talking about?"

"You're talking about Grandfather?" said I. "Was it Grandfather who played the gramophone?"

"No, no," said my mother. "That was your father. He played the gramophone and changed the records. He'd be running up and changing the records all the time. And he'd be dancing all the time. He was a great dancer, a great gallant. . . . And when he wanted me for his partner, and whirled me round I felt as if I were a child again."

"You felt like a child with Father?" said I.

"No, indeed!" said my mother. "I said with Papa, your grandfather. He was so tall and big, and so proud, with his blond and white beard!"

"Then it was Grandfather that danced," said I.

"Your father danced, too," said my mother. "To the gramophone, with all those women he brought into my house. Danced far too much. He'd have liked to dance every evening. Sometimes I didn't want to go to a party at a line-keeper's cottage if it was too far away. Then he'd look at me as if I'd stolen a year out of his life. But he'd always want us to go to the parties he went to. . . ."

"He? Who?" said I. "Father or Grandfather?"

"Grandfather, Grandfather," said my mother.

47

17

My mother went on for a time speaking about Grandfather, or about Father, or about some other man, at any rate speaking of men, and I was reminded of a sort of Great Lombard. I remembered nothing of my grandfather, except his taking me by the hand and leading me up the paths and steps of this plot of land of his. I imagined him as some sort of Great Lombard—I mean the huge hairy fellow with the little white beard in the train, who had talked about his horse and his female children, and his other obligations.

"I expect he was a Great Lombard," said I.

We had polished off the melon as well, and my mother had risen and was gathering the dishes. "What's a Great Lombard?" she said.

I shrugged. I really didn't know what to reply. "It's a man . . ." I said.

"A man?" said my mother.

"A big, tall man. Wasn't Grandfather tall?"

"He was tall," said my mother. "Is a man that's tall called a Great Lombard?"

"Not really," said I. "Not because of his stature."

"Then why d'you think he was a Great Lombard?"

"Because," said I. "Wasn't he blond, with blue eyes—Grandfather?"

"Is that a Great Lombard?" said my mother. "Someone that's blond and has blue eyes? It's easy to be a Great Lombard!"

"Well," said I. "Perhaps it's easy, perhaps it isn't. . . ."

Shrouded in her scarlet blanket, my mother firmly installed herself in front of the table, her arms folded under her withered breasts, and gave me her squinting look.

"It's easy for a man to be blond and have blue eyes," she remarked.

"True enough," said I. "But a Great Lombard needn't be blond."

I remembered that my father had blue eyes, but wasn't blond. And since I also regarded him as a kind of Great Lombard, declaiming *Macbeth* and all his other tragedies at

48

table for the benefit of railwaymen and line-keepers all along the line, I said: "It can be someone just with blue eyes."

"What about it?" said my mother.

I recalled what, in fact, the Great Lombard was like—that is, the man in the train who had spoken of his other duties—and he seemed, as I thought nostalgically about him, not to have blue eyes, but just an abundance of hair.

"Well," I said, "a Great Lombard is a great hairy fellow. Did Grandfather have a lot of hair?"

"A lot of hair?" said my mother. "No, not a great deal. He had a great beard, white and blond. But he had no hair on the top of his head. He wasn't a Great Lombard!"

"Indeed, he was!" said I. "He was a Great Lombard all the same."

"But could he, if you say a Great Lombard's a great hairy fellow?" said my mother. "He didn't have much hair——"

"What does the hair matter?" said I. "I'm sure that Grandfather was a Great Lombard. One has to be born in a Lombard place."

"In a Lombard place?" exclaimed my mother. "What's a Lombard place?"

"A Lombard place is a place like Nicosia," said I. "You know Nicosia?"

"I've heard of it," said my mother. "It's where they make the bread with the hazelnuts on top. . . . But my father wasn't from Nicosia."

"There are many other Lombard places," I said. "There's Sperlinga, there's Troina. . . . All the places in the Val Demone are Lombard."

"But he wasn't from the Val Demone!" said my mother. "He wasn't a Great Lombard!"

"There are Lombard places even beyond the Val Demone. Aidone isn't in the Val Demone, yet it's a Lombard place."

"Is Aidone a Lombard place?" said my mother. "I once had an oil pitcher from Aidone. . . . But he wasn't from Aidone."

"Where was he from?" I asked. "I suppose he was from the Valle Armerina. From this neighborhood. There is a Lombard place even in the Valle Armerina."

"He was from Piazza," said my mother. "He was born

49

at Piazza, and then he came here. Is it Lombard, Piazza Armerina?"

I was silent for a moment, pondering, and then replied: "No, I don't think Piazza is Lombard."

My mother was triumphant. "You see, so he wasn't a Great Lombard!"

"On the contrary, I'm certain he was!" I exclaimed. "He couldn't help it!"

"But if he wasn't from a Lombard place!" said my mother.

"What does the place matter?" said I. "Even if he was born in China, I'm sure he was a Great Lombard."

My mother laughed. "You're obstinate!" she said. "Why precisely d'you want him to be a Great Lombard?"

I, too, gave a short laugh. I said: "From the way you talk about him I think he must have been one. He seems to have thought about his other duties. . . ."

I said this most seriously, recalling nostalgically the Great Lombard whom I had met in the train, and the many men who were like him, of my father in *Macbeth*, of my grandfather, and of the man like him in my imagination. "He must have thought about his other duties, I think," said I.

"Other duties?" said my mother.

"Didn't he say, these present duties of ours are too old? That they are putrid, dead, and there's no satisfaction in performing them?"

My mother was disconcerted. "I don't know. I don't think so."

"Didn't he say that we are in need of other duties. New duties, no longer the customary ones? Didn't he say that?"

"I don't know," said my mother. "I don't know. I didn't hear him say that."

Once more my presence there seemed to leave me indifferent, being in my mother's house, and on a journey instead of pursuing my daily round. Still nostalgic, however, for the Great Lombard's company, I asked: "Was he content with himself? Was he content with himself and the world, my grandfather?"

Flustered, my mother looked at me for an instant, and was about to say something. But she changed her mind, and remarked: "Why not?"

Again she looked at me. I said nothing. She kept staring at me, and, changing her mind again, she said; "No, at bottom, he wasn't."

"Ah, he wasn't?" said I.

"No, he wasn't with the world," said my mother.

"And was he with himself?" said I. "He wasn't content with the world, but he was with himself?"

"Yes, I think he was with himself . . ." said my mother.

"Didn't he think of his other duties?" said I. "He was content?"

"Why shouldn't he have been?" said my mother. "He felt like a king riding on his horse in the cavalcade. And he had us three beautiful children! Why shouldn't he have been?"

"Well," said I. "Perhaps you don't know whether he was or he wasn't. . . ."

18

Then my mother began to wash up. There was no running water, and she washed dishes in an earthenware basin filled with hot water; at the same time she began a spasmodic whistling.

"Will you give me a hand?" she said, as she picked the first plate out of the hot water. I rose and prepared to do so. She scrubbed the place with a little ash, handed it to me and, pointing to a pail of cold water, told me to rinse the plate and wipe it. We proceeded in this way with the other plates and dishes, my mother whistling and singing, and I watching her.

She sang old tunes without the words, softly, sometimes humming, sometimes whistling, with an occasional trill. She was a strange sight, this woman of some fifty years, with her face that didn't look old; though rather withered by the years, yet not old, even youthful; with her chestnut, almost blond, hair; with her red blanket around her shoulders, and Father's big shoes on her feet. I looked at her hands, large, worn and rugged, completely different from her face, for they could be the hands of a man who felled trees or tilled the soil, while her face was somehow that of an odalisque. "These women of ours," I thought, not meaning Sicilians, but women in general, whose hands were without softness in the night, and, perhaps, at times, unhappy on that account, jealous and savage; to have the heart and face of an odalisque, yet not her hands with which to bind their men to them. I thought of my father and myself, and of all men, with our need of soft hands to caress us, and I seemed partly to understand our restiveness with women; how we were ready to desert them, our women with their hands rough and bony, almost masculine, so hard in the night; and how the odalisque woman by her mere touch could enslave us like a queen. It was this, I thought, that rendered alluring people reared in luxury, the entire bureaucratic-military structure of society, the hierarchies and dynasties, the princes and kings of the story books; the notion of the woman with soft, tended hands. To know that they existed was enough to enable us to perceive what they were like, these women, and to see them remote and inaccessible with their horses, their banners and eunuchs. And that was why, I thought, fairs and seraglios were liked, with their trumpets and flags. Amidst all the fun, our gaze would wander from our own womenfolk to seek other women—I, my father, every man—to seek something else in those other women, without for a moment supposing that it was the caress of soft hands that we sought. How mean we were, I thought, as I looked at my mother's shapeless hands, her shapeless feet clad in the old pair of men's shoes—parts of her other nature that had to be ignored and remain nameless. But all this while my mother was singing, singing like a bird, humming and whistling and giving an occasional trill. Her hands and feet did not matter, even her age did not matter. All that mattered was that she sang and was a bird, the mother-bird of the air and—among her eggs —of the light, the mother-bird shedding light.

"Well," said I, "I expect you pass your time like this when you're alone."

"Like this?" said my mother.

"Yes," said I. "Singing."

My mother shrugged her shoulders and looked as if perhaps she wasn't aware that she was singing.

"Don't you mind being alone?" I added.

She gave me her squinting look of perplexity, wrinkled her brow, and said: "If you think I should feel the loss of your father's company, you're mistaken. . . . What makes you think that? Because you're lending a hand?"

"Why?" said I. "Wasn't he a good companion? I expect he also used to help wash up."

"That doesn't mean I should feel lonely without him . . ." said my mother.

"But he was a nice man!" said I.

"I don't need a nice man about the house!" said my mother. "That was my misfortune, his being nice!"

"I wish you'd explain yourself better," said I.

"Your grandfather, you see, wasn't nice . . ." said my mother. "He didn't call the women queens, he didn't write verses to them."

"I expect he didn't like them," said I.

"Didn't like them?" said my mother. "He liked them ten times more than your father did. But he didn't call them queens. When he liked one of them, he carried her down to the valley. There are many here in the village who still remember him. And many at Piazza, too."

"And you complain of Father?" I said. "I think that with your character you might have been worse off being Grandfather's wife. . . ."

"Worse off?" exclaimed my mother. "How worse off?"

"Well," said I. "Grandfather carried them down to the valley, and Father wrote poetry to them. I think you'd have found those escapades in the valley more painful than poems. . . ."

"Not at all!" said she. "I wouldn't have minded if he'd only carried them down to the valley."

"What?" said I. "He'd carry them down to the valley and write verses as well?"

"Of course," cried my mother. "And call them queens,

treat them like queens. He was a nice man. And if any woman had a nice name, like Manon, for example—he seemed to go quite mad. And that was ridiculous at his age."

"Who was called Manon?" I asked.

"That was the equestrienne in the circus," said my mother. "It was on her account I sent him away. . . . Because her name was Manon. But he always treated them like queens. He was a nice man."

There was a pause, but I didn't speak. My mother seemed to be waiting, so I said: "He was a nice man."

"That was the worst of it," said she. "I wouldn't have minded if he'd just carried them down to the valley. Instead he'd come and tell me: 'My dear, if you were a girl, you could be called Manon.' "

"What's wrong with that?" said I.

"What was wrong was that he treated them like queens, not like dirty sows. And God only knows what he made them believe. That's the worst of it. I couldn't look down my nose at them."

"Ah, you couldn't look down your nose at them?" I said, thinking to myself: Strange woman!

"He made them believe God only knows what, and they would look at me as if they were God only knows what. . . . They'd come to my house, railwaymen's wives, peasant women. They were calm and brazen. They wouldn't lower their eyes. They'd look at me as if they were God only knows what. And I couldn't look down my nose at them."

Strange woman, I thought.

"That was the worst of it," my mother went on. "He made them feel they mattered far more than me! And they looked at me as if they did matter far more than me! He called them queens. He didn't let them think they were just dirty sows. And I couldn't look down my nose at them. . . ."

That's what she said, and I kept thinking: Strange woman! Strange woman! And I almost laughed to myself. I knew what we men were like, perhaps odious—like my father and myself—yet right, after all, in our enthusiasm for women's company, and in encouraging them to think God only knows what. And internally, I almost laughed.

19

Taking up the broom, my mother moved about the place sweeping. She was luxuriating in her role of mother and woman, while I, almost laughing to myself, kept thinking that she herself might well have been one of those she called dirty sows, a queen—despite her rough hands—for other men, mysterious, a queen bee and mother of enthusiasms.

Why not, I thought to myself.

Hers was too rich a maternal sense to have let her play the role of a mere wife, an insignificant, wretched creature worn out in keeping track of her husband's enthusiasms for other women. She had too much old honey in her, moving about the kitchen as she now did, so tall, with her almost blond hair, and the red blanket about her shoulders. She was too full of old honey to have ever been a pathetic creature. And almost laughing to myself, I said: "You're a strange woman! So you would have liked them to know they were sows?"

"I would," said my mother. "I would have liked to laugh at the matter. . . ."

"You're a strange woman!" I said. "You'd have laughed at the matter?"

"Naturally. I wouldn't have minded at all! I'd have laughed at it. But he didn't treat them like sows. . . ."

"Why should he have done that?" said I. "They had husbands like you and children like you."

"That's all very well," said my mother. "No one was forcing them to behave like sows. . . ."

"Was it so dirty, what they did? Didn't they do the same as you did with him? Or were they doing something else?"

"Something else?" cried my mother.

She stopped sweeping for a moment.

"What d'you mean, something else?" she said. "They did the same thing, of course. What else could they do?"

"Well, then?" said I. "They had husbands like you. They had children like you. They were doing nothing dirtier than you did with him . . . Why should he have treated them like dirty sows?"

And! my mother said: "But he wasn't their husband, he was my husband. . . ."

"That's the difference, is it?" I said. I laughed to myself. I saw her standing bewildered in the middle of the kitchen, with the broom in her hand, having stopped sweeping, and I laughed to myself. "I don't understand your reasoning," I said.

And, laughing to myself, I resolved to hazard the blow. "I don't understand your reasoning," I repeated. And I added: "Were you a dirty sow when you did the thing with other men?"

My mother did not blush. Her eyes kindled, her mouth closed, hard, her whole body went hard, and the old honey within her was stirred. She did not blush.

And laughing inwardly, I said: "Because I assume you also went down to the valley. . . ." I was happy to stir the old honey within her and, laughing inwardly, I became loquacious.

"You haven't passed all your time in a kitchen," I said. "You've also been down in the valley with someone!"

"Oh!" said my mother. She stood like a stone image in the middle of the kitchen, the old honey stirred within· her, but not blushing, not ashamed. "Oh!" she said, looking down her nose at me.

When she said this, she was more than my mother, she was a mother-bird, a mother-bee, but the old honey in her was too old, and it calmed itself, and lay still, crafty, and I, after all, was a son of twenty-nine, almost thirty years, unknown to her during half of my life, during the past fifteen years, just a stranger from the street as to that half of me; and so, continuing to sweep, she said: "Well, I expect he deserved my going with other men once or twice!"

Laughing to myself, I thought: Ah, the old sow!

I said: "Of course he deserved it!"

Then I asked: "Several times? With several men?"

"Oh!" my mother exclaimed. "D'you think I put myself out for those men?"

"Of course not," I said. "I wanted to know if you'd been with one or two. . . ."

"With one! With one!" said my mother. "It was a mistake, the other time; it doesn't count."

"A mistake?" said I. "How a mistake?"

"It was with a chum of ours while we were at Messina," said she. "After the earthquake. . . . It was a mix-up, really. I was very young, and it wasn't mentioned any more."

"Oh, really!" said I. "And with the other man?"

"Oh!" said my mother. "With the other man, that was by accident!"

"Was he also a chum of ours?" I asked.

My mother said. "It was someone I didn't know."

"Someone you didn't know?" I exclaimed.

"Is that so strange?" said my mother. "You don't know everything that went on."

"I expect he must have raped you!" I said.

"Raped?" said my mother.

The tone in which my mother said this made me laugh to myself. Then, observing her as if from some other spot in the world, and not from there in her very own kitchen, and in her very own Sicily, I asked: "But where was it? Were we already living in the line-keepers' cottages?"

20

"We were at Acquaviva," said my mother.

I was listening to her now from some other place in the world, and I imagined Acquaviva to be somewhere very remote, a lonely spot lost in the mountains. But I said: "But we were all grown-up at Acquaviva. It was after the war."

"What d'you mean by that?" said my mother. "Ought I to have asked your permission because you were grown-up? You were eleven. You used to go to school and play games. . . ."

So it was in those solitary places, Acquaviva, San Cataldo, Serradifalco; the children would be at school, packed off on the goods train, or playing in the hollows of that undulating countryside, the men busy with the hoe, the mothers with their washing or something else, everyone wrestling with his own devil, alone under that limitless sky. It was marvelous—so far away in space. My mother said it had been a terrible summer. Not a trickle of water, this meant, in all the torrent-beds within a radius of some sixty miles, nothing but stubble everywhere, from east to west. And not a house to be seen for ten or fifteen miles in any direction, except, along the railway track, the line-keepers' cottages engulfed by the solitude. A terrible summer also meant not a single patch of shade throughout those hundreds of miles, crickets exploding in the sun, snail shells emptied by the sun, everything aflame with the sun. "It was a terrible summer," repeated my mother.

She had finished sweeping and was putting things away in the kitchen. She wouldn't talk of her own accord but was willing to reply to my questions. "Was it morning? Was it afternoon?" I asked.

She said: "I think it was afternoon. There were no wasps, no flies, there was nothing. . . . It must have been afternoon."

"And what were you doing?" I asked.

"I had made the bread . . ." she said.

So it was like this: for miles and miles around the odor of serpents dead in the sun, and then, all of a sudden, the smell of freshly baked bread about a solitary house.

"I had made the bread," said my mother.

"And then?" I asked.

"I was washing," my mother said. "We had a tub outside by the well, and it must have been the afternoon because it was just the tub that cast a shadow. . . . I always used to wash in the afternoon."

So it was afternoon, and there was the smell of freshly baked bread about the house. There was a well, with water that had come by train in a cistern-truck, and a woman washing. But my mother would not tell her tale, though she replied to my questions. I asked: "And he?"

"He was a wayfarer," said my mother.

"A wayfarer!" I cried.

"Yes, someone who traveled about on foot," said my mother.

"Those miles and miles without a drop of water . . . without a cottage. . . ."

My mother said: "Yes. With a small haversack containing a change of clothes, and wearing a soldier's uniform without any stars, with an old reaper's cap on his head. He had taken off his shoes, and carried them, tied together, on his shoulder. . . ."

"Had he come from far?" I asked.

"I think so," said my mother. "He told me he had passed through Pietraperzia, Mazzarino, Butera, Terranova and a hundred other places. But he seemed to have come directly from where the war had ended. He was still dressed like a soldier, but he didn't have on any stars."

"All the way on foot?" I said. "Through Terranova, Butera, Mazzarino, Pietraperzia?"

My mother said: "On foot . . . by that day he'd been going forty-eight hours without seeing a village or a living soul."

"And he hadn't eaten for forty-eight hours? Hadn't drunk for forty-eight hours?" said I.

My mother said: "Longer than that. . . . The last place he'd passed was a cattle farm. There the dogs didn't allow strangers to approach. That's what he told me, and meanwhile he'd drunk a pailful of water."

She stopped, as if she had nothing more to say, and I asked her: "He only wanted water?"

"He wanted anything else he could get," said my mother. "In fact he didn't ask, but I gave him a small loaf of bread that I had baked less than an hour before. I seasoned it for him with oil, salt and marjoram, and he sniffed the air and the smell of the bread and said: 'God be praised!' "

Once again my mother stopped and wouldn't proceed with her tale, though she answered my questions. I asked her something—I no longer know what—and my mother said that she didn't want the man to hunger or thirst for anything; that she wanted to see him sated, and it seemed a Christian and charitable act to appease his hunger and thirst for other things.

59

"Blessed old sow," I thought to myself.

"But, after all, he just stopped on his way!" I said.

"No," said my mother, "the man came back on other afternoons."

"He was from these parts, then?" said I. "He wasn't a wayfarer?"

"He was a wayfarer. He was on his way to Palermo and he'd crossed the whole of Sicily."

"Was he going to Palermo? Or did he go to Palermo?"

"He was going, but didn't go. He went as far as Bivona. He found work there, in a sulfur mine, and stayed on."

"At Bivona?" said I. "But Bivona is far from Acquaviva. . . ."

"It's the other side of the mountains. About twenty miles. . . . All the places are about twenty miles away from Acquaviva."

"No," said I. "Casteltermini is less than twenty miles away. Why didn't he stop at Casteltermini?"

"Perhaps there was no work at Casteltermini. Or perhaps he wanted to go on to Palermo, but having got to Bivona, he changed his mind."

"He did twenty miles on foot to come and see you?" said I.

"Twenty coming, and twenty going. He was a wayfarer. . . . And he came back on the seventh day after that afternoon."

"Did he come back several times?" said I.

"Various times. He used to bring me little gifts. Once he brought me a honeycomb. It perfumed the whole house."

"Oh!" I exclaimed. And I said: "How's that he didn't come back?"

"That's it," said my mother. She was about to continue, but she looked at me and said: "You don't ask me if it was the Great Lombard?"

"Oh!" I exclaimed. "Why? What's he to do with it?"

"I think it was him," said my mother. "I think he used to think of his other duties. Isn't a Great Lombard someone who thinks of his other duties?"

"He thought of his other duties?" I exclaimed. "He? The wayfarer?"

60

"Yes," said my mother. "Toward the winter there was a strike in the sulfur mines, and the peasants were also rioting. Trains passed by full of the Armed Police. . . ."

Now my mother was talking freely. There was no need to prompt her.

"The railwaymen didn't come out on strike," she went on. "The trains passed full of the Armed Police. More than a hundred died at Bivona. Not of the Armed Police. Of them. . . ."

"And you think he was among them?" said I.

"That's what I think," said my mother. "Because otherwise wouldn't he have come back?"

"Ah!" said I. I observed my mother. She had nothing more to do in the kitchen. She was quiet and placid, and with her hand she was ironing her dress against her leg. Blessed old sow, I thought to myself once again.

PART THREE

21

A mournful bleat stole in from the afternoon outside; it did not die away but rose, turned to music; it was the pipes.

"Now the Novena time begins," said my mother.

And she added: "I must go on my round."

She sat down on a chair to change her shoes. She pulled off the old pair of men's shoes, and slipped on a pair of lady's boots that stood under the table.

"Your round? What round?" I asked.

"I'll take you with me," my mother replied.

The boots on her feet, she rose, taller and more oscillating, and went into her room to dress for going out, and spoke from there to me, through the music of the pipes. She told me that she had begun to give injections. She felt that she could not expect to get anything from my father, she said, so she had begun to earn a living in this way, by giving injections.

Dressed in a black coat, with a large bag rather like a midwife's slung on her arm, she led me into the cold sunshine of the winter afternoon, and the journey in Sicily was resumed.

22

Passing behind the house down a sloping lane and pursuing our way between garden walls, we came to a door and knocked. The door was opened.

It was dark inside, and I did not see that the door had

been opened. There was no window; there was only a fan light with a blackish pane above the door, and I could see nothing, not even my mother.

But I heard her speaking.

"I have my son with me," she said. "How is your husband?"

"Same as usual, Concezione," a woman's voice replied.

"What a big son you have!" it exclaimed.

From the depths said a man's voice: "I'm here in bed, Concezione."

The voice was cavernous, and spoke again: "Your son, is he?"

"It's Silvestro," my mother said.

They were speaking far away from me, all three voices, belonging to invisible things. They spoke about me, too.

"You've reared him to be big like yourself!" said the woman's voice.

They saw me, yet they were themselves invisible; they were like ghosts. And, like a ghost, my mother gave the injection, in the pitch darkness, talking of ether and needle.

"You must eat," she said. "The more you eat the quicker you'll get well. What have you eaten today?"

"I ate an onion," the man's voice answered.

"It was a good onion," said the woman's voice. "I roasted it for him in the ashes."

"Good," said my mother. "You must give him an egg, too."

"I gave it him on Sunday," said the woman's voice.

And my mother said: "Good."

From the depths of the darkness she called to me: "Let's go now, Silvestro."

I was caressing the warm skin of a goat before me. I had advanced a step or two on the uneven floor of bare earth, and, groping forward with my hands, I had encountered its warm skin. I stood still in the icy dark, and proceeded to warm my hands in that live pelt.

"Let's go now," my mother repeated

But the man's voice from the depths detained her a moment longer.

"How many more injections must I have?" he asked.

"The more you have the sooner you'll recover," my mother replied.

"But I have another five to come," said the voice.

And his wife's voice said: "D'you think he'll be cured with those five?"

"Everything is possible," my mother replied.

Then the door opened and my mother became visible again, with the midwife's bag dangling on her arm, on the threshold.

We went out and continued our way between garden walls to the next house on my mother's round. We turned into a second lane that ran downward under the first. Facing us were the open spaces of the valley and the mountain shaggy with snow. On one side were little houses which, set in their kitchen gardens, stood out against the sky and the distant mountain; on the other, basking in the still brilliant but waning sunshine were rows of dwellings carved in the rock and, higher up, another line of dwellings in their gardens. The kitchen gardens were tiny; among the roofs, on the higher levels, they looked like vegetable bins. In the lane goats were dawdling in the sun. The tinkle of their bells mingled with the music of the pipes in the cold air. It was a little Sicily all heaped up in a pile: medlars and curving roof tiles, hollows in the rock, black earth and goats, with the music of pipes fading behind us and merging in cloud or snow above.

"What is that man suffering from?" I asked mother.

"Like the others," my mother replied. "Some have a touch of malaria. Some a touch of consumption."

23

We had not walked more than a minute or two when my mother knocked at another door, and once more I found myself in darkness, standing on bare, uneven earth, with the smell of a forsaken well around me.

"I have my son with me," said my mother again.

And again I heard people I could not see, speaking about me, and among the voices I discerned the tiny voice of a baby.

"Have you the little phials?" said my mother.

"We have them," a man's voice replied.

"Light the fire, Teresa."

"Fetch the straw."

The man's voice and the baby's voice exchanged words. The owner of the man's voice was carrying his son aged a year or two in his arms. My mother said something about the injection, and the man answered, made various noises, opened a drawer, still holding in his arms the baby with the little, high voice.

The flame of a match flickered in the well's deep darkness. I saw my mother's hands, and when the instant of light upon them passed I heard her ask:

"Well?"

"Well?" she repeated two or three times.

Then she asked: "How d'you feel?"

The man's voice asked loudly: "Concezione is saying: 'How d'you feel?'"

"Eh?" came the reply then.

My mother asked: "What have you given her to eat?"

"We'll give her chicory tonight," replied the voice that was the man's.

After a discussion as to how many more injections were needed, we took leave of those ghosts and went on our way. My mother said that it was lucky the woman was ill, and not the man; because it did not matter if a woman fell ill, whereas if it were a man, then it was the end. . . .

"How the end?" said I.

"They stop eating, winter or summer," said my mother.

As a rule, she said, the woman was quite at a loss when her man fell ill. She would not even be able to gather a little chicory in the valley or to look for snails on the heath. All she could do was to get into bed beside her husband.

24

Sheer cloud or snow, the music of the pipes was far away on the village peak, and from the valley's depths mounted the roar of a torrent.

We entered a darkness that was asphyxiating. It was dark and smoky, yet the voices of the invisible spoke no less calmly than in the other dwellings. Even my mother's voice was not troubled by the smoke.

"I have my son with me," she said.

She made the same remarks as on the other occasions; she spoke about me and then about the little phials and the needle. The flame of a match illumined her hands, and when it blew out, she asked:

"Well, how are you?"

"Ah, well!" came the reply.

"What have you given her to eat?" my mother asked.

"We'll be eating now," was the reply.

"We're cooking," said another voice.

There were many voices.

We came out again, and my mother said quite the contrary of what she had asserted previously. It was a misfortune, she said, when the woman fell ill, the mother. It was better when the man fell ill, she said. Because in winter the men did not work, and were useless, and if the woman fell ill, it meant the end. Because the woman, she said, could always go and gather some chicory in the valley or look for snails on the heath. It was the woman, the mother, that kept the house going.

Again we entered a dark dwelling, again my mother became invisible and spoke invisibly.

She spoke about me: "I have my son with me!"

Then she spoke of the little phials and needle, and gave the injection by the flame of a match which lighted up her hands for a moment. Then she asked whether the patient had eaten, and she was told that he would be eating something that evening or the next day. We went out, and my mother became visible again and maintained the opposite of her previous remarks, saying that when the man became ill, that meant the end. . . .

Again we walked down the dark ditch of the lane, now wholly out of the sun's range and immersed in shade, with the tinkling of goats' bells around us, the roar of the torrent, and the cold. Again we entered places that were dark and smelled of disused wells, or dark and smelled dark, or dark and smoky; and my mother would speak about me as a preamble, then about the little phials and needle, then ask the questions about food; and always, while she was about to leave, there would be a little hesitancy on the part of a preoccupied voice that wanted to know how many more injections were needed to effect the cure, and whether more would not be necessary than a specified number, such as five, seven or ten.

In this way we looked over our assembled pile of miniature Sicily, its medlars and curved tiles and roaring torrents outside, and its ghostly denizens in the cold and darkness inside. My mother, as I accompanied her, was a strange creature that seemed to come alive with me in the light, and with those others in the shade, without ever losing her way as I lost my way somewhat each time I entered or emerged from the darkness.

Every time we came out she would say the contrary of what she had said before. Once she said that when the man fell ill it meant the end. . . . Another time, that when the woman fell ill it meant the end. . . .

She would also say: "One has a touch of consumption, another has a touch of malaria."

Once she would say that it was better to have a touch of malaria than a touch of consumption; another time, a touch of consumption was better than a touch of malaria.

"When it's malaria there's no need to go to Enna for the medicine," she would say.

She related how calamitous it was to have to go to Enna to get the medicines for consumption from the Dispensary; to have to make a long journey and spend thirty-two lire, and also run the risk of being locked up in the hospital. People, she told me, went to Enna once, and never wanted to go again. They weren't able.

"But when it's malaria it's the Commune that hands out the medicine," she said.

Yet the next time she said: "If it's consumption you need only go to Enna and you have all the medicine you want." She recounted how disastrous it was to have to depend on the Commune for the medicines against malaria. The Commune was poor, did not dispose of much medicine, and never issued more than one packet. How could anyone be cured with one packet?

"But with consumption it's the Enna Dispensary that gives out the medicine," she said. "It's big, it's well off, it's run by the Government," she said.

Every time she said the opposite of her previous assertion.

25

When we were very near the roar of the torrent, we entered a house where there was light.

It was not a house hewn out of the rock; it was a stone house standing in its kitchen garden on the edge of the lane. It had a window at the back which let in a little light.

"Good evening, I have my son with me," said my mother as she entered.

She did not become invisible and I saw the people in the house, seeing in them all those whom I had not seen before. I saw the patient in his bed, a man, with shut eyes in his dirty, bearded face; and I saw five or six women looking like nuns who, by the bed-foot, were seated round a pail.

As usual my mother spoke first about me.

"I have my son with me," she said.

And I watched how she spoke the words, how the others observed me upon those words.

"You have a big son!" said one of the women.

"All mine are big, and this is the biggest," my mother said.

"Where's he come from to see you?"

They discussed me as usual, my mother and the women, and I noticed that the pail was full of black snails, which they picked one at a time and sucked. They were young and old women, dressed in black, and when they had finished sucking they would fling the shell back into the pail.

"Good appetite!" my mother called to them.

She began to talk about the phials, needle and ether, opened her bag, turned the patient over, and gave him the injection.

The patient, I saw, remained lying on his face.

My mother addressed him: "Well?"

There was no reply, and again my mother said: "Well?"

An elderly woman replied: "It's no good . . . He doesn't talk."

"He doesn't talk?" my mother exclaimed.

"He doesn't talk," another woman replied.

The five women at the foot of the bed continued sucking snails, and the oldest called out loudly: "Say something, Gaetano. It's Concezione."

The patient slowly turned on his side, but did not reply. The oldest woman turned to my mother.

"D'you see? He doesn't want to talk," she said.

My mother bent over the patient, and I saw her place her hand on his shoulder.

"What's this I hear, Gaetano!" she said. "You don't want to talk?"

Slowly he turned from his side on to his back, and showed his face, but again he gave no reply. Nor had he opened his eyes yet.

"It's useless, Concezione," said the oldest woman. "He doesn't want to talk. . . . Since early yesterday he doesn't talk."

"Has he eaten?" my mother asked.

The woman pointed to the pail, and the oldest replied: "Yes, he has eaten."

Then the patient suddenly spoke. He cursed.

I looked at him and saw that he had opened his eyes.

He kept them fixed on me, scrutinizing me while I scrutinized him, staring into those eyes of his. For a moment we seemed to be confronting each other alone, man to man, regardless of the circumstance of his illness. Nor did I note the color of his eyes, but saw in them only the human race.

"Where d'you come from?" he said.

"I'm Concezione's son," said I.

The man closed his eyes again, and my mother said to the women: "You must keep him cheerful."

And to me: "Let's go, Silvestro."

26

Some time before this I had been very ill for months. I had a profound knowledge of what it meant, that profound misery of miseries of the working class; particularly when one has already been confined to bed for twenty or thirty days, and has to stop within the four walls of his room, he and the bed linen, the metal of the kitchen utensils, and the wood of the chairs, table and cupboard.

At such times there is nothing but these things in the world. You look at them, these pieces of furniture, but you cannot do anything with them, you cannot make soup of a chair or a cupboard. Yet the cupboard is so large that it would provide enough to chew for a month. You look at these things as if they were edible; and perhaps that is why children become dangerous and set about smashing things. . . .

The baby has the peg of the baby chair in his mouth all day and shrieks if his mother tries to take it away. Mother, wife, or even perhaps a mistress, she scans the bookshelf and picks out a volume occasionally and proceeds to read it. She spends hours reading or glancing over its pages.

"What are you reading?" asks the sick man.

The woman does not know what she is reading; yet a book can be anything, a dictionary or an old grammar.

Then the sick man says: "Must you choose this moment to acquire your culture?"

The woman replaces the book, but later returns to scan the shelf of books, not of eatables—and again chooses one, and perhaps leaves the house and spends a part of the afternoon out.

"What did it fetch?" the sick man asks her later.

The woman says that it fetched one lira and fifty centesimi. The sick man is discontented. In the fever's unrelenting grip he never fully grasps the situation, lying on his side in his bed that is unmade for the past three days. Yet he wants something, apart from the book that was his since his youth; and he expects a little soup, and bawls at his wife who, instead, has bought bread and cheese for herself and the children.

"Hawks!" he yells at the children.

They get a plate of soup every day at school. This reveals good initiative, providing a plate of soup every day at school for children of the people who are dying of hunger. But it seems to serve as appetizer. After that spoonful of soup the boys return home ravening. Deaf to reason, they are resolved to eat at any cost. They are like wild beasts, they devour chair pegs and they would like to devour their father and mother. Should they find the sick man alone one day, they would devour him. On the table by the bed-head lie the medicines. The boys arrive from school, ravening, wrought up, their appetites whetted. Prowling like wolves they approach the sick man, they want to eat him up. But their mother is at home, so the boys leave the invalid alone and fall on the medicines.

"Hawks!" cries the sick man.

Meanwhile the gas man has cut off the gas, and the electricity man has cut off the light, and the lengthy evenings are passed in the sick room in total darkness. Only the water has not been cut off; the water man comes every six months, and thus there is no immediate risk of his arriving and cutting off the water; they keep drinking as much water as they can, water cooked in every form, water boiled and even unboiled.

But there is the landlady who comes every day and demands to see the "sick gentleman," demands to see him

71

in person, and, entering the sick room and seeing him, she says:

"Well, my sick gentleman—far too extravagant, paying no rent and stopping in bed . . . at least send me your wife to wash up for me. . . ."

So his wife goes to the landlady's to wash her pots, to wash her floors, to wash her linen; all in lieu of the unpaid rent; and the sick man passes the long hours at home, alone with his inexorable fever, which batters at his face, keeps battering at him, rending him as if taking advantage of his solitude.

His wife returns, and he asks her if she has brought anything from the landlady's house.

"Nothing," says his wife.

She always brings nothing.

"But why don't you at least go and pick some wild vegetables?" he asks.

"Where?" says she.

Down the lanes she trudges and goes to the park. Grass grows on the fields, green foliage on the trees. Vegetables! She tears out some grass, tears out branches of fir and pine. She goes to the gardens and plucks some flowers and returns home with vegetables—the leaves and flowers hidden in her bosom. She flings all this on the sick man, and he lies with flowers strewn all over him.

"There you are," says his wife. "Vegetables!"

27

I knew all this, and more besides. I could understand the misery of a sick member of the human race of toilers, and of his family around him. Does not every man know it? Cannot every man understand it? Every man is ill once, halfway through his life, and knows this stranger that is the sickness inside him, knows his own helplessness against it. Thus every man can understand his fellow. . . .

But perhaps every man is not a man; and the entire human race is not human. That is a doubt that arises on a rainy day, when a man's shoes are tattered and water seeps into them; when his heart is no longer captive to anyone in particular, when he no longer has a life of his own, when he has accomplished nothing or has nothing to accomplish, nothing to fear, nothing to lose, and there, beyond him, slaughter is being perpetrated in the world. One man laughs and another cries; both are human, the one who laughs has also been ill, is ill; yet he laughs *because* the other cries. He is a man who persecutes and massacres; and he who, in his hopelessness, sees the other laugh over his newspaper headlines and his placards, does not seek his company but that of the other who cries. Not every man, then, is a man. One persecutes and another is persecuted; not all the human race is human, but only the race of the persecuted. Kill a man, and he will be something more than a man. Similarly, a man who is sick or starving is more than a man; and more human is the human race of the starving.

I turned to my mother: "What do you think of them?"

"Of whom?" said my mother.

"Of those you injected."

"I think they won't be able to pay me perhaps," said my mother.

"That's all very well," said I. "You go daily to them all the same, give them injections, and hope they'll be able to pay you in return in one way or another. But what d'you think of them? What d'you think they are?"

"I don't hope," said my mother. "I know that one can pay me and another can't. I don't hope."

"Nevertheless you go to all of them," said I. "But what d'you think of them?"

"Oh!" my mother exclaimed. "If I go for the sake of one, I can go for the sake of another. It doesn't cost me anything."

"But what d'you think of them? What d'you think they are?" I said.

73

My mother stopped where we were in the middle of the street, and gave me a faintly squinting look. She smiled too, and said: "What odd questions you ask me! What must I think they are? They are poor people with a touch of consumption or a touch of malaria. . . ."

I shook my head. I asked strange questions. My mother could see that; but she did not give me strange replies. And that is what I wanted, strange replies.

"Have you ever seen a Chinese?" I asked.

"Certainly," my mother said. "I've seen two or three . . . They come this way selling necklaces."

"Good," said I. "When you have a Chinese before you, and you look at him and see he's got no coat on, though it's cold, and his suit's tattered and his shoes torn, what do you think of him?"

"Oh, nothing special," my mother replied. "I see many others here in our village who haven't got coats on when it's cold and have tattered suits and torn shoes. . . ."

"Good," said I. "But he's a Chinese, who doesn't know our language, can't speak to anyone, and doesn't even laugh ever. He travels about among our folk with his necklaces and ties and belts. He hasn't bread, he hasn't money, and he never sells anything, he hasn't any hope. . . . What d'you think of him, when you see that he's such a poor Chinese without any hope?"

"Oh!" my mother replied. "I see many others who are like that here among us . . . poor Sicilians without hope."

"I know," said I. "But he's Chinese. He's got a yellow face, slit eyes, a flat nose, prominent cheekbones, and possibly he stinks. He is more hopeless than all the others. He has absolutely nothing. What d'you think of him?"

"Oh!" my mother answered. "Many people who aren't poor Chinese have yellow faces, flat noses, and possibly stink. They are not poor Chinese but poor Sicilians, yet they have nothing."

"But look," I said. "He's a poor Chinese who happens to be in Sicily, not in China, and he can't even boast of having a good time with a woman. Now a poor Sicilian could. . . ."

"Why can't a poor Chinese?" asked my mother.

74

"Well," I said. "I expect a woman would give nothing to a poor wayfarer who happened to be Chinese instead of Sicilian."

My mother frowned.

"I wouldn't know," she said.

"You see?" I exclaimed. "A poor Chinese is poorer still than all the others. What d'you think about him?"

My mother was irritated. "To the devil with your Chinese."

"You see?" I exclaimed. "He's poorer than all the rest and you send him to the devil. And when you've sent him to the devil, and think of him so poor in the world, hopeless and dispatched to hell, don't you think he's more human, more a member of the human race than all the rest?"

My mother looked at me still irritated.

"The Chinese?" she said.

"The Chinese," I said. "Or even the poor Sicilian who lies ill in bed, just like those you gave injections to. Isn't he more of a man, more of the human race?"

"He?" said my mother.

"He," said I.

"More than who?" my mother asked.

"More than the others," I replied. "The one who's ill. . . . He's suffering."

"Suffering?" my mother exclaimed. "It's the illness."

"Only?" I said.

"Cure the illness and all is well," said my mother. "It's nothing. . . . It's the illness."

Then I asked: "And when he's hungry and suffering, what is that?"

"Well, it's hunger," my mother replied.

"Only?" I said.

"Why not?" said my mother. "Give him some food and all's well again. It's hunger."

I shook my head. I could not get any strange replies out of my mother, yet I asked again: "And the Chinese?"

Now my mother gave me no reply; neither a strange one, nor one that wasn't strange; she shrugged her shoulders. She was right, of course. Cure the sick man of his sickness, and his pain vanishes. Give the hungry man food, and his pain vanishes. But what is man in sickness? And in hunger? Is not hunger the whole pain of the world that goes hungry? Is not the man in hunger more of a man? More a member of the human race? And the Chinese . . . ?

28

Now we were no longer descending the mountainside studded with houses, but climbing another slope from the bottom of the valley, climbing toward the sunshine and the music of the pipes, as cloud or snow, above.

"Have you ever been ill?" I asked my mother.

"Once," my mother replied.

"What was it?" I asked.

"I don't know," my mother replied. "I didn't want the doctor and I didn't know what it was. I recovered by myself."

"You recovered by yourself?" said I. "Always something special about you. . . ."

"Special," exclaimed my mother. "How special?"

"I mean that perhaps you thought yourself different from the others," I answered. "Isn't that so?"

"I didn't think anything," my mother said.

"Wasn't Father ever ill?" I asked.

"He certainly was!" my mother replied. "He was falling ill every moment. He had malaria."

"There you are," said I. "Father wanted the doctor."

"He certainly did!" said my mother. "He was like a baby. He'd shiver and run a high temperature. We knew it was malaria, yet he'd want to see the doctor all the same. . . ."

"Father was a humble man," I said.

"He was afraid," said my mother.

"He was a humble man," said I.

I was a little tired; the mounting road had a parapet on one side, and I stopped and leaned against it. I had traveled from the haven of my hopelessness, and I was still traveling;

76

the journey was also conversation; it was present and past, memory and fantasy; it was not life for me, but it was movement, so I leaned against the parapet and thought of my father—not Macbeth nor the king—so weary and with his blue eyes.

Ailing, he was laden with all the world's grief; he was willing not to be Macbeth, he asked for the doctor, he wanted to get well, he was like an infant.

Is a man more of a man when he is like an infant? He is humble, he avows his own misery and cries out in his misery. Does he become more akin to the human race?

"He was a humble man, at bottom," said I again.

I looked at my mother and drew away my hand from the parapet. "And was Grandfather never ill?" I asked.

"He was very ill," my mother replied.

"What d'you mean?" I exclaimed. "He, too?"

"Why not?" said my mother. "He was about forty, and I was seven or eight."

"I expect he didn't want the doctor," said I.

"No," said my mother. "He got well by himself. . . . The almshouse doctor came once, but he didn't come again. Your grandfather didn't want him."

"Precisely!" said I. "He decided to be unusual."

"What nonsense!" said my mother. "He decided not to be ill."

"There you are!" said I. "He decided to be unusual, to be above getting ill—someone like himself! He was a proud man!"

My mother straightened her back and was proud.

Certainly. He was a proud man," she said.

"And what was wrong?" I asked her. "A touch of consumption or a touch of malaria?"

"Of course not!" my mother exclaimed. "He was very ill," she added. "He died and returned to life!"

Now I was not leaning on the parapet, but on my mother's arm. I pondered on men, myself, my father, and grandfather, men humble and proud, and I pondered on humanity, on pride in misery, and I was proud to be the progeny of man.

Certainly some men are not men; and not all the human

race is human. But not because he is humble is a man not a man. Not even because he is proud.

A man could cry out in his misery, like a child, and yet be more of a man. He can deny his own misery, be proud, and yet be more of a man.

A proud man is a Great Lombard and recalls, when he is a man, his other duties. This makes him more of a man, and his illness becomes death and resurrection.

"It was pneumonia," my mother related. "Or something of the kind. And he didn't want the doctor. Said he wasn't ill. He sent away the alms house doctor. Bread was dear for the poor, he told him. Every mouthful costs a day's work. And he sent the doctor away. We must work, he told him. And he continued to do his fourteen hours a day. Until one night he died and came back to life."

"He was a great man—Grandfather," said I.

"A great man," said my mother.

Emerging from the shaded valley, we found ourselves in a little lane, high up in the sunshine.

"But tell me how I give injections?" asked my mother. "Well, eh?"

"Very well," said I.

"You see?" said my mother, gratified, triumphant.

"You see?" she continued. "I can earn my own living."

We were far away from the roar of the torrent, standing in the sunshine, facing the sun that was about to set. There, on the summit of the village, the snow or cloud of pipe music seemed to dissolve in our path.

"Now let's go to the widow's," said my mother. "That's someone who's got money. Pays cash."

29

The widow was a woman of about forty with a beautiful complexion. Her abode was on the first floor, containing two or three rooms with high ceilings.

"They call her the widow," said my mother, "but she isn't one really. She's a woman who's been kept by a fine gentleman. . . ."

"And why does she have injections?" said I.

"Because she's a lady," my mother replied. "Ladies and gentlemen have injections. And she's got into the habit of doing things like them. But perhaps she's got a touch of consumption, too."

At any rate, she turned out to be a charming creature, with her beautiful complexion. She seemed to live all on her own in her vast rooms. She came herself and opened the door to us.

"I was expecting you, Concezione," she said. "I knew that one of your sons had come. Is this him?"

The house, from the front door beyond, seemed to smell of must that had been left to ferment all the autumn. It is the smell of the richer town houses of Sicily, a smell that does not intoxicate, but nauseates. It is the bedfellow of darkness.

The widow received us noisily and full of laughter. She had a rich chest-voice that rose from her ample bosom, and she had black eyes and black hair.

"I suppose I was right to bring him along," said my mother. "Handsome fellow, isn't he?"

"Tall and strong," said the widow. "Worthy of you, Concezione."

With her uproarious laughter she led us through her rooms that smelled, like the front door and the stairs, of must and also a little of cinnamon. There was an aged look about them, rather bare of furniture, and nothing but fans made of picture postcards on the walls; the rooms were dark, moreover, receiving little light, as their balconies looked westward on to a walled-in garden.

My mother continued to talk of me.

"How did you know that he'd come to visit me?" she said. "I expect I'd have been wrong not to bring him along. . . ."

"Oh," answered the widow. "I'd have been curious to meet him."

She insisted on offering us marsala and cakes.

From the table where she set out the refreshments one could survey the entire floor—two or three rooms with many doors, all of them wide open, a table in every room, and in one an immense bed with a crimson bedspread.

"Such is life!" said the widow.

And she gave her noisy laugh. She put some questions to me about Northern Italy. And she asked my mother whether she had taken me along to all the houses on her beat.

"Of course," said my mother. She was gratified at having imposed my presence on so many households. She added that she had wanted to show me how good she was at injections. The widow laughed. She looked at me, the man, with her dark eyes. Her rich voice that came from her vast bosom, spoke:

"But not with me, Concezione."

"What, not with you?" said my mother.

"You won't show him how good you are at injections with me."

"Why not?" said my mother.

The widow laughed and said: "I won't be injected in front of him."

"Why not?" said my mother. She was full of her resolve to impose me.

"Why not?" she said.

"Because it isn't necessary, Concezione," the widow replied. "It isn't necessary here. There are so many rooms. He doesn't have to wait in the street."

"That isn't the point," said my mother. "I want him to see how I give the injection."

"He has seen that often enough," the widow replied. "He doesn't have to see that here, too."

Turning to me, she laughingly said: "That's true, isn't it, Signor Silvestro?"

"Yes, I expect so," said I. But I liked to have myself imposed.

"What, yes?" my mother asked me. "Don't you want to see how I inject the lady?"

"Oh, yes," I replied.

"There you are!" said my mother. "He does want to see."

"But, Concezione!" cried the widow. "I don't want him to see me."

My mother laughed.

"Ah!" she said. "But he's my son. He's like myself...."

"But he's a young man," said the widow.

"D'you think he's never seen a woman in his life?" said my mother.

The widow said nothing more then. She laughed and yielded. With a gesture toward me, she said with a laugh: "There he is waiting, the rogue!"

She lay on the bed, and my mother undressed her.

"This is using force, Concezione," she laughed from her pillow.

My mother dug in her needle with gusto, then looked at me triumphantly, and pointed to the flesh: "See how well-made she is?"

The widow wriggled on the bed and laughed. "Oh, Concezione!"

"And she's almost forty," said my mother.

I paid the widow some compliment.

"Oh, Signor Silvestro!" cried the widow.

Her resolve hardened and she tried to force herself up. But my mother held her down and uncovered more of the upper part of her body.

"Wait till he sees you properly," she said. And to me: "Look, Silvestro!"

"But this is using force!" said the widow, and again she struggled, trying to get up.

At last my mother let her, and the widow, laughing and red in the face, said to me: "You're a great rogue, Signor Silvestro."

She wished us goodbye cordially. My mother and I went out into the street, into the music of the pipes and the sunshine. The sun opposite was just about to set. We laughed, and my mother said that the widow had created such a fuss because she had been a kept woman, and was embarrassed by her irregular position.

"But she's a good woman," she said. "And she's well-made,

81

isn't she?" she added, looking at me and winking, while we crossed the street.

"Oh, yes," said I.

"And her skin is fresh," added my mother.

"Oh, yes," I said.

"She's one of the best-looking for her age, here in the village."

"I expect so."

"But there are others better than her at her age," said my mother. "I was better than her," she added. "And now that I'm fifty I don't think I compare too badly."

"Oh, no."

"Still fresh and blooming, aren't I?" said my mother.

"Oh, yes," said I. "You haven't a single white hair."

"You ought to see how fresh I am underneath."

"You can be proud of yourself."

"Of course," cried my mother. "That's what I used to tell your father. 'You ought to be proud of a wife as fresh as myself at my age. . . .' But he understood nothing about women. He only spoke about fine hands and fine eyes and so on in his poetry."

"I expect he was incapable of speaking about anything else."

"But he might have considered the other things, before composing," said my mother. "He would have been proud of me had he considered the other things. My father was so proud of me and his other daughters. . . . He used to say that no girl in the whole of Sicily had such a shapely back as ours. Ah, he was proud of me, my father!"

30

At a spot higher up, facing the setting sun, we came to another front door like the widow's, yet smaller and less pretentious, with one of its knockers broken.

"Now we're calling on a friend of mine," said my mother.

"To give her an injection?" I asked.

"Yes," my mother replied. "I want you to see how fresh she is. ... Perhaps more than the widow. And she's almost forty, too."

"Is she also a widow?" I asked. "I mean—has she also been kept by a fine gentleman?"

"Oh, no," my mother replied. "She's a married woman. She has four sons. . . ."

Through the worm-eaten front door we came to the landing, and there, by the stairs, again we got that old smell of must typical of wealthy Sicilian households. But inside there was an even greater emptiness, and everything was extremely old, furniture, floor tiles, curtains, blankets on beds, everything was extremely old and dead, smelling of dust more than anything else.

"What d'you inject her for?" I asked. "Is she ill?"

"No," said my mother. "She thinks she's a bit anemic."

"And will she allow herself to be injected in front of me?" I said.

"Why not?" said my mother.

"But if she's unwilling, don't insist," said I.

"But of course she'll be willing," said my mother.

It was a little boy of five who let us into the flat. Two other little boys came toward us, one perhaps seven, the other eight or nine, wearing long hair and long aprons, so that one couldn't tell whether they were male or female.

"Concezione! Concezione!" they kept yelling, and they led us back and forth through all the rooms which were in complete darkness. Then on a little terrace we ran into a girl of fifteen or sixteen, and she also proceeded to call out: "Concezione! Concezione!"

At last we encountered the lady that was my mother's friend.

"Concezione! Concezione!" she cried.

She was rather small, and not in the least anemic to look at, but charmingly plump, youthful, with a beautiful skin. She flung her arms round my mother's neck and kissed her, as if she had not seen her for several months, and, amid the delighted screams of the leaping children, she cried: "I knew you'd bring your son!"

"You knew he'd arrived?" said my mother.

"Yes," replied her friend. "I knew it at once. So I thought you'd bring him. A handsome fellow!"

The little boys shouted, and the girl spoke, while we stood in a room with a very elevated double bed, and my mother told her friend: "Go on, jump on the bed!"

"Are you going to do it in front of him?" said my mother's friend.

"Why? D'you want to send him out?" my mother exclaimed.

"I didn't say that," her friend replied.

The three boys were in the room, as well as the girl, and the lady that was my mother's friend said: "He gives me ideas. He's so big!"

My mother laughed, and her friend laughed with her. The girl laughed, too.

"But it's I who made him so big," said my mother. "You shouldn't get ideas."

My mother's friend flung herself on the bed.

"I expect he has already seen so many women!" she said. She uncovered herself, and while waiting for my mother to prick her with the needle, she said: "I expect he has seen more appetizing ones than me."

The boys leaped about and yelled and my mother, who was not quite ready with the needle, said: "Are you afraid of giving him an appetite?"

She laughed, and the girl laughed with her, and while the boys leaped all over the place, my mother's friend laughed from her pillow and cried: "Oh, no, Concezione! I know perfectly well I'm almost old enough to be his mother."

Then I said: "I don't think that matters. . . ."

She was good-looking; I wanted to pay her a compliment.

"What d'you mean by that?" she shouted.

"D'you mean that she gives you an appetite?" my mother shouted.

"Why not?" I said.

"Oh!" shouted my mother's friend, laughing.

"Oh!" shouted my mother, laughing.

The girl laughed with them. When the injection was over, my mother's friend got up to speak to me. She laughed and wagged a menacing finger under my chin. "D'you know what you are?" she said. "You're impudent."

We had hardly left, when my mother said: "Did she really give you an appetite?"

"Why not?" I replied.

"Oh," she cried, laughing.

"A woman ten years older than you!" she said, and added: "Did the widow give you an appetite, too?"

"Of course!" I replied. "A bigger one still. . . ."

"Oh!" cried my mother.

She laughed and said: "Had I known I wouldn't have let you see them."

But she was chuckling to herself, seeming somehow triumphant. Up that ascending lane, we came to a sort of clearing that overlooked the entire valley and the waning sun.

My mother looked at the sun, then she turned to me: "When was the first time you saw how a woman's formed?"

31

There the music of the pipes could still be heard in the cold, sunlit air; and it was alive now, not snow nor clouds, but very close, and mingled with the tinkling of goats' bells, no longer occasional, but a full and sustained tinkling, as if a procession of flocks was passing behind the houses.

"When was the first time?" I said.

I began to think, trying to remember in order to answer my mother's question.

"Yes, the first time you saw how a woman's formed."

I tried to remember. I was delighted to remember, and it was easy to do so.

"I think I always knew how a woman's formed," said I.

"Even as an urchin of ten jumping from moving trains?" cried my mother.

"Yes," said I. "I knew quite well at ten how a woman's formed."

"Even at seven?" cried my mother. "Even at seven, when you were a tiny tot and my friends made you sit on their laps?"

"I think so," said I. "Even at seven. Where were we then?"

My mother calculated.

"It was the first year of the war," she said. "We were at Terranova. We were living in a line-keeper's hut about half a mile from the town."

"At Terranova?" I said.

There, when I was seven and eight and nine years old, I had read the *Thousand and One Nights,* and many books of history and travel in olden times, and Sicily, for me, meant also that—the *Thousand and One Nights,* ancient lands, trees, houses, and people of the remotest past encountered in books. Then, during my years of manhood, I had forgotten, but the knowledge was still within me, and I was able to remember and recapture it. Lucky is he who has something to recapture!

It is fortunate to have read books during one's boyhood; and doubly fortunate to have read books of remote epochs and lands, books of history and travel, and the *Thousand and One Nights* in particular. A man can recall what he has read as if he had somehow lived through it. Together with the memory of his own childhood, he contains within himself the history of mankind and the world; thus he knows Persia at the age of seven, Australia at eight, Canada at nine, Mexico at ten, the Hebrews of the Old Testament with the Tower of Babel and King David during his sixth winter; the Caliphs and Sultans during a February or September; and the Great Wars of Gustavus Adolphus and others across Sicily and Europe during a summer in Terranova or Syracuse, while every night trains were bearing soldiers away to the Great War that surpassed all wars.

It was my good fortune to read a great deal in my

childhood, and Terranova in Sicily, for me, embraced Baghdad and the Palace of Tears and the Hanging Gardens. There I read the *Thousand and One Nights,* and other books, in a house that was full of sofas and girls, the daughters of some friend of my father's; and there I remember the spectacle of woman's nakedness; like the nakedness of sultanas and odalisques, concrete, certain, heart and purpose of the world.

"Yes," said I, "I knew how a woman's formed better than ever, at seven."

"Better than ever?" said my mother.

"Better than ever," said I. "I knew it, I saw it. I had it always before my eyes, how a woman's formed."

"What d'you mean?" my mother exclaimed. "You used to think about it?"

"No," said I. "I didn't think about it. I knew it and saw it. That was all. Enough, isn't it?"

"Whose did you see?" my mother asked.

"Every woman's. . . . It was very natural to me. It wasn't cunning."

So it was. It was not cunning. Indeed, it was Woman I saw! At seven one does not know the evils of the world, nor grief and hopelessness; one is not possessed by abstract furies; but one knows woman. Never does a male know woman better than at the age of seven or less. Then she appears before him not as solace, not as delight, not even as a plaything. She is the certainty of the world, immortal.

"Once, when I was seven," I related, "the daughter of one of our friends fell ill and died. She was like your patients, whether humble or proud I do not know. I went on visiting her home. I often used to spend hours at a time by her bedside. I had known her for a long time. She used to play with me and take me on her lap; she used to change her chemise in front of me. While she was ill a woman used to come every day and give her injections. And I'd be there and watch her just as I now watched the widow and your friend. Of course, it wasn't the same thing. There was no question of appetite. But one day she told me: 'I'm going to die!'"

"And then?" cried my mother.

"Nothing," said I.

"How nothing?" exclaimed my mother. "She was a friend of ours, an Aladino. She was a beautiful girl. . . ."

"It was a house full of beautiful girls, wasn't it?" said I.

"Yes," my mother related. "Their father used to go to Malta and return with cargoes of resin. Sometimes one of the daughters used to go with him. Then one remained at Malta and married a goldsmith. . . . Another married a broker. And that third one died. . . ."

My mother ended her tale, and then asked me: "Well? You were speaking of when she died. . . ."

"That's all," I replied. "She died and I continued to go to the house. I looked at her sisters instead of her."

"Weren't you sorry when she died?" my mother asked.

"I don't know," said I. "I used to see the others, naked like her. . . . It was never again so beautiful."

""What?" said my mother. "You haven't seen better-looking women than the Aladinos?"

"I didn't say that," said I.

"And your wife?" cried my mother. "Isn't she at least like the Aladinos, your wife? What sort of wife did you marry?"

"I didn't say that," I repeated.

"There's little of women you've seen!" cried my mother."

"I didn't say that," said I, for the third time.

"Come," said my mother. "Now we'll go to Signorina Elvira's. You'll see how well made a girl can be at twenty."

In the crimson glow of the dying sun she quickened her step, striding ahead of me, among the goats and stray people, while the stirring wail of the pipes filled the air.

"Whenever I give an injection to Signorina Elvira," said my mother, "I always think that perhaps my sons have never seen the like of her."

PART FOUR

32

But by now I was sick of these patients and these women. I opposed my mother, and I would not go up with her to the young woman's.

We stood in front of her mansion halfway up the mountain, and I told my mother: "I'll wait for you here."

"What's this nonsense?" cried my mother.

She swung round as if to strike me, like an outraged mother, but I turned out to be a man of thirty, not a boy, and almost a stranger. She argued and shouted. "What a fool!" she cried. But I won the day, for I really did not want to go up there, the wheel of travel having stopped revolving within me at that very moment. What was the use of seeing yet another woman? Or another patient? What good would it do me? What good would it do them?

Death or immortality I knew; and Sicily or the world was the same thing. I looked at the mansion, and thought of the woman inside ready for my mother's needle, for my stare, for a man; and I refused to consider her more immortal than any other woman, than a patient or a dead man. So I proceeded to sit down on a stone and told my mother once again: "I'll wait for you here."

Then, while waiting, I saw the boy's kite rise from the valley below and, following it with my eyes, I saw it sweep over me into the light high above. I asked myself why, after all, the world was not always the *Thousand and One Nights*, as at the age of seven. I heard the pipes, the goats' bells, the voices from the tier of roofs and the valley, and I kept asking myself the question as I gazed at the kite in the sky. This sort is called the "Flying Dragon" in Sicily, and in those skies it somehow suggests China or Persia, sapphire, opal, geometry; and as I watched it I could not help asking myself why a seven-year-old's faith did not endure for ever in the man.

Or would it perhaps be dangerous? At seven, one sees miracles in all things; and from her nakedness, from woman, the boy derives his certitude of things, just as she, our rib, I expect, derives it from ourselves. Death comes, but in no way does it impair that certitude. At that age the *Thousand and One Nights* of man never offers an insult to the world. A boy asks only for paper and wind, and desires only to launch his kite. He goes out and launches it, and it is a cry that rises from him. The boy carries it through the spheres with a long and invisible thread, and thus his faith glorifies and feeds on his certitude. But what will he do with his certitude afterward? Afterward he knows the insults offered to the world, the impiety, enslavement, and injustice among men, and the profanation of mortals at the expense of mankind and the world. What, then, would he do were he always to possess that certitude? What would he do? he asks himself. What would I do? I asked myself. What would I do?

The kite vanished. I looked down from the sky and saw a knife grinder standing in front of the mansion.

33

The lane overlooking the valley was bathed in sunlight. Black-faced as he looked to my sun-blinded eyes, the knife grinder gleamed from various points of his person and his wheelbarrow.

"Sharpen, sharpen!" he yelled at the windows of the mansion. His harsh cries beat on the glass and stone. He was some wild sort of bird, I saw, with headgear such as one sees in the countryside perched on a scarecrow's head. "Nothing to sharpen?" he shouted.

Now he seemed to turn to me, and I, rising from the stone, crossed the lane in the direction of his voice.

"I'm telling you, stranger," he shouted.

He was big with his legs like a plucked fowl's, and he seemed to be roosting on his trestle, revolving the grinding wheel backward and forward as he tested it. "Have you brought nothing to sharpen to this village?" he shouted.

Now the wheel of travel began once again to rotate within me, so I rummaged in my pockets, first in one, then in another, and while exploring a third the man added: "Haven't you a sword to grind? Haven't you a cannon to grind?"

I drew out a penknife, and the man snatched it out of my hand, and set about furiously sharpening it, looking at me, his face blackened as if by smoke.

"Haven't you got much to grind in this village?" I asked him.

"Nothing much worth while," the knife grinder answered. He was looking at me while his fingers leaped about holding the little blade over the whirling wheel. He was laughing and amiable, this thin, young fellow, under his old scarecrow head-gear.

"Nothing much worth while," he said. "Nothing much that's worth the trouble. Nothing much that gives any pleasure."

"You would sharpen knives well. You would sharpen scissors well," said I.

"Knives? Scissors? D'you think that knives and scissors still exist in the world?" said the knife grinder.

"I had an idea they did," said I. "Don't knives and scissors exist in this village?"

The knife grinder's eyes gleamed like white knives as he looked at me, and through the wide open lips in the black face there issued a rather raucous voice with a bantering intonation. "Not in this village, nor in any other," he cried. "I've been round to several villages and I have fifteen to twenty thousand customers, yet I never see knives or scissors."

"If not knives or scissors, then what do they give you to sharpen?" I asked.

"That's what I always ask them," said the knife grinder. "What have you got for me to sharpen? Have you a sword?

Have you a cannon? I look them in the face, in the eyes, and I see that what they've got can't even be called a nail."

Then he was silent and stopped looking at me; he bent over the grinding wheel, worked the pedal faster, grinding with furious concentration for over a minute. At length he said: "It's a pleasure to grind a true blade. You can throw it, and it's a dart; you can clutch it, and it's a dagger. Ah, if only everyone always had a true blade!"

"Why?" I asked. "D'you think something would happen then?"

"Ah, it would be a pleasure always to grind a true blade!" replied the knife grinder.

He resumed his furious knife grinding for some seconds, then, slowing down, he added in an undertone: "Sometimes I think that it will be enough for everyone to have their teeth and nails ground. I'd grind them into viper fangs and leopard claws."

He looked at me and winked, eyes glinting in the black face, and said: "Ah! Ah!"

"Ah! Ah!" said I, winking back.

He leaned toward my ear and whispered. I listened, laughing and saying, "Ah! Ah!" and whispered in his ear. And we both kept whispering in each other's ear, laughing, and thumping each other's back.

34

The knife grinder gave me back my blade, pointed like an arrow and a dagger. I asked him what it cost, and he told me forty centesimi, and I drew out four coins, each of ten centesimi, and put them on the ledge of his trestle.

He opened a drawer, and I noticed that it was divided into three compartments with ten and twenty centesimi pieces in each, amounting perhaps to five or six lire.

"Poor day, today!" I said.

But he was not listening. I saw him move his lips and

murmur something. He was absorbed in his own thoughts. His fingers juggled with my coins. Little by little his murmur grew audible: "Four for bread," I heard him mumble. "Four for wine...." Then suddenly: "And the man with the mustache?"

Once again he began more loudly: "Four for wine. Four for the mustache...." Then suddenly: "And the bread?"

Whereupon I said: "But why don't you lump it all together and then divide it?"

"Too risky," said the knife grinder. "Sometimes I'd spend it all on food, sometimes on drink...." Scratching his neck, he gave me back ten centesimi, gazing up at the sky. "Take it," he said. "I wanted to charge you ten centesimi too much, but God opposed it. It's these ten that confused me."

Laughing, I put the ten centesimi back in my pocket. He lowered his eyes from the sky to the ground, and, with a satisfied air, divided the three remaining coins among the three compartments. "Ten centesimi for bread, ten for wine, ten for the mustache," he said.

His hands free, he seized his old barrow by the shafts, and started up the mounting lane in the light of the sun that had just set.

I did not hesitate to follow him. "Going up?" I said. "I'll come along with you."

Though gratified to have solved his problem, he was now no longer merry, but sad, and did not speak. He looked about him as he strode, wagging his head under the ancient scarecrow headgear, from right to left and left to right. Everything about him was rather scarecrowish; black face, gleaming eyes, huge thin mouth, patched-up jacket, threadbare trousers, tattered shoes, and those ossified movements of his long legs and his elbows.

Suddenly he said: "You must excuse me. I thought I could do it because you're a stranger."

"Oh, it's nothing," said I. "Ten centesimi more or less...."

He said: "The question is one doesn't know how to deal with strangers. Perhaps there are knife grinders who charge forty centesimi, and one risks spoiling their business by charging only thirty. Don't you agree?"

With the knife grinder's spirits somewhat restored, and

myself amused, we walked on in silence for a while. The sun had vanished below the horizon, and a tinkling of bells rose from the housetops.

The knife grinder cleared his throat. "The world is beautiful."

I, too, cleared my throat. "I suppose so," I said.

The knife grinder said: "Light, shadow, cold, warmth, joy, no joy...."

And I: "Hope, charity...."

The knife grinder: "Childhood, youth, old age...."

I: "Men, children, women...."

The knife grinder: "Beautiful women, ugly women, the grace of God, roguery and honesty...."

I: "Memory, fantasy."

"What does that mean?" exclaimed the knife grinder.

"Oh, nothing," said I. "Bread and wine."

The knife grinder: "Sausage, milk, goats, pigs and cows...mice."

I: "Bears, wolves."

The knife grinder: "Birds, trees and smoke, snow...."

I: "Illness, cure. I know it, I know it. Death, immortality and resurrection."

"Ah!" the knife grinder cried.

"What?" I said.

"It's extraordinary," said the knife grinder. "Ah and Oh! Ih! Uh! Eh!"

"I suppose so," said I.

"It's too wicked to insult the world," said the knife grinder.

I said nothing more. I was pursuing the thoughts that had occupied my mind before I met him, when the kite flew through the sky, just as if he were that kite. I looked at him and stopped, and he stopped too and said: "Please tell me this, if a man finds great pleasure in knowing someone, and then charges him ten centesimi or ten lire too much for a service—a service which he should have rendered gratis in view of his great pleasure in making his acquaintance, what is that man? Does he belong to this world? Or does he insult this world?"

I began to laugh. "Oh!" I laughed. And it was natural enough.

"Isn't he one who insults this world? Is he of this world? Does he belong to this world?"

"Oh!" I laughed lightly, since it was natural.

"Ah!" he laughed.

He raised his hat and bowed. "Thank you, friend," he said. And again he laughed: "Ah!"

I laughed again: "Oh!"

"One sometimes confuses the trifles of the world with the insults of the world," he said.

Then he began again to speak in my ear: "If there were knives and scissors...."

He spoke in my ear for a minute or two, but I did not speak in his. Now it seemed to me as if my kite were talking.

35

We reached a very high point in the village, a sort of square, where no longer were there sunshine, goats' bells, pipes, my mother, or any other woman. The knife grinder pointed to a shop.

"D'you want to meet someone who owns an awl?" he asked.

A horse's head in painted wood surmounted the stone arch of the shop-front. On the sides of the entrance, on the doorposts and the open shutters, I saw suspended, ropes and leather straps, with tassels, bells, and multi-colored plumes.

The knife grinder left his old barrow in the square and leaped ahead of me as we entered the shop. "Ezechiele!" he cried. "Ezechiele!"

Inside was a long corridor with its farther end plunged in darkness. Hanging on its walls, and even from the ceiling, as on the shop-front outside, were ropes, straps, tassels, terrets, and plumes, as well as reins, crops, saddles and every kind of riding equipment.

"Ezechiele!" the knife grinder shouted again as we advanced into the shop.

Someone came up running behind, collided gently with us, passed on, and a boy's voice screamed:

"It's Calogero, Uncle Ezechiele!"

We continued our way down the narrow passage among the trappings and the rest; soon we were groping forward in complete darkness, descending into the very heart of Sicily. It was a good smell in that heart of our land, the smell from the invisible leather and ropes; like that of a fresh coat of dust, earthy, but not yet contaminated by the insults to the world that are perpetrated above. Ah, I thought, ah, if I really believed in all this.... I did not seem to be going underground but moving in the trajectory of the kite; my eyes saw the kite, but at the same time they saw nothing but the darkness; saw my heart as it was in my childhood, a Sicilian heart yet belonging to all the world.

At last a tiny light gleamed ahead of us, the tiny light became twilight, and emerged a man's shape, seated at a small table with reins and crops about him, and the shadows of reins and crops dangling about his head.

"Ezechiele," the knife grinder called out.

The man turned round. His face looked plump, and his tiny eyes glistened as if to say: "Yes, my friend, the world has been insulted, but not inside here, yet!"

He spoke in a melodious voice: "D'you want the awl, Calogero?"

Then he saw me, and his tiny eyes dilated and looked worried, until the knife grinder, my kite, said: "I don't need it this evening, Ezechiele. I found this friend, and he had a blade."

"Oh, really?" the man exclaimed, and stood up. He was short and plump, and had blond curls and dimpled cheeks, and his tiny eyes gleamed again as if to say: "The world has been insulted, but not inside here yet."

He looked for something—perhaps chairs—behind the curtain of leather and ropes and tassels around him, set the little bells tinkling all over the place, and, having found or achieved nothing, he resumed his seat.

"Tell him I'm very pleased," said he to the knife grinder.

The knife grinder stretched out his hand and leaned

96

against a little ladder, which stood beside the table and was almost concealed by the trappings suspended from the ceiling. "He's very pleased too," he replied.

"Very pleased," said I.

And the man smilingly scrutinized me, feeling quite sure that I liked him, though it was because the knife grinder—and not because I—had said so. It was with the knife grinder that he went on talking.

"He looks it all right, I think," he said, still scrutinizing me.

"I saw it at once," the knife grinder replied. "There's no mistaking."

The man Ezechiele: "No, there's no mistaking."

The knife grinder: "He suffers."

The man Ezechiele: "Yes, he suffers."

The knife grinder: "It's for the woes of the outraged world that he suffers. It's not for himself."

The man Ezechiele: "Not for himself, of course. Yet each one suffers for himself...."

The knife grinder: "Yet there aren't any knives or scissors, there isn't anything ever...."

The man Ezechiele: "Nothing, no one knows anything, no one notices anything...."

They stopped talking and looked at one another; the eyes of the man Ezechiele were filled with sadness, and the knife grinder's gleamed whiter than ever in his black face, as if he were almost terrified.

"Ah!" said the knife grinder.

"Ah!" said the man Ezechiele.

They leaned across the little table and whispered in each other's ear. Then the knife grinder drew back and said: "But our friend has a little blade. It's for the woes of the outraged world that he suffers."

"Yes," said the man Ezechiele. He looked at me, his tiny eyes shining sadly as if to say: "The world is outraged, very outraged, more than we ourselves realize."

Then he looked around at the knife grinder.

"Have you told him how we suffer?" he asked.

"I had begun to tell him," replied the knife grinder.

The man Ezechiele: "Well, tell him that we don't suffer for ourselves."

The knife grinder: "He knows that."

The man Ezechiele: "Tell him that we have no reason to suffer for ourselves, no calamities to bear, no hunger, yet we have much to suffer, very much!"

The knife grinder: "He knows it! He knows it!"

The man Ezechiele: "Ask him if he really knows it."

The knife grinder turned to me: "Is it true that you know it?"

I nodded. The man Ezechiele rose to his feet, clapped his hands, and called: "Nephew Achille!"

From beyond the depths of the trappings peered the boy who had dashed into us in the corridor.

"Why don't you stay here and listen to what we're saying?" the man Ezechiele said to him.

The boy was very small, and had blond curls like his uncle. "I was listening, Uncle Ezechiele," he said.

The man Ezechiele registered approval and turned again to the knife grinder.

"Then," he said, "your friend knows that we suffer for the grief of the insulted world."

"He knows," said the knife grinder.

The man Ezechiele began to recapitulate: "The world is big and beautiful, but it has been greatly outraged. Everyone suffers and each for himself, but not for the world that has been outraged, and so the world continues to be outraged."

He looked around him as he spoke, and his tiny eyes closed in sadness, then they eagerly sought the knife grinder. "And did you tell our friend that I write about the woes of the outraged world?"

In fact, a sort of notebook, inkpot, and pen lay on the small table.

"Did you tell him, Calogero?" he said.

"I was about to tell him," said the knife grinder.

"Well," he said, "you can tell it to our friend. Tell him that I spend my days like an ancient hermit with these papers, writing the history of the insulted world. Tell him that I suffer but I go on writing; that I wrote about all the outrages one by one, and about all the outrageous faces that laugh at the outrages they have inflicted and are going to inflict."

"Knives, scissors, pikes," cried the knife grinder.

The man Ezechiele placed his hand on the boy's head and pointed to me. "D'you see this friend of ours?" he said. "Like your uncle, he suffers. He suffers for the woes of the outraged world. Learn from this, Nephew Achille. And now, keep an eye on the shop while I accompany Calogero and our friend to Colombo's for a glass of wine."

36

We came out, and the air was brown and the bells for the Ave Maria were tolling.

The knife grinder seized his perambulating table by the shafts and pushed it along. I walked with him, and the man Ezechiele walked between us, wrapped in a muffler, small and taking short steps.

"The world has been greatly outraged! The world has been greatly outraged!" said his eyes, looking around him sadly. They rested on the knife grinder's advancing table.

"What have you got there on your mill, Calogero?" he asked, stopping.

"What can it be?" the knife grinder said, also stopping.

"It's a piece of paper," said I.

The knife grinder let out a yell. "Bloody hell!" he yelled. "Again!"

"Fined again?" asked the man Ezechiele.

"Again!" yelled the knife grinder.

He lifted his hands to the skies, executed two or three extravagant leaps through the air, bit his hands, tore off his scarecrow headgear, and hurled it on the ground. "But really!...But really!..." he kept saying.

"It's the third time in a month!" he shouted. "Scissors, awls, knives, pikes, and arquebuses; mortars, hammers and sickles; cannons, more cannons, dynamite and a hundred thousand volts...."

Finally Ezechiele made the gesture of Joshua when he stopped the sun.

And the knife grinder stopped.

"Friend," said Ezechiele.

"Yes, friend?" the knife grinder replied.

"Why are we suffering?" Ezechiele asked.

"Why?" answered the knife grinder. "For the sorrows of the outraged human race."

"Not for ourselves, then, " said Ezechiele. "For the sorrows of the outraged world. Not for ourselves...."

"Not for ourselves, of course," said the knife grinder.

He was silent. Again he gripped the shafts and continued to heave the barrow, while we fell into step beside him once more.

"But how am I to pay it?" he muttered.

At this point he seemed to hear something that worried him, and he stopped again. He shook the barrow while he listened. "I don't hear the coins," he said.

It was almost dark in the late twilight, and his eyes flashed like the white blades of sharpened knives in his black face. He opened the little drawer, peered inside, opened it further, drew it out altogether and turned it upside down. Nothing fell out, and Ezechiele said:

"Remember, we don't suffer for ourselves, but for the woes of the outraged world."

"I remember," murmured the knife grinder.

"How much was there?" asked Ezechiele.

"There was bread," answered the knife grinder, "there was wine, there was tax money, sixteen centesimi, sixteen centesimi.... Hadn't been a bad day."

"Well," said Ezechiele. "You'll drink wine with me now at Colombo's, and—with your permission—I'll offer you bread this evening at my table...."

"Yes," continued the knife grinder, "my head is covered

100

by my grandfather's revered hat, my shoulders are shielded by my father's blessed jacket, my shame is concealed by the priest Orazio's trousers, and my feet...there is much kindness between man and man, much kindness, and my roof at home is warmed by Gonzales's milch cows. Why does a man pursue three vocations? In order to live on charity, as the Nazarene enjoined upon us...."

"But, my son," said Ezechiele, "think that perhaps it was a poor wayfarer who took your money. Perhaps he hadn't had anything to eat or drink for days. You must be happy that you've helped him to satisfy his hunger and thirst."

The knife grinder was silent. Heaving a sigh, he began again to push his barrow, speaking as he walked.

"Quite right!" he said. "Quite right! These are not the outrages to the world for which we can suffer. These are mere trifles between one poor man and another. Knives! Scissors! There is much else that outrages the world!"

"Much else!" murmured Ezechiele.

"Much else! Much else!" cried the knife grinder. "And the trifles are only trifles, little jests between man and man. He who hasn't played a little jest on his fellow, let him cast the first stone....I myself played one today on our friend!"

"Oh, yes?" exclaimed the man Ezechiele, and laughed.

"Yes, a tiny jest worth ten centesimi," said the knife grinder, also laughing.

I laughed, too, and the little jest was recounted, and we all three laughed like little children together.

"All the same," said the knife grinder, "that wayfarer could have left me the money for the taxes."

He paused in his laughter and his eyes glinted like the white of keen knives.

"The awls!" he yelled. "And if that wayfarer happens to be the same policeman and sleuthhound who served the notice of fine? It's not the first time my day's earnings vanish just when a notice turns up."

The man Ezechiele seized his arm and held it.

"Just a coincidence!" he cried. "This is not the kind of outrage to the world for which we suffer."

101

37

The cold air was serene, and the birds no longer flitted through the air, but were still in their nests. But the color of things could still be discerned in the little lane, and I saw something and cried: "Look! A flag!"

"Flag?" said the knife grinder.

"What flag?" said the man Ezechiele.

"On that door," said I.

"Oh, that's Porfirio!" said the man Ezechiele. "He's the clothier!"

My two companions laughed, and I remembered the Sicilian custom of indicating cloth shops by hanging a strip of cloth outside the entrance. The color did not matter, it could be green, yellow or blue; but a piece of cloth displayed outside meant a clothier's shop, where one bought materials. This strip happened to be red, and the knife grinder said to me: "But Porfirio has half a pair of scissors."

"Oh, yes?" said I.

"Yes," said the knife grinder, "and as I don't always like to bother Ezechiele for the awl, I sometimes ask Porfirio for his scissors."

Here Ezechiele suggested: "Perhaps we ought to introduce our friend to Porfirio."

"Perhaps so," said the knife grinder.

They led me inside while the knife grinder again left his ramshackle barrow in the street.

The shop had little depth, being a sort of alcove with the materials heaped in great piles on chairs near the doorway.

"Please enter," a clear voice sounded invitingly from the darkness within.

"Good evening," they greeted. "Good evening."

"Good evening," the voice went on. "I was just going to lock up."

"And you're leaving the cloth hanging outside?" asked the knife grinder.

"No, I'm just going to take it down," replied the voice.

"Red again today," said the man Ezechiele.

"Yes," said the voice, "I've been putting out red for some time now. But tomorrow I'll change it to blue."

"Certainly!" said the man Ezechiele. "The world is changeable."

"Changeable! Beautiful! Big!" said the voice.

"And very insulted, very insulted!" murmured the man Ezechiele.

Then the knife grinder said: "Tell him about our friend, Ezechiele."

"What friend?" asked the voice.

A human form stirred about that voice in the darkness. It seemed as if the entire darkness itself was stirring; the form was gigantic. Issuing from that human vastness as it approached me in the lit doorway, the rich warm voice asked again: "What friend? This gentleman here?"

"This gentleman," the man Ezechiele replied. "Like you, Porfirio, and like Calogero the knife grinder, like me, and certainly like many others on the face of the earth, he is one who suffers for the woes of the insulted world."

"Ah!" cried the huge man.

He drew still nearer and a tepid breeze, his breath, ruffled the hair on my forehead.

"Ah!" he cried again.

His great hand descended from above, sought mine and shook it with a shake that, despite everything, was kindly. "Delighted," he said above my head.

He turned to the others: "He suffers, you say?"

He breathed his hot sirocco about my hair, and still clasping my hand with gentle vigor, he repeated: "I'm delighted...."

"Please," I replied. "It's nothing."

"Oh?" the man said. "It's a great deal. I'm most honored."

"The honor is mine," said I.

"No, entirely mine, sir."

Again he turned to the others, while my hair was wafted about in the wind of his breath, and asked: "So he suffers?"

"Yes, Porfirio," the man Ezechiele replied. "He suffers and not for himself."

103

"Not through any worldly trifle," the knife grinder elucidated. "Not because they've fined him, not because he tried to play a little prank on his neighbor...."

"No," said the man Ezechiele. "It's for the universe's woes that he suffers."

"For the woes of the outraged world," said the knife grinder.

The vast Porfirio now touched my head and my face in the darkness, and exclaimed again: "Ah!" Then he said: "I understand and appreciate."

The knife grinder gave a yell: "Scissors and knives!"

"Scissors?" Porfirio repeated softly.

He was a great mound of darkness. Some part of his body exuded a warmth that blew about us like a beneficent Gulf Stream, while his gentle, deep voice, that was a lofty wind, said, "Knives?" His sweet, deep voice continued: "No, friends, neither knives nor scissors, we want nothing like that, nothing but live water...."

"Live water?" murmured the knife grinder.

"Live water?" murmured Ezechiele.

Porfirio continued: "I've told you a thousand times and I tell you again. Only live water can cleanse the outrages inflicted on the world and quench the thirst of outraged humanity. But where is live water to be found?"

"Where there are knives there's live water," said the knife grinder.

"Where there's sorrow in the world there's live water," said Ezechiele.

Now we were engulfed in the night, and we lowered our voices so that no one could hear what we said. We were close to one another, with our heads huddled together. Porfirio was like a great black St. Bernard which kept itself and all of us wrapped in the warmth of its coat. At last he spoke of the live water; then Ezechiele and the knife grinder spoke; and their words were like the night and we were like shadows, and I seemed to have strayed into a conclave of ghosts. At last Porfirio raised his voice:

"Let's go," he said. "I'll stand you all a glass of wine at Colombo's."

He dragged down the red cloth, bolted the door, and down the street he led us enveloped in the warm current of his breath.

38

It was not until we were inside Colombo's that he assumed shape and color. Clad in brown haircloth, he was over six feet tall and three feet broad, with a fine head of pepper-and-salt hair, blue eyes, chestnut beard and red hands, in fact a huge St. Bernard of magnanimous aspect.

"Greetings, Colombo!" he called as he entered the tavern.

The knife grinder brought in his barrow, too.

The room was lit by acetylene lamps and some men were singing: "And the blood of St. Barbara."

Colombo, behind the counter, had a yellow handkerchief, tied pirate-fashion, round his head.

"Hullo!" he replied.

"Wine," said Ezechiele. "These gentlemen are my guests."

"Yours?" Porfirio protested softly. "I invited you all."

The men sang seated on a bench against the wall, without a table before them, holding little iron beakers in their hands, and all in a row swaying from the waist.

"But," exclaimed Ezechiele, "I invited you first."

"Here's the wine," said Colombo, putting down four over-flowing beakers on the counter. "This can be Signor Ezechiele's round. And Signor Porfirio can stand the next round."

"Of course," said Ezechiele.

"I understand and appreciate," said Porfirio. He raised his beaker: "Highly honored."

Ezechiele bowed. I also bowed. The knife grinder cried: "Long live!"

A brazier burned in the middle of the chairless room. Before it squatted two young ploughmen who were warming their hands. Colombo poured out fresh rounds of wine from a cask, the men on the bench swayed and sang softly, and the floor, the walls, and the dark vaults poured forth the odor of wine added to wine through the centuries. Man's entire vinous past was present about us.

"Long live what?" asked the man Ezechiele.

"Long live this!" answered the knife grinder, raising his beaker.

"This?" said the man Porfirio. "What is this?"

He drank, they all drank, I drank too, and we clattered our empty beakers down on the drenched, zinc-plated counter. Colombo produced more wine from the cask.

"The world," cried the knife grinder. "Earth, wood, and dwarfs in the wood; a beautiful woman, sun, light, night, and morning; the scent of honey, love, ecstasy and weariness; dream without outrage, world without outrage."

"And the blood of Saint Barbara," sang the raucous voices on the bench.

We were at our second beakers and a deafening buzz of chatter filled the tavern.

"I don't think so," said the man Porfirio.

"Nevertheless," said the man Ezechiele.

"No, it needs live water," said the man Porfirio.

"Hurrah for live water!" cried Colombo the tavern-keeper. "Here's live water! Isn't this live water? Drink, chaps. Joy, life, live water...."

The man Porfirio shook his immense head, but drank. Everyone drank; I did too; the two ploughmen by the brazier drank with their avid eyes, and the men on the bench sang into their drained glasses.

"Trees and fresh figs, pine needles," the knife grinder went on, "hearts in honored breasts, beer and incense, sirens of the deep; free legs, free arms, free chests, hair and skin free in the wind, free race, and free struggle! Uh! Oh! Ah!"

"Ah aah! Ah aaah! Ah aaah!" sang the men on the bench.

"Ah! Ah!" said the two huddled by the brazier.

Others came in. Colombo cried "Hurrah" and poured out more wine and helped himself to some. And below in

106

the dark vault there was nothing but the naked wine that had lain there through the centuries and the ghosts of men exposed in their alcoholic nakedness through the ages.

"Drink, friend," said the knife grinder, handing me my third beaker.

Porfirio observed: "Our friend is a stranger."

"Yes, he's a stranger," confirmed Ezechiele.

"He met Calogero first."

"He's got a blade," cried the knife grinder. "He's got live water. He suffers for the outraged world. The world is big, the world is beautiful, the world is a bird and has milk, gold, fire, thunder, and floods. Live water to him who has live water!"

"Here's live water, fellows," said Colombo. He drank also, and was naked with a drunken nakedness, a dwarf in the wine-producing mines.

"I'm not such a stranger," I answered Porfirio.

"Not such a stranger?" said Ezechiele.

"How not such a stranger?" asked Porfirio.

Slowly sipping my third beaker, I explained how I was not such a stranger, and Ezechiele's tiny eyes gleamed with satisfaction.

"Ah! There you are!" exclaimed Porfirio.

"Didn't you know he's a son of the Ferrauto?" said the dwarf Colombo.

"The Ferrauto has many knives," cried the knife grinder. "Long live the Ferrauto!"

Everyone had drained his third beaker, while I was only halfway through mine. The knife grinder emptied my beaker on the floor, saying that I had to join them in the fourth round.

"I knew your grandfather," said Porfirio.

"Who didn't know him?" cried the knife grinder. "He had live water."

"Yes" said Porfirio. "He came here with me, we used to drink together...."

"He was a great drinker," remarked the dwarf Colombo.

From the bench against the wall the men's singing now

struck a melancholy note. They still sang, "And the blood of Saint Barbara," swinging from the waist, mournful and naked in the depths of alcohol.

"He, too, suffered for the outraged world," said Ezechiele.

"Outraged world? What outraged world?" cried Colombo, wine's shameless dwarf.

"I also knew your father," said Porfirio.

"We were friends," added Ezechiele. "He was a poet and a Shakespearean actor. Macbeth, Hamlet, Brutus.... He once acted before us."

"Ah! he was magnificent!" cried the knife grinder. "Knives and tridents! Red-hot irons!"

They were all at their fourth beakers, while I held mine in my hand still unsipped, hearing about my father's drinking exploits.

"We used to come here together to drink," said Porfirio.

"It was here that he acted," the immodest gnome remarked. "He appeared in a red cloak and told me that I was the King of Denmark."

"He told me I was Polonius," Ezechiele murmured in a tone of humility. "Ah!" he added. "He suffered greatly for the outraged world!"

At this point the knife grinder again cried: "Long live!"

"Long live what?" Porfirio inquired.

"Long live! Long live!" the knife grinder cried.

"Long live!" cried a drunken man.

"Long live!" cried another drunken man.

"Long live!" murmured humbly the man Ezechiele.

"Long live, long live, long live," chanted the doleful men swinging on the bench.

Those who suffered for their personal troubles, and those who suffered for the sorrows of the outraged world, alike found themselves in the naked sepulchre of wine. They were like spirits freed at last from this world of torment and indignity.

The two young ploughmen, squatting on the floor by the brazier, were weeping sober tears.

108

39

"Another round for me and my friends," ordered Porfirio. He unbuttoned the enormous haircloth garment in which he lived, exposing his limbs. Ezechiele undid his scarf. "This will be the last beaker," said Porfirio, "but a beaker all the same."

He had already drunk six, Ezechiele and the knife grinder five each, and I was still at my fourth, which was almost full. Immense with his red face and hands, his chestnut beard speckled with white, his pepper-and-salt hair, Porfirio held sway in that subterranean world of wine. Unlike Colombo the gnome, he did not belong to that realm, but came like some great victorious monarch to dwell in the strange world that was his conquest.

Yet he denied that wine was live water, and he did not forget the world. "Don't have illusions, don't have illusions," he kept saying.

"About what?" said the knife grinder.

Ezechiele's tiny eyes peered about him, with sudden alarm. "No!" his eyes seemed to be screaming.

Then Porfirio, tightening his red hand on the handle of his seventh beaker, affirmed that wine banished the trivialities of the world.

"But the outrages against the world? The terrible outrages against humanity and the world?" asked Ezechiele.

I, myself, let me repeat, was still at my fourth beaker. Something had stopped me when I'd had my first sip of it. I could drink no more. I did not dare immerse myself any deeper in the squalid, remote nakedness of wine.

"Drink, friend," Porfirio incited me.

I took a sip, trying to drink; between my lips the wine tasted good, but I could not swallow it. All man's past within me made this product of sun and soil appear something that was not alive, but a sad phantom squeezed out of age-old caverns. What else, indeed, could a perpetually outraged world produce? Generation after generation of men had drunk wine and poured their griefs into their cups, seeking self-exposure in wine; one generation drank from another, from the squalid, wine-steeped nakedness of past generations, drank from their torrent of griefs.

"And the blood of Saint Barbara," sang the doleful men on the bench.

By now everyone's head was drooping, everyone was sad. The knife grinder was sad, but his eyes were explosive. Ezechiele was sad, but his eyes were full of terror, looking about him in haunted panic lest he discover again the ghosts of the outraged world.

He had played Polonius before my Shakespearean father. And Porfirio? What role could Porfirio have played to my father's Hamlet? He alone was serene, because he alone was without illusion. Yet the grave responsibility was his. He looked at us, at me, Ezechiele, the knife grinder, and the drunken men at the counter, the two young men squatting by the brazier and weeping, and the chanting men on the bench. Sad, they swayed their heads as they sang, and it seemed as if they swayed it as some do when they cry, and their singing seemed a raucous dirge. Porfirio stared long at them, then again at Ezechiele, at me, the knife grinder, and the two weeping young men who had drunk nothing all the evening. I thought that perhaps he was full of consternation at having dragged so many men in his wake into the squalor of that subterranean empire of his. Instead he was quite serene, isolating himself in a supernatural interchange with the gnome Colombo.

Now he was looking at no one. His smiling face saw nothing but the naked happiness of the wine-gnome Colombo. Then he himself lay down in the womb of wine, and he was naked in blissful slumber, though still standing on his feet; he was the laughing, slumbering ancient who sleeps through the centuries of man's history, Old Father Noah of wine.

I recognized him, and put down my beaker. It was not in this that I wanted to believe. There was no world in this. I came away, I crossed the little lane and returned to my mother's.

40

Her house stood on the brink of the tier of roofs overlooking the valley. I mounted the outside flight of steps and paused on the landing. I did not want to have to go in, I knew, to have to get myself a meal and a bed; I wanted to be on my train instead; so I waited.

The cold was intense, and lights shone below in the valley, as well as above on the mountain, lights in small scattered clusters of four or five; and the air was blue. And in the sky a great star gleamed, icy and forlorn.

It was night, in Sicily and in all the still world. The outraged world was shrouded in darkness; the living had shut themselves up in their rooms with their lights on, and the dead, all those who had been killed, sat up in their tombs, meditating. I pondered, and the vast surrounding night seemed to me a succession of nights. Those lights below and above, that freezing darkness, that glacial star in the sky, were not a single night, but an infinite number; and I thought of the nights of my grandfather, the nights of my father, the nights of Noah, the nights of man, naked in drink and defenseless, humiliated, less of a man than ever a child or a corpse.

PART FIVE

41

It struck me that for Sicily, the Street of the Beautiful Ladies had an excessively nocturnal air about it. So the street close by was named after its ghosts.

There of a night a defenseless man encountered spirits, the Beautiful and Wicked Ladies who mocked and molested him, and trampled upon him—they who were the phantoms of human actions, of all the insults to the world and humanity, who came back from the past. They were not the dead, but phantoms, creatures who no longer belonged to this earth. And they were wont to prey upon a man rendered helpless by drink or by some other means.

Imagining himself to be king or hero, such a man would let his conscience be subdued and accept the old insults as if they were honors. Yet another, were he Shakespeare or my Shakespearean father, would subjugate them and enter their bodies, lift them from the mire and inspire them with dreams; he would force them to confess their sins, to suffer, weep and plead for man and to become symbols of human liberation. It might be someone sober or someone drunk: a mighty Shakespeare in his limpid nights of fearless meditation or my humble father in the mad blindness of his wine-sodden nights.

That was the worst of my father, he was exposed and crazy in his cups, an unfortunate Noah who needed a wretched rag to hide his nakedness, and not a man of portents and miracles.

Anyhow, I did not know this.

While we would wait by the window, night would fall at last and cover the undulating country that was bare of all foliage. Already garbed for his performance, my father would appear, followed a little later by his men.

"Ready?" he would say, snatching his horn of head line-keeper off the wall.

Noiselessly we filed into the handcar, we Hamlet-men. My mother installed herself in the middle and we sat at her feet, while my father worked the handlever, and the two men pushed from behind. That is how the handcar was run: by day, to provide a shovel service along the line: by night, for Hamlet. The two men would push for a time, then leap on themselves when it ran down a slope. We would all be silent, while, in winter, the handcar would roll on its own momentum toward some station waiting room, and, in summer, toward a level stretch of the line. There, in the open, the recitation took place, amidst the reapers from the wheat fields, amidst flares, amidst cries from the spectators, with my father obsessed and strutting about his stage that was set up on sleepers.

Ah, then the night! Everywhere, from the ends of the earth, dogs barked. Jasmin blossomed in the seven invisible heavens and on the mountains of the Milky Way. Ten or fifteen stars appeared, yet the fragrance of a million filled the air.

My father blew the horn as the handcar started.

Then something sounded warningly in his ear, and he would cry: "Who goes there?"

It was another handcar on the line, ahead of us.

"Polonius," came the reply.

Or perhaps: "Fortinbras."

Or: "Horatio."

And they were all naked and crazy men who, by virtue of their wine, mastered those phantoms.

Recalling this, I cried: "Oh, outraged world! Outraged world!"

I expected no reply except from my memory; instead one came from the ground at my feet.

"Hm!" said a voice.

42

Another knife grinder, thought I to myself.

I looked down and searched, but could see nothing. Only the customary lights gleamed in the icy stillness.

"Who's that?" I called.

"Hm!" said the voice again.

I looked again, my eyes probing harder. I noticed that the lights were not the usual ones that shone from the dwellings of the people who had locked themselves in for the night. Those lights were out. These others glowed ruddy in the night, like railwaymen's lanterns set on the ground throughout the valley. But I continued to look for the man who had said, "Hm?"

"Hm!" said I. "Hm?"

"Hm! Hm! Hm!" answered the terrible voice.

I resolved to look for its owner and, walking downward, found myself among those lights that were like abandoned lanterns, and I saw that they were the lights of the dead.

"Ah, I'm in a cemetery," said I.

"Hm!" the voice replied.

"Who are you?" I asked. "Are you the gravedigger?"

"No, no," answered the voice. "I'm a soldier."

The voice sounded near, and my eyes peered hard to make out its owner. But the lights of the dead shed no gleams. "Strange!" said I.

The soldier laughed. "Strange?"

"Perhaps you're on guard here?" I asked him.

"No," said the soldier. "I'm resting."

"Here among the tombstones?" I exclaimed.

"They're most comfortable," said the soldier.

"Perhaps you've come here to remember the dead," said I.

"No," said the soldier. "If anything, to remember the living."

"Ah," said I. "Your sweetheart, I expect."

"A little of everybody. My mother and my brothers, my friends, my friends' friends, and my father in Macbeth."

"Your father in Macbeth?" I exclaimed.

"Certainly, sir," answered the soldier. "The poor man always liked to play the role of a king."

"How's it possible?" I cried.

"Oh, yes!" said the soldier. "They think that the gods tolerate in kings what they abhor in common people."

"But how's it possible?" I cried again. "My father's also like that...."

"Oh, well," observed the soldier. "All fathers are like that. And my brother Silvestro...."

I gave almost a yell. "Your brother Silvestro?"

"Why d'you shout?" asked the soldier. "There's nothing extraordinary in having a brother Silvestro, the poor boy."

"No," I answered, "but Silvestro is my name."

"What about it?" said the soldier. "Names are so few and men are so many."

"Is he thirty years old, your brother?" I asked.

"No sir," the soldier replied. "He's a boy of eleven or twelve. He wears shorts, he has a fine head of hair, and he's in love. He loves, he adores the world. He's like me at this moment...."

"Like you?" I murmured.

"Yes," the soldier replied. "Nothing can harm us in our love, him as a boy, and me...."

"You what?" I murmured.

The soldier laughed. "Hm!"

I stretched my hand. "Where are you?"

"Here," said the soldier.

I approached, groping with my hand, but found nothing. The ungleaming lights of the dead formed a long lane behind me, and there were others around me and ahead of me.

"Where are you?" I asked again.

"Here," said the soldier, "here."

"Ah, on the other side," I exclaimed.

"Certainly," he replied. "On the other side."

"What d'you mean?" I cried. "To the left, then?"

"Hm!" said the soldier.

I stopped. Perhaps I had reached the bottom of the valley. The gleamless lights of the dead were now shining above me. "Now then," I cried. "Are you or aren't you here?"

"That's what I ask myself at times," answered the soldier.

"Am I or am I not here? In any case, I can remember; and see...."

"What else?" I asked.

"That's enough," said the soldier. "I see my brother and I would like to play with him."

"Ah!" I exclaimed. "You'd like to play with a boy of eleven?"

"Why not?" the soldier replied. "He's bigger than me. If he's eleven, I'm seven."

"What?" I cried. "You're seven and a soldier?"

The soldier sighed, and said in a reproachful tone: "I think I've suffered enough getting as far as this."

"This?" said I. "To become a soldier?"

"No," he replied. "To be seven years old. To play with my brother."

"Are you playing with your brother?" I asked.

"Yes sir," he replied. "By your leave, I'm also at play."

"Also?" I observed. "What else are you doing?"

"A lot of other things," he replied. "I'm talking to a girl. I'm pruning a vine. I'm watering a garden. I'm running...."

"Ah, you forget you're in the middle of these tombstones," said I.

"Not at all," he replied. "I know quite well that I'm here as well and that nothing can harm me.... Yes, as to that, I'm quite at ease."

"So you're happy," I observed.

He sighed again. "How can I be happy? I've been lying on a field covered with snow and blood for the past thirty days."

"What's this nonsense you're talking?" I exclaimed.

The soldier did not answer at once, so that I was able to listen to the great silence that separated him from me.

"Hm!" the soldier said.

"Hm?" said I.

"You are right," said the soldier. "Forgive me. It was just a metaphorical way of speaking."

I heaved a sigh of relief and again, instinctively, extended my hand.

"Where are you?" I said.

"Here," said the soldier.

116

43

As before, I looked for him for some minutes, right and left, and then gave up the search.

"It's too dark," said I.

"Quite," he replied.

I proceeded to sit down on a tombstone, beside a dead man's light. "It's better to sit down."

"Yes, it's better," said the soldier. "Particularly as there's the play."

"The play!" I exclaimed. "What play?"

"Haven't you come to see the play?" asked the soldier.

"I know nothing about a play."

"Well, sit down and see.... Here they arrive."

"Who are they?" said I.

The soldier: "All sorts of people; kings and their adversaries, victors and vanquished...."

I: "Is that true? I don't see anybody...."

The soldier: "Because of the darkness perhaps."

I: "Then why do they act?"

The soldier: "They must. They belong to history...."

I: "And what do they act?"

The soldier: "The deeds through which they won glory."

I: "What d'you mean? Every night?"

The soldier: "Always, sir. Ever since Shakespeare stopped putting them in his verses, and he avenges the conquered and pardons the conquerors."

I: "What?"

The soldier: "I told you."

I: "But then it's terrible."

The soldier: "It's frightful."

I: "I expect they suffer much. The unsung Caesars, the unsung Macbeths."

The soldier: "And their followers, their partisans, their soldiers as well. We suffer, sir."

I: "You, too?"

The soldier: "I, too."

I: "But why you, too?"

The soldier: "I act, too."

I: "Do you act? Are you acting now?"

The soldier: "Always. For the past thirty days."

I: "But didn't you say that you were playing with your brother of eleven?"

The soldier: "Yes. And I am talking to a girl, pruning a vine, watering a garden...."

I: "What else?"

The soldier did not reply.

"What else?" I insisted.

"Hm!" the soldier replied.

"Hm? Why hm?" I shouted.

Again the soldier did not reply.

"Hullo there!" I called.

"Hullo!" replied the soldier.

I: "I was afraid you'd gone."

He: "No, I'm here."

I: "I wouldn't like you to go away."

He: "I'm not going away."

"All right," said I.

I hesitated. Again I said, "All right." And again I hesitated. Yet again I said, "All right." Finally I asked: "Is it horrible?"

"Alas, yes," he replied. "A slave in chains and stabbed more brutally each day on a field covered with snow and blood."

"Ah!" I cried. "Is that your role?"

"Precisely," the soldier replied.

"And do you have to suffer much?"

"Much," said he. "Millions of times."

I: "Millions of times?"

He: "For every printed word, for every spoken word, for every quarter-inch of erected bronze."

I: "Does it make you cry?"

He: "It makes us cry."

"But," I said, "you play with your brother and speak to a girl, and do all the other things.... Isn't that a consolation?"

"I don't know," the soldier replied.

"Isn't it enough?" I observed.

"I don't know," the soldier replied again.

"You're hiding something from me," I said. "You seemed to be so peaceful, as if nothing could harm you...."

"That is so," the soldier replied.

"Then it's not true that you weep," I shouted.

"Alas!" the soldier sighed.

With humility I asked him: "Is there nothing I can do to console you?"

He replied again that he did not know.

"Perhaps a cigarette," I suggested.

I delved into my pocket for a cigarette. "Shall we try?" I added.

"Let's try," he answered.

I held out the cigarette. "Here you are," I said.

But the cigarette remained in my hand. "Where are you?" I called out.

"I'm here," said the soldier.

I rose to my feet, advanced a step, then another, still proffering the cigarette, but it remained in my hand.

"Well, do you want it or not?" I shouted.

"I want it, I want it," the soldier replied.

"Take it then," I shouted.

The soldier did not reply. I continued to shout. Then I began to run, and found myself outside the valley, standing once more on the threshold of my mother's house. Far away below, I saw the cemetery with its lights.

44

I slept through the rest of that night, and I forgot. But when I awoke it was still night.

Sicily and its snow-covered mountains lay under a shroud of cold ash. The sun had not risen, nor would it ever rise again; it was night, yet night without peace or slumber; crows flapped through the air; and every so often a bullet shot up from a rooftop or a kitchen garden.

"What's it?" I asked my mother.

"Wednesday," she replied.

She was calm, as usual, her blanket draped about her shoulders and a man's large shoes on her feet, but in a sullen mood, disinclined to talk.

"I'm off today," I told her.

My mother shrugged her shoulders. Seated she was, and on her head were the ashes that shrouded Sicily.

"But what's happening?" I shouted.

I rose and went out on the landing; my mother came slowly behind me. She seemed to be keeping an eye on me.

Bang went a gun.

"What are they firing at?" I asked.

My mother had stopped by the door and was gazing up, where the crows were flying.

"At them?" I asked.

"Yes, at them," said she.

Again there was a burst of rifle-fire. It rent gaps in the ash filling the air, but the crows cawed on invulnerable.

"They're laughing," I remarked.

"Haven't you got over your drunkenness?" asked my mother.

I looked at her. She stood there, I repeat, as if she were keeping an eye on me.

"Was I drunk?" I asked.

"You ought to know it at least!" said my mother. "You came back exactly like your father when he used to return home drunk. Somber. And you flung yourself on my bed, so I was forced to sleep on the sofa."

There was another burst of firing.

"I don't understand what comes over you both," my mother went on. "Your grandfather used to sing and joke when he'd been drinking."

There was a fourth burst from a kitchen garden, then a fifth, but the crows flew on unscathed through the ash high up in the sky, never faltering in their flight, cawing, laughing.

"Why these crows?" I cried.

My mother had become attentive now, watching and waiting for one of the birds to fall.

"But are they really shooting at them?" I asked.

A sixth burst, a seventh, and my mother grew vexed.

"It's useless. They don't hit them," she said.

She vanished into the house and came running back with a double-barreled gun, and herself began to fire.

Bang! Bang!

But the crows flew on unperturbed, out of range.

"They're laughing," I remarked.

"Bang-bang-bang!" my mother replied.

A stout woman shouted from the foot of the stairs. She had brought a message for my mother, and, between the firing and cawing, she called to her: "Fortunate mother!"

45

My mother returned to the kitchen without a word, and sat down.

The brazier smoldered in the middle. Slowly she picked up the tongs, shook, swung them, then dug them in the ashes and turned over the embers one by one. Then she rose and went to the stove. I thought that she had not understood anything.

"Will you have a bite with me before you leave?" she asked me.

"As you please," said I. "As you please."

I kept thinking that she had not understood anything. I would even have been prepared to do something for her, although the journey to Sicily was now at an end. Dear old woman! Fortunate mother! She asked me if I would be content with a herring, as on the day before, and if I wanted some chicory. She asked me if I would like a cup of coffee meanwhile, and set about getting it ready. I watched her as she busied herself about the coffeepot and the stove, isolating herself in her tasks as every woman does, and I shuddered at the thought of her solitude, of mine, of my father's, of my brother's who had died in battle.

"What time d'you leave?" my mother asked me.

Sicily had become concrete, and this made me suffer. I answered that I wanted to reach Syracuse in time to leave it the same evening. She was grinding away at the coffee, and simultaneously reckoning the times of the trains and mails.

At length she said: "You won't get called up at least, I hope."

Then I realized that she had understood everything.

"Oh!" I exclaimed.

"You will come another time," she added.

"Are you happy I came?" I asked her.

"Of course," she said. "It makes one happy to talk to one's son, after fifteen years...."

She finished grinding, and the fizz of the water as it boiled over drew her back to the stove, to all those objects that filled her solitude.

"The years," she continued, "come and go; sons come and go...."

The crows kept cawing outside the window. "Those crows!" she said.

"But what brings them here?" I asked.

My mother shrugged her shoulders. "They turn up every so often."

There was a silence, and I asked her: "Who was it?"

My mother looked at the things of our childhood that were scattered about the kitchen, and her gaze traveled far, then it drew nearer and nearer, and she replied: "It was Liborio."

"Ah, the third of us?" said I.

"He hadn't seen anything of the world, and he was happy when he was called up," she said. "He sent me postcards from the places he went to. Three last year, two this year. Lovely cities. He must have liked them."

"Were they cities mixed up in the war?" I asked.

"I think so," she replied.

"And was he happy?" I shouted.

I was really shouting. Then I added: "That's a grand idea, for a boy!"

"Don't think ill of him now," my mother said.

"Ill?" I shouted. "What put that into your head? He must have been a hero."

My mother looked at me as if I had spoken with bitterness.

"No!" she said. "He was a poor boy. He wanted to see the world. He loved the world."

"Why d'you look at me like that?" I shouted. "He was brave. He was victorious. He was a conqueror."

I yelled even louder. "And he died for us. For me, for you, all of us Sicilians, to make all these things go on, for this Sicily, this world. He loved the world!"

"No!" said my mother. "No! You were boys together. You were eleven and he seven. You—"

"Give me that coffee," I shouted.

"Yes," she replied.

She filled a cup and brought it over to me. Setting it down on a table before me, she added: "If he'd have come back, I don't think he'd have been the same. Poor boy! He loved the world."

46

I saw her burrowing herself in that idea: the poor boy who loved the world and nurtured within himself the yearnings of every boy—to see the world, to visit beautiful cities, to meet women. While I sipped the coffee, my mother stared at me as if I were looking very strange; as if I were sipping the coffee with terror and rage. In fact, I think that I contradicted the thought in her that he was a boy to be pitied, and the idea in me that he was seven. I did not want a soldier to be seven years old. So, with real terror or real rage, I exclaimed: "Hell!"

My mother again seated herself on the chair by the brazier

and, very softly, remarked: "There's only one thing I don't understand. Why did that lady call me fortunate?"

"But it's obvious," I replied promptly. "She does you honor because of his death."

She: "His death does me honor?"

I: "In dying he has done honor to himself...."

Again she looked at me as if I had spoken with bitterness. Indeed, whenever our eyes met she assumed, without fail, a certain look—of suspicion, of reproach. She said, with reproach: "And is that my good fortune?"

"His honor reflects on you," I said obstinately. "You bore him."

"But I've lost him now," she said, still reproachful. "I ought to be called unfortunate."

"Not in the least," said I. "Losing him brought you luck. You are fortunate."

Bewildered, my mother pondered for a moment in silence. She still kept looking at me with distrust and reproach. She seemed to feel herself at my mercy.

"Are you sure that woman wasn't making fun of me?" she asked.

"Oh, no," I replied. "She knew well enough what she was saying."

"She really thought me fortunate?" she asked.

"Certainly," I replied. "She would have liked to be in your place."

She: "In my place? What d'you mean?"

I: "In your place, with Liborio dead.... It would have made her proud."

She: "Then she was envying me...."

I: "Every woman envies you."

My mother continued to watch me with undiminished distrust. Obviously she felt herself at my mercy. Now she burst out: "But what are you saying?"

"I'm saying the truth," said I. "It's also written in the books. Don't you remember anything of your school books?"

"I only studied up to the Third Form," she said.

I: "You've studied a little history?"

She: "Mazzini and Garibaldi!"

124

I: "And Caesar, Mucius Scaevola, Cincinnatus, Coriolanus. Don't you remember anything of Roman history?"

She: "I remember what Cornelia, the mother of the Gracchi, said."

I: "Good! What did Cornelia say?"

She: "She said that her jewels were her sons."

I: "D'you see? Cornelia was proud of her sons."

Now my mother laughed. "What a fool!" she cried. "But Cornelia's sons weren't dead."

"Quite!" said I. "They weren't dead as yet. But why was Cornelia proud of them, do you think?"

"Why?" observed my mother.

"Because she knew they were ready to die.... Cornelia was a Roman mother," I said.

My mother shrugged her shoulders. She was bewildered again, and continued to look at me with distrust.

"Do you see?" I went on. "That lady considered you a kind of Cornelia. Wouldn't you like to be a sort of Cornelia?"

"I don't know," my mother replied with distrust. "What was she like, this Cornelia?" she asked.

"Ah, she was a great woman!" said I. "A noblewoman, a matron...."

"A beautiful woman?" asked my mother.

"Beautiful and wise. Tall. Blond. Like you, I think."

"Now, really!" cried my mother. "Why do they write about her in books?"

"All because of her sons," I shouted.

"Fortunate!" cried my mother.

"D'you see?" I shouted. "You're fortunate like that, too...."

She started. "I?" Her face crimson, her blanket-draped figure quivering with excitement, she cried: "D'you mean they'll write about me, too—in books?"

"More or less," said I. "Of you and your son. Already you both belong to literature."

My mother was overcome. She was slow to regain her composure; and she had lost her feeling of distrust.

"To literature?" she shouted. "To literature?"

"To history," said I. "Didn't you know that leaving this

125

world, he entered the realm of history? And you with him."

"I with him?" my mother cried, overwhelmed.

"You with him," I shouted. "You with him."

"You think you still belong to the world?" I shouted. "To this country, to this Sicily?"

"No, my dear," I shouted louder. "You'll see, they'll send for you, and they'll give you a medal."

"A medal?" my mother cried.

"Yes, to pin on your bosom," I yelled.

Then I lowered my voice, and continued in a calm tone: "For what he has done for the world. For those cities. For Sicily."

"A medal to reward his deeds," I concluded.

But at this point my mother began to break down. "How's it possible?" she said. "He was just a poor boy."

I began to be afraid. I began also to remember.

47

What did "poor boy" mean?

I looked about me in the kitchen, and saw the stove with the cracked earthenware pot on it, and next to it the bread bin, the water jug, the sink, the chairs, the table, and the old clock said to be my grandfather's on the wall; and looking about me I was filled with fear. With fear, too, I looked at my mother. Enveloped in her blanket amidst her possessions, she was like each one of them: redolent of time, of past humanity, of infancy and so on, of men and boys, yet nothing to do with history. There, inside the kitchen, she would continue her days, forever roasting herrings on the brazier and her feet clad in my father's shoes. I looked at her and was afraid.

And I asked myself who was more of a poor boy.

Who was more of a poor boy?

I was afraid, I repeat. And I began to remember. While

126

doing so I took out a cigarette and lit it. It was my first cigarette of the day, the only one I possessed, having saved it from the night I got drunk. I lit it, flung away the match, and, recalling what cigarette it was, I slowly realized that tears were falling on my fingers.

Still smoking, I went out of the house. "Cra, cra, cra," screamed the crows in the ash-teeming sky. I went down into the street, walked along the streets of the Sicily that was no longer in motion as on a journey, but was standing still, and while I smoked, I wept.

"Ah! Ah! He's crying! Why is he crying?" the crows shouted one to another as they followed me.

I walked on without replying. A dark old woman began to follow me and asked: "Why are you crying?"

I did not reply, but walked on, smoking and weeping. Then a porter, waiting in the square with his hands in his pockets, asked me: "Why are you crying?"

He, too, followed me, but I walked on, still crying, past a church. The priest saw us—me and the others who were behind me—and asked the old woman, the porter, and the crows: "Why is that man crying?" He joined us, too.

Some boys saw us and exclaimed:

"Look! He's smoking and crying!"

"He's crying on account of the smoke!" they added.

And they followed me like the others, bringing their playthings with them.

Similarly a barber joined my train, then a cabinetmaker, a beggar, a girl with a scarf round her head, and another beggar.

They would notice me and ask: "Why are you crying?" Or they would ask my followers: "Why does he cry?"

They all became my followers, a drayman, a dog, men and women of Sicily, and even a Chinese.

"Why are you crying?" they would ask.

But I could think of no reply. I did not cry for any reason. At bottom, I did not even cry; I remembered, and remembrance seemed tears in the eyes of the others.

What could I do? I continued on my way. At length I found myself standing at the feet of the nude woman in bronze

who was dedicated to the Fallen, and I found myself surrounded by all my friends of the previous days, by all those
Sicilians whom I had encountered and spoken to during my
journey.

"There are other duties," the Great Lombard told me.
"Don't cry."

"Don't cry," said my friends who had been ill.

"Don't cry," said my women friends.

And my little friend with the oranges, he, too, told me:
"Don't cry."

There was the man from Catania, and he said: "The
gentleman is right. Don't cry."

"Eeh!" said the tiny old fellow with the voice like a dried
reed's.

"But I'm not crying for your sakes," said I. "I'm not
crying."

I sat on a plinth at the feet of the bronze woman, and
around me stood my friends thinking that I was crying on
their account.

"I'm not crying," I went on. "I'm not crying. I'm sleeping
off my drunk."

"What does it signify?" Mustache asked No Mustache.

"There's something he's hiding," said No Mustache to
Mustache.

"I don't cry," I went on. "There's nothing I'm hiding."

"The world is very outraged," cried Ezechiele.

"But I'm not crying in this world," I replied.

"He's crying for his mother," said the widow.

"He's crying for his dead brother," said the other woman.

"No, no," I replied. "I'm not crying within myself. I'm
not crying in this world."

Again I asserted that I was not crying at all, not for anyone
or anything, not in Sicily or anywhere in the world. Then
I bade them goodbye, telling them to go away and repeating
that I was just sleeping off my drunkenness.

"Where did you get drunk?" asked the knife grinder.

"In the cemetery," I replied. "But we mustn't talk about
it."

"Ah!" said the knife grinder.

I finished smoking and remembering. Then I stopped crying.

48

And I lifted my eyes to the naked bronze lady of the monument. She was a beautiful young woman, double life-size with smooth bronze skin. Well made, my mother would have announced, furnished with legs, breasts, back, stomach, arms....She was endowed, in fact, with everything that makes a woman womanly, as if she had freshly emerged from the rib of man.

Mysteriously she suggested sex: long hair adorned her neck with sexual grace, and she smiled a smile of sexual subtlety that came from all the honey within her, and from standing naked right in the middle there in bronze twice as large as she need have been.

I rose to my feet and walked round her in order more closely to scrutinize her. I stood behind her, beside her, and then again behind. My friends watched me, the old ones winked, while the women and girls looked at each other with lowered heads, and the Great Lombard solemnly cleared his throat.

"It's a woman all right," said I.

The knife grinder drew near, planted himself beside me on the pedestal, and likewise lifted his gaze.

"Certainly," he cried. "It's a woman."

We both turned round before her, our eyes still fixed upward on her.

"She has milk there," remarked the knife grinder, and laughed.

The girls laughed, from the foot of the monument. And the Great Lombard smiled.

"It's a woman," I said again.

I stepped back a pace or two on the pedestal, the knife grinder followed me, and we both regarded the woman's figure in its entirety.

"Not bad, eh?" said the knife grinder.

I drew his attention to her smile, and he gave me a gentle nudge with his elbow. "Ah! Ah!" he said.

The woman stood erect, with one arm raised to the sky, and the other arched over her bosom as if reaching for her opposite armpit. She was smiling.

"She knows everything," said the knife grinder.

A girl at the foot of the statue laughed, and the knife grinder added: "She's as smart as you make them!"

"Smarter than that," said I. "She knows that she can't be harmed."

"Really?" cried my questioner.

"Of course," said I. "She knows that she's bronze."

"Ah, that's it!" cried my questioners.

"One can see that, can't one?" I went on.

"One can see that," they acknowledged.

I descended a step and sat down. They all retreated a pace or two and sat down.

"This woman is for them," said I

They all agreed.

"These are not just ordinary dead folk," I went on. "They don't belong to the world, they belong elsewhere, and this woman is for them."

"Hm!" the soldier interjected.

"Is it not noble on our part to dedicate this woman to them?" I continued. "In paying homage to this woman we pay homage to them."

"Hm!" the soldier interjected. "Hm! Hm!"

"And in this woman," I went on, "in this woman...."

I stopped myself, and the soldier spoke within me, loudly: "Hm!"

"Hm?" asked my questioners, who were seated round me.

"Nothing," said I. "I only said 'Hm!'"

But again the soldier spoke within me: "Hm!"

"Something wrong, eh?" Mustache asked No Mustache.

"It's a code word," I answered.
The Sicilians looked from one to another.
"Ah!" said the man Porfirio.
"Quite," said the man Ezechiele.
"Certainly," said the knife grinder.
The Great Lombard nodded assent. Everyone nodded.
Someone said: "I know it, too."
"Know what?" asked Mustache.
"Know what?" asked No Mustache.
Above us, the bronze woman was smiling.
"And is there much suffering?" asked the Sicilians.
The woman burst into clanging laughter.

Epilogue

That was my conversation in Sicily, lasting three days and nights, and ending as it began. But I must point out that something happened after it ended.

I had gone to my mother's cottage to say goodbye, and I found her in the kitchen washing the feet of a man.

He sat with his back to the door, and he was very old. She, kneeling on the floor, was washing his old feet in a basin.

"I'm off, Mama," I told her. "The mail is here."

My mother, who knelt facing the man, looked up. "Then you're not eating with us?" she answered.

The man did not turn, neither at my words nor at hers. His hair was white, he was very old, and he kept his head bowed, as if he were rapt in thought or asleep.

"Is he asleep?" I asked my mother in an undertone.

"No," she replied. "He's crying, the fool. He was always like that," she added. "He used to cry when I was in labor, and he's crying now."

"What d'you mean?" I exclaimed in a whisper. "Is it Father?"

All this while he paid no attention to us.

I drew near to look at his face, but I saw that he kept it hidden with his hand. Anyhow, he seemed too old to me; and for a moment I almost thought that he was my grandfather. I even thought that he might be my mother's wayfarer.

"Has he returned, then?" I asked in an undertone.

My mother shook her head with disapproval.

"He's crying," she said. "He doesn't know that I'm fortunate."

At this point she left the man's old feet in the basin, rose, and drew me aside.

"So," she said, "you fooled me about that Cornelia. It wasn't on the field her Gracchi died."

"It wasn't on the field?" I exclaimed, still whispering.

"No," continued my mother. "While you were out, I looked it up in the books you used to read as boys."

"Good," said I. And I kissed her on her brow. "So long."

"Him—don't you want to greet him?" my mother asked.

I hesitated, looking at the old man, then said: "I'll greet him another time. Let him alone." And I tiptoed out of the house.

THE TWILIGHT OF THE ELEPHANT

(Il Sempione strizza l'occhio al Fréjus   1946)

1

In our family we are a houseful of people, and the only one
who works and earns anything is my brother, Euclid. For
a long time I have been out of a job. My mother's new husband
was already out of work when she married him and brought
him home last autumn. My sister, a store clerk, was fired
this summer; so, along with my grandfather, we all depend
on the little my brother earns at repairing bicycles for his
boss who is a mechanic.

Every Saturday night he brings home his money. My
mother takes it, sits down and counts it in her apron.

"For bread," she asks, "do you know how much of this
it takes?"

With eyes fixed on her, my brother's girl asks: "How
much?"

And my mother: "All of this."

Anna is the girl's name. "Let's see," she says. "How come?"

So it goes every Saturday night. Our house is out on
the edge of town, with the Lambrate woods in front of the
kitchen, and the light comes in from back there as if we were
in the middle of the country. Actually, we've never lived in
the real country. My grandfather was a mason. He worked
during the last century, and this one too, on almost every
one of the buildings which have made our city great. Often
my mother turns to look at him.

"But don't any of you ever look at him?" she asks.

Anna looks at him. My girl looks at him. Euclid and I
look at him, too.

"Don't you see how big he is?" my mother goes on.

We can't deny it. The man sits in his chair, his stick in
his hand, and even his head is very big, with white hair and
a white beard.

We see his hands on the stick handle.

"He used to take an iron rod," our mother often tells
us, "and twist it with his bare hands."

His knuckles are like tree knots on his fingers. Now, he

137

can no longer entirely open or close them, nor can he squeeze hard, and if he stands up, he can't straighten his back.

He gets up only to drag himself to the table or to the bed. He is like an elephant, my mother says. He sits in his chair, one leg crossed over the other, his knee like a tree trunk, the stick between both hands, and his bent head is full of weight, his eyes never open beneath the brows. He sits turned toward the wide door which looks out on Lambrate park toward the woods. And the night enters while we talk, passing over his shoulders with the dimming green of the trees and with their perfume.

He's like an elephant, my mother can well say. And we all think so too, ever since my mother began to say it long ago. When we were children we thought of the elephants we read about in school—the elephants of Pyrrhus and Hannibal's elephants. Or the elephant from a circus that we had once seen passing through the streets with placards hanging on its flanks. We thought of all the qualities which celebrate the elephant.

2

Talking again about bread, my mother says: "Half a kilo goes just for him every time he eats."

And Anna: "You see?"

And my mother: "The devil I do. Do we or don't we want him to eat?"

"Let him eat, let him eat," Anna says. "But half a kilo every time is a kilo and a half a day."

"And what is a kilo and a half for him?" my mother exclaims. She runs to grandfather and shakes him. "Tell them," she yells. "Tell them!"

My grandfather slowly raises his face. It is wondering. It is mild.

138

"How many kilos did you used to eat?" my mother yells at him.

My grandfather doesn't ask of what. He keeps his face raised a moment longer, then little by little lets it sink, crushing down into the old beard.

"Am I getting on your nerves?" my mother yells at him. She leaves him and turns to us. "A man like an elephant!" she tells us. "He could go up the scaffoldings with an iron girder tucked under his arm. What is a kilo and a half for him? He used to eat nine kilos. He used to eat ten kilos!"

Here Elvira, my girl, takes sides with Anna. "The fact remains that we have to buy too much bread on the black market," Elvira says.

"That's right," Anna says. "I don't say anything different."

And my mother: "But he only eats bread. What does he eat? Boiled chicory and bread."

"Bread's all any of us eats," Anna says.

Elvira adds that perhaps we might eat a little meat once in a while if we bought less bread, and my mother's husband even speaks of the wine which we might have—a glass once in a while—if we bought less bread.

"Light the light!" my mother bawls at my sister. The electric light blinds her, but her eyes are already fixed on her husband. "What are you saying?" she demands. "All you have to do is work for your share since you're talking. You get a job, and we'll be able to think about wine."

My mother's husband crosses himself. "Dear Jesus!" he starts to moan. "And now who's to stop her?" he moans. "Now I'll be a bum. Now I'll be a murderer. Now I'll be a thief."

"You are only a blabber-mouth," my mother tells him.

And my mother's husband: "Do you hear her? So I'm a blabber-mouth. Sure, and I'm a dim-wit, too. What else? Is it my fault if I can't find work?

And my mother to him: "Is it anybody's fault if we can just buy bread?"

These conversations, which go on forever, wear the children out. They get nervous. Already they're whining. Already they're nagging. They are getting to be pests. And our old man, too, seems to get tired. He uncrosses his leg, gets up, sits down, gets up, sits down, makes himself noticed, almost at every pulse-beat of ours, by the creaking of his chair and the shuffling of his feet.

Is he an elephant?

Oh imagine the time when, perhaps, we were all like elephants! We have a hint of those times in the freshness that enters from the park, and we think of the time when we were happy over such a thing—over the freshness, over the sun in the sun, over the night in the night, over a girl's large hips to be embraced, nuzzling her under the leafage in the woods....None of us men had to buy bread then. We were satisfied with grass, happy with dew. But we have never known those times. My grandfather, whom my mother calls elephant, did he ever know them? I mean, does she call him elephant because of a happiness that he once had? Or for an entirely different reason? For what reason?

3

In the morning, since it is useless to look for work, I accompany my brother Euclid to the shop of his boss, the mechanic, then come back along some grass-covered railway tracks and enter the woods of Lambrate park.

This is certainly not Africa. You are in the middle of trees and yet you hear the noise of street-cars. You come to the edge of a swamp, but also to cast-iron fountains. You pick a branch of broom, but you also kick an empty sardine can. You go up hills of sand, up dunes, but what you see, near and far away, is the line of steel telephone poles. Across the park runs a telephone wire loaded with conversation, and if you get down and listen it may be that you hear a squirrel or a hare, but more likely you will hear voices asking for a number. "Who is it?" one voice asks another. You hear them calling each other; you can even hear them knocking on doors. Or you hear the sudden whistle of a train and imagine the cry of thousands of fellows like yourself who pass on the trains...and your own cry as you feel them passing...

Nevertheless it is here that I come to try to learn what it must have felt like in the time when we were really elephants. Elephants in the way grandfather may have been one? Elephants in the way grandfather is one?

I carry with me my morning hunk of bread (which I have thanks to my brother Euclid) and walk among leaves and dew. I soak myself with dew, I soak myself with leaves. I walk along and find myself thinking how wonderful everything can be. Red berries on plants are pricking the green under my feet—berries of red coral. And the grass itself seems to be springing up around me, spurting up, leaping with a fan-like motion that is a crackling transmutation of grass to crickets and of crickets to grass, of crickets to dew, of crickets to leaves.

And soon I find myself thinking that right here and not far away—not in Africa, not in virgin forests—everything should be wonderful; because this is city (the tracks drowned by nettles) and is like a cheek leaning against the city, not merely a cheek leaning on the plants. And I wish that a time would come in woods like these—in woods of Milan or Paris and now in the day of cities, not like the time before them—when men would really be like elephants, serene like elephants...But they must be free and not belong to somebody else, not from a menagerie. I wouldn't even mind if they were heavy like elephants, thick and clumsy, smoking cigars too, and no longer the graceful ballet dancers or tricky magicians that we are.

Such a time can never have been. But perhaps it may come. And when it comes I don't want to be alone.

Now it is a shame to me to eat my morning hunk of bread. I get it out of my brother Euclid's work, and from the hunger of my grandfather, from the hunger of our children. I come here not to be seen while I eat. In the morn-

141

ing, at noon, I am here, curved over the jet of water from an iron fountain, and I soak the bread under the water. I soak and eat, then bend down farther to drink, and if a man sees me as he passes I don't care because *he is a stranger.* I would blush if it were somebody I knew.

How different it would be if the new time were to come! Then we would hardly eat except to be seen. As if we were saying: we're eating to give others the pleasure of watching us eat!

4

I risk being seen by my own mother as I eat my bit of bread by the fountain.

A woman wearing an Allied military coat passes by. She is tall and big, her face is still fresh even with her white hair; she carries a wood basket on her shoulder, and she is my mother. "Mother!" I call.

I pocket my bread and cross over the ferns toward her.

"Is it you?" she says to me.

From the face bent over with carrying the basket, she scrutinizes me with her hard eyes, and then once more begins to look around in the grass.

"Shall I help you?" I ask her.

I'm afraid she may have seen me with my mouth full and I'd like to know.

"Yes, help me," my mother answers.

"Did you just get here?"

"Do you think I start work this late?"

"I've been here quite a while."

My mother is quiet a moment. She leans over, picks a plant and tosses it back behind her head into the basket. "I know it," she says to me.

"Didn't you see me? Why didn't you call me?"

"It didn't occur to me."

I hunt around and find a little plant of chicory. "I'm

finding something, too," I tell her. I pick it. But I'm ill at ease, and want to carry her basket.

"All right," my mother says. She lets me take it from her, then helps me with the straps.

"It's already heavy," I tell her. It's a large basket, good enough to carry half a quintal of wood when full. But chicory is light. "How come it's heavy? And it isn't even full. What have you put in it?"

"Wild greens," my mother says. "What else could I put in it?"

"It feels like rocks," I say.

"Maybe it's because I've pressed it down a little."

"You must have pressed it down a lot."

"A little or a lot..."

"I'll say so. Like in a press! Like a bale of hay!" Then I ask her: "Are you thinking of cooking it all today?"

"Of course," my mother says. "Tomorrow I'll get more for tomorrow."

"You've got enough for a manger. Enough for a clothes boiler."

"Not yet. We still need another armful." And she bends and picks.

"You're overdoing it. We don't eat any. The children don't eat any. It's too much stuff for grandfather."

"Too much?" my mother yells.

"It makes his stomach swell up," I point out.

"Too much stuff for a man like your grandfather?"

"It can't be good for him."

"Too much, with the little bread that's his share?"

"It'll give him cramps. It can't be good for him."

My mother stops with that I-dare-you-all expression on her face. "But you've never looked at him!" she screams. "A man who is like an elephant!" Her eyes are almost contemptuous. Of whom? Of us, since we are not, although we are her sons, the man grandfather was?

"Ah!" she tells me. "I would never have believed that in my old age I wouldn't see him still as I saw him in my youth."

"What?"

143

"What?" my mother screams. "What! What!" And she says to me: "A man who is young as an elephant! A man who pulls off his shirt and does things an elephant does! A man who can uproot a tree...."

"That," I interrupt her, "no elephant has ever done."

"They do too," my mother goes on, "with their trunks. And he could do it with his hands. That is, with the strength of his arms. And he could break down the wall of a house, just pushing with his shoulders...."

I interrupt her again. "But that's crazy. All the rubble would come down on top of him."

"And how could that hurt him?" my mother says. "He'd shake himself and be clean again. His skin was so smooth," she goes on. "And at the boring through of the Fréjus Tunnel, he was the best among thousands of workers. He was the favorite of all the engineers. They used to bicker over him. And at the boring through of the Simplon it was the same."

Now she's started and she will go on; we can't avoid going back every day to hear again what our grandfather has made in his lifetime: tunnels and buildings, bridges and railroads, aqueducts, dikes, power plants, highways.

And the Duomo?

Yes, the Duomo!

And the Colosseum?

Yes, the Colosseum!

And the Wall of China?

Yes, the Wall of China!

And the Pyramids?

Yes, the Pyramids!

If we asked, my mother wouldn't say no to anything about where grandfather had worked. He is like an elephant, she says. All has come about through his effort, and he is beyond it all because of his mildness, because of his bowed head. "He did it," she says. "He's the one!"

She may mean to say more than we guess she means. She's not dumb. Certainly she means nobody except grand-father, the mass of him sitting there. It is only he whom she calls "your grandfather." But there is no reason why she

144

should not use the name of grandfather for all the others in the world who are like him. Are they not also "the grandfather" for us, all those others who were at the Simplon and the Fréjus with him? And all those who were at the building of the Duomo, as grandfather was at the Fréjus? What but our grandfather is each one, who, like grandfather at the Fréjus, was at the Colosseum? And each one, over and over again, who was at the Great Wall of China? And each one who was at the Pyramids? What about them? Isn't it so?

5

A surprise, at times, can come even to our family.

It happened while we were returning (my mother ahead with her Allied military coat and I behind with the basket) that a voice called us, excited and festive, and somebody from the house ran toward us. So it is that we return every time, hoping at any moment to hear the ring of a festive voice, and see somebody running and waving familiar arms in great signals.

"Listen!" my mother says.

We stop to listen, but there is nothing, or only the distant rumble of vague sounds from the city which blunt themselves against the woods. And my mother says: "I thought it was your sister."

Then she answers: "We're coming!"

She speaks low to me and shouts at the top of her lungs to my sister.

"It's not from home," she says to me.

And to the voice: "Where are you?"

"Mama!" sister calls. "Oh, Mama!"

"She must have been hunting us a long time," my mother says to me. And yells: "What is it?"

"Mama! Mama!" comes from my sister.

145

"Idiot!" shouts my mother. "What is she yelling 'Mama' for?" she says to me. But her eyes are smiling; and she repeats my sister's call. "Mama! Mama!" she calls, mimicking her. "What's that?" comes from my sister. Then I raise my voice. "We hear you," I yell. "What is it?"

"Hurry!"

"Hurry?" my mother yells. And now she is yelling even when she speaks to me.

"She wants us to hurry," I say.

"I don't suppose she wants *us* to start running," my mother yells. "Why doesn't *she* run?"

Nevertheless, she hurries.

"Yes, she *is* running," I tell her.

"Do you see her?"

"I see her. She's on the other side of the marsh and she's running." I point toward the white line of the shore to show her. "And she's going toward the bridge. Now she's making signs to us. We'll get there just about the same time."

And so I keep telling where I see my sister.

"Don't you think I see her?" my mother asks.

She starts signaling like my sister, and begins to run too. "Hey!" they call to each other. "Hey!" they answer each other.

My sister is practically dancing by now. She runs, signals, calls, but all of a sudden she bends and whirls around, dancing.

"Potatoes!" she yells while she dances. "There are potatoes, Mama! There are potatoes!"

"Potatoes?"

"Potatoes! Potatoes!"

"Sweet potatoes?"

"Oh, no. Real potatoes,..."

"Potatoes to cook on the coals?"

"To eat with salt, Mama!"

"Good Lord! To eat with salt!"

It looks to me as if they were both dancing. But if she's not dancing, my mother is certainly prancing...

"A lot of them?"

"Lots!"

146

"Half a kilo?"

"More! A kilo and more…"

"Good Lord! A kilo of potatoes!"

As soon as they meet on the bridge, my mother wants to know where they came from.

"It was your husband," my sister explains.

"Him?" my mother exclaims. "I always thought he must be good for something. I'm glad of that."

At the turn before coming to the house we find my mother's husband waiting for us. It's like the day when we accompanied them to register the marriage. He laughs as he did then. "Well!" he had said to us then, "Aren't you glad that your father's widow is no longer a widow?"

Now he laughs the same way. "Well!" he says to us. "Aren't you glad?" He rocks a little as he laughs, and he hugs my mother, keeping step with her. "I did it," he says.

"Don't you know we can tell it a mile away?" my mother answers.

My mother's man had raised an arm to circle my mother's waist, but now he lets it fall. "Look!" he says. "She almost treats me like I'd been bragging…"

My mother interrupts. "I know all right how good you've been," she tells him. "But I was just thinking…"

And she thinks silently. What? There's a threat in my mother's thinking. Don't think, Mama. Let us do the thinking.

From within ourselves, we beg her. Let the potatoes be as we've said. Let them be cooked on coals for all of us! Let them be eaten with salt by all of us. Let them steam in our hands! Let them taste charred between our teeth! Don't think, Mama! Don't let her think!

And my mother does try not to think. "I'll bet," she tells her husband, "that you could have had all the wine you wanted for yourself instead."

"Sure, I could," he answers.

"And instead you yourself, you'd rather have potatoes? Didn't you say you'd rather have potatoes?"

"That's what I said. Potatoes! Absolutely—potatoes!" My mother's husband feels big again, and starts laughing.

Again he raises his arm and circles my mother's waist.

147

"Well, my widow!" he tells her. He wants to keep step with her. He shifts his stride. "Well!" he tells her, continually changing pace, like a recruit, to keep step with my mother.

"But did your grandfather see them?" my mother asks.

All of a sudden our house appears, like a game warden's lodge, at the end of the green plain on which the park opens. But it might also be a shed with the long wall and broken windows of an abandoned storage place. Under the corrugated metal eaves we see the black, wide-open entrance to the kitchen. There, our grandfather is seated, one leg over the other, stick between his legs, turned toward us from the darkness inside. He himself is that darkness, and my mother has asked her question just at the instant when the house appears.

My sister, with a choked voice, answers. "I don't think so. I don't know."

"Because if he's seen them," my mother says, "if he's seen them, then goodbye..."

"Goodbye?"

"Ah yes, daughter! He is a weight on us."

"Goodbye to the potatoes?"

"He's a man who won't let others live, because of what he needs himself."

My sister almost moans. "Oh, Mama!"

"He could have died ten years ago," my mother continues. "And instead, no. He has to go on living like an elephant."

6

So it is often by way of grumbling that my mother calls grandfather an elephant.

It is not only to praise him. It is also to blame him. To say that he's heavy, to say that he's burdensome, to say that he's inert, to say that he won't ever die, to say that she's sick and tired of it. But the reasons she blames him for are the same she praises him for. Because he's so big, because he needs so much to eat, because he's so serene, so untouchable, so resistant.

At times there's disgust on my mother's face when, stopping a moment to watch him from behind, she observes the nape of his neck tight with health. Or there is dark anger in her face when she is bent over in front of him, shining the vast surfaces of his bronze-like shoes, like the shoes of a figure on a monument that is not able, being bronze, to move the legs to be more accommodating to her service. What does she say, even then, to show her disgust and her anger? "Elephant," is all she says. "A man like an elephant." Even to show her contempt.

"You understand," she now says to my sister, "we can't deny them to him if he's seen them."

"But he hasn't necessarily seen them," my sister says. "He always keeps his eyes shut."

"Or if he's heard you speak of them..."

"He doesn't even hear what you tell him. He never answers."

"He hasn't eaten any since Easter, and if he's heard you speak of them we'll have to give them to him. He likes them so terribly."

"Well," my mother's husband says, "we could let him have a couple."

"A couple?" my mother says.

"I think there's a couple apiece," my mother's husband says. "Couldn't we give him just a couple?"

"A couple for a man like him?"

"The same as for a man like me," my mother's husband says, "and the same as for my widow..."

"The devil the same!" my mother exclaims. She points toward the bottom of the meadow, where sits the dark shadow of our dwelling. "Have you ever looked at him, blond man?" she says. "Have you ever measured your little finger next to his thumb? Or your knee next to his wrist? Come, tell me, blond man!" she screams.

My mother's husband has let go of her waist, and shrinks his head into his shoulders, grumbling that now she'll ask

149

him if he's ever measured his fists next to grandfather's balls.

"Certainly I can ask you," my mother screams. "Or have you measured your full self with his member? I ask you this, little blond man. Have you ever considered what you're like, your full self, next to his member?"

She doesn't wait for him to answer, while she screams. She goes on. And he reddens, not knowing what to say except: "Madonna! Oh, Madonna!"

"There's more satisfaction," my mother continues, in soaping his parts, old as he is now, than to milk yours, you little blond fellow, when you come on top of me. There's not even any comparison, little sailor!"

"Oh, Madonna!"

"And it's a good thing for you to keep it in mind, the next time you come after me, instead of thinking that you're making God knows what kind of impression on me, you little sailor!"

"But why little sailor?"

"So that you'll learn the fear of God before a woman who is the daughter of a real man with a real tool and not with one..."

"Of what?" her husband stops her, his hands in his hair. And he looks at my sister, looks at me. "Forget that she's your mother," he tells us. "Forget that she uses such language in front of her own children."

"They don't have to forget anything," my mother says. She looks at us with prideful assurance, certainly thinking of how lucky we are to have her for a mother, made in the proportions of our grandfather. But her fury has passed, and shaking the hair out of her eyes, she says: "Two potatoes for a man like him! What sense would it make? It would be like kidding him."

No one answers her, nor does her husband walk at her side. We're going Indian file, I last with the basket, my sister in front of me, my mother's husband in front of my sister, and we are all three silent, and somewhat humiliated. My mother leads and keeps on talking. "A kilo is the least you can give a man like him....We can't offend him! A man who

150

would take an iron girder with one hand and toss it up to the next floor of the scaffold!"

She walks and keeps on talking. "A man who...a man who..." And I, marching last in the file, can hardly understand the real meaning of what my mother is saying about grandfather. Everything in the world has been built by him, from the Pryamids to the Fréjus Tunnel, yet he is a stranger to everything, shunted aside by everything, an old man sitting on a chair, out of everything. The same holds for all men who were *he*. The same is true for those of us who are still *he*. And why can this happen?

It is because of this that my mother speaks of grandfather: for the pleasure of seeing him in all the things he could do, and for his own satisfaction in being able to do them, for his delight in his own strength, in his own effort and his own power. Otherwise how could it be?

It is in this that we get our compensation. There is no scope for us in the Pyramids which we raise, for we remain outside, but for each block of stone that we roll we have our recompense in knowing that we've been able to roll it. The greater the mass we roll the greater our compensation. Follow us as we roll it. Nothing else concerns us except the obligation to succeed in rolling it, for our scope is in it, and our meaning is in it. Don't you hear what my mother says? "A man who...a man who..." This is what she says.

7

But the compensation for the little blond men, what is it?

There are also these men among humanity, like the husband my mother has taken, whom she herself calls "blond man" in order to call him something the opposite of the "elephant" she calls grandfather.

151

They are more like monkeys than like elephants. They run and run, carrying buckets of mortar up and down the Pyramids, and I don't mean to say that theirs is not effort. But in the compensation of which I speak they don't seem to share. There are so many of them—the exact half of ourselves, and perhaps even half of our inner selves. Nor do I say that they do less than we, but I ask myself what is their compensation, if it seems that they don't share in the only one known.

Look at my mother's husband and how he is kept on the outside.

What is his hand in comparison to my grandfather's hand? Don't make me laugh. All of him is nothing in comparison to one of my grandfather's fingernails, and all he can do just makes you want to laugh. It is all nothing. He carries buckets back and forth and it's nothing. He comes home with potatoes and it's nothing. He gets on top of his wife every night and it's nothing. Everybody says that everything about him is nothing.

Where, then, is his compensation? He himself never takes any. He gets offended, pouts, and at the same time is the first one to laugh at himself and at anything he may be able to do. "It's nothing," he says. He can say it to himself. Is that his compensation?

He doesn't do what he does, I mean to say, as if he were an elephant. His cheek doesn't sweat against the block of stone. They call him "blond man" and he takes it, "little blond man," and he takes it. And yet, he gives a shove, too. You can't deny it.

As small as he is, he shoves without having anybody notice. He has the other's sweat on him, and the obstinacy of the other sets up an obligatory rhythm for his own shoving. He understands by observing the big one what his compensation may be.

And is this, perhaps, his only compensation? To see in the other what the "compensation" may be?

My mother's husband bends over, gets down before grandfather, and looks at him a long time—how big he is, how big his hands, how big his wrists, how a man is made who has done this thing and that thing. He studies in grandfather what my mother says about him, studying the "compensation" in him. Is studying the "compensation" his own compensation? He is the half in us which looks and studies, and by now, we, too, see something of what he sees. By dint of scratching his head after having seen, he has taught us something. May his compensation be to make us see what he sees?

8

About two hundred yards from our house, toward town, they're repairing a long stretch of road. They're asphalting it. They have a road roller, and night and morning, to put it away or get it out, they pass by with it between us and the park. It crushes the grass, the tractor and the roller behind, with two sooty workmen aboard, and after it has passed, there comes into the house a strong odor which seems squeezed out of the woods.

One of the workmen, not the one seated at the wheel, but the one standing up, waves each time they pass and smiles with the white teeth of a man whose face is smutty black.

At which one of us?

Perhaps at all of us. At our wide open door, at the many women in our family, at the mass of the old man seated a step beyond the sill. I've tried to get work with them and know what they're like. They've finished rolling their stone. They greet us from the roller. And right afterward comes that powerful smell of crushed grass.

Coming back together as usual, my mother and I smell the freshness of that odor on the meadow. "How come they've stopped at eleven in the morning?" my mother asks.

We enter the house, and have the answer. We get it from

the man who has greeted us every day from the tractor. "We've finished, lady," he says.

He isn't young, we see, now that he is near; the smoke on his face no longer makes him the boy that he had seemed to be. It makes him youthful, heartening to see, but it doesn't hide the many years of his small face. And how little he is! He is smaller than our little "blond man."

"Are you going to work somewhere else?" my mother asks him.

"We don't know yet," he says. "But we've finished here. It may be I won't get by here again, and so I took this liberty. I wanted to say goodbye to this gentleman and to all of you, if you will allow me..."

"Ah!" my mother says.

The one with the smoky face is already seated. They've given him a stool next to grandfather, and he's sitting on it, leaning with one hand partly covering grandfather's knee. His hand pats grandfather's knee.

I see her look sidelong at that hand, and at the man from head to foot.

"Oh, well!" she says.

"I've told him that we're honored," the husband of my mother offers.

"Please! Please!" Smut-Face says.

And my mother: "Absolutely, good man! A kind thought is a kind thought."

But she keeps on looking sidelong at that hand, and at the little man from head to foot.

"It's only a question," he says, "of our having become sort of friends."

My mother looks around. "You and who?" She looks at her husband.

"The gentleman and myself," Smut-Face tells her. Again he pats my grandfather's knee. "You understand," he adds. "Passing every day, I saw him, he saw me, and we became sort of friends. We used to wink."

"You winked?"

"Oh, yes. Perhaps I was a bit forward with a man that

154

old. I have some years to go yet. I might be his son. But I started it and he answered."

"Papa answered?"

"Sure, he did. You see, I was coming back from work, and he in his day used to come back from work....I didn't lack respect."

"But you didn't pass nearby," my mother says. "Did he see you? I doubt if he saw you." And she turns loudly to grandfather: "Did you see him, Papa?"

Smut-Face doesn't speak, but he smiles and waits.

One can see him thinking: "Have you got to yell that way?" He watches grandfather as he lifts his face, with its large cheeks, ample beard, and then his glance as it comes out from under the heavy weight of the lids. It falls first toward my mother, who has called him, and then shifts, as it lowers under his white tufted crown of hair, and comes toward him, toward the one who waits. "See, lady! You thought he wouldn't notice me?"

My mother detaches herself from grandfather. "Maybe," the word comes out of her mouth. "And you saw that he saw you?"

Smut-Face doesn't answer her right away. He has his laughing eyes fixed on grandfather's face, as if in colloquy in some secret way with him. Grandfather has not resumed his usual position. He lets the weight of his head come down, the beard crushed against his chest, but his profile is not directed toward his own foot. It is directed toward the visitor. And Smut-Face, because of the low stool, is completely under the steepness of his stare, that is, if grandfather still has his eyelids open.

"Those things don't happen that way," Smut-Face finally answers. "It's not a question of optics. It's a question of having a habit. And I can say that the gentleman here saw me just like I saw him." He turns again to grandfather. "Isn't that right, sir?"

Meanwhile the stool creaks under him. It has creaked several times as he turns; it is broken in one leg and could fall apart under him if he didn't watch his equilibrium. His little smile returns to my mother: "It's the same when I say that he winked at me just like I winked at him. It's not that I saw him wink! But he winked at me, and I know that he winked at me. Otherwise how would we have made friends?"

His glance makes a complete circle, looking at our faces, and then he again pats grandfather's knee; he is again with grandfather. The stool crackles under him. With his other hand he holds the broken stool, my mother notices. She seems about to speak. Instead, she goes toward the chicory emptied out of the basket onto the floor.

"We've got to hurry here," she exclaims. "Anna! Elvira!"

But she doesn't entirely leave Smut-Face.

"Well," she tells him. "A kind thought is a kind thought. Would you like to stay with him a bit? I'd like to have you stay. Make yourself at home."

9

At this, my mother and the three girls begin to clean chicory. Kneeling around the big pile, they make two piles each, one of refuse and one of clean chicory. Their hands move fast, as if in sewing. All of them are so absorbed that for five or six minutes it looks as if they weren't aware of having a visitor in the house. But my mother, herself, remembers. "Only it's too bad he's deaf," she suddenly tells him.

"Deaf?" Smut-Face repeats.

"That's right. He doesn't hear much."

"I don't know," the other one says. "You can't be sure."

"We have to scream in his ears."

"But you see," he says, "you can be tired of listening rather than actually be deaf. It happens. Then you don't answer. But that doesn't mean that you don't hear."

My mother, listening, has quit sorting.

I know that she may think the same thing about grandfather's hearing. At times she herself says that grandfather is deaf, and then at times, she denies it. "Am I boring you?" she usually yells at grandfather if he doesn't answer. So she observes: "There's something in what you say." And she peers at me, at her husband, daughter-in-law, and daughter, as if to say, "He's not so dumb, this Smut-Face." Meanwhile she notices the creaking of Smut-Face's stool. "You gave him the broken stool!" she exclaims. "Is it the broken one?" her husband says. And she: "Change it. Give him a chair." But Smut-Face stops us. "It doesn't matter," he says. He doesn't care about changing. "I thank you, lady," he adds quickly, sweetly, "it makes no difference."

He speaks as if, suddenly, something occupies him which doesn't allow him to pay attention to anything else. Does something occupy him that is happening to grandfather? Something grandfather is doing?

My mother turns and goes over to the old man. Grandfather, his big head always lowered, but rather toward his shoulder than toward his chest, is moving one of his hands. He has already released the stick and his hand is raised, neither open nor closed. It searches toward Smut-Face. What does he want to do to him?

A moment passes in which it seems as though the hand wants to light on his arm. It goes further up and seems as though it is about to touch the shoulder, then goes on up, reaching to the height of the face. What does it want to do? Give a caress?

We might even expect it to push him away. But Smut-Face doesn't look as if he expected this. His chuckle is cunning.

"But imagine!" my mother says.

The hand stops, not entirely open, uncurled, and two fingers go over the cheeks, first one, then the other, and then withdraw.

What on earth has he done? It was like a caress.

Meanwhile the hand withdraws, palm up, the fingers turned toward the beard and the lowered gaze.

"Yes, it doesn't come off," Smut-Face says to grandfather.

We all laugh a bit, and my mother, laughing, says: "He had taken you for a Negro."

"No, lady," Smut-Face tells her. "He just wanted to know whether it came off."

Then he goes on with grandfather, rather lowering than raising his tone of voice. "It's such a crazy smut," he says. "I don't know what it's made of. I have to use vaseline to get it off."

There is a movement in the vastness of my grandfather's beard.

"That's right, vaseline," Smut-Face repeats. "Sure." And he laughs. "It makes you laugh, doesn't it?"

But we don't laugh. We look at grandfather, at the new movements of his beard, and we listen to something we know is his laughter, coming out of his hundred years.

It is a sound like a rivulet inside of him, deep in him, far away among the riffles of the years. From where does it come? From the time when he was an entirely different elephant? We are used to it. He laughs about three or four times a year. But it never fails to impress us every time.

10

When my brother Euclid arrives just past noon, my grandfather's chicory is always ready in the big pot.

My mother introduces my brother Euclid to the visitor. "This is my oldest son," she tells him. And to my brother Euclid: "He's a friend of grandfather's."

Smut-Face is very polite: he gets up, bows, and shakes hands with my brother. "Your mother flatters me by calling me a friend of the gentleman here...I am full of respect." Then he sits down again with creakings from the stool.

"You try and get him to change the stool," my mother whispers to Euclid.

She has removed the pot from the twig fire and signals to the girls to set the table. "Stop woolgathering," she tells them. "Hurry." And she comes with the pot, putting it on a plank on the floor next to my grandfather. She puts it down and straightens up, her hands on her hips. She looks at the steam clouding grandfather's mass, around his head, coiling around his head, and she sees Smut-Face's black face damp and gleaming there in the middle. "Excuse me," she says. "That's the way I get him to the table." And she adds at once: "Now we'll eat. But I wouldn't want you to go because of that. If you eat at noon too, you can do it here just the same. If you can stand what we have."

"But please, lady," answers Smut-Face, his hand on his heart. He has risen and is standing in the middle of the copious steam, damp with vapor as if he himself had stepped out of the pot. "Lady," he says, "I don't like to trouble you, but I do appreciate the invitation. As a matter of fact, I have nobody in town. And today I can't even eat with my gang. I'd have to eat alone, sitting on some step somewhere. I'll stay then. But, pardon me, why are these children crying?"

"Always at mealtime our kids begin to cry. It's just as soon as they see their grandmother bring up the pot. Pay no attention to them," she tells Smut-Face. "We don't. Others cry all day but these just at this time."

"Isn't it strange?" Smut-Face comments. "Other children cry all day, I imagine, because they'd like to eat. Then they usually quit at mealtimes. But these, why do they cry right now?"

"You shouldn't eat with us," my mother replies. "I'd say that it wasn't wise. Why they don't cry during the rest of the day, I myself don't know. Perhaps it's because they have a certain capacity for bearing up. But why they cry just at this time you can see with your own eyes. We're going through a bad time, my friend."

"Ah!" Smutty exclaims. "I'm sorry. You mean to say that they'd like a more substantial meal at this time, if I've understood right..."

"You've certainly not exactly misunderstood," my mother

159

tells him. "But you'll understand better." She signals for him to move aside. "Make room, there. Our old man wants to pass."

Our old man, in the fog of vapor, stands up with all his mass, upright, not curved, and Smutty has to raise his light eyes high in order to seek out the big face. The old man has stopped because Smutty is underfoot. But as Smut-Face draws aside, grandfather places a hand on his shoulder, and leaning on him, accomplishes the second of the two steps which separate him from his place at the head of the table.

My mother then takes up the conversation with Smut-Face: "If you realize that only my son Euclid works, you'll be able to excuse us."

"But lady," Smutty says. "I'm just a workman, too. I've seen it like this too, and worse." He's very timid and ceremonious in his conversation with my mother, even though always jovial. "I've seen it, too," he repeats.

"Not me," my mother interrupts, "I hadn't seen it before. With the strength he had in his day, that old man at your right would bring home the wages of three men, and he always had a job..."

Here she stops, but not because she's through; only because she hesitates. She looks at us and doesn't quite know how to spare us. She'd like to, but doesn't know how.

"While now with three men here," she continues, "not counting the girls, they barely bring home the wages of one."

"Excuse me," Smut-Face protests. "I wouldn't talk that way if I were you. And please excuse me, all of you. But I believe I must say that the lady, here, isn't quite fair."

We agree, all right. But my mother's husband agrees more decisively.

"Have it your way," my mother says. "It's just that I don't hide my thoughts."

"I have the greatest admiration," Smut-Face continues, "for a workman like the old man must have been. I could even see it from a distance... He must have been the pride of his crew, and of those working with him and of those working near him..."

"And for whoever watched him work," my mother adds. "And for whoever was of the same blood, my friend. And for whoever cooked for him and for whoever washed for him. And for whoever sewed for him and ironed for him."

"I don't doubt it," says Smut-Face. "But I don't believe that a workman," he says and laughs, "has to be a champion to earn a living..."

"That's the point," my mother's husband shrills.

He jumps up and shakes hands with Smutty across the table. "Good!" he shrills. "You've told her off!"

"Good next time!" my mother comes right back. "Till now, he hasn't told me a thing I don't know."

"Just so, exactly," Smut-Face says and laughs. "I haven't said a thing she didn't know. And I'm not ever likely," he says laughing, "to have anything to say that she doesn't know."

"Then say so and don't laugh," my mother says.

"Lady, I'm not laughing," Smut-Face says and laughs. "But it is certainly not because they're not big and strong that your sons don't have work."

"Of course that's not the reason," my mother says. "They're big and strong. Furthermore, my son Euclid does have work."

"Therefore, they're not to blame," Smutty says, and laughs.

"And whoever said they were to blame?" my mother exclaims.

"That's right," Smutty says. "Absolutely."

"And that goes for us, too," says my mother's husband.

"For us?" Smut-Face says, and laughs.

He is very small. Grandfather can make him disappear from sight by passing his arm in front of him. Smut-Face now points to himself and to my mother's husband. "For us?" he repeats. And he shrugs his shoulders just as my mother tells her husband: "You keep quiet, blond man!"

11

In honor of the guest my mother wanted the table set better than usual. And so we have not only plates and glasses, but also an oil cruet, even two fruit dishes, and two plates, dinner plate and soup dish, with spoon, fork and knife, as if for soup, meat and fruit. Furthermore, we all have to stay put in our places, though usually if I have already eaten my bread in the park, I sit down and get up as often as I feel like it, and swallow my bread near the sink, wetting it at the faucet.

"We might just as well do without pretending that we are eating our antipasto," my mother says. "Because here, sir," and she turns to the guest, "it is a question of make-believe. We make believe that we are having a second course..."

"And we also pretend," my mother's husband adds, "to drink wine." He lifts his empty glass. "To your health!" he says. And he carries it to his lips.

"Let's not exaggerate, silly," my mother tells him. "You can fill your glass with water." Then she turns again to the guest.

"At times we make believe we are even eating fruit, but not always... I'm glad, because of my children, to do so. Not just for fun. If we didn't," she explains to the guest, "someday when there might really be something to eat, how would they behave? Like little barbarians...."

"Oh, I understand," the guest murmurs.

"They might even eat with their hands," my mother continues. "Perhaps they might even suck it up from their plates," she goes on. "They would be like barbarians. And always would be... So it's necessary for them to learn manners even now when they don't eat."

"Learn a trade and put it aside," my mother's husband says.

"Just like the proverb," my mother continues. "Come one day they might have to eat, and they must know how."

"I understand," the guest murmurs.

He watches the youngsters sobbing. His smile never leaves his black face, and he watches the way they are nailed to their chairs even while they sob. "But it's certainly clever," he murmurs. Then he asks: "Have you already taught them to eat everything?"

"We teach them according to their age," my mother's husband answers. "So both the bigger and the smaller ones know how to eat soup. The same with fried potatoes. The same with greens. And they all know how to drink water with a drop of wine. He turns toward the sobbing children. "Why don't you drink, dears?" he exhorts them. "I put wine in the water."

"Silly!" my mother says.

"Why?" he says. "While meat," he immediately adds, "must still be cut for the littlest one."

"And chicken?" the guest asks. "Have you already taught them how to eat chicken?"

"Of course! There's this little fellow," my mother's husband answers, "who knows how to eat it as if he were a little prince. And the young lady facing him knows, too. As if she were a little princess. And when they have a helping of chicken and face each other, they look almost as if they were dancing a minuet, with all their little gestures."

Even behind his smile, the guest is very interested. Nor does he mind my mother, who would like to cut it short. He doesn't hear her tell her husband again: "Silly!"

"Don't they eat it with their hands?"

"Heaven forbid!" my mother's husband answers. "They know it would be a nasty thing to do!"

"They take it apart with a knife and fork?" the guest asks.

"But naturally," answers my mother's husband. "Perhaps helping themselves by pushing with a small piece of bread, if the chicken is cooked hunter's style...."

My mother yells at him, "Stop. I told you to stop."

"Lady," the guest murmurs. "Only one last question." Then he asks my mother's husband: "And are they able to take it all apart?"

163

"They don't leave a crumb," my mother's husband answers.

"Well!" the guest murmurs. He thinks about what he has heard. "I'd like to know how to eat a chicken wing myself," he says, and laughs. "Never have had the chance to learn," he says, laughing.

"Do you mean to say," asks my mother's husband, "that you've never eaten chicken?"

"Never had the chance," our guest says and laughs.

"But today you can," my mother's husband says. "I believe that today our second course just happens to be chicken." And while the children sob loudly, he looks questioningly at my mother. "Isn't it chicken today?"

"Yes," my mother says. "There's chicken."

12

A blow on the table, as if a weight had fallen on it from the ceiling, makes us turn toward our grandfather.

"He's right," my mother says.

We see his beard tremble, while his fist, not trembling but red, withdraws. Smut-Face's eyes are appreciative, looking at the fist.

"You and your make-believe," my mother says to her husband. "This way we forget that our old man is too patient." And to all of us, to Smut-Face: "Let's go on to the soup."

Grandfather has a soup plate before him. My mother takes it, and with a wooden serving fork fills it with chicory. She drains the broth and adds some more, goes on draining the broth and adding more. When there is a mound of chicory, she places the soup plate in front of grandfather.

"All right?" she asks.

Grandfather glances at the steaming greens. If he's satisfied he begins on them without further ado, without

164

motion except for his solemn hand. If not, he lifts his face toward my mother.

Now he lifts it.

"What?" my mother says. "Doesn't it seem enough to you?"

But my grandfather means to say something else. With a finger he points to our guest, to Smut-Face's plate.

"He's worried about you," my mother tells him.

"And I'm grateful to him," says Smut-Face. "I'm grateful to him."

"But do you want some of it?" my mother asks. "We can't get it down. We were able to for a couple of months. Then we had to quit. Even in this, we ought to be like him; we should be able to eat chicory without oil every day and never get tired."

Here she's about to end up with: "Like an elephant." I can see it on her lips, but Smut-Face interrupts her first.

"I, too, in my small way, am the same kind of man," he says.

"Can you, too?" my mother asks. "Can you eat chicory every day without oil like he does?"

"I say, in my small way," says Smut-Face. "I say that I'm also that kind of man in my small way. I, too," he says, laughing, "eat my chicory every day. And I might almost say that all of you eat yours every day."

"Not at all," my mother says. "We could for a couple of months and then had to stop. Now we only take a ladleful of broth in our plate."

"In order to torment the children," says my mother's husband.

"To keep them in training how to eat soup," my mother says.

"And what's that?" Smut-Face asks. "Isn't that chicory every day?"

"Maybe," my mother says.

She thinks about it and adds: "Certainly I don't say that it might not be." But she thinks also of other things and usually ends up saying that our grandfather was or is an elephant, "like an elephant." I can see it the way her lips move, at the thought of "all the rest." I also notice that she hasn't said it once yet since our smut-faced visitor has been in the house. And now once again Smut-Face interrupts the course of her thoughts.

"So for forty years," he says, "I've had my chicory, in my small way."

"For forty years?" my mother says.

"Since I've been working," says Smut-Face, "I have an anchovy every day at noon," he says and laughs. "I used to have oil with it, but these last few years without oil, just the way the gentleman has his greens."

"But an anchovy!" my mother exclaims. "By Heaven! An anchovy is an anchovy!"

"An anchovy isn't like chicory!" my mother's husband exclaims. "But let's be more explicit," he goes on. "Do you mean to say a salted anchovy?"

"Yes, salted," Smutty replies, but answering low and rather timidly.

"Well, then!" my mother exclaims. "Here you were saying you were made like grandfather, and you can eat a salted anchovy every day!" Then she adds, her eye fixed on Smutty: "It takes nerve!"

"Indeed, yes," my mother's husband says. "You must admit it takes a certain amount of nerve!"

Meanwhile the word circles the table: "Anchovy! Anchovy!"

Smutty shrinks into his shoulders. "That's true," he says and laughs. "But in my small way. I must admit that the gentleman is something else again…"

13

My mother had already poured the ladleful of chicory broth into each plate. Smutty's plate, too. And so now we go back and forth with the spoon, four or five times, from plate to mouth, and the soup is finished.

There was silence while the soup was eaten, a rest of some minutes. Each one of us had withdrawn into himself. Grandfather remains withdrawn in his enormousness, as he always seems to us, bent over the soup dish, and each one of us has perhaps had a thought of his own. We ask each other as we turn to look around: What have you thought? What has he thought? What have all of you thought? And I, what have I thought? What have we all thought?

It is with this written on her face that my mother looks at our guest. But the questions pass, one after the other, on her face. They are never strange questions which will be uttered. We're all back at the starting point, and my mother says to our guest: "Perhaps you have today's anchovy with you...."

Our guest is again openly chuckling.

"What?" he answers. "Certainly I have today's anchovy with me."

"And don't you want to eat it?" my mother asks him. "Go right ahead if you'd like to eat it...."

"Sure, go right ahead," says the husband of my mother.

"Oh, I don't mind not having to eat it for once."

The voice of my mother's husband becomes choked as he says, "We'd be happy to watch you eat it."

"But don't you insist," my mother tells her husband. "You can't make him eat it so that you can enjoy watching him eat it."

"Would he like to watch me eat it?" the guest asks.

"Now he feels obligated," my mother tells her husband. And to the guest: "Excuse it. Excuse it. I've got a husband like a child."

"But I don't say he'd actually have to eat it," says my mother's husband.

"No?" the guest asks. "Did you mean to say something else?"

"Don't pay any attention to him," my mother tells him. "He never knows what he wants."

"I don't know what I want?" asks my mother's husband.

"Perhaps he does know," the guest says. He waits and smiles, looks at my mother, and then unbuttons his jacket. "Perhaps he meant something else," he adds and smiles, "but perhaps he knows what he meant." And he searches with one hand through the inside pockets of his jacket, waiting and smiling.

"No, he doesn't know," my mother tells the guest. "You don't know," she tells her husband.

"Do you really think so?" her husband asks her.

The guest looks at both of them, waiting, and can't make up his mind to pull his hand out of the pocket it's in.

"Perhaps it is so," my mother's husband says. He has lowered his eyes before my mother's eyes, and has lowered his head, too. "Perhaps it's like she says," he adds in a choked voice. "Perhaps I don't ever know what I want," he says.

At this the guest takes out his hand, and he has a little packet held between two fingers. The paper has oil spots on it. It is a page from a used copy-book with faded words on it, in a childish handwriting. But the packet is so thin that it might contain nothing, or perhaps only a toothpick. The man with the laughing smutty face holds it between thumb and forefinger, and lifting it, seems to want to open it.

"Just imagine," my mother tells him. "Why should he want you to eat the anchovy? He only talks to hear himself talk...."

Then Smut-Face lowers his hands, and with one hand flaps the packet against the back of the other. He plays with it for a moment, then drops it on the table, beyond his plate, abandoned.

My mother's husband clears his throat. "Humph!" He clears it rather furiously, and lifting his head, even defies my mother's glaring.

And now grandfather seems to be searching too. He has

raised his mouth and beard. His whole face is raised, and he no longer eats, and he moves his nostrils as if he were searching. Good Lord, how he sniffs!

He is smelling what makes him think of barrels and salt, of the holds of ships, of waterfront storehouses, of the sea itself and journeys, of his journeys on foot or by rail, in his time. He thinks of the smells of his journeys, the smells of the people with whom he has traveled, and he looks at Smut-Face seated by him. He looks at him, accepts him, and soon returns with tranquility to his soup dish.

So my mother's husband quiets down, too, after the excitement and anxiety which had seized him on seeing how grandfather sniffed. Now he's the one who sniffs. He does it loudly, wanting it to be noticed. But it's clear he doesn't smell anything. Good Lord! What had the old one been sniffing? The young one should be able to smell better, being so much younger.

He stops trying, and raises himself somewhat, his elbows on the table. His interest is fixed on the faded words written on the copy-book sheet in which the anchovy is wrapped. "What?" he murmurs. "What is it?" He turns his head, trying from the right, then from the left, wanting at all cost to read, turning his head here and there.

"Worse than a child," my mother says.

My mother's husband sits down again. "I just wanted to see what's written there."

"Do you want to see what's written?" Smutty asks him.

He holds out the thin packet and my mother's husband finally has it before him. But he doesn't read right away. First he sniffs at it from one end to the other, very near.

"Well?" we ask him. We all want to know what's written there.

"It's the same word written over and over again," my mother's husband answers.

"But what word?" we ask.

"I don't know," he answers. "I can't make it out."

Meanwhile he feels it, suddenly squeezing the packet. "Open it, open it," Smutty tells him. Actually, he has already made us a present of his little packet and its contents. You can see it, in a way, from the pleased look in his eye. The only thing is, he doesn't quite know how to tell us to consider it our own.

"Oh, no," my mother's husband replies. "Why open it?" He hands me the tiny packet, and we all pass it around. "Give it here," my mother calls out. "And is the anchovy in it?" she asks Smut-Face. She unfolds the used copy-book sheet, and the anchovy is in it. We all stand up to look. "You see?" our mother says to Smutty. She points us out to him. "We're very greedy in our family," she tells him, "and I don't know what they'd give for one anchovy." She wants him to understand that we'd really prefer one anchovy even to pork steaks. "If you don't eat it today," she tells him, "shall we let them eat it?"

Smutty's eyes are radiant. He would like to have tomorrow's anchovy in his pocket to give us that one, too. Then he asks if there isn't a bit of chicory left. "Ah!" he tells us. "I don't know what I'd give for a plate of chicory!"

14

While the anchovy, still intact, makes the rounds of the table, and each one of us has had just a sample of the odor and of the salt on our piece of bread, our grandfather, for the second time, perilously raises his head filled with the weight of years.

Certainly he is big and hulking. My mother always says it. And we see him that way ourselves, but we think it is because of his years. How many years? We don't ask ourselves. We judge them to be numberless as we look at his enormous hands. We know only that he worked before the last war, before our birth, and in the last century, before our mother's birth. It is another century itself which is raised with his head. And his eyes, in all their mildness, are for us the eyes of names learned in school—of Mazzini, of Garibaldi—as well

170

as his own. That is why we now stop and look. Could we be lacking in respect toward another century?

The great bearded face is again lifted and again searches around, but searches blindly. He doesn't even bat an eyelash. Only his nostrils quiver, nothing else. But how acutely! To the shore of his olfactory sense come the most distant seas …and again the holds of ships, which fly the flags of long crossings, releasing the brine of voyages and more voyages, filling ports and shops. They fill the avenues of our city and the wharfs of every place in the world with the odor of the world in every part of the world.

Smut-Face is carried away looking at grandfather. What on earth happens to an odor sniffed across so many years? Grandfather again studies Smutty as he had before. But now he bends toward him for a long time, sniffing him, almost in his hair. And again he sniffs the air, moving his nostrils to do it, and turns his face restlessly, giving himself no peace.

Then he bends over the man on his other side. This is my mother's husband, who withdraws gradually as grandfather's face approaches. In fact, at a certain point, he leaps up. He leaves his chair and takes a step back.

At the same time grandfather rises. He won't want to go after him? Slowly, first placing his hands on the table, leaning against them, he pushes himself up; then he moves between the table and Smutty's chair.

"But where do you want to go?" my mother yells at him. "Papa!" she yells. "You haven't finished your chicory!"

Smutty's eyes are excited and he helps grandfather get down again. For that's what grandfather does: he sits down again right after my mother's yelling. With a rumbling, though, that grows out of his whole big head. Are rocks sliding in the caverns of that big head?

"He's grumbling," my mother says. She takes the anchovy, on the plate, and holds it out to grandfather. "Was it this," she asks, "that you smelled?"

Grandfather doesn't even look. He grumbles, but his face is mild, and his head lowers.

"It's an anchovy which I offered," Smutty tells him.

The arch of the brows is raised and widened in grandfather's face, as the face inclines. There is wonder in him that he has heard. Then a greater mildness, as if by now, to hear or not, could no longer matter to him.

Certainly there must have been something that did matter. But what was it? He doesn't know; and he's stopped grumbling. Perhaps it was this thing they are speaking about. Perhaps it wasn't really so. Or he might have just believed it to be so, and then it might not have been. Could it have been only a question of eating? The mildness in his bent-over face turns to sadness. It is just as well for him to eat his chicory.

15

But my mother has pushed the plate with the anchovy next to his hand, behind the dish of chicory, and now no one will think of being able to have any.

Goodbye anchovy, is the thought that runs around the table. Even though Smutty is appreciative, looking at us with an exultant little smile from his pale eyes, it is bitter for us, with our empty plates.

We are in the same fix as we are every day: a hunk of bread, half a stick-loaf each, with "chicken" to be eaten properly with the tip of knife and fork. It may be roasted, and may be served with fried potatoes, or even with pickled mushrooms. My mother's husband is too heavy-hearted, by now, to ask what it is. And so we point our forks, pitch in with our knives, scraping our plates without knowing exactly what it is we are pretending to eat. Halfheartedly, we entreat the children in a low tone: "It's chicken. Remember that."

Only Smutty remains vivacious. He watches us attentively, in order to follow what we are doing. "Wing," he says. "You've given me the wing. Isn't that so? That's just what I wanted—the wing." He talks and laughs, and the silverware scrapes away, scraping on the plates, and there isn't a dog among us who falls in with his conversation.

Now that the anchovy is there by grandfather, even my mother joins in the bitterness we all feel.

This always happens, after she has sacrificed us in favor of grandfather. She looks at her "blond man," and her eyes are not proud. Her face resting on one hand, she lets her gaze pass over him, as if in tenderness. This time she hasn't even quarreled. She didn't have to fight us for what she gave grandfather. Ah, mother, you don't console yourself through the usual fierceness. She hasn't had to hold us back with her raging, showing us what grandfather is, and telling us of the things he once could do. She deprived us for him without having to show herself as the daughter of the man he once was—of the elephant.

In fact, she has not yet told our guest at all that grandfather is an elephant. And now it is too late to tell him. At this moment my mother doesn't love grandfather. Instead, she loves us and our children, and looks tenderly at her "blond man," and if by chance she looks at grandfather, it is to cast on him, in a flash of resentment, the excess of the torment which embitters her.

"You must excuse us," she says suddenly. She turns toward the stranger who sits with us, looking among the bowed heads for his sooty face, motioning to him to look up and listen. "Our situation," she says to him, "is not precisely what you see."

But Smutty doesn't understand. He doesn't foresee what, suddenly, my mother intends to tell him.

"And don't look as though you had just fallen from the clouds," my mother continues. "Our situation is better than you see it." She asks the others to witness the fact. "Isn't it better than it seems?"

But only Smutty agrees, with a glimmering of his little smile.

"My son Euclid works, and he is a man who really works," my mother says. "And even if there are many of us, we can live on the work of one man. We could have more on our table than we do." She calls Anna to witness the fact, and Elvira. "Isn't that so? They always say that we could even have meat once in a while. And certainly we could have anchovies. We could have one dish or another once in a while, at least on Sunday. Ask them if I'm wrong."

Meanwhile the glimmering of a smile spreads over Smutty. He could tell my mother that she's not wrong.

"And do you know what my husband says?" my mother continues. "You yourself tell him," she says to her husband. "He says," she continues, "that we could even have a thimbleful of wine once in a while." She asks her husband to testify to the fact. "Don't you say so?" Then she says to smiling Smutty: "This is our real situation. Not what you see. And if we can't act accordingly, it is because of what Anna always says. Ask Anna."

Smutty only smiles more broadly.

"Go ahead," my mother insists. "Anna is this one. Ask her."

"Why is it?" Smutty asks. He is smiling broadly. And no one can say whether he has really asked Anna or not. Nor does Anna answer.

It is my mother who answers herself: "It is for bread. It is because we buy too much bread, and all of my son Euclid's work is spent for bread. And why?" my mother yells. "Why do we have to spend all on bread?"

"Because it's so," Smutty answers and laughs.

"The devil because it's so!" my mother yells at him. Then, rapidly lowering her voice: "It's because of him! Only because of him. He eats a kilo and a half, and would eat ten kilos! It's for him. Because he wants everything for himself."

"For him," Smutty exclaims. He looks at the faces across from him, marvel playing over his little smile, then he asks softly: "For whom?"

"For him. For your friend," my mother thunders.

"For the gentleman here?" Smutty asks.

"For the elephant there!" my mother thunders.

174

16

That is the way my mother finally got to the elephant with our smut-faced guest.

He is a little man who has winked from his smutty face at grandfather as, for a solid month, he passed on his machine across the field. Now he has come to us as grandfather's friend. He sits at our table as grandfather's friend, and yet my mother has been led to speak to him of the elephant in a way scornful of grandfather.

"Elephant?" Smutty murmurs. "Did you say elephant?"

"Isn't he like an elephant? Look at him! Look at him!" my mother says to Smutty. "You yourself can see how he's like an elephant!"

Smutty hasn't waited to have my mother tell him to look. He is already looking at grandfather, and grandfather has his chest stuck out and head turned toward him in order to be admired. "Oh, Lord!" murmurs Smutty. "And here I was asking myself what this man reminded me of. I winked at him, asking myself. I was getting acquainted, and I kept asking myself. And all along this is what he looked like."

He stares with a fascinated smile. "Just what I thought!" he says. "Just what I thought, but I couldn't say it! You know, that's it! You certainly hit the nail on the head."

"Sure, I hit the nail on the head!" my mother replies. "It didn't take much guessing for me. Me, I've been cooking all my life for him and washing and ironing for him…"

Here Smutty is suddenly perplexed. "I didn't mean to say anything wrong. Excuse me! Sure, it's as you say, but I didn't mean it the way you did. I wouldn't want to offend this gentleman."

My mother stops him. "Don't you think any more that I hit the nail on the head?"

"Excuse me," says Smutty. "I don't mean to say that he's got a nose like an elephant or ears like an elephant. I only mean that he is one."

"And that's exactly what I say," my mother tells him.

175

"Naturally," Smutty murmurs. He remains perplexed. However, in a remote way, his little smile is enchanted, and somewhere, in his remoteness, there is a secret about the man, about mankind, and he has just now discovered the importance of it. "Naturally," he murmurs.

He is perplexed and would like to straighten out between himself and the others the possibilities of misunderstanding that cause his bafflement. He is fascinated and would like to be able to let my mother and the others know what it is that fascinates him. "But the elephant," he says, "is the noblest of the animals."

"I know well enough that he is a noble animal," my mother says.

"Don't you see, you say it too," he says. "All his qualities are noble and all the qualities called noble are noble only when one has them like he does. Take strength, for example..."

Here he is aware that he has launched a conversation that may run on and on. He stops a moment. Perhaps he asks himself, in his perplexity, if he can let himself go on. But he is also fascinated, and so he does go on. "What is strength if it is not like it is in him? If it is generous and tranquil like it is in him, then it is noble. But if it is not like it is in him, it isn't at all noble. The same with gentleness. It is a noble quality when it is the way it is in him. And the same with humility. The same with patience. They are noble when they are the way they are in him."

He sees now that we're attentive. Even our kids are attentive, because of the curiosity they have for anything regarding this big elephant animal that my mother constantly points out to us as if it were visible and immobile somewhere outside the window—a mountain or something out there —while now instead here is the fact of the almost subterranean qualities in the man. Is that it? And it's a stranger who is telling us. But we're not satisfied with what we ourselves have learned about the world and about ourselves. We're always waiting for a stranger to come and tell us something more. And "something more" means "the rest of it," and that's what we need most; we miss it.

So go ahead, stranger! Even our children are listening, and even my mother waits for you to tell her what my grandfather is, and what she herself is, beyond what she already knows she is—her life, her years, her great expenditures of self, what of herself is honey and what is gall on her tongue, the hunger she has, and the hunger she sees.

"Isn't it almost cold?" Smut-Face asks. He turns to look at the kitchen door flung wide open on the woods, behind his shoulders, but he doesn't want my mother to get up and close it.

"That's not it," he says. "I've been chilly since I first got up this morning and it doesn't pass. It's just me. It's nothing."

Still he speaks of it. And he speaks of it on seeing our attentiveness, as if to indicate that he might get colder if he stayed much longer with us.

"No," he says to my mother. "I don't want to be in the way."

My mother has closed the door, and he says that the best way is to warm up inside. He'd like wine while he talks. He'd like to be warm and comforted, and then to speak. "People who eat don't like to have people just drinking. They call them drunk. But does that make any difference to us?" He motions to the biggest of our kids. "May I send him?" he asks.

As before, he hunts through the inside pockets where he had found the anchovy, and puts on the table some ten-lira bills, a fistful, then two or three more.

"You must allow me," he says. "I know very well I am in your house, but I am also at home. There's a reason why I came in this morning. I was cold. I'm cold now, and since I've started talking with you, I'll tell you the thing...Some day or other I would have had to say it. It's only my own story but no one else could give it quite the same way, after me. So may I send the boy?"

He brings the knuckles of two fingers near the boy's cheek. He'd like gently to pinch his cheek. "But my fingers are frozen," he tells him. And he asks the boy for his name, and asks him, too, if he likes roasted chestnuts.

"You'll have to allow me," he tells my mother. "I had

177

already decided that when the day came to say something
I would spend my last wages with those who would listen
to me. Now I've begun and you are listening. But you've
got to let me get warm. Will you allow me?"

He points to the ten-lira bills that he has stacked one
on top of the other. He's pulled out another five or six, quite
a stack in all, maybe fifty, and begins dividing them in bunches.
He shows them to my mother's husband.

"Anyway, later, I wouldn't have any use for them, and
instead, one time, I'll have eaten hot chestnuts and drunk
wine in good company, and it will be the most amazing time
of my life. Do you all like hot chestnuts? A little party of
people to talk to is the wish I've always had and never fulfilled.
It's a kind of vow I made. And wouldn't you want me to fulfill
it?

"I don't have children or nephews in the world near at
hand. I don't know where any relative may be. And any good
I ever wanted, I don't know where it is. I've lost my wife,
and two daughters are in Australia, so I can say that I have
my star in heaven.

"But this isn't the story I started. It's just that this has
to be said, too. If you begin, you wind up by telling, and
it's in telling that little by little you find the true story, in
the middle of things like this...So then, hot chestnuts...Does
the gentleman like hot chestnuts?"

His eye measures our old man. He looks into the soup
bowl, then he counts us with his eyes and decides that two
hundred lire are necessary for the chestnuts. In vain we say
"no," as we see his little smile unfolding more when he says
that an extra hundred lire is for anchovies. This, too, is
decided. The anchovies are necessary. He laughs. For the
wine, he asks the boy: "Can I trust you?" He explains that
it should be red but clear against the light, as if it came from
his home district.

"Maybe it's better for me to go with him," my mother's
husband says. And getting on his way, he asks: "From what
part of the country?"

"Oh, it doesn't matter!" the guest answers. "Just let it
come from some famous place! Get it from your own region."

17

It seems for a moment that now Smut-Face would like to wait in silence for the return of my mother's husband and he shrinks into his small shoulders, being really cold. But the little smile of his light eyes wanders toward grandfather's face, and he is again in the fullness of a secret, smiling in fascination.

"Ah!" he resumes. "I certainly thought that the gentleman here had something to tell me, and the lady had already hit the nail on the head. How long have you known this, lady?" he asks.

"I mean to say, one person accumulates in his head the making of a whole Bible, to reach a single meaning, and another person can get at the same meaning with just one word. It happens sometimes," he continues, "that they ask us if we believe in God. Hasn't it ever happened to you? Sure it has. I imagine that hundreds of times it must have happened to this gentleman. He is the ideal type to ask whether he believes in God. He's so imposing!"

He turns to our old man. "Haven't a lot of people asked you?"

And he lays his hand a moment on grandfather's arm. "But let them come! Let them come and ask me at the point where I am. Now, I could almost answer them. Do I believe? Don't I? As if it had anything to do with this! It may mean to leave in peace, but it does not mean to go in peace. We, too, have sought, and it is necessary for us also to have found something if we are to go in peace."

With one hand he holds grandfather's arm and with the other an arm of my brother Euclid, who sits by him. "You see," he says, with those two hands like claws of a roosting bird on their arms, "I understand what it was like in ancient times, how in the early days of mankind, they could adore, sometimes a bull, and sometimes a horse, or a swan, and so on. It was one thing after another, sought and found down through the ages. But that didn't mean true adoration. It meant that men were aware of certain qualities we ourselves have, of certain facts in us, and they saw how there could be great and prodigious qualities, great facts in us. Like the horse! they said. They saw these qualities in ourselves, suddenly, in the same way they could see them in the horse, and then they would point to the horse! That's the idea. It was the horse! But it was those qualities, those facts in us that they pointed at in the horse. They didn't actually mean the horse."

There isn't even a second while he speaks when the little fascinated smile isn't flickering from his pale eyes. Yet, you can see that he speaks wearily. He's cold, he's sick. Probably he came to our house because he felt sick, not because of the friendly feeling he said he has for grandfather.

That doesn't prove that he doesn't have that feeling, in the way he said. But certainly he must have been afraid to be caught out on the road with his illness, and that's why he's with us now, and why he is talking, despite the remoteness of his little smile. He stops often, with long pauses. Is he waiting in fear? He looks around, and seems impatient for the wine to arrive.

"Instead," he adds, "what do they mean in showing us God? Not things to be learned ourselves. And I wanted to find out something that I had not found already. Something else..."

He begins again, a thing at a time, as if he hadn't stopped. He has a thread that he doesn't lose.

"They might even ask us the question. Do you believe? Don't we believe? But not, for example, at the point of death. Be careful," he says to grandfather. "They'll come, they'll ask it of you, and then, if you are concerned, you'll stop thinking about what you wanted to find out, and you won't have your story in hand. You won't go in peace."

On saying this, he shakes grandfather's arm. And grandfather shakes himself and looks at him sidelong, but nobody can be sure whether or not he is listening. However, Smut-Face continues, talking just to grandfather. Is he sure that he's listening? He is certainly the kind who might say all this that he's saying just for grandfather and nobody else. And if

180

grandfather doesn't hear him? If grandfather, let us suppose, is really deaf?

"Lucky," he tells grandfather, "it isn't lost, that old way of things men had when they were boys. Whether you believe in God or not, you don't lose the pleasure of drinking wine and water, of thinking, of resting, of being a man and woman together...And so you don't lose that old way of knowing. In fact, it has developed.

"This is my satisfaction for today, and it ends my story. Do you understand me? I might have been your apprentice, bringing you the mortar bucket, and I would have been what I am today, one who learns from you without having you say a word. We can understand each other with little winks. Isn't that so?

"Perhaps this is the biggest satisfaction of my life...To be able to tell you my story which I have just finished learning from you exactly, and to have understood the two things at the same time, thanks also to this lady, your daughter. One thing I've learned today is that the old way men had of adoring an animal, a mountain, a tree, a thing, was like I said it was. And the other thing, that it still goes on and still is the most vital way we have deep inside ourselves of knowing and of progressing."

Has he stopped? He has just spoken like a public speaker at the end of a speech. But it may be that he has only finished what was meant specially for grandfather.

In the other room, where the door opens on the street, there is the sound of my mother's husband coming back with the boy. The guest looks over, rubbing his hands, as if the cold he feels were pleasant now, since he's on the verge of comforting it with hot chestnuts and wine.

The two of them enter, the boy with the packages and my mother's husband with two flasks, one in each hand. And I could swear that my mother's husband hadn't gone on the errand just to get a taste first himself. And he must have run back.

"He hasn't said anything while I was gone?" he asks my mother.

181

She sees him panting while he takes his place.

"Nothing, or hardly anything," my mother answers him.

18

But the guest is not the type to get upset on hearing his half-hour conversation labeled a "nothing."

Rather, he looks at my mother with an approving little smile. "Now I want to watch you eat anchovies," he tells her and laughs. "I hope that in all this eating make-believe stuff you haven't forgotten how to eat a simple thing. Do you still have a little bread? I have here today's ration of two loaf-sticks." He pulls them out of his coat and offers them. "Put the anchovies in between and eat with your hands. Wine is better if you drink it on top of anchovies."

He is excited, as he gets up to fill the glasses. His hands tremble, and he fills up more glasses than there are people to drink.

"Go easy," we could tell him. There comes from him a kind of pleasant whining, like a dog being patted. But in our family we aren't drinkers. My grandfather wasn't one. A glass lasts us through an entire Christmas dinner, for a whole evening, and it will be our guest and my mother's husband, one facing the other, who drink what's left of the first flask and then all the second one.

"Shall I pour?" they ask each other.

"Go ahead. Thank you."

"May I serve you?"

"Much obliged."

They don't pour any more for us, since they see that our glasses are always full. Our guest tries once to refill grand-father's glass, but my mother stops him.

"It's useless," she tells him. "He doesn't like it the way he does water."

"Really?" our guest exclaims.

"Really," my mother tells him. "He can drink only one glass of wine, while he can drink a bucket of water..."

The guest is quickly persuaded. He looks at our old man. "I understand," he tells grandfather. "In water itself you can love the same thing we need to find in wine in order to love it. You can go to the well, a man like you, to draw water, and can be happy there, or at a fountain, the way the rest of us are happy at a tavern table."

He says "you" and "us." Does he split mankind in two? I ask myself how far he'd go in splitting them. Absolutely into two principles? No, since he's spoken of many things as his that are also ours.

But with that "us" he speaks both of himself and of half of mankind: of himself and of my mother's husband, the little blond ones who carry buckets back and forth, who hear all they do called "nothing" and all they say called "nothing," and who don't observe each other, and who don't start friendships among themselves because they are already bound, since always, by friendship born of their wine.

"Clink," one touches his glass against the other's glass, the old ceremony which we don't approve.

"Your health," says one.

"Your health," says the other.

Health is in the world where the sun shines, it is at the well from which you draw water, in satisfied hunger, in the embrace that has become sleep. But this health in darkness which many men wish each other, men just like us, always disturbs us a little. What do they wish each other? That specters will pacify them and put them to sleep?

We see them, glass by glass, as if they were going down toward some subterranean world. But we don't know whether it disturbs us more to see that they are capable of descending there, or to see in them that such a world exists, and that it is as real as the other, a half of the other in the same way that night is half of the day.

"To the health of the gentleman here," our guest says.

I would like to stop him, at least him. Is the cold he felt now passing? A specter of heat will envelop him. And I wouldn't want him to disappear below. We want him to

183

stay with us. He had things to tell us. And we, even the kids, still have our attention fixed on him. There was a moment when we expected not a little from him. Has that moment gone?

19

All of a sudden he sets down his not yet empty glass, putting one of his small dark hands on top to cover it, and turns toward my mother.

"But why do you say that he's an elephant?" he asks her.

"Papa?"

"The gentleman here."

"Certainly. I never said it about anyone else."

"Why do you say he's one?" he asks her. "As a good thing? Or as a bad thing?"

My mother answers him that it's as a good thing and as a bad thing at the same time, for what grandfather was, good and bad both, and for what he continues to be, with his massiveness, and all his needs and all the bother he knows how to cause.

"That's right," the guest says.

But he lets my mother go on. She repeats the usual story of grandfather, of everything grandfather could do and of all the jobs on which he worked—the Fréjus, the Simplon, the buildings of Cordusio, the cupola of the Arcade, the reclaiming of the Ferrara swamps, the iron bridges over the Po (and the Duomo? And the Pyramids?). Only, she doesn't get as excited as with us, nor does she exaggerate so much. It's as if she were trying not to be the person who is talking, but rather the person who happens to want to listen. And at her every phrase the guest says: "That's so."

"And do you know everything about elephants?" he then asks her.

Of course my mother knows everything. For example,

she speaks of grandfather naked to the waist, and tells about the way his skin would dry up right away even after the most profuse sweat...

"Have you noticed their patience?" the guest asks her. "You bother them, tease them with silly tricks, or tickle their ears, and they just look at you. With a twitch they flick away the fly that you are, and then simply look at you. They don't pick you up bodily and toss you aside."

My mother answers that grandfather used to lift things up bodily and toss them aside. He had even picked her up and tossed her aside, once or twice.

"But that is their anger," the guest says. "Have you ever noticed the way it really is? It doesn't fall on whoever is really to blame. It falls on other people who happen to be around, on things that are around. This doesn't happen because they are inclined toward injustice. It's because they love to moderate themselves and in injustice they can moderate themselves. Beware, if they show anger justly against anybody! And if once or twice he picked you up and tossed you aside, you may be sure that the fault was rather in somebody else."

My mother answers that she doesn't know. She smiles; she could tell some things, but there are too many children around, and then she doesn't want to carry the conversation around to herself.

The guest understands my mother's smile. "What should it mean?" he says. "No father on earth has ever known for sure if there is evil in such things and in what way, even for a young girl, or if, perhaps, the worst evil is that people wait to see them punished."

Here my mother's husband calls the guest. He wants him with him in the wine-drinking. He doesn't want him away. And he grunts from the wine. "How? How? What does my widow say she did?"

The guest uncovers the glass, brings it to his lips, and takes a sip just to reaffirm his companionship. Then, having poured some more out of the flask, his small hand falls on the glass like a cover.

"Instead," he continues with my mother, "you should ask yourself if you didn't do something really wrong one of

185

the times when he picked up and tossed aside somebody who was in his way to the right or left of you."

Again, my mother's husband calls to the guest. "Who?" he asks. He doesn't want to drink alone.

And he grunts from his well of wine. "What in the world for are you wasting time with my widow? She'll never confess..."

He recalls his guest to their former communion. "Are you or aren't you going to pour for me? Do I have to pour for myself?" He grasps the flask and leans the neck of it right down into his own glass.

"Don't you spot my tablecloth," my mother yells at him.

"Well, you take it off then," her husband answers. In fact, he himself lifts the cloth from his corner, and with the precision that you never expect of drunks, but that they always have, he takes every item, one by one, from the head of the table where they are sitting, he and the guest, on either side of grandfather, and one by one, he sets everything on the bare wood, pushing the tablecloth farther on down the table as each bit is released. "Everything my widow says," he grunts meanwhile, "is that the fault was mine. And she'll never confess it." He repeats "never" many times, while he's shifting things from the tablecloth to the bare wood of the table top. "Oh, never!" He repeats this in sing-song.

"And papa?" my mother yells at him. "Don't you see that he doesn't like it?"

The hands and the beard of grandfather are twitching in irritation. He notices what my mother's husband is doing before him, and with irritation he touches the bare boards where now his plate sits with the heap of chestnuts.

He hadn't noticed anything since they put the plate of chestnuts in front of him. Over them he had placed his hands with their befogged touch, picking up a chestnut, foggily peeling it, bringing it to his mouth, then picking up another chestnut, peeling it, carrying it to his mouth, and the same with a third, and sometimes even a fourth. And then, with three or four in his mouth, he would dedicate himself for several minutes to chewing.

But now he looks here and there about the table, moving

his hands in irritation here and there about the bare boards.

"Don't you see you're bothering him?" my mother yells at her husband.

And my mother's husband groans. "Do you hear her? When something goes wrong it's always my fault."

He stops shoving the tablecloth, since the table is clear between the guest and himself, on both sides of grandfather, and again grasps the flask by the neck. "You wanted me to pour for you," he grunts, "and now you don't let me pour for you any more."

He calls to the guest to be his companion again. "Come on," he says to him. He wants to go all the way down to the bottom. But just because of this he wants to be sure that the one with whom he started the descent is following him. It may be that he is afraid to find himself alone in the deep labyrinths of wine. "Come on," he says. And he pours wine over the small hand of the guest as it still covers the glass.

And so the wine spills over the table boards.

"Now do you see?" my mother yells. "Now do you see?"

Meanwhile the guest looks at grandfather, who has again taken chestnuts up in his befogged hands, peeling the chestnuts one by one, putting chestnuts into his mouth.

20

Smut-Face says to my mother: "Have you noticed the way elephants are when you aren't nice to them?"

Of course my mother has observed that about them too. She says that if you weren't nice to grandfather he would quit whatever he was doing and sulk for about ten minutes, and then go on.

"Ah!" the guest says. "It looks as though they have a melancholy disposition, they get excited so little and make such little noise. But inside they have a joyful disposition that nothing can really disturb much."

My mother says that it is because of this, because of their joyful disposition, that they never need to get excited or to talk.

And the guest says: "Yes, it's because of the good disposition they have inside them. It envelops them with its freshness and it has its own movement and murmur as if it were a brook inside them." He ends up by saying that elephants are happy. "Ah, they are really happy!"

And my mother says that they also make others happy. She says that in my grandfather's good old days it seemed as though the house were full of canaries that sang whenever grandfather came and sat down to read the paper.

"That's the happiness of elephants," the guest says. "They make you happy. They don't even whistle or move a finger to give you happiness, and yet they give it to you just from watching them."

He says that's why it was his dream ever since childhood to be a sorcerer.

"A sorcerer?" my mother exclaims.

Perhaps he's at the good part of the story he wanted to tell us. Our kids prick up their ears. Is this his story?

Well, he had wanted to be a sorcerer. "You know," he says. "One who could talk to them, to elephants, and one they would talk to. It's so rare that you really talk in this world. You hardly ever talk. And I've always wanted to know the secret of making people talk a little."

"Is that what you call a sorcerer?"

"It's that and other things. I was a small child when I saw that it was impossible to confide in anybody in the world. I tried and tried, and I could not succeed, and then I thought that the first thing to do was to learn to enchant them."

"Enchant them how?"

"In one way or another. I thought of this, too. That there certainly must be lots of ways and I must choose one of them. But I knew that, generally, sorcerers play some kind of instrument, and I decided that I would enchant, too, by playing an instrument. The only thing, I had to find some music."

"Did you find the music?"

"That was exactly the most difficult part. What makes

188

the enchanting is in the theme. It has to be a special theme, not just the first one that comes to hand, and learning to enchant really means looking for the theme. You must know about snake charmers. They have a theme for rattlesnakes, and one for cobras, different for each kind. You must know that."

"For what were you looking for a theme?"

"For elephants, of course. Though, to tell the truth, I didn't know it right away. I started looking. It had to be special. It had to be for one kind of thing and not for another, and yet I didn't know for what kind the theme I was looking for had to be."

"And then?"

"And then, I looked. I was a little child, and I pulled out my fife and looked. And I was a young man, and I went into lonesome places, and sat down on a rock, and I played and sought."

"Even when you got married, did you keep looking?"

"Even then. I couldn't be in the house where my wife was. After all, among other things, it was for my wife's sake that I was seeking. I used to go out into the open country at night, as soon as my wife was sleeping, and there I'd go at my fife, looking for my theme."

"You've looked for it all your life?"

"All my life. The urge used to come on the streets, in my work with tar, at mealtimes, and I used to eat in a great hurry, and then would go aside somewhere to seek with my fife."

"How could you find it if you looked where there wasn't anybody? Snake-charmers do it with snakes in front of them..."

"It isn't said that it must always be done this way. It's enough for you to think about the way things are, the way you've seen them, and you can hunt with the certainty that you'll always end up finding it."

"But you haven't found it."

"What do you mean, I haven't? One day it came, and all at once I felt it there. But I wanted to be careful. I set myself to repeating it in order not to risk forgetting."

"And did you try it on somebody?"

"I would have tried it some day. The important thing was having it. From that moment on, the only thing that bothered me was making it perfect. I kept on with the habit I had of going off into some lonesome place every day. Sometimes I'd go early in the morning, sometimes toward night, and now I have it like a diamond. It can do miracles."

"What a strange story!" my mother says. "And is it," she asks him, "for enchanting elephants?"

The man takes the full glass in his hand. He laughs and empties it. He has said before that he didn't know for what he was seeking his theme. Now he answers my mother. "Why, yes, lady. It's for enchanting elephants."

21

One would like to know what his little smile means at this moment. Is it the same as it has been? Still a little smile that can be ironical and rapt at the same time, questioning and satisfied? Or is it hallucinated?

He tips the flask, looks inside for wine, pours some for his companion, and then for himself. But again, he doesn't drink, again lowering his hand to hold it over the mouth of the glass. As if, in this way, through some need of his, he would like to bewitch his wine, some way or other, before drinking it.

"I've known them for quite a while," he says. "In strength and gentleness, in patience, in courage, in their joyful disposition, in their happiness, yet I didn't realize it."

"Ah!" he tells us. "I didn't understand what it was that I liked in being very quiet near a working companion, or on the train near a traveler, near anybody who isn't talking, or near a young fellow, near a vile beggar, and the whole thing was that I like being near an elephant."

He turns to my mother. "Is it an elephant, you say?"

190

He answers *yes* to himself. The thing is that he likes to stay with elephants, and the theme he's been preparing all his life he's prepared for them, for "the gentleman here," for elephants.

He lifts his free hand. He looks through his inside pockets once again, and this time he puts a reed fife on the table. "There," he says. But not because he's showing the fife. He's not at that point yet, and his little smile hasn't changed.

"We're so many things," is what he says. "Anything you want. Tigers and little dogs, little pigs, and baby chicks. We are mountains, we are rivers, we are gnomes no taller than mushrooms. But we are also this, and the lady can be witness. Even elephants. And it doesn't matter whether big or little. Even elephants."

He lifts up the hand holding the fife. "You see here?" Now his little smile changes. And how it changes! It's like the joy of youngsters showing a toy. "It's for those who are elephants that I've found my theme."

The reed fife has holes rimmed in metal. It is ringed around about seven times by the same metal, and we look at it. It's an old fife, brown in color. One can imagine that our guest really has had it since he was a boy seven years old. Is all his life in that pipe?

From the end of the fife hangs a bit of red rag.

"What is that for?" my mother asks.

The guest's little smile is wise. "That?" he says. "That does extraordinary things. That shows right away whether the person for whom I play is an elephant or not. And it shows how much of a one he is. Oh!" he exclaims. "You'll see!"

He has taken his hand away from the mouth of the glass and has grasped the glass.

"Would you like to play it here?" my mother asks.

"To the gentleman here," the guest answers. "I almost didn't play it for anybody, and instead here I am..." He drinks a sip, wipes his mouth and lifts the fife with both hands up to his lips.

"You're sure nothing strange will happen to him?" my mother says. "He's already such a burden to us. I wouldn't want him to be heavier on us, on account of your music."

The guest smiles. "Just the contrary, he'll be lighter."

"I wouldn't want him to get more of an appetite."

"There's not the least danger."

"Or that he'd get a stroke and be bedridden."

"But Mama!" we say.

"What do you know about it?" our mother demands.

"He might even take it into his head to want this music every day."

And again we say: "But, Mama!"

The guest laughs and says, "You'll see!" and he begins.

22

Is he really playing?

At first it hardly seems so. We see him blowing, a little moan comes from the reed, and that's all. But his blackened face is concentrating and the smile in his eyes disappears under furrowed brows. Grandfather does as we do, looking only at him, while he has laced his fingers, one hand with the other, on the table.

The old reed moans. Is that the tuning up?

And still it is just a reed. It sounds like a cane in cane-brake, with water running near it into sands and sea, over laundresses' arms, cracked and seamed by the beaten linens.

Little by little Smut-Face pushes himself back in the chair, always blowing, tuning up. He doesn't look at us once he has begun, and from the time he's stopped looking at us he no longer has the little smile on his face.

I have said that he is frowning. Better to say that one eye is out of focus. But it always points down. He pushes himself back still further. In fact, with his foot he pushes back his chair a couple of paces, and then sits down again, without having stopped blowing his reed or looking down.

Because of the way he keeps looking down, more and more, we can't quite tell what his eye is like. Is it scowling?

Perhaps worse than scowling: it is flecked with blood. And he has wanted space around himself, a circle around him. He sits with the chair under him tilted back, but his feet look as though they were nailed to the floor, as though they had penetrated it with claws.

But shall we have the theme?

We all look at the fife, waiting for the theme, wondering if it is only this moaning as when it used to be growing in a cane-brake, and we see that the little red rag at the tip no longer hangs limp and inert. It is unfurled and lifted. Just that: it is lifted. It's carried by the wind from the holes of the reed and flies high, as if it were a flag, almost waving.

There certainly is something going on now. The sound is full. It is the cane-brake catching the wind, and it is thick on the bank of the waters with the wind inside, along all the rivers, all the seas, even in Africa along all the lakes. It is a cane-brake and becomes an organ: subtle in every note, rather shrill, but in its full sound very deep. Then suddenly it stops.

Was that the theme and is it over?

The man is sweating and his eye wanders. He wavers toward the table, looking for his glass. His drinking companion offers it to him. "And this, then, is all your theme?" my mother asks him.

"Not bad," we say.

"It's a theme like any other," my mother says.

He has taken a drink and wiped his mouth. A bit of his smile returns to his face, even in his squinting eye. "I only played it for the gentleman here," he tells us. "He's the only one able to hear it the way it really is."

"But what has it done to him?" my mother asks. She looks at grandfather. "I don't see that it's done anything."

"Oh, no?" Smut-Face says. "Didn't you see?"

He also watches grandfather, ponders a moment, then begins to play his reed again, standing up now and continuing to watch grandfather. The little red flag, this time, lifts up at once. He sways a bit as he plays, perhaps rocking a bit, continually shifting from foot to foot, and the theme comes forth almost at once. I mean, the reed seems young, as in the cane-brake, and suddenly the cane-brake is the world itself. At once it is like an organ.

We all watch grandfather. What is there to see in him? His head is bowed the way it is when he's seated at the door opened toward the woods, and his hands, with the fingers neither open nor shut, are laid large on the table. There is nothing to see in him. I would almost say he is asleep.

But Smut-Face twists his head while he plays, twists his shoulder down, sweats from his brow, and his breath twists inside the reed, twisting upward the beat of the little red flag. He's really not firm on his feet. He rocks forward as though he might knock against the table. He wavers back and forth, bending his knees, then suddenly jerking himself up sharply, jerking out the sound of the cane to a shrill note.

He appears to be signaling to us in some way—with his head, with the reed, with his elbows...

Is he really signaling?

He wants us to look at grandfather. And we look at him. Don't get excited, little man, we're looking at him. We're looking at him...

But what's happening? Grandfather is beating those fingers of his on the table. By Heaven, he's beating time! Grandfather is drumming on the table with the fingers we thought petrified, and he marks with taps the time of the music.

23

"Ah!" my mother says.

The theme stops, and the little man, withered, sits down.

"And this is all?" my mother asks.

But he doesn't notice what she says. With his wandering eye, he searches for his glass, his hands numbed. Again, his drinking companion puts it into his hand, and sweating, exhausted, he drinks with short sips.

"Mama!" we say to our mother.

"It's not much if that's all there is to it," she says.

The little man drinks another sip. His eyes close while he sips, but he opens them again, and carefully puts down his glass. "You know," he tells us, "I've been a bit sick for several years. I've always been somewhat sickly, but more so for the last several years. They say it's T.B. I should go to the hospital. Perhaps I'll go, and perhaps not. At any rate, I've had my party with you. I've said the thing I wanted to say. I've played my theme to this gentleman, and for all this I want to give you my sincere thanks. Thank you, children, thank you, ladies and gentlemen, thank you, lady..."

"You're welcome," my mother says. "But why do you want to go?"

We all murmur something too, but against her. "Why do you treat him badly?"

And reaching across the table, her husband takes his drinking companion by the arm. "No," he tells him.

My mother looks us up and down, those of us who were the chief ones to murmur. "I?" she exclaims. "Since when did I treat him badly?"

"Since when?" the little man echoes. "That's the word for it. Since when? Actually, I owe her more than anybody else, and I thank her, aside from the gentleman, more than anybody else. After all, I haven't said I'm leaving, although in a while I'll have to say it. Now," he tells us, "I've worked to the last. You see it from my face, and whether or not I go to the hospital, it doesn't mean that I'll have much time merely to sit on a chair.

"But it isn't death that comes, as people say. It is we who go to it. When we've found the little we could find, then it's over. There's nothing left," he says, "that means anything to us. We drink some more wine, but we don't look for anything further in it, and it doesn't say anything further to us. Nothing says anything further to us. The air we breathe doesn't say anything further to us. The rest at night doesn't say anything further. That is, we accomplish nothing further, and whatever our age, we can think of ourselves as already dead. Otherwise, we are dead and foolish both."

"And isn't it good it's that way?" my mother interrupts.

195

Our guest feels taken down. "What?" he asks.

"What you were saying," my mother replies. "That a man who has worked to the last, when he's through working he's through living."

"I didn't say that," our guest observes. "That can be a good thing but, at times, may not be..."

"Why not?" my mother exclaims. "Then he doesn't weigh on anybody else. He doesn't eat off anybody else. He doesn't need anybody else to dress and undress him."

Our guest looks at grandfather. He has also made a motion across the table, as if to stop my mother's words before they reach grandfather. "How do we know when a man's a weight and when he isn't? A man can be the only one to bring food home and still be a weight. While a child, for example, is never a weight. We can't judge according to such things."

"However," my mother insists, "the thing you were saying is a good thing." And she looks hard at grandfather, while she speaks. "You're lucky not to have much time for sitting down, I can assure you on behalf of your daughters..."

Our guest looks from my mother to grandfather, then from grandfather to my mother, and again from my mother to grandfather.

"But I never said such a thing," he answers. "In fact, I'll tell you," he adds, "I was a very grieved man this morning when I came in here, and I came in just because I was so grieved. I was cold," he tells us, "I was ill, I thought my days numbered, and yet I didn't think I was through. I wasn't sure I had found..."

"You had found your theme," my mother tells him.

"That was some time ago," the guest says. "But for whom? I didn't yet know for whom I'd found it..."

"After all," my mother says, "you've said that you're glad you worked to the end, and now you want to uphold the opposite view."

"I don't mean to uphold the opposite view," the guest says. "In fact, I would be glad only to have the time to clean my face of the dirt from my work...But I do say that we ourselves know when we are dead, and that then we must hold ourselves ready. I didn't mean anything else."

196

24

"Well!" my mother says.

She is thinking. Reflectively she looks at grandfather once, also at her drunken husband. Finally she comes out with the question: "Elephants...do they or don't they die?"

"Oh!" the guest exclaims.

With his little smile, he rises to his enchanted sphere. He said a while ago that his dream was to be a sorcerer. Didn't he mean, rather, that he wanted an occupation in which he, himself, could become enchanted?

"You wish that they wouldn't die?" he exclaims.

"I don't know," my mother says. "Certainly though," she hurries on to add, "they work so hard when they're young! After all, it's right that later they should have a long time for doing nothing."

But her face denies that this is right. Her face is dark, made so by the things she has heard that now oppress her within. "Well then?" she asks. And her face seems to ask again whether they do or do not die. "You know about it, don't you?"

The guest says he does.

"Then you must know, on the average, how old they get to be."

The others, the girls and my brother Euclid, begin to talk too...

"They don't last so long."

"No herbivorous animal lasts long."

"I think they generally die at twenty-five."

"At twenty-five years?" my mother says. "Or twenty-five centuries?"

The guest, with his rapt smile, finally speaks. "The elephant, among all other animals," he tells us, "is the one that dies with the greatest wisdom. That is, it is the highest example nature gives us as to how you can know when you are dead, instead of being dead and not knowing it."

Here he touches grandfather's arm—which is a strange thing for him to do during such a speech—but he has been carried away, gently rapt in his enchantment.

"Are you listening?" he asks grandfather. "It's a wonder, the way they die. As soon as they realize they are worthless and are a weight—there!—they cut the cord. They consider themselves dead, and they die."

He tells grandfather this, and with fervor, with inspiration. Yet before, he hadn't wanted my mother's words to reach grandfather. He had turned their meaning through his own words, and had seemed to try to stop them with gestures, across the table. Why, all at once, is he so eager now to say all this to grandfather?

"And you should see with what precision they pick the right moment when they would become a weight. They are aware of it to the minute."

Is grandfather listening? He doesn't show it, except for the fact that his face is turned toward our guest. But that might be just by chance. His beard doesn't stir. His head is bowed as if in sleep, and neither his hands nor even the big veins marking them, respond to the pressure the guest puts on his arm.

"Never, in all of Africa," the guest continues, "do you see a dead elephant in the woods or in the paths. Nor can it be said that they bury their dead. They have secret cemeteries that they don't even know themselves while they're alive, where the old elephants go when they think it's time to die. Do you understand this?"

He is silent a moment. But not because he wants a reply. It seems to him that he has said something that won't let us break his silence, it's so extraordinary.

We keep looking at grandfather. Is he listening? And does he understand if he does hear?

My mother breaks the silence. "But what do they do?" she asks. "Do they kill themselves?"

Smut-Face starts to laugh. "Nothing violent," he answers her. "They get on their way, reach their place, stretch out and wait to die. Nothing else."

"But if they walk they're still spry," my mother says.

"Naturally, they're still strong," the guest says and laughs. "And you must realize that they don't exactly know where the place is. They must look for it. They must walk days and days."

"But they could stay with the others and live a bit longer," my mother says.

"What would be the use?" the guest asks and laughs. "To weigh on the others a little longer and then die like dogs alongside the road?"

"Well!" my mother says.

"Here is their wisdom," the guest tells her. "To know at a certain point that all they have left is the strength necessary to reach the place where they can stretch out."

"I don't know," my mother says.

25

Then my mother turns to the guest with a whole run of questions.

Has he traveled much?

He hasn't traveled much.

Has he always hunted in the same place?

He has never hunted anywhere.

And what has he done? Has he been an ivory merchant?

No, he says, he's never been an ivory merchant.

"Then how," my mother asks, "did you know all these things about elephants?"

He begins his story once again. "You see..." he says.

And he is happy to be for a moment more the man he would have liked to be, once in a lifetime, to speak of himself, with listeners around, holding forth with a speech full of the things of his own story. "In my town," he tells us, "there's a great rock that you can see from the windows at the end of the bare country. On a line with the hills, it is higher than any, and you can see its profile clearly for many miles, from the windows, as if it had the wild ears and trunk that, they say, elephants have. For this very reason it is called The Elephant. From a distance it seems to be the size you think elephants are, and nearby, much bigger—a colossus of rock and elephant.

"At first I merely used to look at it—just what I could see of our rock from the porch of my mother's house—looking at it and thinking of these animals and their qualities. Then I began to go across the fields and up to the hills where The Elephant stood, even right under where he was, and I thought about such animals as I sat under him. I used to climb as high as I could along one side of him, and I used to pat his flank, or pet him as if I were his caretaker and he really had the qualities of elephants—the great strength and gentleness, the humility, the patience, the courage, the happiness, which are so noble in these animals.

"I did this for many years, until the day that I left our town, so now I can say I know all there is about them."

"About elephants?" my mother asks.

"About the qualities you think of as theirs, and therefore, also about them. I thought about it all the time, and learned how they were. I knew them. Yes, lady, I also found out this way about their habits and about their death."

"But then you must have seen them in Africa," my mother insists.

"I've never been in Africa, lady," the guest repeats.

"And you've never seen them in a menagerie, or a circus, or in a zoo?" my mother asks.

"Never have been in such places."

"Good Lord!" my mother exclaims. "Do you realize what a big nerve you have? I couldn't begin to tell you how much!"

26

Even while the little man still laughs, his teeth begin to chatter.

He wanted to pour himself some more wine, but has found the bottle empty, and has taken his hands from the table and stuck them into his pockets. He is all huddled up, closed in his little shoulders, and yet he still laughs, at times looking at grandfather, at times at his drinking companion of today, at times at my mother, looking at them with his little smile while his teeth chatter. "I've certainly talked too much," he says. "And you know, in our town they say that when you talk too much, once, without being in the habit, it means that you are near dying..."

My mother interrupts. "You don't mean to tell me you don't have the habit of talking!"

The little smut-faced man narrows his shoulders even more. "Of talking too much?" he says, his teeth chattering. "As you wish. But I hope just the same you'll forgive me, and remember, that after all, it was you who let me. And this gentleman, of course!"

He silences his chattering teeth. He gets up, wavers, turns to sit down, then again stands up. "Maybe the people who eat are right," he says, "when they say that those who don't eat shouldn't drink, and call us drunkards. They're quick at defining speeches like mine and then washing their hands of the whole thing. Drunkard's talk, they say. Don't they say it?" he asks, and his teeth chatter. "Go ahead and say it too, and then wash your hands of it."

"No," moans his companion of the wine.

My mother's husband lifts his face as though from an ensnaring fog, up from the table, and looks as if he were lifting off cobwebs with vague motions of his hands. He moans from sleep and wine: "No, brother."

But his hands stop, his face sinks between them, and again he is withdrawn from what goes on between us and his companion. He says nothing more.

His companion, Smut-Face, still wavering, has taken a few steps. He is going toward our kitchen door, which is now closed against the woods. He finds the chair on which grandfather sits all day, when he's not at the table, and sits down, somewhat bent over, pressing his hands against his stomach.

"The only thing left for me is to talk like they make drunkards talk in movies," he says, with chattering teeth. "But I wouldn't want you to keep me. I've thanked you. I've said goodbye, and I really need to go."

He speaks with his face turned to us, but he raises it toward my mother, who has followed him.

"Really!" he adds, his teeth chattering.

With a hoarse moan, his companion of the wine, at the table, still tries to call him. But he can't tear away from the fog of cobwebs that is the sleepiness of the wine. He doesn't even moan "no." He moans "m-m-m." And he is the only one in our family who would like to keep the guest.

My mother, following Smut-Face, has an ironing-table cover over her arm, as if she were thinking of covering him up with it. It's just a thought crossing her mind—to make him lie down for a little. But that's all, and she doesn't tell him to stay, and nobody else does, except his bottle-and-a-half companion. What is our fear? That he'll get drunk in our house, the unknown one, and that he may vomit in our house? Or that he may die in our house?

"I don't just have T.B.," Smutty says, his face not entirely without his smile, even now, in the act which raises him toward my mother. "Is it T.B. alone which strikes men? There are many other illnesses. And maybe I have some others, too. Perhaps I have cancer."

He speaks of this very softly, as if only to my mother, in order to confide in her something that will make her decide to let him go, even without letting the others know. But we are all only afraid that he won't go soon enough. We wouldn't want to see his vomit or anything else on the floor of our kitchen, between grandfather's chair and the woods. And so my mother goes silently to open the door for him.

"Well!" she says to him.

Smutty stands up, walks straight to the door sill, then crosses over.

From there he turns to make us a farewell sign the way he used to do those days when he was passing by, standing erect on the tractor of the road-roller. Is he winking now, too?

My mother leans out to look after him. "Well!" she repeats. And she calls after him: "Come back to see us, if you happen to be passing by."

27

A day passes, and another comes. The spree has made my mother's husband sad, and grandfather is the way he's always been, sitting on his chair in front of the woods, with his old stick between his legs.

But there's something new between my mother and her husband. They are together a great deal, and he accompanies her when she goes for chicory. They hardly fight any more, and they exchange long glances. This develops after the sadness which overtook him from the spree. But is it really something new?

Other times we have seen them getting along this way, she towering above him, like a mother whom he alone can render benign and tender, and he, little, with his minute face, getting in the way of her housewifely chores.

Then there are periods when he wants to repair everything broken in our house; and he's good at doing it even without a single proper tool. He can repair faucets, washbowls, light switches, and all such things, so that they really work, or he can get back our electric light when the man from the Electric Company has cut it off. In fact, his buzzing about the house is the first sign that he and my mother are getting along. You can tell from the hammer blows, or from the racket of the iron. By Heaven! you say, they're getting along.

And why does it always somewhat surprise us? Why, each time, does it look like something new to us?

We think of our mother only through her own words: of what she tells us about how grandfather was. Nor is there any doubt that they indicate a great deal about her. Nevertheless, she did marry her little "blond one."

Why did she marry him? Why has she taken a man just like him into her large bed?

And it is not the first time, either. Her first marriage, too, was also with a "little blond one." My father, too, was a man like that: smallish, with a minute face. And we bear an imprint of it, especially my sister. Why don't we take that into account?

203

This time, however, we see them getting along without having the house echo with hammer blows. He is a sad husband getting in her way all day long. And she is a silent wife brooding over him, as if she, too, were trying to be sad. So the thing really does seem new to us now.

But the really new thing is what happens to grandfather.

He sits in front of the door that opens on the woods, and all day long he is the same as before, yet, either morning or afternoon, there isn't a single day when he doesn't start talking. It had been two years since he uttered a single word. We'd forgotten his old man's talk. And now, this novelty.

From the kitchen there seems to come a deep rumbling, and it is our grandfather talking, with a voice hoarse as if there were rocks in a deep throat.

Of what?

What does he want?

We learn from our mother who runs up to him to listen and reply.

"What was he saying?" my mother yells. "Who was saying what?" Then she repeats: "Ah! What was the little man with the reed fife saying?"

She repeats it, and yells: "But what was he saying about what?"

She yells: "Ah! About elephants!"

She yells at him some of the things the little man told us about elephants. But grandfather beats his stick on the floor. That isn't what matters to him. This is not what matters to him. The man said something else. My mother yells other things to him that the little man said. And grandfather again shakes his stick. He beats it against the floor.

It isn't this. Not this. He speaks in a more resentful tone out of the rumbling of rocks in the deep throat, like the dry tearing away and fall of rocks on a cliff-face.

"Ah!" my mother yells. "The way he spoke of their death?"

My mother's husband has gone behind her. "Sure, the way he spoke of that."

He's on the other side of my grandfather, and grandfather has turned his face away from him. Grandfather doesn't even want to know he's there. He doesn't even want to know he's talking. He never wants to know he's there.

Grandfather has turned further toward my mother, but he doesn't hear her yelling at her husband, the way she does when she isn't getting along with him: "You! Mind your own business." Instead, my mother and her husband remain there exchanging a deep glance. "He wants you to repeat it," her husband says to my mother.

Nor has grandfather shaken his stick, although he's turned three-quarters of the way around.

That's what he wants. "Repeat it to him," her husband says to my mother.

28

Now, on Saturday evening, when my brother Euclid brings home his week's wages, and we are gathered around my mother's apron, we still talk about the things we could buy if we didn't have to buy so much bread.

Usually, it is the girls who begin. Then they go on, and say a lot, but my mother doesn't stop them as she once did. She listens, and lets them say all they want. And so we talk about how much better we could live if it weren't for grandfather. Good Lord! A kilo and a half less of bread to be bought every day. Good Lord! It would mean no black market bread! It would mean 190 lire a day to spend for something else every day!

Can you think of that, you folks?

It would mean meat once in a while—some Sunday! Or, on a Friday, dried cod! To have beans, some evening. To have anchovies! Will you think about that, you folks? With fifty lire you can get one hectogram of anchovies...

At this, we turn to look at grandfather's mass, and the rumbling of rocks comes from him, deep from the harsh valleys. It is evening, and autumn. The door is closed in the kitchen, against the forest, but it has glass panels, and beyond

205

the glass you get the confused darkness of trees and of the deep woods out there. "What?" my mother asks.

She's gone toward grandfather.

Her husband steps behind her, drawing closer also, to listen. "You know very well," he tells her. "He wants to know what that man said about the elephants."

My mother bends over grandfather. "What he said about the elephants?" she asks him.

Grandfather says yes, that's what he wants to hear.

And my mother asks: "About how they are strong, and at the same time gentle?"

Grandfather shakes his stick. That's not it, damn it!

"But you know what he wants," my mother's husband says.

He goes to the other side of grandfather, where he can look straight into her face, and grandfather makes only the sign of turning his head away. The first time he had moved away, a bit less the second time, and not at all the third. Grandfather makes a slight motion, as if to move, but by now, he, too, is listening.

"What he said about their death?" my mother asks.

That's what grandfather wants. What did he say? And my mother begins: "That they are very wise."

With a sign of his hand, her husband tells her to go on. It's not enough for grandfather to hear that they are wise.

"They understand at once when they're not able to get around any more," my mother continues.

She hesitates. She could say the whole thing in four words. But she keeps stopping. So her husband goes on: "When they are a weight to others."

Here, my mother makes a decision. "Yes. They even understand that quite a bit beforehand. Then they don't wait until they are without strength. They lift their trunk, trumpet their final blast, their farewell, and then start on their way."

My grandfather lifts the heavy weight of his brow. And he waits for the rest.

"The question," says my mother's husband, "may be simply one of pride."

He speaks as if the thing were up for discussion, and as if he had it in mind to explain motives, to discover them for himself and for others.

"Isn't it so?" he asks, uncertain. "They don't want to make ugly sights of themselves. They're too heavy to be in the way when the gloss is off their hide, or the elasticity, and so on. Who wouldn't lack respect for them? And that's what they don't want. Isn't that pride? Certainly it's also sensibility with pride. They feel what must happen to them, so they lie down, and decide to die."

My mother's husband, in the mellowness of these last days, is not loquacious except when grandfather wants to know what that little man had said about elephants. And he's very serious even in his loquacity. He says things he has apparently thought out during the rest of the day while he's been quiet and silent. They are certainly not the first thoughts that have come into his head. And he repeats them, every time, almost always the same.

As a matter of fact, my mother doesn't answer grandfather very differently. She, too, repeats the same thing every time. And how could she avoid repeating herself?

The argument doesn't change. The scene is the same. It doesn't change. Nor does grandfather ever change the order of his questions, either the spoken or the silent ones. All that happens is predisposed, on both sides. My grandfather, on his side, has what he wants. And on their side, my mother and her husband have the same from him: what they want from him.

"Do they lie down?" my mother says. "Before, he said that they get on their way, and that they go on and on to find the place where they lie down, going on for days and days, even months."

Grandfather is very attentive. From behind him, we notice the alertness of his ears.

"Exactly," my mother's husband says. "And that's one proof more that they don't want to be ugly sights, that they don't want to give any, or to see any. They don't want ugly carcasses along their paths."

Here, grandfather speaks again. How? How?

"They don't like," my mother explains, "to have the dead along the paths."

"You ought to say," her husband corrects, "that they don't want help to die. They like to die hidden, except from the other dead."

"And it's because of this," my mother continues, "that they have secret places where they go before it's too late. To disappear, before it is too late, from the eyes of the living, and to wait, stretched out there, to be dead."

At this point grandfather speaks for the last time. He asks how it is possible that they stretch out for dead before they are dead.

"He said it that way," my mother answers. "I just repeat to you what he said."

Grandfather, then, lowers his forehead.

"That's what's remarkable about them," my mother's husband says to him. But he has come too near, and grandfather moves his face away, with disdain.

29

Suddenly, one day, it is not merely just hard to eat bread dipped in water from a fountain—it becomes an eternal torture, and you are condemned for an eternity.

Besides, chewing and swallowing give you a strange sense of nausea. In the long hours when you don't chew you are dizzy. You are empty inside, and the taste that was bread or will be for the next meal, comes up to take you and rock you over emptiness. How, then, at mealtime, can you face that taste?

My sister bursts out crying.

"You! You!" my mother tells her. She mocks her, making a whining and sobbing sound.

"Shame," she tells her.

Anna gets up. "We've reached the point where we have to make a decision."

She, as well as Elvira, speaks of our children.

"We've reached the point where a girl begins to be a whore."

It would be well, here, for my mother's husband to say: "Let's not exaggerate." He's there, pulling at his cheeks between his fingers. But he doesn't even whisper, and the ugly word lingers among us.

"Oh!" my sister moans. "Is that what you want to bring me to?"

No one is saying, they tell her, that she ought to do it.

"Then who are you speaking for?" my sister moans. She says that Elvira and Anna are certainly not speaking for themselves. They have their men who wouldn't let them. Therefore, they speak for her.

But at this point my mother comes forward.

"If anyone has to be a whore," she says, "I'll be the first one."

"What?" her husband says.

He, too, comes forward, but not to pull at his cheeks. It's to speak. Hasn't she, like Anna and Elvira, a man who won't let her?

His question lingers a long time in the look, first from him, which passes from one to the other. Finally, it goes toward grandfather and we all look at his back, at his neck, and out comes the rumble of rocks which is his voice.

"You want to know," my mother yells at him, "how that fellow talked about the elephants?"

And my mother's husband goes to my mother. Together, she on one side and he on the other, they begin the story about how elephants die. But my brother Euclid arrives.

Dark has fallen a short time before, with his evening return. The light is not yet lit in the kitchen, and my brother himself lights it. He has a piece of newspaper in his hand.

"Remember that old fellow?" he asks us.

"That man who was here last week?"

"The old man with the fife?"

209

"That little man of the elephants?"

My mother turns away from grandfather, and her husband draws nearer.

"That's the one," my brother Euclid says.

"What's happened to him?"

Grandfather doesn't grumble at having been left in the middle of the story. He waits, turning to us the back of the great massiveness that he is, but his ears are alert for what we say.

"He's dead," my brother Euclid says.

He's dead?

My brother reads to us from his piece of newspaper about how such and such a man was found dead before the hospital gates, the morning after.

"The morning after what?" my mother asks.

"Why, the morning after he was here," my brother Euclid answers.

"And they say that," my mother asks, "in the paper?"

"They don't say exactly that," my brother Euclid says. "The paper is two days later and it says—yesterday morning..."

He explains that the paper was hanging on a nail, in the shop's toilet, and that he, glancing at it by chance, had found the two-line notice.

"But it doesn't tell us anything that's got to do with him," my mother points out.

"Nothing!" my brother exclaims.

"It says that such and such is his name," my mother continues, "but we don't know what his name was."

"But we know his face was black with smut," my brother Euclid answers. "And the newspaper says that they found him dead with his face black with smut from his work. That's what it says."

"You see?" my mother's husband moans.

He moans at my mother with a tone of reproof, the same as that day when he was moaning in his cups.

"See?" he repeats, after five or six minutes. And after five or six more: "You see?"

210

Nobody says a word in the long minutes that pass between one and the other of his moans.

Somebody goes to the glass door, opens it wide, and the dark outside is already night in the trees, in the woods, between the two arms of sound which gather it in, from the invisible city, on both sides. A bit of moonlight runs over the trees, bitter over them, and the semicircle of the city is also glowing, but glowing in reflection, without showing lights because of the woods between. Except on one side, a reddish glow lights up and dims. We know it comes from an advertisement, a big disk, at the depot exchange, but here, among the trees, it is like a lighthouse for men toward the forest for those men who go through.

"See?" my mother's husband moans again.

My mother has returned to grandfather and has begun telling him what he wants to know: how the little old fellow who played the fife died—not, this time, how elephants die.

30

Other days come, other nights come, and one night there is a noise that awakens us—someone in the kitchen has opened the door toward the woods.

We think my mother has gotten up. Is it already daytime?

But my mother is asking herself who has gotten up before her. She rises, puts her Allied military coat over her night-gown, and goes into the kitchen.

The door is wide open and outside the last darkness is lifting, like the foot of a walker lifting smoothly from the grass of the field, vanishing toward the paths, among the trees.

My mother lights the light. What's this all about? She leans out of the door, calling, not loudly, first Anna, then

Elvira. Then she doesn't call again, and her silence is long and strange. Nor has anybody answered.

We come down to see.

Well?

My mother stands at the door sill, her arms hugging her breast, her hands under her armpits, inside the Allied military coat. She's looking toward the woods, but she turns. "The only thing I don't get," she tells us, "is how he got up alone. How he got dressed alone."

"Who?" we ask.

And my mother points him out to us, with a motion of her chin.

It is our grandfather of the Fréjus and the Simplon who is walking away in the first uncertain light of day, already near the paths that lead among the trees, at the end of the field. He is all dressed, even with his coat and shoes on, his hat on his head and in his hand the stick on which he leans. It's as if he were just going to take his place in his chair. He is moving with the same calculated step, even if he's a bit more straight in the back now.

"Hey, grandfather!" we call to him.

My mother stops our calling. "Let him alone!"

Why let him alone?

My mother begins all over again telling us of the man he's been—all the jobs he's been on, how he was there, how he could lift this, how he could fling that, what an elephant he was. By God, if he wasn't! She holds us still, telling us his story. But we can't let him go, just go away like that.

"Isn't he an elephant?" my mother says.

We say that an accident can happen to him. In the woods there is the bridge over the Lambro. There is the marsh. We call again: "Hey, grandfather!"

Grandfather then turns around at the edge of the woods which he has reached. To his right, in the already clear sky, the red eye of the big disk is lighted. He raises his stick. Shaking it, he salutes. And the red light of the disk blinks on and off.

"We, too, are elephants," my mother tells us.

212

With this she refuses to let us run after him and bring him back home. She re-enters the kitchen. We go in with her, and in the electric light, which pales with the light of day, her face is smiling.

"You don't understand a bean," she says. "It's not the beginning of night. It's the end."

She shows us the time by the old pendulum clock.

"You see? It's half past six. Already the workmen are crossing the park to go to work. They'll meet him and bring him back. But meanwhile, let him get disenchanted!"

LA GARIBALDINA

(1950)

1

The sun was setting, it was June, the year was 19——, and a soldier, a bersagliere, had just crossed the first two tracks of the railway station at Ragusa in Sicily. The train for Terranova, Licata and Canicattì was waiting on the third track just the other side of the second platform. It was loaded with people who had taken up a refrain that they sang sometimes by the dozen and sometimes by the hundred, their voices coming and going in snatches. The bersagliere looked the length of the train at arms waving out of windows of carriages whose doors were tight shut. He noticed the tattered berets some were waving, and the yellowed, ragged bits of clothing others waved, and he saw everywhere the dark bearded faces of the region continuously coming and going at the windows.

"What's the matter with them?" he asked.

He had turned to a brakeman who was walking back and forth the length of the train, his whole body up to his hat in the shade but his hat right in the bright sun. The brakeman barely swerved enough from his course to glance at him and immediately resumed his unhurried walk, tapping dryly along on enormous hobnailed boots. He got to the upper end of the platform where white steam flowed in a long jet from the lower body of the engine. And, as if he wanted to lean against it, he touched the cast-iron pipe that watered the parched coal in the tender. The soldier watched him from the place where he still stood and saw the sun light up all the buttons of his uniform and the shiny visor of his cap; he followed him with his eyes as, little by little, the brakeman retraced his steps along the platform.

The people inside the train hurled insults at him, or perhaps they were merely apostrophizing him or calling out to him. It looked as if a frantic tussle were going on from compartment to compartment, and the contestants were in desperate need of someone like him. But then the song would billow out again and it was always the same song, and the brakeman would not look anyone square in the face. Instead he answered the soldier.

"They're wating for the train to leave."

He stopped suddenly, and stood with his arms crossed on his chest, exposing a rip in the elbow of his jacket sleeve. "They've been waiting for an hour and a quarter," he added.

The soldier nodded vigorously; whether or not he remembered what he had asked before, he now looked more florid and smiling than ever. He pointed to the dark-green railway cars as they stood there in the sun that caught them squarely from the windows up, and to the ragged passengers overflowing every compartment. "Oh, of course!" he said. And he said that he had been unwilling to bring so much as a box lunch with him. "You see how I've made the trip? Empty-handed! Just to be able to travel as comfortably as possible."

The brakeman, arms still crossed on his chest, was screwing up his face in an effort to catch the soldier's words against the clamor of what was going on in the train. But why was he putting himself through such an ordeal? One would have thought that talking to the bersagliere would have made as little sense to him as walking back and forth along the platform. He looked ill. His color was greenish, as if he were suffering from malaria. Yet he went on standing there, even listening to the details of the three-day pass the soldier had managed to wangle. And it was only when asked if they were waiting for a "connection" that the brakeman started to move off.

"I thought I heard a bell ring," the bersagliere added.

He saw the brakeman's arms fall, but this time he did not follow him with his eyes. There was an old woman who was signaling him from the train, and a man who was calling him amid a flag-waving of rags as he leaned far out his window. He ended by going toward them.

The passengers set up more of a ruckus than ever, and the whole carriageful yelled louder, then the whole train yelled louder. The soldier hastily drew back, repelled also by the furnace-like heat that burst on him from above. But he had

218

not wiped the kindly smile from his face, nor the pleasant expression he had at the thought of going home for three days and the brakeman, as he came back again from the rear end of the train, planted himself once more before the soldier and crossed his arms on his chest.

"There's a later train that's made up here," he told him gloomily.

"Does it go as far as Terranova?" the soldier asked.

"As far as Licata."

He told the soldier that the train that was waiting was for the riff-raff, migrants who were going wherever there was a harvest to get in, men and women on their way back from the orange groves with their wages in kind piled up to the rafters...and hungry bums and vagrants, too many penniless vagrants.

Even when the brakeman was talking, he looked as if he were about to take off again. He rose on his toes and fell back on his heels, rose and fell, and said, falling back, that instead of this one the train three hours later was just what a fellow needed who wanted to travel in comfort.

"Yes, but it's in three hours," the bersagliere said.

The passengers had begun to stamp their feet rhythmically on the train floor so that hundreds together sounded like a single drum. Two or three words could be made out of the song they kept repeating, "lousy," "ground," "lousy," "ground," and the soldier caught himself trying to make out the rest.

"Food's lousy..." he picked up.

He saw that a few young louts were pointing at him amid great bursts of laughter while the old woman went on trying to tell him something. The man was still there with the rags like flags waving and he had not stopped addressing him. A third with a moth-eaten conical hat had decided to apostrophize him too. What could he be wanting to tell him? The bersagliere seemed to realize that, at bottom, none of them had anything very specific to tell him even if he did draw nearer, so he had scarcely taken a step in their direction when he turned his smiling blond face back toward the place he had last seen the brakeman; now a little old man stood there.

He too was a trainman but he was all oily and bare to the waist, with a double flag, red on one side, green on the other, tucked under his arm. He had just crossed the tracks and now stood there watching him. "Having fun, eh?" he asked. He winked and went on his way, waving the green side of his flag in answer to a whistle which shrilled from a distance where the tracks, beyond any shade, glared naked in the sun.

But now the brakeman was back a third time.

"I think I'll wait the three hours," the bersagliere told him. "I didn't want to take anything with me, not even so much as a box lunch, because of the long way from the station at Terranova to town. I didn't want to be bothered with anything, have to think about it, worry that someone might steal it from me. I haven't been home since Christmas and almost all my gear needs something done to it, a stitch here or there, but I preferred to leave everything as it is until a long leave just to have three days without anything to worry about, and I wanted to start off with the train trip itself completely free from worries of any kind. You get worn out in the army. Oh, I don't deny the fact that you can have a hell of a good time, but you get worn out. You sleep badly, indeed you do, and I was thinking that if I could sleep on the train most of the way…that's why—if, as you tell me, the other train leaves almost empty—I'll wait another three hours and sleep those extra three hours in the waiting room.…"

"You won't have such a long time to wait," the brakeman answered.

Rising and falling as before, he showed him the station clock.

"There's only an hour left," he added, falling back on his heels. "What with the time lost en route and the waiting time in the station, we're already a couple of hours late.…"

He walked away uttering a raucous cry.…Already a couple of hours, already a couple of hours…

The bersagliere was too pleased with his own lot not to admit a brakeman might want to utter a cry like that of a peacock. He was only too willing to accept any strange possibility that might befall that train. For instance, he accepted the fact that blows sounded from within as if someone were beat-

220

ing against the doors with sacks of grain; that rumbling sounds could be heard; that a band of monkeys, for instance, might have been let loose inside the carriages to pull all the old women's hats off, and all the old men's beards; and that even in the midst of it all, the passengers found it possible to clap hands in time to their song.

"...he sleeps on the ground," the bersagliere made out.

The young toughs who had pointed to him before were now hopping up and down at the carriage windows fairly bursting with laughter, and the soldier caught another word.

"Can they be making fun of me?" he could not help asking himself.

The boys were now trying to make their voices harmonize but their efforts were continuously broken up by gales of laughter, and men and women interrupted them too, either from behind—within the carriages—or from the neighboring windows from which they cursed the racket.

One of the boys was conducting, his arm raised. "No," he would yell at every false start, "no, no! Back to the beginning." And they would start in all over again, he beating time and the others singing in unison: "...His food is lousy/he sleeps on the ground...his food is lousy/he sleeps on the ground."

The bersagliere felt someone pull him by the sleeve.

"Having fun?" It was the little old man with the flag once more. "Don't take it to heart," he told him. "They aren't sore at you."

And the train kept on singing what it is like to be a soldier.

> Here's a soldier
> Still safe and sound.
> His food is lousy,
> He sleeps on the ground.

"But don't take it personal," the little old man said and he too burst out laughing. Still laughing, he pointed out that the fellows who were singing ate badly too, and that they too slept on the ground. "Like me," he said laughing, "and like the brakeman there." That meant that the youngsters were making fun not of the soldier only but of themselves, and of him, old man that he was, and of the brakeman too.

"As far as we're concerned," the bersagliere said, "we don't eat so damn badly...." He laughed along with the little old man. "Besides, there aren't any wars we have to go to any more: the wars come to us!"

While they were still laughing, they noticed that a train had pulled in to the station. The locomotive drew in, passed them, then one freight car after another passed with decreasing speed.

In high boxes the brakemen could be seen giving the last turns to the brake wheels. Their eyes looked white in their smoke-tanned faces. They jumped down as if alighting from a trapeze. A trainmaster, trumpet in hand, ran the length of the platform. The red hat of the stationmaster appeared.

The bersagliere climbed up the little ladder to one of the brakemen's boxes, and stood on top of the great freight looking at the bellowing train, at the roofs, still sunlit, at the gardens and rocks, the windowpanes reflecting the last rays up there on the crest of the city with its monasteries and churches.

Looking down at the platform between the two trains, he recognized the brakeman with the malarial face. He called to him gaily at the top of his lungs:

"Hey, colleague! Hey, *paesano*!"

But he could not make himself heard. He dropped down on the other side of the freight, crossed the last track still to be crossed, and went to plant himself on the threshold of the third-class waiting room.

There he found himself bellowing what the whole train had been shrilling. "His food is lousy. His food is lousy."

"So you've finally learned it?" the little old man with the flag asked.

He stood before him once more, having jumped down from the step of a luxury car which was now passing with its splatter of red plush; it was hauled by a station engine along the first track.

"Funny you should have to hear it from the peasants," he said laughing. "What kind of thing d'you sing in the barracks nowadays? In my time, they used to sing it."

On his way to attend to something, he added:

"Could be you eat better'n we did and you don't go to wars any more..."

Whatever else he said was lost in the racket and the soldier started to hum once more, "Food's lousy, food's lousy"; then suddenly he was aware that there was no more din coming from the far side of the freight train. The only sounds were whistles blowing and the banging of cars as they knocked against each other. And crickets chirping in the gardens that were scattered amid the now-sunless rocks.

When the freight pulled out not long after, he saw that its tail light was already lit. Did this mean that night would have fallen before he reached his next stop? The soldier saw all the tracks empty before him and could not help fearing that there would be no later train for Terranova.

But the brakeman had not misled him.

There was a freight leaving at 9 P.M. in the direction of Terranova—and a duke who had holdings at Donnafugata, another with interests from Chiaromonte to the lower Mediterranean, a third whose castle was at Falconara had pressured the National Railways into adding one carriage to this freight train, a luxury car with the inevitable red plush.

Further, they had gotten officialdom to agree to let the train travel at passenger speed and not at that of the other freights. Influential people from Napoleone Colajanni's party and from the Socialist Party hollered that it was an outrage. Protests rose from Caltanissetta to Girgenti, from Caltagirone to Modica. This train, they all said, should be hauling water cars to provide drinking water for some of the villages between Ragusa and Licata that had none. But moving at the speed of a passenger train, the "special" could not perform this service, and so the fountains of Comiso or Licata stayed dry until two in the afternoon by which time they were flanked by long lines of women and boys who had come there to draw water from as far as twelve kilometers away.

The carriage with the red plush served the fine gentlemen

who had obtained permission for it, a convenience one of them might make use of as often as once a month while it was a toss-up if the others found use for it as regularly as once a week. But they liked to be able to count on its being there. Moreover they liked to impress with their power the businessmen and lawyers who had occasional use for the train. "This is the way business is courted in our part of the country..." the lawyers wrote the Palermo papers for which they acted as stringers. And though the opposition ran articles on page one of the same papers telling what was going on around the fountains of Licata, the protests were in vain.

During the last pre-election rallies, they did use the comment made by one of the dukes in question: "But I always see the animals drinking troughfuls..." he had said. And the Socialists picked up ten or a dozen additional votes when they explained to the long lines waiting at the fountains just what the duke had said. All the same, the train ran at its own privileged speed and according to its own privileged schedule.

And the railway workers on the Ragusa-Licata line, the brakemen, switchmen, linemen, men like the little old man with the flag, or like the malarial brakeman with the ripped sleeve, liked it better that way. Who knows what ungodly night duty they might have to face, otherwise. And the bersagliere liked the fact that at last he could climb aboard and walk the length of the car without running into a single soul. The upholstery on the long, facing seats promised an even better sleep than he had dreamed of, a comfortable trip, and the assurance that his three days without anything to worry him had at last begun.

"I was so right," he said to himself, "not to bring along so much as a box lunch."

And he walked the full length of the corridor, looking into the compartments for the wooden benches he had gotten used to from all his previous train trips. Then, since there was nothing but plush to sit on, he sat on plush. It was already dark in the compartment; lights were on in the huddled brilliance of the city, and he leaned back against the arm rest of the upholstered bench looking out as the white set-backs of the mountains disappeared, fading gradually into the perfume of the jasmine, the song of the crickets, and the intermittent glow of the fireflies.

He fell asleep and woke. There were voices of people getting into the car and he woke only to fall asleep again. Then jerks and jolts broke the rhythm of "his" car and he awoke anew only to drop off once more.

His face was a peaceful blank.

They looked him over by the light of a lantern and saw the insignia on his military collar and shoulder tabs.

"But he's not a carabiniere."

"No. He's just a bersagliere."

They shook him. "May one ask, Honored Sir, how you happen to be here—*Signor* bersagliere?"

He woke then with the light of the lantern full in his eyes. "This is it?" he mumbled. "Are we there?"

"Well," they ragged, "that all depends on where you're going."

Then they asked for his ticket.

"Tell me where we are, will you?"

"In the tunnel under Donnafugata..."

A wavering violet light came from the small oil lamp let into the ceiling. But the only true illumination came from the lantern which now shed its beam on the hands of the two men who had wanted the ticket. Otherwise they were in stark darkness as they stood before the bersagliere in the smoky air that came from the compartment windows. The windows had evidently stayed open all the time he had been sleeping, until the conductors' arrival.

"I thought we were already at Terranova," the bersagliere said.

"You'll not see Terranova tonight, you can bet," they answered.

They had raised their voices a bit, talking to him in turn but so rapidly that it seemed as if they were speaking in unison.

"You'll see plenty of Donnafugata tonight."

"But doesn't this train go as far as Terranova?"

"The train? Sure, the train goes as far as Terranova. The train can go there all right. It's you that can't go there."

"The train can go there all right, but I can't?"

"The train has its papers all in order just so's it can go there. Now what kind of papers have you? You haven't the right papers to travel on this train and you know it. It's you that can't go there, see?"

The soldier stretched out a hand and touched the ticket the two of them held under the beam of the lantern.

"Isn't my ticket for Terranova?"

He heard an answer that implied there were two Terranovas, one toward which the yelling, crowded train he had passed up was headed, and the other, the one to which this train with its plush lined compartments was permitted entry.

"On a military pass, get it, you've got to take the regular train," they told him. "This train is a 'special,' and first class at that. You'd have to have a first-class ticket."

They went on talking, talking, but the long and short of it was that the bersagliere had to get down at Donnafugata, pass the rest of the night at Donnafugata, pass the morning there, the afternoon too, and pick up—after a lapse of twenty-four hours—the same screaming train he had not taken at Ragusa that afternoon. He moved a hand over his face.

"I should have figured that the idea of wanting to get there the easiest, most comfortable way was no good!"

Then he expostulated anew:

"If I'd only brought a box lunch with me! I'd have taken the right train if I'd brought me at least a box lunch!"

"What's all that crap about a box lunch?" they asked. They told him again that what he needed was a first-class ticket paid at the regular rate and not a box lunch.

"It's all the fault of that brakeman with malaria!" the bersagliere exclaimed. "He's the one that told me to take this God-forsaken train....I didn't even know the train existed. I was as good as on the other one already."

2

Meanwhile the door to the nearby compartment opened a crack, then all the way, and a new face appeared out of the smoke.

"Who has that beautiful voice?" the face said. "What a beautiful voice!"

It came forward slowly, solemnly, one might say amply, as if it were in some fashion on horseback. The head of an animal came along with it. "Are we on the platform?" The face sniffed and coughed, yet managed to look up at the lone flicker of the overhead lamp which, showing the veils and wisps of hair, revealed that this was a woman of a sort.

The tone of voice in which she now sang out reinforced this impression. Pointing a finger at the bersagliere, she said:

"Is *he* the one with the beautiful voice? An angel in the heart of a mountain...that voice brought back the young tenor I heard at La Scala."

She had pushed her way between the two trainmen by now, accompanied by the quiet animal which seemed perpetually mixed up in the fringes of her shawl.

"Let's have a look at him," she added.

And she seized the hand of the man carrying the lantern to raise the light to the right height.

"Why, he's fresh as a daisy! He's a fine one to lean on, in spite of the fright Don Carlos here gave him...." Turning to the bersagliere, she went on: "Don't pay any attention to him. He's only Don Carlos, he's no lion."

Then she discovered that her angel was a soldier.

"A soldier can stop armies! And there you sit, soldier, afraid of my Great Dane. It's true that he doesn't bark but then he doesn't bite either. He's absolutely useless....You know, if you'd been born fifty years earlier, you'd have sounded the trumpet under the walls of Calatafimi."

At this point the trainmen tried to interrupt, addressing the woman as "baroness." They wanted to tell her something, perhaps only that the soldier was just a bersagliere, neither more nor less, but they did not manage to utter a word.

"And what were you doing to him?" she cut them off. "He was talking as if someone had insulted him. And as for you fellows, you sounded as if you were trying to play him one of your tricks.... 'What tricks?' You can see perfectly well that he's innocent. What were they doing to you, innocent?"

The trainmen pointed out that it was "him" who had tried to play the trick.

"He?" the old woman exclaimed. "Can't you see his mother's milk isn't dry on his lips! What kind of trick could *he* ever play?" And she imposed silence on the two trainmen: "Let us hear what he has to say."

At this the bersagliere blushed visibly even by the wan light of the lantern.

"Ah God, what a rose!" the old woman cried. "He's blushing; perhaps he's afraid of my hoary locks, and here these heathen try to convince me he's played a trick on them!"

She broke off because of the smoke. "Can't you open the windows any wider in here? We're suffocating...."

The trainmen pointed out that more smoke would come in if they opened the windows wider.

"Then let's get on with it," the old woman ordered. "It's because of you that I'm here," she said to the bersagliere. And she addressed her dog which was now whining: "Shut up, you fool!" Then, turning to anyone else who might hear her on the train or over the entire surface of the earth, she said: "Will we never get out from under this mountain?"

A far-off whistle came from the engine; everything slowed down and once more picked up speed as metal plates seemed to fly open every so often to reveal iron doors spaced throughout the endless course of the tunnel.

"What if we were to go into my compartment," the old woman suggested. She said there was no smoke in there. "Let's go."

But only the two trainmen started to follow her.

"Hey, you," the old woman bawled, turning in the doorway. "Didn't you understand what I told you? There's no smoke in there."

"Well, I have to get down anyway," the bersagliere answered.

"You can tell me in there what they were doing to you. D'you want to get out at Donnafugata?"

"I'm not the one that wants me to get out there...."

"Who else does?" the old girl thundered, taking a step back into the compartment. "You mean you don't want to get down there but you have to?"

"It's all because I didn't want to carry so much as a box lunch," the bersagliere answered. "I decided I wanted to travel in comfort, but I even took the wrong train."

Then the trainmen explained the situation as best they could, piecing the story together between them and liberally sprinkling each phrase with "Signora Baronessas."

"Aren't you ashamed!" the old woman exclaimed. "This...this *innocent* here was good enough to bow before your tricks and threats. I knew he looked like a lamb ready to be led to the slaughter. I could see it in his face. ...So, he can't ride on this train? This train is such a national outrage that, if only Garibaldi were alive today, he'd get right up out of his grave at Caprera to protest. And you two dare talk about tickets, you dare ask whether they're in order or not! Why, if ever in its entire history this train has been of the slightest real use to anyone, it will have been tonight because it gave a poor soldier a ride....For whom do you two vote, anyway? The Bourbons? Do you ever ask if *my* ticket is in order? Or Don Carlos's here? Do you ever ask if my dog's ticket is in order? He should ride in the stock car, given his size—not even in the baggage car—but instead he rides in the compartment with me and no one of you has ever made the slightest fuss about that."

At this point, a locomotive's whistle sounded high and shrill. Even the noise of their train's wheels seemed absorbed by the other sound. The trainmen rushed one to one window and one to another, dropping the casements open on a wooded

229

night in which a disk of light could be seen drawing nearer and nearer. The men could not take time to answer the old woman they had addressed as "Signora Baronessa."

The train slowed.

The night was suddenly white with stones as they passed a dried-up stream bed, and the train slowed still further. There were the fireflies once more, and the crickets could be heard, and the fresh scent of the hills covered with locust trees rose to the nostrils.

The trainmen opened the doors now too, one on one side and one on the other, and they leaned out ready to jump down as soon as they could.

"So you're running out?" the old woman said.

One was swinging his lantern and a platform whitened the night as acacia leaves brushed, passing, against the man's head. He jumped down with a shout, landing between train and high white cave-like wall of the station.

"Donnafugata," he cried out to the desert.

The station wall was spectral white against the black columns of the woods, and the bersagliere searched in vain for a more formal station either at his feet or under some nearby roof; his eyes sought a light, some sign of life.

"Do I get down here?" he asked.

"I cooked their goose for 'em," the old woman answered. "Didn't you hear me handle 'em? All they could do was run out on me...."

"Then you'd say I could stay?"

"Obviously. As long as Don Carlos here can stay, you can stay....They won't even come back...."

"What about my ticket? If they don't come back, they won't return my ticket."

"They they'll come back just to return it. What kind is it, a round-trip fare? They can't keep any part of a ticket you can still use."

But the bersagliere was not completely reassured. "Let's hope they come back soon," he kept saying.

"Why?" the old woman asked. "Where do you have to get down? At Comiso?"

230

"I'm really going to Terranova, but if I can't stay on that long..."

The old girl snorted with satisfaction. "Terranova?" then she cried out, raucous-voiced: "You can stay on as long as you jolly well need to. I couldn't guarantee it if you'd had any further to go. But I get off at Terranova myself, and nobody's going to make you get down a minute before I do. Come on. Let's go. Let's close these windows out here on account of the tunnels up ahead...."

And she flung herself about making all sorts of attempts to close the windows, but she was hampered by the black web of her shawls and veils and by the enormous dog which always managed to get in the way, flattening himself against her, on one side or the other.

In the adjacent compartment where she wanted them to go as to a place already "hers," she kept nagging until the bersagliere had opened all the windows, nor would she agree to sit down until he had stretched his hand out each of them into the night to prove that, indeed, they were open.

"You're here now to keep me company, and no one will try to put you off the train any more," she told him.

She settled herself with a squeaking of springs. "Aren't you going to sit down? Don Carlos here, he'll stretch out on my side of the compartment and you can sit opposite." She worked herself into a comfortable position. "You'll see: they'll leave you alone and that's a fact. You can get ready to sleep on it."

"That's why I took this train instead of the other one. I wanted to sleep the whole trip."

"Well, in here," the old girl said, "you can sleep the whole trip.... It's ten o'clock now and they'll take at least three hours what with the waits at every grotto we pass. Then there's that other train that's up ahead now. We'll have to wait here till it leaves Comiso, though God only knows how they can tell when that'll be with this station that looks like the mouth of a tomb.... But you can be sure we won't reach Terranova before one.... You can count on that."

The bersagliere tried to find the best possible position,

placing not only his head but one cheek carefully against the velvet pile of the upholstery. By his smile he must have found things almost perfect. But at the mention of Terranova the old woman's voice had resumed its raucous tone of excitement.

"How does it happen you're going to Terranova? If you were born there, you must know who I am. I know everything there is to know about Terranova. And believe me, I'd remember having seen a face like yours among all those…those Carthaginians. Do you have relatives there or are you going back to your garrison? Well, in either case, you'll have figured out who I am…."

"Truly…" the bersagliere said.

"Truly what? You're not going to tell me you know my life from *a* to *z*, but I'm sure you know something about Italian history. Didn't you go to school? You'll have gone through Fourth Grade. You'll have learned about Cornelia, mother of the Gracchi. You'll have learned who Lucretia was. You'll have heard of Anita who died during Garibaldi's flight to Rome. And that's why you'll have heard of me, the one who followed her spouse into exile! Now do you recognize me? Don't you recognize me?"

She threw herself forward with such vehemence demanding his reply that the bersagliere was shaken from his position and raised his head. He readjusted himself as best he could in his former place, and repeated, "Truly…" Then with more candor than wit he said that he could not guess who she was. "I just know they called you 'Signora Baronessa.' "

"That's a title the unimaginative vulgarians tack onto me," the old woman exclaimed. "It's my daughter that married a baron. Not me. I kept right on being a republican even after Garibaldi met up with that…scion of the house of Savoy."

Meanwhile the train had begun to move again. There was the noise and then there was the night air that came in in gusts. "Remember to close the windows when we go through the tunnels," the old woman cautioned him. But this was no more important to her than the gesture with which she adjusted her coils of hair during the black night ride,

232

for she was waiting—and with no attempt to hide it—for the bersagliere to give some indication that he had understood. She showed this if by nothing more than the pose in which she still held her head rigidly erect. And she now told him that in history she bore only her own first name "as a woman," just as had Lucretia or Anita. "Do you know what my name is in history?" she exploded.

But the bersagliere had rushed to close the windows as smoke came pouring in.

"It's Leonilde!" the old girl shouted.

The soldier went back to his seat pleased at having been able to prove himself helpful, and the old woman, now armed with a pair of opera glasses, prepared to use them as if to probe the dark. It was on him, once more withdrawn into his shadowy corner, that she trained them.

"Doesn't the fact that my name is Leonilde mean anything to you?" she asked.

The bersagliere, who continued to smile more or less, shrugged.

"I can see, I can see," the old girl checked him, "that much I can see without another word from you: Leonilde means nothing to you. But then Cornelia, mother of the Gracchi, means nothing to you either."

She plucked a confirmation from the bersagliere that indeed Cornelia meant nothing to him either.

"Perhaps Clelia? I mean the Roman virgin who fled with all the other hostages from the camp of the enemy! Does *she* mean anything?"

The bersagliere indicated sleepily that not even Clelia meant anything to him.

"What about Camilla? She was that warrior maid who had something to do with Aeneas. Does Camilla mean anything to you?"

Not even Camilla meant anything to the bersagliere. He murmured "Aeneas?" softly but gave no other sign that even

233

Aeneas meant anything to him, and the old woman was appeased.

"Now I know why my name means nothing to you," she crooned. "*No* name means anything to you. You are as innocent as the angels the Good Lord used to send to earth to punish us poor mortals with their flaming swords. I thought so the moment I laid eyes on you. That's just what you're like. And you have the same pure heart and unmarked mind as they, in order to be pitiless...."

From the arm of the seat against which the bersagliere was leaning and from the springs under him and at his back squeaks rose in a steady crescendo as he twisted and turned in embarrassment. The train burst from—then re-entered—the mountain; its whistle shrilled down a gorge, and the bersagliere leaped staggering to his feet to reopen the windows on the night. But the whistle was once more swallowed up underground, raucous still as it was stifled by the tunnel's gaping maw, and the bersagliere dropped down again without having been able to open them.

"Not only do you have their voice and their face," the old woman went on, "but you're all pink and nice. Just like those paintings in which they stand smiling as they kill. And they are always blushing."

The bersagliere interrupted, all of a sudden, to tell her that "those two" had come back into the car.

"Back again, eh?"

The bersagliere reminded her that "those two" had not yet returned his ticket.

"Well," the Signora called out, "why don't you come in here?"

The compartment was a double one, with a corridor running along one side and aisles that separated the sections one from another. The trainmen were standing in shadow in the farther aisle. "Why don't you come in?" They did not answer, but a streak of light passed under the seats, cast by the lantern they had placed on the compartment floor. Were they coming in or were they not? They talked it over between themselves.

Don Carlos had placed one great paw on his mistress' black lap and this made it hard for her to get up. But she managed to heave herself to her feet and then turned, kneeling on the seat, and faced the two of them over the top of the backrest.

"Baroness..." one of them began.

"To hell with the 'Baroness' business!" she interjected. "When you want to pay me a compliment, just remember I've worn the colors; I've been an officer...keep those tuppenny-ha'penny titles for those who enjoy 'em. Now why don't you just hand over the ticket that belongs to the soldier here who's accompanying me...?"

"The ticket...yes, of course...we can hand it over..."

"Can? You *must*! What's all the fuss about, anyway?"

"There's no fuss, Ba...."

"I've already told you, I'm no Ba! Now where's that ticket?"

The ticket passed from one to the other trainman to be examined all over again, turned and re-turned under the bluish light which shone thinly from the night lamp suspended from the ceiling. The old woman reached an arm across the seat backs to take it from them.

"But the soldier," they told her. "He'll have to get down at Comiso."

"The soldier is traveling with me and will accompany me as far as Terranova."

"*If* he pays the difference he can do it, Signora."

"Difference? What difference? He's paid for his ticket. You wouldn't want him to pay twice, would you?"

The bersagliere rose wearily. "Perhaps I'd better get down at Comiso."

"You are traveling with me," the old girl snapped at him over her shoulder. "You stay where you are."

The trainmen explained to her that they no longer questioned the difference between a military and a civilian ticket; they were now worried about the difference between a third-

and a first-class fare. He must pay the difference or get off the train.

"I'll get off, I'll get off," the soldier said.

"Now what's got into you to want to get off here?" the old woman yelled. "I told you I'd take you as far as Terranova and I'll take you as far as Terranova."

She now told the trainmen they should be ashamed to talk to a poor soldier as if he were a feudal landowner, told them again what a national outrage their train was to begin with, and mentioned first Garibaldi, then Don Carlos once more. The trainmen could not get a word in edgewise, and the bersagliere did not say again that he thought it best to get down.

Instead, he opened a window.

"See, I fixed 'em for you once more!" the old woman said.

Soft clean air was coming in the window now, no longer the acrid stench of the tunnels, and even the trainmen were opening the windows on their side. The bersagliere looked out and mentioned that he saw lights.

"Perhaps it's Comiso," he said.

It did not take much to restore his tranquillity; all in all, he was well enough pleased with the comfort of the trip, the soft seats, and the sleep he still promised himself with his cheek against that plush cushion. He felt Don Carlos push up against his back and turned to pat him. He was only a big dog, after all; he knew that from his smell. Like the smell of the night: you could tell just as clear that the train was running through countryside full of prickly pears.

Running? There was the screech of brakes along the tracks. The train slowed. Once more the two trainmen had disappeared from the compartment to the rear. Perhaps they were walking along the outer step, holding on to the handrails of the car. At last, with a croak like a frog's, the train stopped over a flat bed of gravel.

The old girl was still congratulating herself with Don Carlos over her latest victory. And Don Carlos gave as good as he got. The big creature was poking in among her shawls and she was chuckling to him over the things that had been said. She told Don Carlos all over again that the soldier had been all ready to get down, right here at Comiso. "Were you tired of keeping me company?" she aksed the bersagliere. And he found the question laughable. He admitted it.

He laughed with her as he had done with the old man who carried the red flag. He laughed as he told her now about the little old man who was so happy and the brakeman who was, instead, so funereal, and he told her too about the train he ought to have taken. "It fairly howled, all of it!"

He stopped to listen a moment to a sound that was not frogs croaking amid the frog noises. "What's that noise?" he said. It was not the rushing of a torrent nor the threat of an approaching thunderstorm. It was amid the frog noises, all right, as if it were the sound of other animals right in among them.

"We've caught up with it," the old woman answered.

"With what?"

"With the train you should have taken."

3

They were moving again, passing the three or four lights which distinguished Comiso from the cactus-scented dark. The old woman was saying that they were lucky as they would now be in the forward train, that they would no longer have to make long waits at the station stops, and that they could count on reaching Terranova by midnight.

"Because you must know our 'national outrage' does things like this too," she cried. "I've been away from Sicily for the past six months and I'd come to believe they'd put a stop to it, but I see they still do it."

Suddenly, she was indignant. The "national outrage" should have considered it enough to refuse to carry the water needed daily by the town with no water supply of their own. But the idea of catching up with and passing the work train of those poor devils and making it wait until "national outrage" arrived, that's too much....Garibaldi would have withdrawn to Tierra del Fuego in protest had he still lived.

"And what's happened to those two Arabs who wanted you to pay the difference between your ticket and the first-class fare?"

She added that the bersagliere could consider himself lucky. "You were certainly born under a lucky star...."

He said he thought so too, and the old woman told him that he would certainly be furious if he had taken the other train: it would be like having someone spit right in your eye, she said, to sit there and watch this train pass you by.

Then she asked him if he was always so lucky.

"I get good ideas," he answered.

They jerked to a stop and immediately heard the rumble of the "howler." The noise came from right and left, from above and below, yet they could see that the train had drawn up on the track alongside. In the dark, matches flared here and there.

The bersagliere said something the old woman could not hear, and then she said something he could not hear. The noise that surrounded them had a distinct rhythm and the bersagliere could pick out the words.

His food is lousy, he recognized.

He sleeps on the ground. He recognized that too.

Hadn't they ever given the song a let-up? He yelled at the old woman that they were singing.

"What d'you say?"

"They're singing; I said, 'they're singing.' "

His face was radiant, and he wanted to tell the old woman what they were singing. "They're singing about us."

"About us?"

He pointed to himself, touching various parts of his uniform. "About me. About soldiers." And he tried to make her hear the words they were singing.

The old woman nodded vigorously. She too had caught the rhythm and the words of the song, and it seemed as if at some near or remote period in her life she had sung

238

it, and sung it again and again. Her strident voice broke in:

> Here's a soldier,
> Still safe and sound.

At this point the bersagliere joined her.

> His food is lousy,
> He sleeps on the ground.

They wound up together.

Then he told her, as the old man with the flag had told him, that the howlers had it in for themselves rather than for soldiers. "They don't have it in for me, for soldiers like me." And because of the noise, he pointed to himself again, touched his sleeves, his chest, and shook his head in dissent.

"They have it in for others. For themselves."

He was aware that his gestures and words, altogether drowned by the racket, did not convey his meaning and at first he gave up. But then he decided to try it again: "They don't mean to be offensive," he yelled.

He was interrupted by an impetuous rush of sound which rose wildly, no longer rhythmically, in a whoop of triumph.

The old woman too had started to yell. She was shaking her fist out the window and yelling. What had come over her? But even before the bersagliere could gather the facts from her words, he understood that the howlers' train had started to move. This was what was happening. He was in time to see the last car disclose the empty platform on the other side as it pulled away into the night, and he heard the voice of the crowd fragmented by the distance which was swallowing it up as the train disappeared.

The old woman was against the "howler."

"Now I s'pose you'll keep us anchored here until that one reaches Vittoria!" she bawled out the window.

That was why she was indignant. The shadows of train-men with their lanterns in their fists now gathered beneath the window. They answered her, calling her "Signora Baronessa," and tried to calm her fury but she would have none of them: she wanted the stationmaster.

"Baroness here! Baroness there! I'd like to see how you'd jump if Duke Armando had been here, or even that stuffed shirt, Lillo..." she said. "Then you'd have seen to it that this train pulled out first. But there's no one aboard worth taking a bit of trouble over, according to you. That's the point! There's only a poor old woman and a poor young soldier."

The men on the platform answered that this was not so, that there were other people on the train as well as themselves, and they mentioned Don X, Don Y, the son of Don Z. Meanwhile the old woman went on repeating that even if no one but that witless Lillo had been here...evidently extreme proof of the shortcomings of the trainmen.

Then she wanted the bersagliere to express his horror of Lillo. The trainmen assured her in the interim that if her train had not taken precedence over the other it was only because the engine had to stop long enough to take on water. They would leave, the men said, without waiting for the other train to reach Vittoria. In five or ten minutes at most. The engineer would see to it that they did not pile up on the train in front of them....

But the more they said from the platform intending to placate her, the more upset she became. "Irresponsibles! Irresponsibles!" she kept repeating. "Oh, what irresponsible minds! What Muslim irresponsibility! What typically irresponsible Muslim minds!"

At this she drew in her head, leaving the trainmen below on the platform shrugging their shoulders.

"Did you hear them?" she asked the bersagliere. "Now they'll have us pull out before the other train has reached Vittoria. All I had to do was give them a dressing down and they've got us running off after the other one. Hurrah for the Muslim mind! Now mind you, I have nothing against the Sicilians as such, and nothing against the Arabs. In fact, I disapprove of our occupation of Tripolitania...*but* when they start stuffing all their old wheezes down my gullet, that I can't take. Let 'em keep their messes to themselves!"

Once more she wanted the bersagliere to express his horror of Lillo.

"Just think of that Lillo! You know who Lillo is? He's a dwarf, a regular dwarf about four foot high! His nurse dropped him; no, it was the midwife dropped him at birth and he hit his head and his tail. But the floor he went and landed on was that of the richest house on Piazza Armerina, all rose marble. That's why today you have the fine sight of that ridiculous dwarf receiving the judges who bow and scrape before him in open court, or being given a military salute by the commander of the garrison."

She asked eagerly what the bersagliere thought of such goings-on.

"Doesn't it make you sick? All that for a fellow who runs to shut himself up in the broom closet when there's a thunderstorm! And he still wets the bed, though he's almost thirty years old! You know how we can tell when he's 'in residence' at Terranova? We can see the yellow sheets flapping in the breeze over his cousin's rooftop...."

She heard a muffled snort of laughter the bersagliere tried in vain to suppress. But the night was silent now all around them except for a sad humming that might have come from the telegraph wires.

"Makes you laugh, does it?" the old woman said. "It's nothing to laugh at, let me tell you."

But the bersagliere looked as if he were laughing because of everything put together: the mix-up of the trains, the old woman who got indignant first for one reason then for another, then the Lillo business, and more because of the way she told it than because of Lillo himself. He was making manful efforts to keep himself from bursting out laughing.

As luck would have it, the train started to move just then. There was a short blast on the dispatcher's horn, then the splat and strain of the couplings from car to car, a screech of the wheels, an opaque flash of light washing in as they passed an open door; then the dark station dropped behind, and the dark water tower, and Comiso itself was swallowed up in the dark night, heavy with the scent of prickly pears.

"That's really too much," the old woman cried.

The bersagliere saw her leap up and turn her head away. "Have they come back?" he asked.

"At 'em," the old girl hissed to Don Carlos.

It took Don Carlos quite a while to get on guard. He was in a half crouch and the old woman could easily hold him in. A frail voice could be heard addressing her over the top of the seat backs.

Perhaps someone asking alms? But why here? Not a word could be understood but a hunched figure was outlined in the distant night light of the other compartment, shoulders bowed, head bent to one side, white hands gleaming bone-pale in the bluish light as they rested on the backs of the two seats that separated the compartments. Still, the old woman must have known who it was and what he was trying to say.

"You want to thank *me*?" she started to answer him.

She half addressed the cringing figure and half, the bersagliere.

"He thanks me for having got the train started again! A fat lot of work I did! And what if it piles up on the one ahead? Will you thank me then? The trouble is, nothing ever happens in this damned country! What's that? Speak up! Prospero thanks me too? See here, soldier, this old man holds all the hills in Butera. I mean he *owns* them. And he stands there thanking me in the name of three other big landowners sitting over there behind him.... What did you say you wanted? You all want to come in here to keep me company? You just tell them to excuse me. Excuse me! I'm already in good company. Tell them I can well understand their joy at seeing me back in Sicily; tell them I return their greetings but that they could have stretched their limbs enough to bring me their greetings in person. That's to say... What are you doing? Stay where you are!... I was saying I admire the delicacy with which they sought not to disturb me. I don't want them in here, understand? Don Carlos and my orderly are enough. Stay over there.... Stay right there! Just put your

242

rosary of thanks back in your pocket and keep it to yourself!"

Bent and ailing, the man withdrew his white hands from the seat back.

"Thanking me for having heard me sound off!" the old woman exclaimed. "For having got the train going again! It was I, perhaps, who gave a blast on that horn?"

And as the man meekly reappeared, trying once more to say something, the old girl reminded him of the harsh cold of the winter of 1908, of the cold of that January, of the cold of a certain Tuesday of that January.

"What can have gotten into you, Enrico, to come bother me?"

Shaking his meek old head, Enrico disappeared in a halo of faint blue light. The door back there could be heard opening and closing despite the noise of the rushing train. The old woman grumbled to herself. Even Don Carlos, who was still on guard, grumbled. And the bersagliere could contain his laughter no longer.

"Oh, my word..." he managed to get out between one hoot of laughter and the next.

"What's there to laugh about and say 'Oh, my word'?"

"I said, 'Oh, my word, that Enrico...'"

"That's nothing to say, 'Oh, my word' about. He could buy and sell you ninety times over."

The bersagliere tried to check his spasms of laughter.

"I just said...he talks...without saying...a word."

"Couldn't he have lost his voice? Couldn't he have asthma? Or bronchitis? What do you know about his hidden qualities?"

"Of course he could have hidden qualities," the bersagliere said, merrier than ever. He was a little humiliated that he could not stop laughing but not enough to help him check himself. "Of course...one shouldn't pass judgment...on a person one knows nothing...about..."

"Are you blushing again?" the old girl asked. "I'll just bet you're blushing."

She gave him a kick in the leg and told him not to cross himself for what he must have been thinking.

"But I warn you it's no laughing matter," she went on.

243

"He's quite capable of cutting a slice out of your side without letting you feel he's been near you. I had a holding, a mountainside at Butera, and he...made off with it!"

"You certainly put him in his place, though! That's why I was laughing."

"You were wrong. You were wrong. I don't spend my time putting people in their places. If they're out of place, let 'em stay there!"

A gurgle from the soldier told her that he had started to splutter with laughter again. The old woman's language, coupled with the admonitory tone she was trying to assume, was obviously too much for him to resist. It was as if she had tickled him and, despite his efforts, he had succumbed. Now he did not know which way to turn to find an acceptable object for his amusement.

"Oh, my word..." he said again.

"Now what?"

"Oh, this train..."

"What's wrong with this train?"

"Well, my word, it's going right along...Oh! We've scarcely stopped a minute...I mean we didn't have to wait...back there at Comiso..."

He was completely sincere when he brought up this topic for a part of his hilarity did indeed come from this source.

"Is that anything to laugh about?" the old woman interrupted. "Come, come now. Come, come."

At this, the bersagliere whooped it up more loudly than ever.

"Oh, the very idea," he said from the depths of his being, "the idea of calling me your orderly! Oh, the idea of being an orderly to a lady!"

The old woman was now laughing with him.

"You think I couldn't have had an orderly?" she managed to ask him. "There you sit hiccoughing with laughter because, in your innocence, you know nothing of the world of men. If you knew any little thing about us mortals here below you'd know that I've had more than one orderly in my time. It's pretty tight-fisted of this Socialist Monarchy, let me tell

244

you, that they don't give me an allowance for one now."

She laughed with an undertone of bitterness.

"And whoever called it 'socialist'? Just bamboozled with all the fandango they put on. They've failed to recognize my military rank, failed in every way to give me fair treatment, failed to pay me a double pension in the light of what my husband and I stood for. Son, you'd better know it: I've been everything, a soldier like you, then a lieutenant, a captain, a major, finally a colonel.... You think I didn't have an orderly when I was a captain? I had a bigger one for every rise in rank they gave me. And you, dear boy, descended from the right hand of God to play soldier in our Socialist Monarchy, you couldn't have guessed you'd also turn out to be the orderly of an old woman!"

The dark air entering from the window had a brackish scent of green grapes growing on a hillside covered with vineyards, of the far distant sea, and of the shore where a sandy hill ascends in a line of dunes to end in a flat sandbar.

The old woman stood up while the soldier pulled himself together after his irrepressible burst of hilarity.

"And so we're about to reach the next town," she said, thrusting her head out into the black, racing wind. Then she withdrew it, rearranged her hair and added, "I always liked the town of Vittoria. Nothing to it but houses in a row; still the town has something I always liked. Are you familiar with it? But to be familiar with it means little or nothing. It's the countryside.... The town with its overlay of roofs lies there in the midst of its countryside and not even the glow of a single lamp is to be seen. One year after the other, one after the other... nothing ever happens here. You go to Milan and return, and nothing has happened. Once you get back to Sicily, you find nothing has ever happened. Nothing in Giarrantana, in Ragusa, in Terranova. The era in which things happened is over. Stop! Basta! Gone when you were an infant," she said to herself, "not even a little girl, because after all you were only a baby in '69.... Hey there, soldier! Leonilde was only a child when her name marked a page in history. Now she is happy if she can just manage to find

245

something she likes as much as this village of Vittoria....Something here, something there to be liked....A little something everywhere."

She seemed happy, enjoying the invisible countryside spicing the air. The soldier too seemed even happier listening to her.

The train slowed, then started to whistle as it slowed a little more, and the air coming down from the black slopes of the vineyards, and up and down from sandy slopes, from sea slopes, entering the windows, left a little more of itself in the compartment, and the smoke smelled as it does on top of a hill when it plumes up from a railway valley.

The train stopped and started, stopped and started. In the intervals between its whistles, a more distant whistle was heard. A flash of another train could be seen. Then, at the curve, the red lights of the other train were visible.

The howlers' train which had fallen behind again now drew in and the soldier could picture the faces at the compartment windows, looking out into the black night: the boys laughing at him, never tired of repeating their song, the old woman trying to say something to him, the man in rags like flapping feathers, the other man with the shabby cone-shaped hat who had made a long tirade.

Whether he knew it or not, the soldier was excited; he faced the window behind the old lady or turned to the one on the other side, saying that this time no one would get away with spitting at them as people had done at Comiso.

"Would you like to spit at them?" the Signora asked.

"It's not that," he answered, but he was excited just the same and even more so when they passed the howlers' train, or when they stopped alongside it at the Vittoria station.

Scornful laughter came from the shouting crowd, the flares of a match flamed up here and there. Then came the "tam-tam," the rhythm that the crowd's voice never loses, the same repeated song, forever the same, a thousand times repeated during the hours of travel in the sun near Ragusa, at sunset near Genisi, in the night at Donnafugata, Comiso, Vittoria:

> His food is lousy,
> He sleeps on the ground.

The soldier tried once more to tell the old woman that they were not singing against soldiers, not exclusively *against* them, not properly...and he took refuge in mimicry, but black figures in the night moved along their train on both sides, that of the narrow station and that of the howling cars. The soldier was all atremble:

"We fooled them, we fooled them!"

The old lady said he should be ashamed of himself and blamed both sides for the usual "Sicilian Muslimism." She could not be heard, anyhow, and was interrupted by savage shouts, wild roars, and blows on the windowpanes, as people passed their compartment.

"Hornéd bastards, sons of bastards; hornéd sons of bastards, with a ribbon on your horn!"

It seemed to the soldier that the boys howled "bastards," that the old woman screamed too, and that the man with the shabby hat, and the other with his rags fluttering about like feathers filled the whole train with their faces, as many faces as there were windows.

It all seemed possible enough but it was also droll; even their insults were ludicrous; then the soldier laughed, but the old woman, interrupted in her last tirade, was now boiling as she listened to them:

"Oh, the scoundrels! Oh, the wretches," she shrieked, pulling at the soldier's sleeve. "Don't you hear them?" She wanted him to answer them man to man, answer them with a tough, commonplace insult, he who was a common man, but she herself answered instead, thrusting her head from the window before it was too late:

"Horns to you, and may you attach them to your babies' cradles! Attach them to your saddlebags, your packsaddles, you dogs!" The soldier, whistling with two fingers in his mouth, now joined her:

"To you, and you!"

Soon nothing more was heard from the other train for the railway switches were thrown, first one, then a second....Their train was on the move again.

"I never met a man like you," the old woman said. "Didn't you resent their insults? It was *your* mother they insulted, after all....Are you or are you not your mother's son? Have you a mother? I do understand and appreciate innocence but this goes way beyond a pure mind, at this point; it's like having fresh water instead of blood in your veins, or perhaps you really are what you appear?"

And she gave him a sharp little glance, trying to discern on his face the phosphorescent gleam of the divine sign, but the bersagliere answered that he was simply happy. He was happy because he should have been traveling on that terrible train whereas here he was on this peaceful one. He should have stayed back yet he was now up front. He should have stopped at Donnafugata yet he was now running on well beyond Vittoria.

"And all this, thanks to you," he added.

The Signora had to admit he was a gem. "I *deserve* an orderly like you."

The bersagliere was not so sure he deserved it; still, he had had the bright idea of trying for a comfortable trip and now he was having one. He had wanted to sleep all the way, and now...true, he hadn't slept yet but, since their train was ahead and they would no longer be harried by the noises of the other train at the stations, it was likely he could do so now. He had refused to take so much as a box lunch with him, nor had he shouldered his knapsack or carried even a small parcel—this had been the best idea ever. This impulse alone had given him luck for the rest of the trip.

As the old woman kept asking him to explain himself more clearly, he now started to describe the long walk at Terranova from the station to the town.

"Certainly," she said.

"It's a hard climb," he said.

"Of course it is...certainly is."

"Then, too, I'm not yet home at the end of the climb."

"Neither am I."

"I have to cross town and go down on the other side."

"Toward the sea? I have to cross the full length of the town, too. I live near the Capuchins."

"So you can well understand....I didn't want to bring a single thing along. On my arrival, I'll wake up and I'll have only a long walk ahead of me and nothing to carry."

"You are very lucky, indeed!"

"That's so, don't you agree?"

The old woman said that his luck lay in being such a gem, in being her orderly, her squire, her protector, in being everything the Socialist Monarchy had refused to admit its obligation to give her.

But she made it even plainer. From her dark corner, she was searching again for a phosphorescent supernatural sign on that face whose features were scarcely distinguishable in the bluish glimmer of the compartment night light. And she told him that not only would he carry nothing but he would not even have to walk all the way.

"How can this be?" he asked.

"You will not walk!"

"How can I avoid it?"

"You will go by carriage."

"As though going by carriage were nothing! Do you know how much a carriage costs from the station to town? Then down the slope to the big boats? I've never in my life ridden in a carriage; besides, no carriage waits for the night train at Terranova."

"Mine will wait."

"Do you own a carriage?"

"Oh, innocent boy, you think I have no carriage? I hire one for the months of my stay. My relatives have already been notified from Milan, and again from Giarrantana, and then from Ragusa; that's why we'll find their carriage which I have already paid for...."

"But, dear lady, what have I to do with your carriage?"

"Why not you? I—and Don Carlos—can get in, you may get in, too, as my orderly, of course. The carriage will be empty except for Lionheart on the box; my baroness daughter won't be there, nor my baron son-in-law, nor the other little Leonilde whose grandmother I am."

"And you'll take me by carriage all the way to town? After that, I'll continue down the slope until I reach the Barconi district, the big boats, if you'll just drop me off at the square. But first I can accompany you home, if you wish. I can get to the Barconi from the Capuchins just as well...."

"It is nice of you to offer...but you'll go home by carriage to your Barconi, you innocent, you. Innocenzo *is* your name, isn't it? I want you to have the best of luck tonight."

The lady asked him if he knew the fairy tale of a certain boy who had a certain cat.

"I want it to be that way, tonight. I want to be for you what that cat was."

"Do you mean Puss in Boots?"

She nodded. "Well, I too have boots. I'm a female cat instead of a male, and I'm old, Innocenzo, an old cat, but I too have boots...a carriage, I mean. I'll have you jump aboard it, fold the steps, close the door, and there you'll be, inside with Don Carlos, a poor boy transformed as if by magic into another. I'll mount the box beside Lionheart. We'll climb the dusty road where there will be no light, no living soul, but if there were I'd shout to clear the way for the Prince of Donnafugata."

"What then?" the soldier asked.

"What then? Then we'll stop in front of your house...." A full stop was called for at this point to imagine the scene of the arrival: she, descending in high boots from her box seat, unfolding the coach steps, opening the door for him as he, the Prince, was having it borne in on him that his home had not been changed for that of a prince.

"But I'll continue to do something for you. I can continue to do something. Nothing can happen to me, but it can to you. For you, things can be different. I can change something for somebody else, and I'll do it."

The tone of her last words conveyed her decision and the bersagliere did not ask what kind of change she meant; perhaps he did not wish the "something" to happen, perhaps he even feared it. And he continued to stare into the dark corner occupied by the old woman, waiting in a state of suspense which may have been one of hope or diffidence.

"What's that?" said the Signora, suddenly vehement. "You don't care? Obviously, you can't care if you really are what you appear to be. How can you be interested in any change if everything is the same to you? I'll tell you what I think, anyhow. I like you in many ways, just as you are at this moment, without a trace of self-interest. It's because of your beautiful face...your beautiful voice....Are you blushing? You certainly are blushing again. You would not appeal to me if you didn't have this simplicity of heart which does not permit you to feel gratified by praise. But you must not think I wish to seduce you...."

She started to laugh in a submissive yet lamentably prolonged manner which differed from all the other laughs of the evening. Did it make her sound more like an old woman? Less like a lady? Or perhaps just the reverse: less like an old crone and more like a lady?

"Not that I never seduced anyone, mind you. I did seduce many! I really seduced them! I was quite an attractive girl, if I say so myself, both in my military uniform and in a simple skirt. I was a great temptress before I married and then again when I was widowed. You should have seen me at the turn of the century, what a whore I was...."

"Whatever are you saying?" the bersagliere exclaimed.

She went on talking, her voice quavering in the rush of her laughter. "Whatever am I saying? All the traveling men from your villages whispered it. All my lovers and all the others as well, those who only lusted after me; they all said it. What a hot whore she must be! And I was proud of it, I must confess, because I always knew what they call a real woman here in Sicily. Elsewhere, too. A real woman is a whore so long as she likes to go to bed. Isn't that being a whore?"

The soldier admitted timidly that it could be so.

251

"You see? You see? If a woman so much as shows, even a little—from the way she is made, say—that she *could* like it, then she is a whore...."

The bersagliere admitted yet did not admit it. Actually, she could seem to be one without having been; or be one, without seeming to be.

"What do you know about it?" the Signora muttered. "You cannot possibly know anything about it with that blushing face of yours.... I know of some husbands who call their wives whores because they find them hot for love-making. Should I not have been proud of being called a whore?"

"You weren't a paid prostitute," the bersagliere interrupted. "You have no sons by men you don't even know...."

"But I did like men! And I didn't confine myself to devouring them with my eyes from behind a shutter. Oh, no! I wanted to be a woman no matter what they called me. I took part in the war, crossed Italy on horseback, and filled a page in history all to myself by following my husband. I devoured the men with all of me, not just with my eyes... a good few of them even before my widowhood. After I became a widow, one after the other, one after the other.... Never heard of a woman like me? Well, you're young, let alone innocent, and Sicily is full of so-called whores who never leave the house. Have you heard of them? They have filthy minds, if you ask me; even go in for family affairs; they're worthless trash. Now you take me, I wanted to be worth something, dear Innocenzo, with the grace of God I had in my body! You should have seen the breasts I had until a few years ago! Are you raising your hands to heaven? You may well raise them. It was really a sight to raise your hands about; why, people would run and point me out to others...!"

Once in a while, the soldier would try to interrupt her:
"My mother, on the other hand..." but the Signora would not give him a chance to finish.

"You want to remind me that I could be your mother? I don't forget it, don't you worry. A woman like me may have done everything possible under the sun and still not lost her pride. I never stayed with a man whose level I wasn't up to."

"My mother, on the other hand..."

"Your mother, again! As soon as I knew I was old, I refused to go on...some attractions I still had; perhaps, for a few years more; but I broke off my last love affairs right in the middle. In love I never wanted to be above them, but not beneath them either, if you know what I mean."

"My mother..."

"I've had enough of your mother!" And then she sighed, "Well, I put a stone over the whole thing, and now I am alone; nothing more can happen to me in this world in which nothing ever happens anyway...."

"Now, my mother..." the bersagliere finally broke in.

"What's your mother got to do with it, in the devil's name? Your mother, your mother...are you trying to tell me that your mother was a saint?"

"No, Ma'am."

"All you sons want to say your mother was a saint; even my own child, the one who's married to the baron. Little hypocrite! And even Ruggero, although the compliment's more justified in his case given the little he knows about it. Doesn't it ever occur to you children that a mother may not take it as a compliment?"

"That isn't what I wanted to say."

"What then? You could even say it, for all of me...."

"The fact is that my mother was more of a whore than that," said the bersagliere.

"More...than that?"

The bersagliere said that his mother was a real one. Not only had she given birth to him without any husband but she had abandoned him, turning him over to the convent by placing him on the wheel the nuns used for receiving packages.

"You never left a child of yours 'on the wheel,'" he said. "You have no children who are the sons of *things*. Yet that's just what you could call me, a son of a *thing*."

He said this with his usual good humor, in order to

253

explain, not to recriminate. He wanted to say it because it was the truth.

Meanwhile, neither the old woman nor the bersagliere realized that the train had stopped and started again. They were traveling, this much they knew. And they knew they were running through a world of vineyards, with the sea no longer so close as before. This much they must have known from the night itself.

They must have felt through the night the presence of tender hills covered by leaves upon leaves upon leaves. And further on, they would feel the hills turn moldy, then parched, reeking of malaria, stretched out there consumed by malaria, right up to the station at Dirillo with its long, narrow slopes like the tombs of those whom malaria has killed.

The soldier, who had begun to yawn, was talking about the family by whom he had been adopted, his adopted father, mother, sisters and brothers. He yawned as he talked on.

The Manina family?

Yes, the Maninas.

The Maninas from the Barconi district, the big-boat district near the beach?

His voice smothered by weariness, he was saying that all the Manina males were adopted like himself, boys left on the convent wheel, and all the girls were legitimate.

The soldier kept on talking and yawning, talking and nodding. People had come in and sat down in the rear half of their double compartment but the bersagliere went on yawning and talking and it was the old woman who first became aware that the two trainmen were back there for the third time. She must have heard them some time earlier, for one of them kept clearing his throat. Still, she kept her soldier talking, asking him why he had joined the infantry to do his military service and not the navy. He explained sleepily that with the land forces he would be through a year and a half sooner than with the navy, and that old Manina would not have liked to do without his share of the work for an extra year and a half. She kept him talking whether he was yawning or not, nodding with sleep or not, and despite

254

the presence of the two trainmen back there she told him something about herself, told him about what she called her own page in history.

She said that it had all begun when she ran away from boarding school, a flight that became the subject of a patriotic song. That was the period when rumors were rife that Garibaldi's "Mille"—his thousand courageous volunteers —were about to embark to liberate Rome, just as they had done in 1860 for the Two Sicilies. And she, Leonilde, had filled her page in history by searching for the "Mille" in Genoa, in Leghorn, then in Palermo and Naples, until finally Garibaldi was ashamed of being sought out by a little girl who wanted him to do what he had always wanted and never yet accomplished.

Leonilde was Milanese. She spelled it out for the benefit of the two trainmen seated behind her: "Mi-la-ne-se," from Milan. A thousand eight-hundred kilometers away.

And her family had found her and taken her back to Milan after Garibaldi no longer wished to feel ashamed and preferred to do the deed for which Leonilde had sought him out. That was how she had filled her page in history, by encouraging Garibaldi to liberate Rome.

She said it, paying out the syllables one by one as she had when she told him she was from Milan. But once more she stopped to listen to the two back there, and she went on to say that she had further distinguished herself during the expedition that finished at Mentana, speaking as if Mentana had taken place in 1869, and repeating and repeating, and saying that she had disguised herself as a boy in order to be able to join up, that she had been first a private, then had been recognized as the Leonilde who had given her name to the patriotic song, that she had fought as a lieutenant, and had been discharged a captain.

Once her page in history had been opened, it did not close: all Garibaldi's expeditions—from Mentana to Aspromonte and Calatafimi—were jammed in between 1869 and '70. She spoke of them, addressing herself to the two who were still seated back there. She called out periodically,

255

"Do you understand, you two?" Gradually it became obvious that she was addressing herself more to them than to the bersagliere. She leaped to her feet at a certain point in order to offer them, swallowed up as they were in the shadow of the unlighted car, the supreme revelation that her page in history was not confined by national boundaries. Its scope was European, not merely Italian, and it was in France too that she had shone, on soil that was not monarchic, not under Bourbon domination. There she had fought side by side with the volunteers from the Vosges and the Garibaldi legionnaires from Dijon. Yet—and at this she turned back to the bersagliere—she could be considered an historic figure more on the lines of Lucretia, Brutus's wife, than on those of Camilla, the warrior maid.

And she went on to say that it was above all as a wife that she had filled her page in history, that she had filled it by her wifely obedience when she followed her husband into exile among the...the Carthaginians of Terranova. Two years after the end of the Franco-Prussian War, he had wanted to retire, like Garibaldi, to his own equivalent of Caprera. Many men who had been among Garibaldi's intimates had wanted to do the same. Some found their Caprera by retiring to a villa in Venetia, some found it on a farm in Tuscany, some, by returning to the provincial cities of their birth. He had chosen to look for his in Terranova in Sicily which he had never seen before. "Are you following me?" she rapped out. And she, Leonilde, had taken it "like an ancient Roman" who considered it her supreme duty to remain united to her spouse even in exile. Thus she had filled her page in history by supporting, at twenty, the decision of her husband of forty-nine who may, yes, have found the respose he was seeking but in a place where Leonilde—especially after her French sojourn—had found only self-sacrifice.

Paris, Milan, Terranova....The war on horseback, and now only this sulky night train. The times of great events had flown by; all that could "fly by" now were these old tumble-down hovels called stations, like Dirillo....

The old woman wanted to ask if they had already passed it.

Whom should she ask? Those two back there?

The bersagliere?

The soldier was asleep.

"Don't you know it's dangerous to sleep in malarial country?" she roused him. She had him get up and close the windows. "Never breathe the night air where there's malaria." And he might still be exposed to it for hours: after all, there were those two back there certainly plotting to have him get off the train at Dirillo. Then brusquely she asked him if he had slept well, if Leonilde had lulled him well with the rocking of her song.

"What song?" the bersagliere exclaimed.

"My page in history, oaf!"

"Oh, I listened to all that..."

"You did not!" she screamed. "Watch out, soldier; I don't like to be cheated."

"But I did listen to it."

"Let's see, then: where was I born?"

"In Milan, Ma'am."

"Did I mention what year it was that I filled a page in history?"

"You mean 1869?"

"Of course. 1869. Now tell me, *how* did I make history?"

"In the Mentana and Calatafimi campaigns."

"You mean, first with my escape from school. But, really, how did I fill my page in history?"

"You made Garibaldi feel ashamed of himself."

"I made history as a wife who followed her husband into exile," the old woman exclaimed. "It's so simple! And I hope you won't tell me we went into exile in Paris."

The bersagliere did not have to tell her anything about Paris or anything else just then, for people had arrived in time to cut off any further reply. Don Carlos growled.

"You back again?" the Signora said.

The cringing Enrico was once more trying to talk to her with his fading voice and his hands that resembled those of a corpse.

"What d'you want now?" she asked him. "I don't wish to give offense...but I never feel glad to return here, that's all....And I don't like to see anyone until that state of mind has passed...."

Don Enrico had no assignment to learn by rote, no questions of history to listen to and answer. He could wash his hands of the whole thing, yet he kept on fluttering his ghostly hands, excusing himself and blaming others. He stopped to answer Don Carlos's growl with something like a growl, then went back to excusing and blaming, pointing over his shoulder, and finally, turning to indicate others behind him, he brought out the name, Prospero, and then another name, Filippo.

The voice of a young man said that many of them wanted to pay their respects to her before she reached her destination. "Well! Well!" she said. He went on talking and she said that it didn't matter, he kept it up and she said there was no reason to go out of their way, and he talked on and she repeated that she had meant no offense. And so it went until three or four of them were trying to make themselves heard over Don Carlos's growls and the old woman's comments, and they said at last that they were all planning to go to Butera from Genisi for the hunting.

The old woman shook her head when she heard him mention the hunt. They were always special in Sicily! In June the animals were always in heat, so no hunting in June....But the Sicilians, always special, hunted anyway, the improvident fools, the dilettantes....However, why should she bother her head about it? She didn't have to pay the piper. It was clear that she did not intend to be drawn into a discussion of the subject.

But then the men said they hunted only the birds that were using the flyways northward, birds of passage, in short, no native strain, and above all no game. They were gentlemen. They knew enough not to fire unless there were quarry in season. That was why they were not stopping over at Genisi.

They were leaving. And their only reason for going to all that trouble was that there were no birds of passage winging their way over Genisi. That was exactly why they were going to move on to Butera, to see if the big flights north had begun. The heavy influx was usually toward mid-June. The skies were black with birds heading north. And they wanted to look over the lay of the land to see which hilltops were best as cover.

"Yes, yes," the old woman was saying to each in turn as he added his word. "Yes, yes. Yes, yes." She spoke to them as to a bunch of children she was in a hurry to dismiss. She did not want to become involved. Still, at a certain point, she said that the flyways over Butera were not necessarily any more infallible than those over Genisi and that, if she had been they, she would have gone to Piazza Armerina.

"Well, then, let's go there," the gentlemen said. "Come along with us," they said. And they even called her "Zia" in the local fashion. Enrico kept on gesticulating with his corpselike hands, like a priest celebrating mass, and the names began to spill forth again, Prospero, then Filippo, then Michele, but the old woman said she had too many things to do to think of leaving Terranova and her own property just then.

"I'm not a lady of leisure, you know," she said. She grew more interested, though, and after protesting once more that she only went hunting at the right season and not at any old time of year like a savage, she started asking about guns, cartridges, hunting dogs, and which boys of the district would be used as beaters to start the birds. Were there good beaters at Butera? What about Genisi? Sharp eyes were needed for such a job. Still, she had her orderly who could act as beater if she went hunting.

She pointed her finger at the bersagliere as she said this, and she added that his eye was infallible where such things were concerned. "That's true, isn't it?" He could see clearly even looking into the sun, she said, and he could sight a flight ten miles away.

The bersagliere did not say a word about whether it was true or not. Instead, he leaped to his feet. On the skyline

259

he had seen where the stars began to be transformed, first one, then another, then a third, into quivering red lights as they steadied, then grouped on the summit of a distant hill. He lowered the glass in the compartment door. It must be Terranova.

"What are you saying?" she exclaimed. "It's impossible." They still had to stop at the Dirillo station. How could they see the lights of Terranova before they had stopped at Dirillo?

But she too saw the moving thread of lights far away in the night, stretched between earth and sky. And she rose to her feet as the gentlemen sought to kiss her hands. Once more, they invited her to join the hunt at Butera or, if she preferred, at Piazza Armerina. Leonilde was furious with the trainmen who had not forewarned her. "Quick, hurry, the small valise must come down; now the sack up, up here, the hamper, quick, out of that corner." All this while she was turning and twisting, trying to put Don Carlos on the leash. Everyone was helping her and joking about the amount of luggage.

"Don't bother, please, my orderly is here. Innocenzo, Innocenzo!" As the train slowed, the flash of a street lamp lighted a yellow wall. There lay the whitish reflection of a sidewalk, running before the already opened compartment door. The railway men jumped down and the wheels screeched under the pressure of the brakes.

"Goodbye, goodbye..." "See you at the Butera hunt..." The old lady tapped one of the gentlemen's arms to greet them all, as the soldier, about to take his leave, stood thanking her from the sidewalk.

"But I told you we have the carriage!"

Leonilde was standing on the step and looked for all the world like the statue of a saint, carried out of some church with all her shawls and necklaces about her. She even had flowers.

"May I help you?" asked the bersagliere, as the railway men eased her down. Leonilde, standing there with her dog as big as a horse and the four pieces of luggage scattered about her, was still berating the two railway men because they had asked the soldier to pay a difference on his ticket.

Finally she laughed at the nasty look they gave him as they jumped back into the open compartment of the already moving train.

The gentlemen were bowing and bowing, leaning far out of the compartment windows as the train passed. Then came the last cars, the baggage van with its red taillights, and the fading rumble as it disappeared. Only a little wind and some straw stirred by the train's passing were left behind: Terranova...

The roofs and walls of the town of Gela, called Terranova for centuries, cover about three miles. The long plateau, elevated some hundred and fifty feet between the plain and the shore, divides the fertile tract of the one from the arid length of the other. This long plateau is a rock formation containing an admixture of both of its flanking elements: on the one side it is richly verdant where it faces the hills, on the other, the sea side, its soil is dry and sandy.

Desert is that sea, like Africa to which it leads; desert too the deep shore for forty miles, plus another forty on the other side. Desert, the interminable retaining wall that stretches for more than forty miles from Terranova to Licata and for another forty roadless miles, to the east, west and north, with its tilled but empty plain, its undulating arid land, its land formless with malaria, dunes white with malaria, and the white valleys of the nearby hills.

Any traveler who ascends toward the village at night must notice this phenomenon just as, later, he will become acquainted with the song of the wheelwright that runs, coming or going, through the Mazzarino road. Even if he remembers cities he has seen there—in days of winter light—crowning the hilltops at intervals some sixty miles apart with their wrinkled precipices all around their sides and their houses piled on top, the traveler knows that Gela rises like the ancient capitals of the first human races, the Chaldean city of Ur or the Hebrew city of Hebron. Those too were surrounded by cultivated fields and by their harvests; they had their steep pasture lands whence the closely kept, compact herds came down for the Monday fair. And on their far side they had the limitless circle—symbol of a world just born from God's

261

hand—fluctuating vaguely between water and rock, united, empty, covered by thorn bushes with small white snail shells attached to them, and snake nests hidden under the stones among their roots.

This unfinished band of earth, called Dirillo and Ponte Dirillo from east to northeast, known as Uomo Morto to the north and as Serra Gibliscemi still further north, called also Manfria and Mongiova, not forgetting Suor Marchesa and Serra dei Drasi, and known in its entirety as the Land of Buterese—unwound, extricated from the malarial slime—faces the seashore and forms with it at night an immensity of darkness on which the quivering lantern of a wheelbarrow gives the impression of armies of enemies or ghosts advancing for a last reckoning, until the traveler hears the creaking of the barrow's wheels.

Either the place in itself or some kind of memory of it seemed to please the old woman for her happiness was clear on her face. The fact of finally having arrived made the bersagliere happy and this was just as obvious on his face too.

The Signora's eyes were smiling at the dry scent brought in by the night where, here and there, the crops of the present season and the hay of the previous year were stacked together. The soldier's eyes were smiling too, round at the thought of three whole days without chores. He pictured a fountain, then saw himself among the dunes with the big boats pulled up on the sand, and he lying under the stern, under the smell of tar of the beached hulls, and farther down along the dunes near the mouth of the Gela River, near the Doric temple, there among the dunes and the bamboo of Betalem.

Their eyes met in secret communication as they silently congratulated each other on having arrived; then the soldier gathered up the luggage.

"What are you doing?"

"I'm taking them to your carriage...."

The sidewalk was deserted under a breath of wind which

flicked up the scattered straw. The feeble light coming from a street lamp and reflected on the yellow wall was like an ember.

"What about a porter…or a guard?"

"But what do you want them for, Ma'am, when you have your own personal attendant?"

"We can make it in two trips."

But the soldier wanted to carry all four valises at once while Don Carlos dragged at the old woman, suddenly blocking her way in an impulse to smell the nether edges of a wall.

"And I was the one who didn't want to carry so much as a lunch box…" the bersagliere kept on repeating as he hinted jokingly at the possibility that the lady had no carriage.

"Perhaps I'll have an automobile. An automobile would be even more appropriate than a carriage for a modern Puss in Boots, wouldn't it, and so perhaps they'll send a car."

By now they had passed the iron exit gate, still open for night passengers, and found themselves on the sidewalk which was as feebly illuminated by its street light.

"As you see, there's nobody here."

"Lionheart is asleep on the box, I'm sure. Lionheart, Lionheart!" she called; then to the soldier: "Just be calm; he is bound to be asleep around here somewhere in the dark."

The bersagliere searched the darkness, almost sniffed at it.

"Lionheart!" repeated the Signora.

"Be quiet, please," the bersagliere put in but, in the sudden silence that followed, no sound was audible except that made by some straws which, pushed by the wind's fingers, were skipping about on the dusty piazza.

"Nobody here," said the soldier. "We would have seen the carriage lights by now!"

4

The soldier put down the blanket-roll, expansible valise, large suitcase, sat down on the edge of the sidewalk with her duffel sack over his shoulder and hid his face in his hands.

"This is just like the baron, my son-in-law. I should have expected this kind of trick from him, the calculating, blood-sucking vampire. Never satisfied, never ready to call it quits. ...I should have known that he wouldn't send the carriage to avoid tiring the horses in case I shouldn't arrive. My son-in-law is like that...he uses the barter system with his peasants and pays them only after he has sold all his corn and tomatoes; that way, he avoids his peasants' competition on the open market. Naturally, he doesn't send the carriage to meet me even though it's my own, and I paid him for the horses, and I pay Lionheart's salary. The baron pays for the forage out of his wife's dowry so it's quite logical for him not to let the horses out to work up more of an appetite just to meet an old woman who may or may not arrive. After all, she's still strong. One who was a soldier and a Garibaldina obviously can walk. Don't forget, Leonilde, you are strong and you can make it on foot; you can carry those valises just as you once carried a knapsack...."

As she talked, she struggled with Don Carlos who tugged her from one side to the other until she finally released him from the leash. The soldier saw the great piebald dog running to and fro over the whitish dust of the piazza. Don Carlos was visible in the dark; behind him was the black outline of a hovel and, farther up, the whitish dust of a road—but way up, like the beginning of the Milky Way, like the Milky Way itself.

"I should have guessed it. A man like that, with a face like a delinquent moron, a man who looks like all his delin-quent moronic ancestors hung in a row in the hallway! A man who hasn't turned those crooked noses and distorted mouths to the wall..."

As she talked, the old woman examined the five black doors facing the piazza and several times attempted to turn the knobs, shaking them and rapping on the panels. Then she went on to talk about her daughter, the weakling, who may have kept her telegram from her husband in order to avoid a scene; she even mentioned her grandchild, Leonilde, the naughty brat, who may have carried off the telegram secretly to put Grandmother to all this trouble.

Meanwhile, she continued to knock at each of the five doors shouting loudly:

"Hey, Stationmaster!"

"What have you in mind?"

"I want to leave the luggage with him."

"Do you think he can hear you? And will he come down to open the door even if he does?" The soldier, seated on the sidewalk surrounded by the valises and with her sack over his shoulder, shook his head.

"Why shouldn't he get up?" she exclaimed. Just the same, she left off calling at the top of her lungs and looked toward the end of the dusty piazza at the huddled dark mass of the houses where the Milky Way began which marked the rise from the town. "But wait, wait, I have an idea..." and she flew across the piazza saying that somebody must have a handcart or a pack-mule.

"You think they'll wake up at this hour, much less get up?" the bersagliere called after her.

The soldier heard her knocking and shouting, then talking with someone for a few minutes, growing angry, grumbling, and returning.

"Now what?" he asked, raising and hefting the large suitcase.

"I'll carry this one..." the old girl said as she took up the expansible valise. They started to cross the piazza, its dust and straw swirling around their feet, and they moved on toward the upward slope which by now was turning as white as the real Milky Way; their goal was the row of five or six street lights that marked the far edge of town up there on top.

"A regular Puss in Boots..." the bersagliere half groaned, "with a carriage...and maybe a car...."

He dropped the phrases one after the other with gaps of silence between like the sound his steps made on the rock, the dust, the straw, and again on rock.

"What do you mean?"

"Nothing, nothing!"

"You said something, I heard you....You don't believe I have a carriage?"

"I don't believe we're riding in one, that's all...."

The old woman swore that the following day her carriage, with Lionheart in his gala livery, would come call at his door. She would put it at his disposal for his three days' leave and he would come to dinner every night; besides, he could have her husband's best suit and all of his underwear.

"It's better for you not to talk while you're climbing; you'll have no breath left."

On their right the road was flanked by a black abyss from which, every so often, a tiled roof emerged. The old woman seemed to be counting those heaps of tile as she struggled along. She was silent for the moment and her breathing was labored. She looked once more at the roofs, stopped and suddenly moved toward a mound of tile and stone in which a door was vaguely discernible; she began to shout at the poor sleeping inmates while the bersagliere continued his ascent. He heard her far behind him calling at each hovel door, and decided to stop and wait for her; he put the valises down on the walk and sat on them to rest.

The rustling of the skipping straw was gone and the Signora's voice came to him between breaks of silence.

"Hey, good people, hey, Christian souls..." Nobody answered but the dog howling from somewhere, then he suddenly reappeared and came galloping toward the bersagliere on ghostly paws.

"Hurry up," said the soldier. "Hurr," Don Carlos answered and he continued his phantom gallop toward his mistress's voice.

The old girl had started to throw pebbles at the hovels as she went on calling intermittently: "Hey, good people, hey,

Christians..." She was afraid of going down into the black ditches by the roadside and so flung pebbles instead of using her hands—or a foot—to knock on the doors. Finally a woman answered her from behind a tight-shut window.

"What do you want?"

"A porter, a handcart, or a mule."

"My husband has the mule with him and he'll only be back from town tomorrow evening. He went to Mirabella and Mazzarino..."

"Well, you can at least store my valises for me even if your husband has gone to Mazzarino, can't you?"

"I don't open the door at night when my husband is away in town."

"I won't eat you; I'm an old woman."

"My husband will kill me if he finds out that I open the door to anyone when he isn't here."

"Your husband will kill you if you open the door to a man, not to a woman. I tell you, I'm an old woman."

"But I'm a young bride, Signora."

"But I'm a woman, dear girl, just like you."

"My husband will never believe you are a woman. Don't tempt me, Signora. There's nothing I can do about it."

"If I were a man you'd do it all right. Who knows, perhaps you already have a man in your bed, someone who knocked before I did."

"What kind of manners do you call that? D'you wake people up in the middle of the night to hurl insults at them?"

"Everybody knows you're a whore; everybody knows when your husband's gone to town you open the door to any man who happens to knock. I'll tell your husband that you refused to open the door to me only because I didn't use a male voice."

"You'll ruin me! And you said you are Signora Leonilde? A lady never calls a young bride a 'whore'; you are no lady; you are the devil disguised as a lady. Father, Son and Holy Ghost! What can this devil want of me?"

At this turn of affairs, the old woman changed her tune.

"If you open the door, I'll say nothing to your husband and show you a beautiful thing."

"Please don't tempt me."

"I have a beautiful soldier with me."

"Oh, please, please, don't tempt me."

"A handsome bersagliere, my girl."

"Don't tempt me."

"Well, perhaps the man who is in your bed doesn't want to see him."

"Go away, demon! Go away!"

The bersagliere had not been able to make out a word of all this. He only heard the old girl talking to someone. and he certainly hoped that she might come up with a mule or, failing that, that they could leave the valises in someone's house overnight.

After all, he must have thought to himself, she's a fine, thoughtful person. It was on his account that she was going to all this trouble. But though he strained to listen, he did not hear a door open and in time the figure of the old woman came into view, black on the whitish road, bowed under the weight of the single valise which she shifted constantly from right to left, from left to right. The bersagliere was still waiting for her.

"It was in the cards," he said.

The Signora, breathing heavily, uttered not a word and for a long while they continued their climb toward the row of six lights now not too far away, toward the emerging out-lines of houses with their black windows and doors...

"You said your house is at the Capuchins?"

She hesitated but finally answered, "Yes. My daughter lives near the Capuchins."

"The long and the short of it is that that's where we have to go," he muttered, then sighed again that it was in the cards. They had reached the last stretch of the slope where the road turns slightly and where, on the side of the rise, there is a sort of platform of beaten earth—of mud and ditch-water when it has been raining, dust and straw leavings when it is dry—with a scales let into it to weigh vehicles. They reached the first street light, haloed by a dusty glow which served to outline the vast shadows around it.

"Yes, it was in the cards all right," the bersagliere repeated and they looked each other straight in the face in the wan light, and as they looked they exchanged a wry grin.

"At least from now on we'll be walking on level ground, but I certainly...had quite an idea...when I decided I'd not carry a thing, not so much as a single parcel, not even a box lunch. It's all really funny," he laughed, "to think I'd wanted to be able...to walk uphill, hands in my pockets!"

The old woman did not protest nor did she try to interrupt or try to alter the tenor of the soldier's lament. She walked beside him in silence, let him add that it was time he get over the idea he was so damned lucky, get over the idea he was different from the others, get over the idea that he'd been well-advised to try what he had tried; let him say that she should stop trying what *she* had tried, too, trying to get someone's attention at almost every house they'd passed. Perhaps after all it suited her better not to be without her things till morning. Otherwise, who knows, she might have run into someone more willing than the night watchman, or the cripple in the square. Yet, who knows, would she have found someone as willing as her good orderly, the bersagliere?

She let him ramble on and laughed with him when he laughed. She had dropped behind a bit and now followed him, listened to him; then, suddenly, she whistled and called Don Carlos to her; the great dog appeared from one of the pitch-black side streets, the only living thing they had encountered uphill on their way to the main square and on the main road of the sleeping town.

Now it was the bersagliere's turn to be silent. His stride had resounded six or seven times before the old girl started to talk in his stead, saying things in an undertone.

It was not true that he had not been well-advised, she said.

It was unkind on his part for him to say that his decision

269

had been ill-advised, for had he not met someone who could help him greatly?

From the very next day, he would be able to gauge how much she could do for him, and she repeated the promise about the carriage, with Lionheart in his gala livery on the box.

She repeated the invitation to dinner, and the suggestion of a dance. She added that there was a beautiful girl he would meet at the ball (it had now become a ball), a girl so lovely that he would be made happy just by looking at her but that he would be allowed to do more: talk to her, pour out her wine, offer her bread.

Here he was, she said, lucky indeed to be walking beside, or almost beside, a person who held the warp and woof of his good fortune tight in her hands.

The tolling of a bell whose tone fell suddenly, reverberating against the paving stones, reminded them both of the task they had in common but it frightened Don Carlos who ran out of one of the alleys. They looked back at the dark town whose bronze throat had given voice. Was it one o'clock or did the sound mark a quarter after an unpredictable hour?

The town too had something that was indefinable. There were wide-open doors, dark wells of emptiness, wide-open windows, wells of emptiness too; and there were other doors and windows closed as if they had been blacked out for centuries upon centuries in a far distant age, before the flood.

The walls were covered with cracked dust and the northwest wind, blowing full strength, raised a yellowish clay of grit from the façades; even the houses with some sort of attempt at a style appeared shapeless with their outlines frayed, their corners rounded and their cornices nibbled away.

The town might have witnessed the coming of Abraham, the pilgrimage of the Three Kings, Roland's passage on his way to Roncesvalles, and Garibaldi's passing....The soldier and the old woman were somehow reconciled. They stopped and decided to rest.

Trying to help the soldier free himself from the sack, the old woman realized for the first time that he was covered with sweat.

"But you're soaked, completely soaked! Don't take your jacket off; it's windy."

But the bersagliere sat on the heap of luggage and took off his jacket; then he started to wipe the sweat from his chest by passing his handkerchief inside his shirt. The old woman said, "That isn't very good manners, I must say!" whereupon he hurried to put his soaked uniform back on. With little protestations and cries of alarm, the old girl made it clear that putting on a wet garment, all weighted down with dampness, was worst of all, and she kept it up, urging him to take his jacket off again. She too was wringing wet from the long effort and they sat there on the heap of luggage side by side, he saying that at home, near the shore, he was used to doing things differently—and that was a fact, he said—she saying at the same time that in wartime things had never been like this. First he would half listen, then talk at the same time; then she would half listen and break into her litany. Finally, she pulled out a gold-colored cigarette case.

"Do you smoke?"

"Sometimes."

The old woman said that her preferred vice would have been taking snuff except that she did not like to reek of tobacco; instead, she limited herself to an occasional half cigar.

"D'you smoke cigars?"

"Oh, I have cigarettes too."

The bersagliere took a cigarette and the old girl had not the heart to search for a half cigar in her things so she took a cigarette too. They lighted up and sat smoking, talking and smoking in the dark night on the main square seated on her pile of luggage.

"Certainly, I could never be a porter," he observed, laughing at his own sweat, at his fatigue, whereas she was once more fresh and dry.

"D'you mean to say that I could be a good porter?"

"I mean to say that I am good at loading sand or pulling

271

boats down to the shore, but that you would beat me at going to and from the station and the town."

"So I could stay down at the station and be a good porter?"

"You certainly could, if you weren't a woman and a lady."

They whistled up Don Carlos who had once more got lost to view in the alleys, and they started to walk again, the bersagliere laden as he had been before, the old woman as before with her small valise, and they moved together from the darkness of the square into the sandy light of the main crossing.

They passed the massive building of the Mother Church with its sandy flights of steps, its gravelly columns, its sand from architrave to architrave amid channels of shadows up to where the pigeons and the bronzes that sounded the hours were fast asleep.

The right-angled roads to left and right appeared as a row of fires suspended in mid-air; on the right, toward the Capuchins, the fires faded to dwindling embers and the last points of light mingled with the stars at Capo Soprano. The old woman herself was stunned to see how far away it looked.

"But we aren't going to Capo Soprano; we're going to the Capuchins," said the bersagliere, looking at the dusty, worn-out, rocky walls of the Municipal Building. Nearby, he felt in the darkness the presence of the invisible alley through which he could slip home in ten minutes.

"You could go directly from here and be home in ten minutes."

"Of course I could," but he didn't look into the alley; instead, he counted the lights in front of him: one, two, three, four, five, six; one every two hundred yards. At the fourth light there was the public park, and at the sixth the Capuchins.

"Since I've got you this far..." he said.

The old woman started to look for a porter once more, a certain Leonardo who was probably asleep behind an open door around the square somewhere, and she shouted: "Leonardo, Leonardo!" But nobody answered from the darkness; only Don Carlos reappeared.

"Don't waste any more time, Ma'am. Leonardo is deaf and you couldn't wake him even if you kicked him. In order to find him, we'd have to search with a lantern behind each door on the square and in each niche of the Mother Church."

"Why not look for the night watchman, then; perhaps, Gallante knows where Leonardo is."

"We'll try to run into him..." but the bersagliere wanted to get on with it, to walk fast, whereas the Signora, far to the rear, was trying to stop him, still looking for somebody.

As they passed the second light they suddenly heard a sound; thereupon the old woman dropped the valise and crossed the road, saying over and over: "This is where it came from, from up there..."

"What do you think it could have been? Someone closing a door, going in or out..."

"Doesn't this give you a ray of hope that 'someone' may help us...." And she was off again, her short steps beating their tattoo, sure of finding help yet not knowing what kind of help she wanted.

"But how can anyone help us?" It could have been someone gone to call a midwife, or a midwife or doctor on the way home, he thought. "Signora..." he called. He got no answer, only a little scream. The Signora had once more disappeared.

The street lamps were separated by long stretches of dark night. The soldier stopped at the last light before the Public Gardens and waited for the old woman to reappear in one of the circles of light. Here and there, night was lifting a little and in the lessening gloom the two stone-faced, closed, unhearing and unheeding lines of houses could be seen.

"But Signora...Signora. ..." he called, with no hope of being heard, and he put down the valises once more and sat on them as he waited for her to come back.

273

5

"She's a real madwoman!" he said to himself. "What can she be up to?"

And he said to himself he'd about decided to dump her things there and go about his business. He reminded himself that he certainly did not want to hang about with her until dawn. He wanted to get a few hours' sleep this blessed night, he told himself firmly. Furthermore, he wanted to get up early in the morning of his first day on leave, he admonished himself aloud.

"Ha! Ha!" he heard someone reply.

Someone was chuckling up over his head, and the bersagliere turned to see where the sound came from, and looked up.

"She's a mad one, isn't she?" the voice went on.

It said, laughing, that perhaps calling her mad was going a bit far; perhaps it would be more exact to say that she had a screw loose.

"She has more energy than a town our size can cope with. She does this, she does that, and she still has plenty left over. That's why she's always having it over the rest of us. What trick did she play on you?"

The bersagliere kept searching for the source of the voice from balcony to balcony, among the great arabesques of shadow that the flowering wrought iron of the balustrade cast against the façades of the houses. But nothing moved in all that black foliage, nothing on the first floor above the street, nothing on the second, nothing on the third, and the man spoke with nearby sleepers in mind; he spoke so low that one could not tell at what height he was standing.

"Well, I can see what she's done plain enough, after all," he went on. "There you are with her valises! She always gets in at this time of day, or night rather, so that someone's got to tote them for her. And each time there's one more. And each time they get heavier. Doesn't it seem to you that they're heavier than they should be? She's quite capable of loading them with earth and stones...."

The bersagliere was not paying much attention to the meaning of the words. He was too busy trying to figure out the speaker's whereabouts. Yet at this point he thought he should intervene in some fashion or other on the old girl's behalf.

"After all, I offered to carry them," he said.

"Of course, you offered," the man continued. "Therein lies her cunning.... In inducing some, excuse me, poor bastard to put himself in a position that gives her a bit of amusement. And she doesn't do it out of meanness. It's because nothing happens in this world any more and one must help the time to pass somehow.... But if you offered your services with the idea you'd be rewarded, get it straight out of your head. She's the tightest fisted woman in the Two Italies and she'll never give you a lira. A lira? What am I talking about? Not a cent... not a red cent...."

The bersagliere protested.

"But I shouldn't have done it even for *ten* lire, if I'd been doing it for the money."

"So you did it out of courtesy, out of an impulse to succor the weaker sex, out of a spirit of compassion.... How perfectly she hit the mark! Would you have done it for a man disguised as a woman?"

"Now you're not going to try and tell me she's a man...."

"How would I know? I'll go so far as to admit she's my cousin, or that she *became* my cousin, but as for anything else I could tell you, I don't even know if her mother was a dressmaker or a *coiffeuse*. And she's quite capable of passing herself off as sixty, if it's to her advantage."

"You won't try to tell me she's twenty...."

"Twenty, no, because as I remember she's been the bane of our existence a bit longer than that. But anything is possible. In any case, however you may look at it, I'd refuse to carry four great pieces of luggage, even for a woman, a lady, if you wish, who's no longer young... luggage filled with stones at that."

This time, the bersagliere felt it was scarcely worth the effort to show his disbelief. By now it was plain as the nose on your face that the queer duck up there was making it up out of whole cloth! But he still couldn't get over not being able to see him, and he continued to look for him, throwing back his head and letting his eyes wander this way and that.

"I'm no ghost," the joker said. "I'm here, all right. I'm here."

The bersagliere's eye was caught by something with a large shadow that seemed to be moving about on a first floor balcony. What was it? He managed to distinguish the bulk of it from its shadow but he still could not be sure of what it was. It looked like the tail of a bird. "Here I am," the fellow continued almost in a falsetto. And at last the bersagliere saw the thing open and close, he saw that it was a fan, he saw the hand that held it, and he saw, further back, the face of the man who had been talking to him.

It swung forward out of the shadows, with white teeth, a mustache, and thick eyebrows arched over two little, close-set eyes.

"Have you managed to locate me?" he said. "Now maybe you'll believe me... I've never been a ghost. It's just that every night I like to chat a bit with the people who go by, provided they don't come from this hole-in-the-wall. Come again. It will always be a pleasure, and it will do something for you, too. You'll learn, as we talk, not less than you'd be taught by the Salesian brothers."

His tone indicated that the audience was over. To emphasize this impression, he had gotten up from the armchair or chaise longue on which he had been sitting and which he evidently kept on the balcony for his own convenience. And the bersagliere saw through the thick, leafy shade, that he was dressed in a garment he knew was called a "Japanese dressing gown" or "kimono."

His mind went back to the old woman.

"Where the dickens can she have got to?" he asked himself none too quietly.

The man on the balcony once more emitted his cackle of laughter.

"Where? You may well ask. Ha, ha! Didn't I tell you?"

The bersagliere interrupted him because he thought he had heard something.

276

"Sssst! Quiet a moment...please..."

In fact, a kind of call could be heard. Did it come from the square? From farther away than the square? But the far-off bells of the Mother Church rang twice just then, and the man on the balcony insisted that must have been the sound.

"No, no..."

The bersagliere wanted a chance to listen again. He heard whisperings more or less everywhere, stifled noises, as if from balconies and windows all along the Corso there were people spying on him as they whispered to one another. Then the voice that had sounded like a call was heard again, only stronger.

"It's up to you to get out of it..." the man picked up again.

"Please!..." said the bersagliere.

He heard the voice for the third time, stronger still, and strident.

"Whatever does she want?" he said.

"Ha, ha!" the man said.

The voice intoned its call the fourth time and now the words were plain:

"Are you talking to yourself?" they said.

The old woman had found someone.

"I've got Romeo here," the bersagliere now heard or thought he heard.

The man on the balcony bounced about in his flowered dressing gown as if someone were tickling him. "Just listen to that, now!" he exclaimed. "She's unearthed Romeo."

The bersagliere asked if Romeo were not the beggar by the Church of San Rocco who moved about on his hands and the seat of his pants.

"The very one. The very one," the man on the balcony answered, and wriggled about some more.

"The one whose legs don't work?"

"That's the one."

The man was trying to repress a spasm of laughter that he finally let out in a long, thin laugh. "That's the one," he repeated. The bersagliere told him that as a child he had always been afraid of Romeo, and the man said once more,

"The very one." Then the bersagliere told him he had thought that one must be dead, but all the man said was, "That's the one."

"Can't you hear me?" the words penetrated the rush of sound that seemed to leap from one balcony to the next.

The bersagliere gave no indication that he intended to answer. Instead, he looked up, from one spot to another, at the dark façades and at those that received a little splash of light from the lamps strung along the street. The bulbs swung back and forth. A few wisps of straw moved on the ground beneath the nearest of the lights. There was a bit of breeze, anyway.

But the man had jumped back and could no longer be seen or heard.

"God only knows what she wants," the bersagliere said. "What's she calling me for? I can scarcely run back and forth with all these bags here...."

"Ssst," the man on the balcony interrupted. "Speak low." He reappeared above the shadows of the railing and, shielding his face with his fan, glanced to right and left at the buildings flanking his own. "After all, Gela was built of the stone from Dionysus' ear."

But he quickly regained his composure, took on all his former ease of manner and repeated out loud, as if uttering a challenge, his dictum on the original sin of the city. He seemed amused by something his sharp hearing had managed to seize from a wrangle which had broken out a few seconds earlier and whose words had been deadened by the depths of the Corso.

"She's priceless," he commented. "Priceless, priceless...."

Then, as if he considered himself blessed with perceptions which multiplied the effectiveness of his every faculty, he started to give the bersagliere a play by play account of what he heard. "She's having a row with Romeo..." he informed him. "She wants him to rouse someone to take care of the luggage....Or to carry it himself, just imagine...." He spoke then fell silent, spoke then fell silent, listened and spoke and had a fresh burst of laughter which he did his best to suppress

278

behind his words and then behind his pauses. He seemed to find it irresistibly comic that the old woman sought "to draw even Romeo into her games," as he put it. But he said that there was little she could do about it: Romeo put no bridle on his tongue, and besides, he had seen she had a soldier in tow; he had seen them go by together; and she had him loaded down all right. What was she pestering him for if she had already collared a soldier?

"I know," the commentator went on, "that it's an ignorant prejudice to consider the place of one serving in the army as the lowest in the social scale....But in these parts it's a prejudice they all hold. Even the porter, Leonardo, would consider being asked to carry the luggage in place of a soldier a kind of insult....That's why Romeo has got it in for you as well as for that old rogue...."

"Got it in for me?" the bersagliere exclaimed, incredulous and upset.

A recurrence of the distant squabble, which now sounded more like a hand-to-hand melée, had revived the murmur running from balcony to balcony like a sort of collective long-drawn whistle or sigh; and the man once more shushed the bersagliere, this time stopping still himself right where he was, with a smile plastered like a slap across his face. His hand raised in a gesture which demanded continued silence, he cocked his head to follow for a good minute whatever was going on down there as well as the murmur which rose and fell every so often from the balconies; then he announced that a third character had come on stage.

It was Galante, he said, the night watchman so like a stone statue whose ghostlike tread stalked all murders, brawls, and breakings-and-enterings that took place in Gela without, however, his having prevented a single one of them. Just what was needed at night, he added: a statue gifted with omnipresence who could bestow the comfort of his company on whoever had been attacked yet who, at one and the same time, in no way inhibited the aggressor. He winked ever so meaningfully as he sang the statue's praises, then once more changed his tune abruptly—though how he could have heard

279

anything in the heat of his own chatter was a mystery—to say that Galante had given a new dimension to the wandering inclinations of the old woman.

"Now we're in for it," he said. "Romeo has just reminded her that the seasonal invasion of the threshers began night before last.... They sleep in the square at Cappadocia behind the little house behind the Registry; there are a good three hundred of them, and *she's* asking for some reliable milksop to look after her luggage.... Yes sir.... Going from here to Cappadocia would be like jumping from the frying pan into the fire with those three hundred sleeping thugs.... It might take from now till dawn but that's just what she's looking for, something to keep her busy, and I'll bet you my tomorrow's dinner that you'll soon have orders to wait for her here; she well knows all she'd get for her pains would be a laugh if she were to wake Giovinazzo to give a soldier a hand. ...What'll you bet? I'll bet my beef-stew dinner.... Let's give her a moment to clear her throat and then we'll hear the trumpet blow: one—two—three—four...."

On the "four," in fact, the sounds of a voice could be heard calling "Don Carlos...Don Carlos!" It was clearly hers. Then she set to calling the bersagliere, "Innocenzo, Fortunato, Innocenzo, Innocenzo, Innocenzo...."A pause. "Can you hear me?" she went on yelling. "I'm just going over the hill for a moment. I'll be right back.... Now don't you move from where you are."

The man on the balcony was now up close to the railing.

"You're surely not going to let yourself be led around by the nose all night, are you?" he asked the bersagliere.

"Of course I don't want to waste the rest of the night waiting on her," the soldier answered.

"Well, you know what you've got to do if you don't.... You've said it yourself."

"What did I say?"

"That you'd put her things down and go on about your business."

The bersagliere wearily inventoried the clutch of bags on which he was sitting. He asked: "Would you keep an eye on them for her?"

"I?" the man exclaimed. "I've never given a soul any cause to laugh at me: I'm a serious person. Besides, that's not stuff that takes looking after. If you come back this way at noon tomorrow you'll find it's all still here. Likely nothing but horseshoes in all four valises!"

The bersagliere got up off the heap. "What are you talking about?"

He shook first one and then the other of the two suitcases, then lifted the big traveling case; last, he seemed to be weighing the rolled case with the plaid blanket inside it.

"I tell you what I'll do," he added. "I'll carry them to her house and leave them in front of the door for her."

"That'll be good for your health."

"Only trouble is, I don't know the number."

"Well, when you've reached the Calvary..."

"The Calvary?" the soldier exclaimed. "But the Calvary is in the other direction. The lady told me she lived near the Capuchins."

"If she lived near the Capuchins, she'd have sent you toward the Calvary," he answered. "Do you follow me or not? It's because she lives east of town that she's sent you to the west."

The silver tinkle of women's laughter, quickly checked and all but stifled, raised louder murmurs and whispers from the balconies on either side. The man said precipitately that he must withdraw now, raised his clenched fist and shook it, muttering against something that prevented his taking a breath of air even at night, and, after making a sign of greeting and farewell to the bersagliere, disappeared.

The soldier, stock still, did not know what to do. He looked opposite, a bit up from the light hanging in the middle of the street, at the balconies from which the squeals of stifled laughter seemed to have come. They had roller shades of rushes, as well as the shadows of the black leafage. Most of them were pulled up high. Some, instead, were halfway down. One, which was directly in the path of the glare from the

281

street lamp, had the blind dropped all the way so that it flapped out a bit from beneath the railing, and the bersagliere centered all his attention on this one. The fall of its tightly interwoven, horizontal reeds seemed strangely like that tinkle of laughter. Then, too, the shade seemed alive with movement. The bersagliere, not knowing what else to do, gathered his trappings as best he could and took them to the other side of the street just beneath this balcony.

"Do you want me to tell you what's up?" a voice began.

It came from the top-floor balcony where a head now appeared and leaned downward.

"Leonilde is a rogue," it went on, "but that man is a worse one who tried to mix you up over there. Just go straight on toward the Capuchins. If she told you 'the palace,' it's because she lives there sometimes with her daughter; the first big building on this side just after you pass the convent. If, instead, she'd told you 'the villa,' that's the place she goes when she wants to be alone and weep for her dead husband, and that's a bit on the other side, at Capo Soprano, but certainly not as far as the Calvary...."

A murmur more or less of agreement seemed unleashed by these words, running from balcony to balcony and even leaping the adjacent dark patch to be picked up by those living level with the next street lamp and across from the Public Gardens.

"Niccodemo is so mean-minded in his resentment," the voice now addressed the others, "that he'd really have had this young man go to the other side of town to spite her. All because he didn't get away with what he tried to pull off with her. Am I right, Signora Eugenia? All because of the iron he still has in his soul a good ten years after..."

The voice of the one called Signora Eugenia now burst forth from a nearby balcony as if the murmur, which had become one of dissent, found its release there.

"Not right at all, Professor. You can't make a saint out of Leonilde just because she turned a man down for once. Is it to her credit that he didn't appeal to her? No thanks to her. Niccodemo was a handsome man, into the bargain, and the fact that she didn't know how to appreciate him is no credit to her. Nor does it seem to me a feather in her cap that she realized she might have to support him. Or has tight-fistedness become a virtue? From whatever point of view you wish to look at it, no, I can't see where you're right."

"But the Professor," a third voice chimed in, "wasn't trying to whitewash anyone. He was just trying to save the young soldier a trip by not letting him go to look for her where she wasn't to be found. And he pointed out the malicious meanness of one who is certainly no more excusable than she."

It came from the balcony directly below the one from which Signora Eugenia had let loose, and this voice was weak, unaggressive in itself, almost spent, yet armed with two shadows that climbed upward, the enormous silhouette of two hands lifted toward the upper balcony as if to grasp and shake it.

"For you won't tell me that Niccodemo is the more excusable because he lives yonder, closing himself away in an entresol and agreeing to come out only in the hours when everyone else is asleep—all this with the aim of concealing what's going on between him and a certain lady who lives on the main floor...."

The murmur from the adjacent balconies, visible and invisible, altered its tone depending on who was speaking. It had first been with, then against, the Professor. Then in complete agreement with Signora Eugenia. Then against the voice of the third person who had spoken. Now it agreed with the last words, and it was not slow to change as soon as a fourth voice made itself heard from a fourth balcony.

"Let's not stray from the subject," the new bell rang out. "I do not deny that what the lawyer has just said has an element of truth in it even if we have scant proof. But we are not talking about Niccodemo here. Here we are concerned with Leonilde. No question of the one who lives in the entresol, but of the one who lives up at Capo Soprano. It's she who has just arrived, she who ranges up and down the Corso, she who yells and storms about and sets the whole town by the ears. Aren't the valises hers? They are. So let's not talk about the wolf who's not there but about the wolf who is; thus the poor boy who's come within range of her fire may take timely warning...."

The bersagliere had a sort of road guide in those voices, in the talk passing from one to the other and from one balcony to the next. Fearing that his old girl might indeed live not in this part of the city at all but right on the other side, he sought continuous reassurance as to which direction he should follow. And the reassurance came from each new voice which led him along, a few yards at a time, toward the lights of the Public Gardens which were now quite near; each move had him gathering up and depositing the luggage in a kind of relay.

A fifth voice, then a sixth, then a seventh and an eighth, a ninth, cut through the dark patch between the street lamps, running from balcony to balcony even where he could not tell if there were balconies, and each voice had terrible things to say about the old rascal yet each voice never managed to get them said. It seemed they were about to tell of murders, thefts, kidnapped infants, and all they brought out was a phrase, perhaps, uttered on a certain occasion or in a certain fashion which proved that she talked like neither a woman nor a lady. A phrase revealed her malevolence toward the archpriest, or lack of respect for the police lieutenant, or perhaps it was for the Bishop of Caltagirone, and so on and so on. Or perhaps she had done some task she should have left to her overseer or the keepers, instead of wandering around on mule-back over her own land....Then again, who had ever seen her embroider a stitch, or sew, or prepare a sweet or a rosolio, and instead who could not swear that she played *scopa* and went hunting? The bersagliere laughed inwardly, recognizing in these comments the old woman he had met and as each one confirmed for the sixth, the seventh time at least that she lived near the Capuchins in her daughter's palace when she was not in retirement at a villa she had up toward Capo Soprano, he kept on going.

Fantastic tales were attributed now to her openhandedness, now to her avarice, and, since these contradicted each other, he concluded that they canceled each other out. He heard it said that she was greedy, that she could out-fast a camel; great wealth she had let her son-in-law, the baron, devour and, at the same time, she had devoured wealth from her baron son-in-law; hatred for her neighbor, pride, yet excessive familiarity, even intimacy with the last person she might have run into. This led him to believe that she was not lying to him when she had given him to understand that she was a woman of power, a real Puss in Boots, and the fact delighted him as he was indeed delighted to hear her called a regular trull, a first-rate old bawd.

What did they hope to accomplish by calling her such names? A pity she wasn't on the spot to hear them and laugh with him about it....

Of course there were things the soldier did not understand very well.

For example, what about the tenth voice's reference to "women of the wagon train," "camp followers," "women who —even today—manage to follow the regiment when maneuvers are scheduled," "the type who gives birth standing in the guardroom doorway while the trumpet shrills the leave call..."

And what about the statements of the eleventh, according to which Leonilde must have been presented to Garibaldi at the time of her first communion? The General "as he grew old, liked 'em young" and "took his consolation prize from one after another of 'em for not having been made King of Italy in Vittorio Emmanuel's stead." He had called the little girls "Garibaldinas," hadn't he, just as she now called herself....

The bersagliere could understand well enough a person's being full of bile and he even understood that one might wish, or at least try, to inflame all the other denizens of the balconies with bile. But he could not assess how really offensive any of these statements might be, and it was only at the twelfth or thirteenth—when he heard himself called a "Maltese" and a "crazy Maltese"—that he began to realize it would be better to have been called a pig or an ass outright.

"Well, if it's a question of *having* one, you've got one all right."

"Who tried to deny it? With that damned cock crowing and the whole bunch of 'em passing the word to each other, I couldn't get in so much as an explanation. 'She's got a soldier, so what use are *we* to the Garibaldina?' Just as if I'd asked them to carry the bags for a donkey...."

The bersagliere laughed. "Donkey or no donkey," he said, "I'm only too glad to finish what I've begun...."

"You say that because you think we're nearly there," the old woman answered. "You say that because you think we're going to the Capuchins...because you wouldn't mind if I went to sleep under the roof of that baron son-in-law of mine on the very same night they refused to send the carriage to meet me. According to you, it would be perfectly all right for me to spend the night there, to knock on their door. You didn't even ask me if I had an alternative, some other house I could turn to. Let me tell you, I don't need to beg at anyone's door: I *have* another house, my dear, and that's where I'm going...."

The old woman paused a moment to look him over and then finished what she had wanted to say, that she'd gone to look for another fellow to lend him a hand so that she could feel free to go where she damned well pleased.

"On the outskirts of Capo Soprano?" the bersagliere asked, "or on the far side?"

The old woman looked him over once more and finally got to her feet, saying that, at all costs, she had not wanted to have to impose on him again, but then she added, "Capo Soprano...midway." And she added, "Worse luck...too bad it's not on the far side...too bad it's not at Montelungo...too bad it's not at Manfria's tower," and she reiterated that, had it not been for her wish not to impose on him, she would have wanted to live far from the smoke of her son-in-law's

chimney pots, in a part of the city out of his sight and thought!
"How many lights away is he?" the bersagliere asked.

He had counted one more street lamp between him and
the Capuchins and he walked, bags in hand, looking at the
lights as they rose a bit before him, trying to count them
from the Capuchins on. He asked if it were the first after
the Capuchins, or the second, or beyond the third.

"We'll see," the old girl answered.

She too was counting now, and she wanted to count the
ones behind her, beginning with the farthest one she could
see. But she could not decide if it was a first star or a last
light and so reversed the count, beginning with the Capuchins.

In the distance, a dog started to bark. The old woman
said, "That fool," and, having broken her count, started all
over again with the street lights only to interrupt herself to
snap out, "Perfect fool," or "What a numskull." Was it even
Don Carlos barking? She snapped out that indeed it was Don
Carlos who had gotten to the palace. "He never barks," she
explained, "except when he gets back home after a trip and
then he just sits and barks for a half hour at a stretch to
inform the neighbors. At the palace, or the villa, or wherever
'home' happens to be at the moment."

"Because, after all," he heard, "one should pay for one's
own stupidity, and whoever manages to fall into a trap after
all the warnings he's had from those who know what they're
talking about has it coming to him.... He would pay through
the nose...."

"But I'm her orderly!" he protested.

From balcony to balcony on both sides of the street
where it was dark, and, further along, facing the Public Gardens where it was dark and, further along, facing the Public
Gardens where it was light a murmur arose in reply, a half-
joking, half-indignant sound that grew as if the packed train
with all its howlers had returned, drawing near, drawing in,
to a station: "Soldier...soldier..." he heard over and over. A
new voice, the fourteenth or fifteenth, had already begun
its own version of "Now, let's be reasonable." Yet the murmur
continued to rise with its refrain of "Soldier...soldier," to right
and left, near and far; and the bersagliere (who might well,

287

at this point, have asked himself if he were not in a strange city or if he were not a stranger in a city in which he had lived until now with his head in the sand) had stopped with the bags around him at that corner where the fence surrounding the Public Gardens begins; his idea was to reply in kind, as a soldier, as he had to the series of whistles loosed against him in the Vittoria station; but just as he had made up his mind to do this, he became aware that the aggressive murmur was suddenly stilled, that it had ceased, or rather that it had been canceled out and that the balcony doors were closing their shutters one after the other.

"It must be the Garibaldina on her way back," the bersagliere said to himself.

And he laughed instead of whistling, first of all out of contempt for those who ran to cover, and then because, hearing the old girl call out, "Innocenzo, Innocenzo," and hearing her tread, and Don Carlos thumping on ahead, he was glad that she was like this and that he had guessed right.

But she was far from the winner this time.

"Nothing doing," she said.

Emerging from the dark with her hat in her hand and strands of hair hanging lank on either side of her face, she told him it was no laughing matter.

"I haven't a single one left."

"One what?"

"Not a single thresher, of course.... At first they wouldn't stir, then some twenty or so followed me part way, and now I'm just forced to depend on you again."

She plumped down on her luggage as soon as she had drawn alongside. "Ouff!" she sighed, and took a moment to catch her breath. Then she flapped open her fan to raise a bit of a breeze and clacked little strokes against the many chains and trinkets that adorned her breast.

"It's all that idiot's fault!" she added.

"What idiot?"

"That Romeo down at San Rocco.... He tells them I

already *have* one soldier. And what a soldier! And what a soldier!"

"Shouldn't he have told them?"

"He said it as if he had been telling them I have a donkey. 'You got a soldier, Baroness? You got a soldier, Garibaldina?' "

Now there were no more unbroken walls to flank the road, but dark masses of buildings of varying heights and degrees of formlessness, and the dog's voice singled out one of them repeatedly as if his bark had been a light flashing on and off. Although she went on saying "Ninny" and "Nincompoop," she seemed rather pleased. Her tone was increasingly lighthearted. "That's where it is," she said, her voice fairly bubbling. And she did not call Don Carlos to heel nor whistle him up but hurried her step like an old horse that still feels an occasional spurt of youth, change of pace, an impulse to hear its own bridle jingle and to feel its harness in place once more.

All the baubles she wore at neck and wrists rattled. "That's where they live," she said. Her daughter, and that other Leonilde who had made her a grandmother, her son-in-law, and his eleven ancestors hanging on the walls of the main hall each with his nose out of joint. They'd all be hearing Don Carlos now; they'd hear him bark and they'd know that she had come back and been able to get as far as the palace, and beyond. "That's where we're going," she added, "just beyond the villa of those English people; see, up there, after the second light; that is, the third, well, let's say between the third and the fourth...."

6

An hour later the bersagliere was retracing his steps from one to another of those lights with the springing step of one who—all things considered—had not had too rough a day of it.

He said to himself, "It must be at the third street light!" And he said to himself, "It must be between the third and the fourth street lights."

But he said it laughing, and he ended up by believing—he said to himself—that he was going to his own home now just as he'd hoped. Wasn't he about to arrive without so much as a lunch box? Hadn't he been right to leave without a thing to load him down? Otherwise, he'd have been walking along now with parcels in his hands. As for the chore he'd just accomplished like a beast of burden, it was over and done with. To make up for it, he'd traveled much more comfortably than if he had taken the howlers' train. And that wasn't all: he'd seen so much he would never forget, learned so much, things that would be useful later on, so much he could tell others....

He said all this to himself and much more, with Don Carlos' bark still ringing in his ears as if the villa itself, on its lonely ledge of rock and behind its iron grillwork, were barking after him from farther and farther away.

"What a character!" he said to himself.

The longer he walked, the more easily the sound of his footfall drowned out the bark of the dog. That was why he would stop every so often and say to himself, "What an old woman!" as if it were she barking after him in the night.

By the time he reached the Capuchins, he was whistling. Now he could have taken a shortcut at this point but he chose to continue along the road lit by the street lamps, on the paving that, after all, he liked to feel under his feet. He whistled, then he broke off to say something to himself, he chuckled about it, then he began to chuckle again. "And what an old skinflint!" he said to himself. "True! I wouldn't have taken anything. All the same, she could have offered...."

Laughing, he said to himself that she had probably thought she'd paid him off with the lees of the marsala and the cracker that smelled of camphor she had urged on him in her dining room where all the furniture was covered with dust-sheets.

"What nerve she has, though!" he said to himself. "How can she live in that lonely house without so much as a single maid? It's plain as the nose on your face, she'd sleep in her husband's tomb rather than give her son-in-law the satisfaction....Think what Mama Manina would do if she were all alone in a big house like that! Why, she'd think the very doors—painted white like that—were ghosts."

Starting to whistle again, he found a strong, lively tune on his lips.

The air was fresh as if that point of daybreak had already come that wakes the animals—the donkeys waiting to be harnessed to the carts, the cocks in the courtyard, the host of rustling warblers in the trees—when he thought he heard, "Hsst! Hsst!" He had gone from whistling to bellowing words. They came out in a warm, resonant voice in time to his step. "Hey, there...blon...di...na, tea...sing Ga...ri...bal... di...na..."

But just at that point he was sure he had heard, "Hsst!" and that it wasn't a bird he was hearing; all in all, he was sure someone was trying to catch his attention. Could the story of the balconies be beginning all over again?

He kept straight ahead, his song muzzled, and he heard, "Hsst!" behind him, above him, ahead of him.

People were trying to catch his attention from at least three places at once. He kept on going beyond the point of the third "Hsst!" but there was a fourth, then a fifth, and a sixth....He could not turn off the damned Corso until beyond the Public Gardens. He hurried his step. But there was still a stretch to go, and he could not keep on pretending that nothing was happening when from every damned balcony visible or invisible there came the shrill undertone of their damned calling.

He stopped. "What do you want?"

One of the reed blinds on one of the balconies moved ever so slightly. "Do you have to yell?" a barely audible voice hissed at him.

"But you're all calling me!" the bersagliere said.

"Just come on over here and talk to me. Don't pay any attention to the others. Will you tell me something in strictest confidence?"

"I'd always spit out anything that could be helpful."

"Sssh! Quiet down," and the voice behind the blind went on in scarcely distinguishable tones.

"What d'you say?" the soldier asked.

The voice repeated a little louder the words it had already uttered.

"What? What?"

The voice repeated for the third time, "What have you been doing with the baroness all this time?"

The bersagliere heard a twitter of laughter run from balcony to balcony. He answered sharply, "With Signora Leonilde?"

"With her. With her," the voice said. Then, in a tone so different that it might have been a different voice, it went on:

"What were you up to all this time?"

"All what time?"

"Almost two hours... I saw you both pass by at two-twenty and now it's past four."

"But I took her all the way to the villa at Capo Soprano. Not just to the Capuchins."

"What of it? You could go there from here in twenty minutes."

"Not if you were loaded down as I was, you couldn't!"

"Well, let's say half an hour. Two-twenty plus thirty makes it ten to three."

"Then there's the half hour back..."

"The way back is downhill and, besides, you weren't 'loaded down.' You know what time you should have reached this spot? Well, I'll tell you: at three-fifteen at the latest."

"Well, what with one thing and another..."

"That's just what I'm asking you. With *what* thing and what other?"

A fresh wavelet of laughter rippled along the balconies, and the bersagliere did not know how to get out of standing there trying to justify himself.

"Well, between the business of the key and the business of the light bulb, and with that dog..."

"What business of the key?"

"The Signora couldn't find it and we had to open the

suitcases to see where it was while the damned dog kept poking his nose into everything, even snatching things right out of our hands..."

"And may one ask what was 'the business of the light bulb'?"

"Same thing. The Signora sent me in ahead of her to turn on the light, up on the first floor, she told me, but there wasn't any light bulb and the light wouldn't turn on so I had to come back downstairs to rummage through her valises where she said she had one, and that meant opening up everything all over again...."

"And what about the dog?"

"I've already told you. He went on scattering all the things from the valises up and down the street the second time we had to open them and I had to run after him to liberate an undershirt he'd run off with...."

"The undershirt belonging to the Signora?"

"One of them. That's the way I lost most time, running after the dog."

The voice behind the blind recognized the fact that the bersagliere might well have spent all the time unaccounted for performing these acts. *Might* have, yes. And they might equally have taken up ten minutes instead of forty-five, or three hours, for that matter. He'd passed his time to no good purpose, in any event, and who could object to that?

"There, you see?" said the bersagliere.

He could go on his way, pleased at having answered calmly instead of having worked himself into a rage even if he heard the voice laughing behind his back and talking with the other voices from neighboring balconies, all of the voices laughing now.

"Hsst! Hsst!" the signals continued thick and fast, coming from invisible beings facing the path he traversed between the two sides of the street.

"Who are you, anyway?" he heard someone ask. "Are you Maltese? Are you from Malta?"

But knowing what they wanted, he could afford to ignore them and concentrate on getting out of the pickle by turning, immediately after the Gardens, down the dark little street where there were no more houses with balconies and no more nosy people who called themselves ladies and gentlemen. He joyously burst out whistling the *Garibaldina* theme again. And why shouldn't he sing it? He reached the Public Gardens in full voice and passed them, still singing despite the guarded catcalls that followed him, through the very trees, despite the birds that the morning freshness had by now awakened and who awaited only the light to take flight from their nests.

But as the lights went out, all of them at once right down to the end of the Corso, you could see that the sky was no longer black. The Corso itself, the asphalt paving, looked blue between the high walls. And together with the sounds one heard, a cock crowing some little distance off, carts creaking into movement still further away, one could see shadows of men coming steadily uphill with metallic reflections glinting at about head height.

The bersagliere soon ran into five or six men walking in line, their black hair curly, their cheeks all but black, their eyes flashing; by their yellowed rags and moth-eaten berets, he could recognize them as the howlers from the other train or men just like them who had now become—as if by magic—quieter than ghosts. They barely glanced sidewise to look him over as they passed and they made no noise, not even with their feet which for the most part were bare, though a few had theirs bound with rags.

Their sickles were over their shoulders and these were what gleamed now and again whenever a reflection struck them as the men shifted their weight. The last in line jiggled his sickle up and down as a sort of greeting. The gesture was repeated by others in the next line and in lines still to come. The calls from the balconies had stopped; the signs the men with the sickles made as they passed were characteristic of the Sicilians, albeit a little on the mysterious side, and the bersagliere no longer felt any urgency about turning off down one of the byways. He continued along the Corso, making in his turn certain small negative gestures which were meant to have the same slightly derisive undertone as those of the reapers.

Was it because he was a soldier? The mocking signs made at him from the windows of the train as it stood in the Ragusa station were more or less the same kind. In any event, he was not intimidated by them; he gave as good as he got but with decreasing emphasis, decreasing frequency, and finally he went back to whistling his *Garibaldina* theme. He whistled on without giving a thought to the foolish remarks he heard from some voice in the line.

"Mmmm..." he heard.

And "Prrr..." he heard.

A loud fart that he heard distinctly provoked only a change of one note in the motif he was whistling between his teeth. And a few laughed at his response. Then came a howl from the steps of the little church where the cripple Romeo huddled night and day.

"View halloo!"

Was this aimed at the bersagliere? It would seem so. Else, who *was* it aimed at and why? The soldier did not turn down a dark lane that opened off the Corso a bit before the church. He was about to do so as the call echoed and re-echoed with stubborn insistence, taken up from afar. But then he decided against it and resumed his rapid stride, resuming too his whistled air of the *Garibaldina*. As he drew level with the façade of the church, he saw Romeo's face with its round eyes fixing him from under the tattered brim of a conical hat.

In the light which already showed lambent and roseate, the bersagliere saw little groups of men gathered along the two sidewalks ؛   flanked the Corso from Romeo's church to the piazza. ʹℓ he men had the black whiskers appropriate to reapers but their hands were in their pockets. Just the same, you could tell they were reapers, that is to say, migrants, by the strange clothes they wore which no regular hired hand would consider wearing. There were the vivid blobs of color from women's blouses or skirts which they did not refuse to use for patches, and the triangular or circular bits tacked here and there on their clothing to transform their mends into ornaments. Then the braid or strips of cloth with which they had bound up their cuffs, shirts, or pants. Or the gilt cord with which a few of them tied back their wild, uncut locks at the base of the neck. And some wore a single gold ring in one ear lobe as proudly as they wore their great mustaches.

Going from place to place in large groups for the sowing, the reaping, the threshing of the grain, for the picking of the cotton, they paid no heed to the impression they might make on others wherever they happened to be, just as an outcast, a Romeo, one who has gone beyond any concept of trying not to displease his neighbor, dared flout the permanent residents of the place. But though Romeo or Leonardo, the porter, might take salacious pleasure in noting the wildly varied condition of the reapers' rags, those who came to overrun the city two or three times a year—some boasting ostrich plumes, a piece of red canonical cloth, the trappings from a discarded police uniform, the bells and trim of a worn-out harness—were known simply as "the sowers," "the reapers" or, generically, "the Calabrians," though most of them came from the northern mountains of Sicily, and the townsfolk let it go at that.

If the bersagliere had reason to notice that they all more or less resembled Romeo, it was because he sensed the understanding that existed between Romeo and them, or rather between Romeo and those groups of men who stayed seated or lounged on the sidewalks, hands in their pockets, leaving it to others to wend their way up the Corso, sickles over their shoulders, in a single line of march which started at the piazza, all black and noisy and marked by a continuous furling and unfurling of the doves which rose, circled and swooped to settle down again in constant rotation.

The sickles of the loungers were stacked nearby with their sacks and cooking pots.

They were not laughing, not joking. Only black, with a dogged expression or with that look beyond doggedness that bespeaks grim boredom.

"Was it you?" a tall man asked, facing the bersagliere down with flashing eyes.

"Of course," Romeo cried, hitching himself upright on the steps. "Who d'you think it would be? Of course it was that one. We don't have any other soldiers wandering around here. I saw him with my own eyes, and the Garibaldina told me so, and he himself'll tell you...."

"Let him tell us, then," cried the reapers. "Let him tell us."

Meanwhile a man on horseback rode up from the piazza, opening a way for himself as the doves rose about him with a whir of wings. The bersagliere looked at him as if, in some way or other, he were coming especially for him. He was an old man dressed in corduroy hunting clothes, one of the best-known hunters in Terranova who roamed the woods of the great estates; his teeth were sparkling white, and the gun barrel, pointed downward, was slung behind him from shoulder to saddle.

"Giovinazzo!" he called.

He was searching in the crowd of reapers gathered around the bersagliere and he rode right into their midst, nor did he rein in his gentle horse with its mule's ears until he had opened the circle along one entire side. "Well, then?" he asked. He was addressing the tall reaper who had questioned the bersagliere. "Well, then, are you going to Settefarine? Or you and another squad can work Ponte Olivo as far up as Sparacogna. But don't forget, it's almost five. Will you come to terms with the other squad leader?"

The reaper, Giovinazzo, was holding the soldier by the front of his jacket. "I come to terms with nobody," he answered.

"Then take your men to Settefarine...."

"Ha'n't I already told you, I'm not going!"

"Don't I pay you just the same as the Garibaldina?" the man on horseback asked. "It's a lira a head we pay. That's the going price here."

" 'Tis not the price," a grumbler muttered from behind Giovinazzo. " 'Tis the treatment that plays its part."

297

"You'll not have me believe," the man on horseback answered, "that that skinflint treats you better than I. She gives you a two-kilo loaf and we give two-and-a-half. She gives a liter of wine and we give a flaskful...."

"Well, from *her*," the grumbler went on, "'tis a liter right enough, and you can thin it to suit. But with you others, those that are giving a flaskful have already thinned it good or they give us water and vinegar...."

"Here's something new," the man on horseback interrupted. "We all know that the wine given the reapers is watered, from the time of Noah, because its purpose is to quench your thirst, not to get you drunk. But since you've brought up water and vinegar, it must be with vinegar that the Garibaldina thins hers. Otherwise why would *you* thin that 'right enough' liter? You wouldn't thin it! You'd drink it off just as it is and you'd get drunk and fall asleep, and get a touch of sunstroke...."

He was speaking now with irritated condescension, looking at the bersagliere instead of the persons he was addressing. "What's happening to me?" the bersagliere might well have asked himself. He saw the man was looking at no one but him, was staring at him with increasing attentiveness, and he might well have asked himself if what was going on between him and the reapers was not pretty serious.

By now he had shaken himself free of Giovinazzo's hand. He had even managed to draw a bit back from the center of the circle, and Giovinazzo too had raised his hands along with the others to protest with outcry and gesture against the implications of the man on horseback. "As if we..." he cried. "As if we..." the others cried.

The man on horseback, his eyes still on the bersagliere, said that he did not wish to stay there indefinitely discussing and cajoling, as if there weren't plenty of able-bodied men in the piazza to call up. He said he had lost enough time already. He said he'd be on his way. The soldier saw the man take his eyes from him just at the moment a reaper turned to cry up to the mounted figure that there was no need to take it like that, and that if Giovinazzo wouldn't go, *he* would go, and with him the eight men in his squad.

"What?" howled Giovinazzo. He asked one reaper after another if it wasn't true that they had all been present when the Garibaldina had let it be known she would pay twenty-two *soldi* that season. But the man on horseback cut in with a reminder that his offer had been made to Giovinazzo, and that he would pay a lira a head for a squad like Giovinazzo's, adding that for men like Trimestrieri's he could pay only eighteen *soldi*.

At this, they all set up a howl. The men of Trimestrieri's group wanted to know why they were worth less than Giovinazzo's. Giovinazzo's men were sure they had this and that advantage over Trimestrieri's. The latter group hurled insults, used rough words. But Giovinazzo's men let them roll off like water off a duck's back—after all, they'd had quite a triumph and all they said was that it certainly served Trimestrieri's men right.

Romeo was laughing from the top of the steps.

He was enjoying the scene, laughing, flinging himself about, and he marked the hours when the five strokes sounded from the piazza, underscored by the thick whir of hundreds of wings as the doves wheeled into the air. Then he commented, laughing, on the departure of the man on horseback. And he cried out as he saw the soldier start to take off.

The bersagliere was caught by a sleeve and brought back into the group.

But Giovinazzo's men were only in a mood to sneer by now.

"What have you got against me, after all?" the soldier asked.

The reapers nudged each other, winked at each other broadly, asked each other what, after all, they had against that particular soldier.

"What have we got against him?"

"There's no doubt we've got something...."

"But what?"

One of the men, with a red bandanna with white polka

dots on it tied around his head, began by asking what a soldier does.

"He sweeps out the barracks," they answered.

"He cleans the latrines," from someone.

"He washes the stew pots," from another.

He answered by telling them that he went on marches, carried a knapsack, but the interlocutor continued to ask the same question while Romeo, hunched down on the top step, twisted in contortions of laughter.

"His food is lousy..." someone added.

"He sleeps on the ground," another said.

The reaper with the bandanna no longer needed to repeat his question. All he had to do was raise his hand as a signal to elicit a fresh answer from the circle of his fellow reapers, and the answers soon became nothing more than "His food is lousy" and "He sleeps on the ground"; in due course the rhythm was established and they picked up the beat, and they all hammered out the chorus.

The bersagliere might have believed himself in the midst of the bedraggled group on the howlers' train, with the young boys and all the others, with the brakeman, too, and the two conductors who wanted him to get down at Donnafugata, but the reaper with the bandanna now turned to him as well to get his answer to the question.

"That's just the way it is," he answered. "He goes to war...and...he sleeps on the ground...."

"And you wanted *us*," the reaper hurled at him, "to carry your bags for you?"

A great roar went up in which Trimestrieri's men joined.

"Just take a look at him!"

"He's not a General!"

"He's not even a non-com!"

"He's only a soldier...."

"And *we* were supposed to carry a soldier's bags for him?"

The bersagliere tried to say that the luggage had not been his, had never been his, and to say all the rest that he could have said, but he did not manage to say any of it for the reapers drowned out his voice with their noise,

300

and they pushed him from one side of the circle to the other, and from one man to another, and then there was Romeo who was choking out from the top of the steps: "I...I...I..." he was saying, all red in the face. Halfway up the steps, below Romeo but above the reapers, the mug of the night watchman, Galante, came into view. He was thin, small-boned, with that grayish cast to the skin and enough white at the temples to make even a man in his fifties pass for old. Just the same, he looked spry and sharp, rather gnome-like, as only those along in years can look. He reminded the bersagliere of the little old trainman who had appeared with a red flag in his hand at the Ragusa station, and that was why the soldier kept on trying to tell his story, directing his gestures to Galante, there on the steps.

He kept on talking and talking, as if aware that he could not be heard but wanting to begin again anyway. Nor was there any dearth of reapers seeking the same thing: five or six of them were, in the selfsame manner, asking the little old man to hear their side of it. Then there were seven, then eight, then nine, and they all were aware of the difficulty of being heard and would stop a bit only to begin again, louder than before. The old man looked at the soldier and shook his head, looked at the reapers and shook his head, but as if he'd already made up his mind what to think about all this. He never stopped smiling, his face sharp and alert, and he made a few gestures to the one and the others to calm down. "Don't take it personally," he finally managed to say to the bersagliere.

The reaper, Giovinazzo, and the reaper with the bandanna on his head were talking to each other in whispers interrupted by great guffaws, and the old man told the bersagliere that it wasn't with *him* they were annoyed. "It's because the Garibaldina doesn't want them after all," he said.

He kept on wrinkling up his face with cunning glances and told him that he should try to put himself in their shoes and pity them. Since they had always reaped and threshed the Garibaldina's grain, they had come back to do the work again this year, and all of a sudden she'd turned them off.

301

They didn't know which way to turn. "I don't know if I make myself clear, but they don't know what to do with themselves.... They're out of work, see."

"What?" the bersagliere asked him.
He could scarcely hear. But behind the little night watchman Romeo's voice now rose, too.
"Whose fault is it, I'd like to know," he cried, "if they're out of work? Whose fault is it if the Garibaldina doesn't want them any more, if she's turned them away? Whose fault is it that they made her angry...that they had to turn her down? It was just so's they wouldn't have to do the bidding of that good-for-nothing soldier and carry his bags for him, so it's plain as the nose on your face it's his fault. Whose fault is it? Whose is it? No one else's but that soldier...."
The old man was shaking his head, smiling. "But they're all over that now," he said. "They aren't offended any longer. It's only that they're out of work, and he must take all this with patience, and feel for them."
He had turned back to the bersagliere who still could not hear him clearly, and was urging him not to take offense, while Romeo, behind him, was imitating him in a falsetto voice.
"Feel for them!" he repeated in falsetto. "But it's those fellows," he cried, "who feel for *him!*"
Meanwhile the reapers, between one guffaw and another, one snort and another, had found a new game to play with the soldier.
"Let's salt him!" was the new proposal.
The reaper, Giovinazzo, and the reaper with the red bandanna had worked it out between them, whispering in each other's ears, and now they loosed it, and the others took it up.
"Let's salt him! Let's salt him!"
Grabbing the bersagliere, they threw him down; the idea was to hold him motionless, unbutton his trousers, and rub his private parts with salt or street filth.
The bersagliere tried to fight back.

"They're salting him!" Romeo howled. And he heaved himself about, imitating grotesquely every twist and turn of the prone bersagliere, and the rags with which he was clad flew around him like ruffled feathers. "And you," he said, turning to the night watchman, "what do you say now? Shouldn't he take it personally now?"

The old man did nothing more than shake his head under his watchman's cap. Of course he disapproved of what he was witnessing, yet he kept on repeating that it was nothing and underlining his words with certain slow gestures which meant to convey the same thing.

But the reapers had neither salt nor street filth to hand. They reached in their pockets, then imitated one another by running to the nearest unpaved lane to pick up whatever they could find, and one of their number had the idea of running to their knapsacks, but by then the reaper with the red bandanna had come up with a third proposal.

"Let's have him carry our knapsacks!" he proposed.

They all considered this the best and most appropriate suggestion yet. "Let him carry our knapsacks! Let him carry our knapsacks!"

Only Romeo was against it. He cried that this was a foolish prank, without any kick to it, that "salting" him was a worse punishment. "At least, salt him first!"

But the reapers were already dragging the bersagliere across the street toward the pile of knapsacks. Red Bandanna was following in their wake and directing them with his hands, as if he were an orchestral conductor. "What does the soldier do?" he asked.

"He carries the knapsacks," they all replied.

Their voices were trying to hit the beat as before.

"The soldier?"

"Goes to war."

"The soldier?"

"Sleeps on the ground."

"The soldier?"

"Carries the knapsacks! Carries the knapsacks!"

This last response, though thundered out, was each time interrupted here and there by splutters of laughter, and when they tried it a third time it trailed off into a murmur. For

303

a horse was coming; the sound of its shoes could be heard, and all the reapers stopped and looked toward the middle of the Corso.

The bersagliere turned around too. All of a sudden, they had loosed their hold on him, he could shake himself, stand up straight and rearrange his clothing, and he saw a white and black horse shaking its head in the air and all the reapers gathered around. He saw that the figure, though covered by a cloak, seemed like that of the old woman; then he heard a voice he recognized, and he saw that it was indeed her figure moving toward him, and that it was "his" old woman on horseback.

"Never in my born days," she exclaimed, "would I have expected to see you all here at half past five in the morning! Giovinazzo, what's our agreement? From sunup to sundown. ...This evening you'll stop the minute the sun drops below the horizon. But meanwhile you're not at the Bruca, getting ready to start work. Perhaps it's your idea that you'll go to work when lawyers go to Mass?"

Giovinazzo, cap in hand, kept on repeating, "Well..." Trimestrieri too. He held the horse by the bridle and kept on saying, "Well..." They certainly wanted to say by that "well" that they must have misunderstood that she had let them go, or that she had expressed herself unclearly, or perhaps had changed her mind at the last moment, but they got none of these things out. They just stood there looking at each other and kept on repeating, "Well..."

"Well, what?" she exclaimed. "I watched from the window to see which squads were passing: Marzapane, yes; Dardanello, yes; you, here, no. So I had to come all the way down here to see what's got into you."

"Well, you see..." they said, and the reapers' faces were red. And not just Giovinazzo's and Trimestrieri's. Those two had already managed to stammer out, "You see, Garibaldina..." That much they had managed to say.

304

"Well, for today," the old woman went on, "you won't get your twenty-two cents. Take it or leave it; you'll get one lira."

The reapers were consulting each other as if they did not consider this at all fair. But the confused sense of well-being that had spread over their faces had not been wiped off. If anything, it seemed to grow.

"Well, then, Garibaldina?" Trimestrieri asked.

And Giovinazzo: " 'Tis to the Bruca, then, we should go?"

And Trimestrieri added, "To the Bruca, they? And us too?"

The old woman answered that they should know where they were to go from all the years they had been doing the job, sowing and reaping and threshing for her. Dardanello was working the Mautana fields, as usual. Marzapane, Cappellania. There was no reason that she could think of why they two, in squads of thirteen and nine, could not work the Bruca, as usual. Or did they want to make a change? But then they should have got together with the other two to work out the change.

"And how much 'tis you're paying Marzapane?" Red Bandanna asked.

The old woman said she had seen him pass with his squad at four-thirty, as she watched from her window. She would keep her promise to them and to Dardanello. They would have their twenty-two cents an hour.

"And why not us?" the reaper asked. "Why're we getting only a lira?"

Each reaper uttered a little sound of protest, but vague and formal as if part of a ritual.

"How often do I have to repeat it for you?" the Signora exclaimed. "Had I seen you pass at four-thirty, as I watched from my window, I would have given you people twenty-two cents an hour, too, and I wouldn't have had to come all the way down here. I could have stayed home and rested a bit after the strain of my journey...."

The reapers were murmuring among themselves, "True

305

enough," and "That's fair enough," but there were those who wanted to say something else and one of their number got as far as trying to say it.

"But, Garibaldina..."

He stopped, silenced by the black looks he caught from some of his comrades. A few nudged him, others tried to kick him, and this left the way open for Red Bandanna to take over once more. "From tomorrow, at least," he half stated, "'tis twenty-two cents you'll be giving us?"

"Listen carefully," the Garibaldina told them. "You go up to the fields now, do as much as you possibly can, and at sundown I'll come by and look things over...."

"Ahhh, Ga-ri-bal-di-na..." the reapers chanted, paying out the syllables one by one.

"And if what I see..." she went on.

"Ahhhh, Ga-ri-bal-di-na..."

"...satisfies me..."

"Ahhhhh, Ga-ri-bal-di-na..."

The reapers did not try to drown out her voice with a cheer. Instead, each one had put his arm around his comrade's shoulder and they were all swaying in unison and moving their heads from side to side, repeating "Ahhh, Ga-ri-bal-di-na" with the long, slow syllables scanning as they fell.

And the scraping of the horse's hooves began again.

Surrounded by the reapers who kept up their chanting and their swaying, the old woman rode in the direction of the piazza. And she was decidedly old, got up in men's clothes, with a little hat on her head trimmed by a long veil, and with her heavy cheeks flabby and a black weariness about her eyes, her hair in disorder, her clothing flung on every which way despite the baubles. But she was wonderful just because she accepted the fact of being—and in no way tried not to be—old, beyond any single thing that recalls youth yet far from beyond the things that make for life. She called

306

Don Carlos, whistled him up, and turned to look back to be sure he was following when she saw the bersagliere following the train, a little behind the others.

"Hey, Fortunato," she cried to the bersagliere.

His eyes were shining. He saw her in her gray veil, and she was as attractive to him as a young girl. And it was just because she was old, not because of some residuum of youth.

She was a lot older by daylight than he could have believed during the night he had just spent with her. But alive in her old age, alive in the same way a young girl is who is on her way, for example, to a wedding. "Now do you believe," she called back to him, "that I have a carriage?"

And she laughed. If she had a horse, he could have no possible doubt that she must also have a carriage. "Besides, I'll send it over for you," she added. "I promised I'd make your fortune and I will...."

One last time she turned back to ask him again where he lived. But the horse had already broken into a trot, the reapers were falling behind one by one, and the bersagliere wanted to cross the street.

He walked faster.

He kept on walking faster, almost started to run, and reached the piazza in the midst of men talking to one another, some on horseback, some on the ground. From the cupola of the sandstone church already touched by the sun the two bronze bells rang out, one long, one short, summoning people to the first Mass of the day. At every two strokes of the hammers, the doves flew out of the bell tower or rose from the cornices, from between the columns, from the steps, but they rose only to settle down again, rose and returned, as if it were they sounding the bronze bells each time they circled into the air.

The bersagliere turned down the street that led to the sea. It was all downhill now with the bells echoing all around him and from every terraced level he could see the sea on the horizon. Above the terraces, the doves wheeled gleaming in the sun with the heavy old breeder leading the flight of males and females. And the bersagliere broke out strong and free once more with the song he had been singing earlier:

You—are—the—bright—star
Of—us—poor—sol—diers
Hey—there—blon—di—na
Teas—ing Ga—ri—bal—di—na....